Ace Books by Walter Greatshell

XOMBIES: APOCALYPSE BLUES
XOMBIES: APOCALYPTICON

XOMBIES:
APOCALYPTICON

Walter Greatshell

ACE BOOKS, NEW YORK

THE BERKLEY PUBLISHING GROUP
Published by the Penguin Group
Penguin Group (USA) Inc.
375 Hudson Street, New York, New York 10014, USA
Penguin Group (Canada), 90 Eglinton Avenue East, Suite 700, Toronto, Ontario M4P 2Y3, Canada
(a division of Pearson Penguin Canada Inc.)
Penguin Books Ltd., 80 Strand, London WC2R 0RL, England
Penguin Books Ireland, 25 St. Stephen's Green, Dublin 2, Ireland (a division of Penguin Books Ltd.)
Penguin Group (Australia), 250 Camberwell Road, Camberwell, Victoria 3124, Australia
(a division of Pearson Australia Group Pty. Ltd.)
Penguin Books India Pvt. Ltd., 11 Community Centre, Panchsheel Park, New Delhi—110 017, India
Penguin Group (NZ), 67 Apollo Drive, Rosedale, North Shore 0632, New Zealand
(a division of Pearson New Zealand Ltd.)
Penguin Books (South Africa) (Pty.) Ltd., 24 Sturdee Avenue, Rosebank, Johannesburg 2196,
South Africa

Penguin Books Ltd., Registered Offices: 80 Strand, London WC2R 0RL, England

This is a work of fiction. Names, characters, places, and incidents either are the product of the author's imagination or are used fictitiously, and any resemblance to actual persons, living or dead, business establishments, events, or locales is entirely coincidental. The publisher does not have any control over and does not assume any responsibility for author or third-party websites or their content.

XOMBIES: APOCALYPTICON

An Ace Book / published by arrangement with the author

PRINTING HISTORY
Ace mass-market edition / March 2010

Copyright © 2010 by Walter Greatshell.
Cover art by Cliff Nielsen.
Cover design by Lesley Worrell.
Interior text design by Tiffany Estreicher.

ISBN: 978-0-441-01845-1

ACE
Ace Books are published by The Berkley Publishing Group,
a division of Penguin Group (USA) Inc.,
375 Hudson Street, New York, New York 10014.
ACE and the "A" design are trademarks of Penguin Group (USA) Inc.

PRINTED IN THE UNITED STATES OF AMERICA

10 9 8 7 6 5 4 3 2 1

ACKNOWLEDGMENTS

To my agent, Laurie McLean; my editor, Danielle Stockley; and all the excellent folks at Berkley/Ace—my sincerest thanks. To my readers—you're the reason I love this job. And to my wife, Cindy—all my books are for you.

To die—without the Dying
And live—without the Life
This is the hardest Miracle
Propounded to Belief.

—EMILY DICKINSON

CHAPTER **ONE**

RODEO ZULU TANGO

In considering why the collapse of civilization occurred with such astonishing speed, we must acknowledge the role of sexism: In almost every recorded instance, men failed to respond with appropriate caution to female attackers. This has been called the Sadie Hawkins Effect, in which radical reversal of traditional sex roles conflicted with assumed male supremacy and clouded the ordinary instinct for self-preservation. Overnight, a world in which women were the "weaker sex"—where they frequently dared not walk alone for fear of sexual assault— was transformed into a world where wholesale violation and murder were being committed upon *men* by *women*, where men were suddenly the objects of violent lust, and where the toughest of tough guys dared not go out in the open for fear of his life . . . and his wife. This was not a condition that most men could readily grasp, to their abrupt misfortune. By trying to retain their perceived sexual hegemony—by leaping in to "take charge"—the males of our species surrendered in droves to the annihilating passion of the Maenads.

—**The Maenad Project**

Marcus Washington, aka Voodooman, sat at the card table and tried to gauge his opponents' blank expressions. You weren't allowed to turn or take your eyes off the game; you weren't allowed to show fear. It was a matter of honor that you had to sit still and play for real in the shadow of death.

Marcus knew these men better than he knew his own family. They were the Dead Presidents Posse, the four of them seated at the cardinal points of the compass:

Righteous Weeks faced north, with the best view; Little Rock faced west; 50 Cal east; and Voodooman himself in the blind position, for which they drew straws before the game—all very cool customers who were not easily spooked. But they were nervous now, all right. The question was, were they nervous enough?

Marcus could hear the dancing clown at his shoulder and the expectant buzz from the stands—he sensed the bull's-eye on his back, knew he had better choose his next move carefully, or it could be his last. Seeing Calvin's frozen grin, he thought, *Boy looks like a long-tailed cat in a roomful of rocking chairs.* Maybe this would be a good time to bluff.

Righteous had just raised two dollars and the others had matched it, so Marcus said, "I'll see your two dollars and raise you five more." He threw his chips in.

The tension swelled like steam in a teakettle—oh, it was going to be close.

Little Rock and Calvin folded, shaking their heads. Righteous disgustedly tossed in the chips and said, "I call, you son of a bitch. Show your hand."

Marcus had no hand to show; it was pure trash. He felt naked in the crazed glare of the stadium lights. If nothing happened in the next instant to prevent it, he was going to have to show his cards, losing gambler cred as well as the nineteen dollars in the pot. Then the skin on his shaved scalp tingled—*Oh damn*—

Something happened.

The other three leaped backward in unison, and Voodooman barely had time to dodge as a ton of pissed-off Black Angus Hereford came barreling through the game like a horned locomotive, causing the cards, the chips, the table itself, as well as the players and their chairs, to explode in every direction.

The audience exploded, too, into gales of laughter—convict poker was the prison rodeo's most popular event. The last event of the evening, and in this instance, the last rodeo event of the year, for this was New Year's Ropin' Eve.

"Shit, man, that was close," said Righteous Weeks, helping Voodooman to his feet and handing him his hat. "You one crazy nigger. Motherfucker got eyes in the back of his head."

"Just remember it's my hand—last one seated. Cattle call."

"You earned it, brother—straight bull flush. Were you really holding?"

"Nope."

Weeks laughed, dusting himself off. "I didn't think so. Shee-it. A'ight, let's put this puppy to bed."

It was almost 10 P.M., an hour before lockdown. Now the animals would be returned to their pens and the weary and battered inmates to their cells—those who weren't already at the prison infirmary or being ambulanced to the state hospital. Now the hootenanny would begin: Bands would play, free men and women would dance and drink until midnight on the red dirt of the arena, then it would all be over but for the fireworks. No inmates invited.

Voodooman was helping corral the bull when the first screams started in the stands.

He looked up in astonishment to see rioting among the spectators: men and women grappling with one another, and the prison guards and trusties rushing to intervene. At first he thought it was a joke, some kind of mass prank: Several hundred women were straddling men—bodily pinning them down—and smothering them with what looked to be passionate kisses. But clearly there was nothing funny about it—some folks were just angry, telling their children not to look, but the ones nearest the trouble were plainly scared about something. Other audience members were frantically trying to pull the pairs apart and shouting for help.

"LADIES AND GENTLEMEN," said the announcer, "I'M AFRAID I HAVE TO ASK YOU TO REFRAIN FROM CAUSING A DISTURBANCE. I KNOW IT'S NEW YEAR'S EVE, AND WE'VE ALL HAD A FEW DRINKS, BUT REMEMBER THAT WE ARE ON THE GROUNDS OF A PENITENTIARY AND MUST ACT IN FULL ACCORDANCE WITH THE RULES—IT'S FOR YOUR OWN SAFETY. THIS IS A FAMILY SHOW. WE'RE ALL HERE TO HAVE FUN, BUT ROWDINESS WILL NOT BE TOLERATED."

Marcus watched as five people, two of them state troopers, managed to wrestle one of the women off, fighting for all they were worth to get her into a headlock and cuffs. Other men were interfering with the woman's arrest, offended by the rough treatment she was receiving. They were trying to be gallant. Meanwhile, the man she had been kissing looked like a broken doll, sprawled on the bench.

Holy shit, Marcus thought, *that man's dead.*

The woman looked . . . strange. Wet with pepper spray, her face was twisted into a mask of black rage—or was it pleasure—her mouth a gaping pit and eyes almost popping out of her head. She was wearing a sexy cowgirl outfit with buckskin fringes, all torn and disheveled now. They were all like that, all fighting like wildcats to get at the men; Marcus could see the tendons standing out in their necks. Their *blue* necks, he noted. All the women seemed to have blue skin.

Suddenly, the dead man burst to life, leaping up and seizing another man who had been checking his pulse. The attacker's face was puffy and purple from strangulation, his tongue black, but his near-death experience didn't slow him down any. Onlookers shouted in surprise, scrambling backward as the two men thrashed between the benches, then tumbled out of sight below the bleachers.

Marcus wasn't sure whether to laugh or scream—this was the damnedest thing he'd ever seen. It *had* to be some kind of stunt—*had* to be.

A shotgun was fired into the air, and an officer yelled, "Everyone stay seated! That's an order!"

The announcer came on again:

"LADIES AND GENTLEMEN, WE ASK YOU TO PLEASE REMAIN IN YOUR SEATS AND COOPERATE WITH THE AUTHORITIES. DO NOT LET YOURSELVES GET DRAWN INTO THIS BRAWL. THE FOLKS RESPONSIBLE WILL BE DEALT WITH SHORTLY IF YOU'LL ALL JUST REMAIN IN YOUR SEATS AND REFRAIN FROM ADDING TO THE CONFUSION. ALL RODEO PERSONNEL AND TRUSTIES ARE INSTRUCTED TO RETURN AT ONCE TO THE STAGING AREA. EVERYONE REMAIN CALM— THE SITUATION IS UNDER CONTROL. WE APOLOGIZE FOR ANY INCONVENIENCE."

The rodeo performers and trusties weren't listening. They had all stopped what they were doing and were calling to their wives and sweethearts in the stands, or just watching dumbfounded as chaos broke out above them. The animals were getting jumpy from the noise.

Reining in one of the ponies, Righteous Weeks called out, "What in hell's going on? Somebody makin' a break I don't know about?"

Voodooman could only shake his head. "I don't think so."

"Be one hell of a diversion."

"You got that right," agreed Voodooman in his Texarkana drawl.

Despite what the announcer said, nothing was under control. In fact, the trouble was spreading like wildfire, doubling every couple of minutes. The number of cops was shrinking by the second, and now some of them were *joining* the fray, crazy and blue-faced as the women, attacking and grappling with anybody they caught, forcing their victims down like spiders on flies and sucking the life breath out of them—a kiss of death. *"Love Potion Number Nine,"* Marcus thought crazily, but there was nothing funny about it. It was all happening so fast. People were *dying*— they were as dead as any corpses Marcus had ever seen, and he had seen a few. But then the weirdest thing kept happening, the ridiculously *crazy* thing. The victims—the corpses frozen in their last death rictus—would jump up and maul someone else. It was like a murderous game of tag: You're *it*.

Voodooman could see the whole deranged business because the crowd was thinning as people fled the stands. They ran down onto the field, scattering in all directions, and the horrible blue attackers followed them. Marcus couldn't believe how many of the things there were already. Another few minutes, and there wouldn't be anybody alive and sane left in the arena. For a moment longer there were isolated bursts of wild shooting, then no more guns, no more guards, no more control.

Frozen with shock, Voodooman said, "What the fuck they *doin'* to 'em?"

"I don't know, brother, but leave us get the hell outta here."

A man carrying a little boy ran up to them, screaming, *"Help us! Please stop them!"*

"What the fuck you expect us to do? We ain't armed."

"Please! They're coming—!" He was suddenly blind-sided by a running leap, taken down by a feral-looking teen-age girl. She was all over him like a snake swallowing a rat—it was if she thought she could burrow down into his body through his mouth. Her teeth broke against his teeth. The little boy was knocked to the ground and lay there screaming.

They could hear the man's chest collapse, like the dregs of a milk shake being drained through a straw.

Voodooman grabbed the kid and put him on the skittish horse, tying a rope around his middle and fastening it to the saddle horn. "Hug his neck good and tight," he said, shaking the child by his shoulder to snap him out of it. *"Okay?"* The boy nodded through his tears. To Righteous Weeks, Marcus said, "Get up there with him, man. Go!"

"You do it—I ain't gonna be nailed with no child-endangerment rap."

"Just ride clear of this mess and drop him off with somebody!"

Before Righteous could reply, the horse suddenly reared up, yanking him off his feet and breaking his grip on the reins.

"Damn," he said, watching his favorite mount escape with the bawling kid on its back.

"Ain't nothing we can do," said Voodooman grimly. "Come on."

They allowed themselves to be swept up in the hysterical mob exiting the field. People were being attacked right and left, or falling and being trampled. As the two convicts crowded through the entrance promenade, they saw their cell-mate 50 Cal galloping toward them on another horse, the warden's big Percheron stallion. Cal had a blue woman lying hog-tied across his legs, and a little girl hanging on to his waist from behind. As he rode, he had to hold down the woman with one hand to prevent her from bucking loose. People beseeched him to stop, to save them, too, but he ignored them, breasting their yearning hands as if they were a cane thicket.

Approaching Voodooman and Righteous Weeks, he shouted, "I roped Darleen! She ain't right, but I'm takin' her and Maybelline!" Before he could reach them, one of the demonic ghouls leaped from the crowd and knocked 50 Cal out of the saddle, taking his wife and daughter with him. The horse reared, kicking someone in the head with a sound of busting crockery.

"We gotta catch that horse!" Voodooman shouted, and the two men plunged through the dwindling crowd after it. Things were going south fast, the ranks of fleeing people eroding around them like a sand castle. The horse was their only hope—Marcus realized that without it, they were no better than sheep: easy pickings for the ravenous wolves at their heels.

But just as they caught up to the plunging beast, and Righteous caught the reins, Voodooman knew it was too late.

The demons were on them.

Out of the corner of his eye, Marcus saw something ugly rushing toward him, a blue-faced scarecrow with a shock of straw blond hair. It grabbed him hard around the neck and toppled him into the horse's haunch, causing the animal to buck, kicking wildly. He felt the force of its hooves rocket past his face, hard enough to snap his neck or crush his skull had they struck him. Instead, they hit the thing on his back: two iron-shod pistons straight to its face. Something wet spattered his neck, and at once the weight was off his back.

He spun to see a whole pack of blue devils swarming in, this final invasion going unnoticed by Righteous, who was too busy steadying the horse to see them coming.

"Look out!" he shouted, just as the other inmate vaulted into the saddle. Marcus grabbed hold of his waist and put one foot in the stirrup, hanging off the side like a circus rider as Righteous kicked the animal into motion.

The horse wouldn't go; it tossed its head in confusion, spinning sideways to see the wave of crazed harpies sweeping in from behind. Its big golden-apple eyes rolled with panic.

"Hah!" shouted Righteous, kicking its flanks. "Run, bitch!"

All at once a huge, humped shape barreled out of the darkness and straight into the thick of the ghouls, running them down or tossing them right and left on the honed tips of its horns—an enormous Brahma bull with blood in its eyes.

"Damnation!" yelled Righteous. "It's Damnation! Somebody musta left his pen open!"

The bull veered around the stalled horse, nearly goring Marcus as it stampeded past him toward thicker concentrations of people in the visitor parking lot. He winced as its horns thundered by, close enough to graze his back. That would be the final irony: if after everything that happened, he was killed by a steer.

But it didn't touch him, kept right on going. The sight of the bull snapped the horse out of its panic, and it immediately broke into a following gallop. Marcus swung himself up over the horse's rump, grabbing Righteous Weeks around the waist, and saying, "Don't get no ideas. This don't mean we're engaged."

"Just hang on."

Weeks reined the horse sideways behind the arena, driving the nervous animal away from the crowd and off the main thoroughfare. A ravening horde of maniacs followed, but Marcus applied his spurs, and the creatures fell behind in the dark. Other refugees were there as well, scattered across the parade grounds and running for the farm outbuildings. When they saw the horse, some turned around to beg for help and were immediately attacked by blue-faced ghouls. There was shooting along the fence line, guards in the towers trying to stop what they thought was a mass escape. No way Righteous was going anywhere near there; get shot trying to escape with his parole hearing coming up next month? Uh-uh. Ignoring the civilians, he called to any convicts they passed, "Stay away from the perimeter fence! Get up inside the main camp!"

Prison buses and trucks with horse trailers were peeling out of the rear staging area, some covered with crazy attackers, some crashing before they got out of the parking lot. The animals were all over the place. Marcus saw a bucking, panicked mare with a blazed face dragging a snarl of concertina wire with people tangled up in it.

Making for the inner gate of the camp—the triple-fortified central compound that contained the main cellblock—Righteous and Voodooman found themselves once again falling in with a fleeing mob, but here there were fewer crazies to be seen, perhaps because all the spectators had reflexively run the opposite way and were bottled up down at the exit. This was a much smaller crowd, mostly prisoners and trusties, not a single one of them female, and some even armed.

The gate guards watched stupefied as men poured through from the farm, unsupervised and completely out of order, babbling incoherently about crazy women and blue devils.

The guards didn't try to stop or interrogate them—leave that for the block captains and the warden, wherever he was. The quick-response team had already been dispatched to the arena with tear gas as well as more lethal munitions. Clad in their imposing black riot gear and shields, resembling a Roman cohort, they'd mop up any trouble quickly, and the prisoners knew it. Emergency procedure during a jailbreak was first and foremost to get everybody under lockdown, and these boys were obviously eager enough to do that for themselves.

Voodooman and Righteous Weeks were another story: Two convicts riding into a restricted area on the warden's prizewinning stud was a clear violation of something, and the guards were quick to draw down on them. "Stop right there!" they shouted. "Get down off'n that horse!"

"You gotta close the gate!" Marcus shouted, jumping to the ground. "They're right behind us!"

Ignoring Marcus, the second guard shouted up at Weeks, "What you think you doin', boy, bringin' that horse up here? Take that back where it belongs."

There was a sudden influx of men streaming through the gate, running wild-eyed from the not-yet-visible threat at their heels, no one wanting to be last in line.

"Can't you see they're almost here?" Marcus screamed, as much to his fellow inmates as to their keepers. "Shut the damn gate before it's too late!"

"Too late for what?" the senior guard scoffed. "All I can say is, you both better have the warden's permission to be riding that horse, I tell you what."

"We do! He sent us to tell you to close the gate!"

"Is that right? Why don't I ask *him* that?"

"He ain't here!"

"He damn sure is."

A manic, burly figure came rushing out of the darkness.

People scattered out of his way, not for the usual reason that he was the warden, but because something was clearly wrong with him. Even from a distance, he looked like a rabid animal.

"Warden!" the guard said in alarm, leaping to help him. "You okay? I was just—"

With brutal force, the guard was slammed backward to the ground, the tails of Warden Henrickson's wool coat covering them both like a cape as Officer Shoney's breath was sucked from his lungs.

Utterly stunned, the second guard stood by helplessly, waiting for something to make sense. Marcus knocked him down and wrestled his shotgun away, shouting, "Everybody inside! Just go!" Righteous rode the stallion through the gate, forcing an opening in the packed mob, followed closely by Voodooman, dragging the guard, and a few dozen stragglers.

Then there was no more time—the men inside heaved the high, sliding gate shut against the cries of frantic latecomers, who were racing up the hill with nightmarish freak jobs all around them. *"Please God, let us in!"* someone shrieked.

"You can't just leave them out there!" one of the prisoners yelled.

Voodooman leveled the shotgun on him, on everyone, forcing the crowd away from the fence. "Ain't nobody touches that gate. All right? Nobody touch the gate!"

"What the hell we supposed to do now?" asked Righteous.

"Go inside and wait until the SWAT team arrives."

"More like the National Guard."

"Or the mo'fuckin' Yoo-nited States Marines. Damn!"

The peals of terror from outside seemed to rouse the guard from his stupor. Shaking free of Voodooman's grip, he grabbed his rifle back, and shouted, "Everyone to your cells!

Go back to your cells and wait there!" He shuddered, then suddenly vomited on his shoes. Trembling, flinching at the sounds outside, he wiped his mouth, and said, "Everything's under control! Everything's under control! Return to your cells at once."

No one made any argument.

CHAPTER **TWO**

DEAD SEA

The American shore, ominously dark as any cannibal coast, was visible in the moonlight as pale cliffs above a thin white hem of breakers. Commander Harvey Coombs knew there were supposed to be houses up there—the famous Newport mansions—but he couldn't see a thing, not a single light. Nor had he seen any other towns or cities: Falmouth, Fall River, New Bedford—all the teeming port settlements of southern New England were dark. To look upon that black coastline now was like peering down a tunnel through the ages. Seeing it the way it hadn't been seen in centuries.

Pilgrims, thought Coombs, lowering his binoculars. *We're pilgrims.*

That was it exactly. This was now the wilderness, the New World.

Coombs rubbed his puffy eyelids as if to remind himself that he was awake, was not dreaming. The freshly stitched incision on his forehead was real enough; the hole in his skull still hurt. Now that he had no clear mission objective anymore, the events of the past few months were growing in his mind like a tumor, a festering glut of unthinkable knowledge that kept gaining mass and crowding out the consolations of faith, hope, or rational thought.

How could it have happened? Agent X, the Xombie horror, Thule and the grim paradise of the Moguls, and now . . . what? There could be no homecoming, no end of the journey. Somehow he had found himself commanding not an Ohio-class submarine, not a U.S. naval vessel at all, but a nuclear-powered ghost ship, a modern *Flying Dutchman*, haunted, lost, and forever doomed to sail a dead sea.

In some part of him, Coombs had expected to come back and find America alight and sane like a beacon on the horizon, though continuous monitoring of every broadcast frequency revealed only dead air, the vacant hiss of static. Even the ambient sounds of the Atlantic Ocean were returned to a primeval state, devoid of human echoes. That pervasive churn of marine technology so familiar to submariners was gone. There was nothing to hear out there anymore but the random clicks and rasps of fish. That and the stealthy rhythms of his own boat. But still he had nurtured this irrational spark that some remnant of America would be waiting for him, like a candle in the window.

But no. It was over. It was truly all over. And in that case, what in God's name were they doing? Every one of them was already dead, they just wouldn't lie down.

Like Xombies.

But what else was there?

His headset crackled: "Commander Coombs. Dr. Langhorne requests permission to speak with you."

"Tell her I'm coming down." He spoke the words with the dry mouth of a man descending into a catacomb, a chamber of horrors. That's what the boat was to him now: a 560-foot-long steel tomb. Harvey Coombs was not a man who had ever put much stock in the supernatural. He was not superstitious or particularly religious beyond what was expected of any career-oriented, socially well-adjusted military officer. In his rational being he had no frame of reference for all that had happened in the four months since he had been assigned command of this nameless ship—his first and last command. He could not comprehend Purgatory, or Hell, or The End of the World. But there was a word for the mood that pervaded this boat and its crew: "dread." Death was afoot belowdecks, quite literally, and the living suffered its unspeakable presence in duty and purest dread.

Dread not, he mused. *Dread not, dread naught, dreadnought. Dreadnaut*—he had to smile at that one: *Jason and the Argonauts, meet Lulu and the Dreadnauts.* Not exactly the stuff of Greek legend; it sounded more like a cheesy cover band. And they already had one of those aboard.

Climbing down through the dank chambers in the monolithic black sail, Coombs thought as he often did lately about the choices, the sheer chance, that had led him into the Navy, and by extension to this strange, infernal place. It might so easily have never happened at all. He might be out there even now, lost beyond that dark shore, amid the blue multitude. The same as everyone else.

He could feel the anxious eyes of the crew on him now as he passed through the control center, searching him for confirmation of what they all felt and what they wanted *him* to feel. So that they could be reassured he was doing something about it, being the cool, competent leader they needed him to be. But he couldn't—Harvey couldn't give them that assurance. He had no such hope to offer.

"Keep to our present heading," he said. "Rich, take the conn for a minute."

"Yes, sir," said his executive officer darkly. "Robles, you and Phil go down with him."

Lt. Dan Robles stood up from his console.

"Stand down, Dan. I don't need an escort this time."

"It's just a precaution."

"I know, but it's been a week, and I think we might let

up a little bit—the good doctor seems to be handling things down there. She's the expert."

"Respectfully disagree, Captain," said Kranuski. "We can't afford to relax our guard, not with *them* aboard. Whatever Dr. *Quinn* down there may think, it's too dangerous."

Richard Kranuski had many disagreements with Coombs about how the ship should be run, and increasingly strong support among the weary, makeshift crew, but Coombs did not think the XO would mutiny—bad as things were, it hadn't yet come to that. Terror was a great bonding agent. "If Langhorne feels safe enough to bunk down there all alone," he said, "I should be able to manage a quick look-see." He patted his sidearm. "I still got the old peashooter."

"Like that'll do you any good if—"

"Nothing will do us any good, Rich, if it comes to that. At some point, we just have to trust to fate."

"It wasn't fate brought those things aboard," remarked Alton Webb from the plotting table.

"Stow it, Lieutenant," Kranuski said sharply, reining in his man. To Coombs he said, "Well . . . it's your call, Captain."

"Thanks for reminding me." Coombs ducked away through the hatch.

Descending the companionway, he deliberately quickened his pace, not giving himself time to think. Alice Langhorne's work area was in the old mission control room, the deck that had once housed the submarine's nuclear launch systems. It was stripped now, an empty shell on the third deck of the command-and-control module—the boat's forward section. The hatch was sealed off and plastered with red caution tape. Someone, probably a teenager, had scrawled, *Abandon hope all ye who enter here*, beneath a large skull and crossbones. Using his command access key, Coombs opened the door.

Half the lights were out in there; it was dim and clammy

as a dank basement. In the center of the room was a small glass coffin bathed in lamplight, with a dead girl inside. She was blue, blue of flesh as well as of dress, with glossy black hair fanned out around her head. The scene was funereal, eerily dreamlike.

Coombs stepped over the raised threshold. The girl was Louise Pangloss—Lulu—Fred Cowper's daughter. Commander Fred Cowper, retired, who had hijacked the sub as a refugee ship, filling it with a bunch of discontented shipyard workers and their teenage sons. Fred Cowper, whom Coombs had arrested for treason and later seen hauled ashore at Thule Air Base to be interrogated about the missing "Tonic"—the stolen antidote to Agent X. Harvey didn't know what had happened to Cowper after that, not until their escape from Thule, when Lulu's lifeless body had been found wedged atop the sail after two days submerged . . . holding Cowper's severed head in her lap.

She looked peaceful now, waxy and unreal. Her casket was a converted trophy case from the wardroom. It had been moved here after the men began to complain about "the dead girl stinking up the mess." Now it looked as though the doctor was using it as a desk: There was a chair beside it, and a box of documents on the floor. Atop the other materials, he could make out a spiral notebook labeled, *Xombies—A True Account, by Louise Alaric Pangloss*, and several computer disks labeled, *Maenad Project—Mogul Archives, Vol. I–VII.* Flipping through the notebook, scanning its dense blocks of minute handwriting, Coombs felt a twinge of pity. Lulu had been a smart girl, "a smaht cookie," as Cowper once said.

There was a rustling sound behind him. "Doctor?" Coombs called, trying to sound officious. "Dr. Langhorne?"

The walls began to move.

Don't panic . . . oh hell . . .

There they were—blue and cold as part of the machinery, as if they had sprouted from the guts of the boat itself. Forty of them, wedged wherever they could fit amid ducts and pipes and empty electronics bays, like toads under a rotting log.

Sensing him, they had begun to stir, swaying into motion like . . . like . . .

Like zombies, he thought. When they looked at him with those bright spider eyes, Coombs had to suppress a whole-body shudder. He had seen things like these take his men, witnessed close-up that nightmarish Xombie kiss: a man struggling helplessly, pinned face to face with one of these blue monstrosities like a rat in the coils of a snake, as the demon's gaping mouth covered his and instantly sucked all the breath from his body. The inconceivable horror in the man's dying eyes. Most of all, Coombs wished he could forget the *sound*—that hideous crunch of collapsing lungs, of crumpled ribs and vertebrae. A human being drained like a kid's juice box.

And then, seconds later, springing back to life as one of *them.*

The Xombies shuffled toward him, crawling, slithering, their unblinking black eyes staring as if fascinated. Closing in. Some of them were men and boys he knew—big Ed Albemarle was there, and Vic Noteiro's grandson, Julian—the naked and the dead. Coombs unsnapped the holster of his gun, flicking off the safety. He began to think that this hadn't been such a hot idea, that maybe this was it, the last mistake he would ever make.

Serves me right. Oh shit . . .

"Commander," said Alice Langhorne, appearing at his shoulder and nearly causing him to discharge his weapon. She waved the Xombies back, saying, "*Shoo*, you guys." As they moved away, she said, "Sorry. They're just being friendly."

"Doctor," said Coombs, his mouth paper-dry. Clearing his throat, he asked, "How's our little Snow White?"

"She's still inert. Still dormant."

"How can you tell she's even alive?"

"Well, she's not, strictly speaking. But as you can see, there's no evidence of physical deterioration, no decomposition. Even in that hyperbaric chamber, the cells of her body are continuing their metastasis. And it's a good thing they are: Without her ability to synthesize the Miska enzyme in her blood, we wouldn't have the means to pacify the others. They'd revert overnight."

"Won't she run dry?"

"She can regenerate indefinitely; all she needs is a little replacement hemoglobin to make up lost volume."

"Hemoglobin? Phil Tran told me you had her on glucose."

"We're out of glucose. Besides, saline and glucose are no substitute for whole blood—we can't take any chances with her. She's our golden goose."

"Where are you getting the hemoglobin?"

"I'm donating my own, for now."

Coombs had noticed that the doctor's face seemed a little wan but dismissed it as nothing unusual. Everybody gets pale on a submarine, it's an occupational hazard. But now . . . "You can't be doing that," he said firmly.

"It's a minimal amount, a couple of CCs a day. There isn't any alternative, unless you want to solicit contributions from the crew. I think we both know how that'll go over."

Coombs could think of nothing to say to that. "What did you want to speak to me about?" he asked.

Langhorne loomed above him, taller and more buff than he was, harshly competent and a good ten years older. Her hair was a platinum flattop, a razored shock of glass needles that jutted from her scalp like a crown. Like everyone else on board, she had a bandage on her forehead where the Mogul tracking implant had been removed—she was the one who had removed them. Without benefit of anesthetic.

For a woman in her fifties, Langhorne radiated a certain intensity. Among the men, she had already developed quite a reputation as a ballbuster, but Coombs was grateful for her confidence, her powerful sense of purpose, which was something he desperately needed right now. They all did.

"What do you think?" she said to him impatiently. "The *plan*, Sherlock. We're almost there, aren't we? We need to go over the *plan*."

"We can't have a plan until we know where to land. Right now we don't even know if the bay is navigable. We won't know that until we can see out there, and that won't be until sunrise."

"It's not that complicated. Just get this boat as close to the city as you can, blow up a rubber raft, and these guys will do the rest."

Captain Coombs looked at the slack-jawed Xombies, aimlessly milling around and staring off into space. Now that they were actually approaching their destination, it troubled him to think Langhorne might be wrong, that he had let himself get caught up in her delusion. *Plan my ass.* Maybe they should just scuttle the sub right now and be done with it—the end result would be the same. "You really think these things are going to be able to get ashore and execute a complex mission?"

"They can hear you, by the way; they're dead, not deaf. And they're not stupid, they're just a little . . . *slow*. Think of them as severely depressed." She smiled grimly. "But then, aren't we all?"

"Okay, great, but have you actually talked to them? I mean about doing this? Are they even capable of understanding?"

"Yes. They don't say much, but they're willing, or at least they're fairly suggestible. Can't you tell? They're more coherent than they look. The problem they have is that they're being bombarded with new sensations—every cell of their bodies is lit up like a Christmas tree from the Maenad infection, and it's overwhelmingly euphoric. They're *stoned*. The modified X enzyme in Lulu's blood acts as a depressant, bringing them down enough to function, but they do need supervision. That's why we'll have a video data link to guide them along the way. The only problem is the time factor: They have no sense of time, and if they're not back within eighteen or twenty hours, the inoculation will wear off, and we'll lose control of them—that is, they'll lose control of themselves. Either way, we'll never see them again."

"Most people on this boat would look upon that as a good thing."

"Yes, because they're morons. These guys are our only connection to dry land—maybe you'd like to try stepping ashore yourself and see what happens."

"No thanks. What makes you think they'll be able to find what they're looking for, this supposed vaccine? Miska's so-called Tonic? I thought he destroyed everything—and what he didn't destroy, the Moguls already picked over."

"The Moguls didn't know Uri Miska like I did. They financed his longevity research, but they didn't work with him every day for ten years. They didn't know everything we were doing, or everywhere we were doing it." She said this with bitter satisfaction, having married and divorced a Mogul, the now-deceased James Sandoval, whose naval contracting firm had refurbished the submarine for exclusive Mogul use.

As if thinking aloud, Alice Langhorne muttered, "Professor Miska had secrets—secrets he obviously kept from

everyone, including me. I admit it. The son of a bitch had
his own agenda, no question about that." She looked at the
angel-faced corpse in its glass casket, and Coombs thought
he detected a gleam of welling tears. "Agent X was just the
tip of the iceberg, I can tell you that," she said. "We still
know a few things, don't we, baby? *Oh* yes. We've still got
a few tricks up our sleeve . . ."

Commander Harvey Coombs, captain of what was likely
the world's last active nuclear submarine, and probably the
highest-ranking American naval officer left on the planet
(even discounting his emergency field promotion to admiral, which he did), now looked at the troubled face of Dr.
Alice Langhorne, perhaps the last surviving PhD, the last
scientist, maybe even the last *woman*, and thought, *She is
nuts.*

And then: *Hey, pal, join the club.*

CHAPTER **THREE**

WATERFIRE

Incomprehensibly vast as the horror was, it began with that most mundane of human annoyances: the persistent ringing of telephones. Seemingly at the exact stroke of midnight, Eastern Time, 911 phone banks began lighting up all over the country— indeed, all over the world. The extraordinary volume of calls would certainly have swamped the ability of emergency call centers to respond, had their operators been capable of responding, but they were not. Such call centers, staffed predominantly by women, were early casualties of the Maenad craze. So the phones rang and rang, unanswered.

Therefore, if the events of New Year's Eve do in fact represent the Apocalypse of biblical prophesy, as some have suggested, then it may truthfully be said that the Angel Gabriel did not herald the end of the world by blowing a trumpet. He notified us by phone.

—**The Maenad Project**

Sal DeLuca lay on a steel bed, dreaming of a steel beach.

He dreamed of sitting in fluorescent green twilight on dunes of granulated steel, surrounded by an immense steel

cylinder that rose fifty feet above him, its top open to a corrugated metal sky. Sal wasn't alone. There were other boys
there: his buddy Ray Despineau, Hector, Rick, Tyrell, Sasha,
Shane, Jake, Julian, and more. He knew them the way one
gets to know people one has been cooped up with in difficult circumstances for almost a month. He knew them too
well.

Working at Finishing was not like working at a lot of the
other departments in the plant. It was dirty. You had to wear
Tyvek coveralls, goggles, and a respirator. The coveralls
started out white and turned black. You had to climb the
rickety scaffolding again and again, lugging all your equipment, moving up and down inside that hull segment like a
cockroach in a garbage can. You took your breaks sitting on
cold piles of lead-colored, lead-heavy blasting grit. Worst
of all, it was a complete waste of time: This huge vertical
cylinder on which the boys tested every pneumatic tool
known to man—drilling, gouging, grinding, blasting—was
intended to house the command-and-control module—the
CCSM deck—of a Hawaii-class nuclear submarine. But it
never would; that sub would never be finished. No matter
how much work they put into it, the thing would just sit
here in its blasting cell, slowly rusting away, monument to
the imperatives of a powerful, lost civilization.

"This blows," said Kyle, a strikingly handsome sixteen-
year-old with intricately cornrowed hair. His mother had
braided it, and he refused to touch it—as though, if he waited
long enough, she might return. "What good is this? We ain't
never gonna need to know how these things are made.
We're never gonna build one; nobody ain't never gonna
build one ever again. This is just busywork to keep us . . .
busy."

From high up on the scaffold, a voice boomed down,
"Busywork?" It was Mr. Albemarle. Big fat Ed Albemarle,

supervisor of the Finishing Department. "Did I hear some-one say they want to trade places with somebody on the out-side?" he bellowed. "Because I guarantee you there are plenty of folks out there who would jump at the chance."

"No, sir. I just don't understand what good it'll do us to know the difference between pastel green and mare island green, or how to mix epoxy for sound damping or relagging or nonsweat—"

"That's *antisweat*." Mr. Albemarle was making his way down to them. "It keeps condensation from forming inside the hull. Keeps *this* from happening." He indicated the rust on the cylinder. "And if you intend this thing to last at sea for twenty years, that's pretty important."

"But this one's never going to sea."

"No, this one isn't. Get up, all of you."

They stood, brushing grit off their papery suits. Ed Albe-marle reached the sandy floor and planted himself in front of them, eyes shaded by his gray hard hat. "I guess there's something that hasn't been made clear to you, so let me try to hammer it in: *Everything matters*. The knowledge that's in your heads might be the only knowledge there is, and all our lives might depend on it. Welding, grinding, fore and aft, above main axis, below main axis, centerline, frame lines, buttock lines"—at *buttock*, the boys smirked for the hundredth time—"*everything*. So that you don't cause a fire and suffocate with your thumb up your butt because you were splicing a cable and cut a boot off one of the pen-etrations and didn't know how to seal it up again!"

Derrick said, "Come on—you guys and the Navy crew will do all that. Like they'd even let us touch it, give me a break."

"Everybody thinks that when they're sitting on the bench—you guys are reserve players. Any one of you could be the difference between life and death for all of us. Believe me, if and when that boat sails, you are going to carry your weight. For all you know, you boys may *be* the damn crew."

They all laughed. Tyrell said, "Cabin boy is more like it."

Albemarle frowned. "It's time to grow up, ladies. This is not Bring Your Children to Work Day. You are not here to play. Your fathers, your uncles, your grandfathers, maybe your older brothers are all working round the clock to earn you a safe cruise out of here. There's no other way out, trust me. Maybe you don't know what that means, maybe you think you don't care, but whether you like it or not, you are going to earn that ticket. Now come on."

Albemarle walked between the massive timbers supporting the hull section and opened the exit door, waiting at the eyewash fountain as the boys filed out.

"Are we finished for today?" groaned Freddy Fisk, a short, stocky boy with stamina issues. Freddie was the son of Arlo Fisk, one of the nuclear experts.

"We're never finished at Finishing."

"But Mr. Albemarle, we clear our cots at five thirty and go to class till noon, then we get a half hour for lunch and work for you guys till six. All we get is a half hour for dinner, then we have to study until lights out. We're missing dinner!"

Ed Albemarle rubbed his temple as if in pain. "Didn't you hear anything I just—? Fine, if you want to go, go!"

A little cheer went up, and the boys started to leave.

Ed raised his voice above the bustling escape: "I just thought you might want to head down to the pier with me and take a quick look at tomorrow's assignment. Your last assignment, really. All the classes are assembling down there right now, but if you'd rather go to the cafeteria . . ."

The boys stopped dead.

Sal DeLuca asked, "Are you serious, Mr. A?"

Ed nodded. "We don't have forever. The noose is tightening. It's time you boys got some familiarity with your new home before she puts to sea. So you want to check it out?"

Twenty-six eager heads bobbed like wake-churned buoys.

"Then let's go."

Sal woke up. At first he thought he was still dreaming: He was high up in a cavernous space, a steel chamber echoing with the avid chatter of boys. *We're home,* he heard them saying. *We're back!*

Home! Sal thought woozily. Then he came to himself and realized where he was: the Big Room—the huge midsection of the submarine, which had formerly housed twenty-four Trident missile tubes and now served as a makeshift dormitory for close to a hundred refugees, most of them teenage boys like himself. *Oh,* he thought, *Providence.*

Like everyone else in the Big Room, Sal DeLuca had made a nest for himself, a pallet of cardboard and foam rubber to cushion the steel-grated deck. Turning stiffly on his side, he peered down off his balcony to the more populated lower levels, half-expecting to see all the faces from his dream down there. He longed to hear the comforting boom of Mr. Albemarle's voice, or Tyrell's wisecracks.

But Ed Albemarle was dead. No, worse than dead. He was a mindless Xombie and Dr. Langhorne's test subject, as so many of the Xombies were. Either that, or they were simply gone, like Tyrell. The lucky ones were gone.

Sal's father was gone.

You can't go home again, he thought.

*   *   *

"Sir, you should come up and take a look at this."

"What is it?"

"Fire. We're seeing fires up here. From downtown."

The boat had spent the whole day traversing Narragansett Bay, painstakingly threading the narrow shipping channel to the exact spot where it had started out months before, then penetrating even deeper inland. Past the bridges and the islands. Past the barren submarine compound that jutted out into the bay like a hunk of Texas panhandle. Right up to the gates of Providence itself.

The coast looked clear. There were no signs of shipping, no boatloads of refugees, no obstructions of any kind. The industrial shorefront was deserted and peaceful, the buildings quiet as tombstones. On the low hills beyond, the first leaves of spring could be seen. The boat anchored in sight of downtown, near where the tugs docked, just outside the highway bridge and the great steel hurricane barrier.

It was no place for an Ohio-class submarine. At almost seventeen thousand tons, she was too big, too broad, and too deep for this harbor. *A total breach of regulations,* Kranuski reminded the captain. The slightest glitch and they could run aground, get stuck in the mud. Die like a mastodon in a tar pit. Without regular dredging, the channel was already changing, shifting, filling in. A vessel their size plowing through could collapse it completely in their wake—they might be digging their own grave. Kranuski's exact words.

Commander Coombs didn't like being bottled up either, in shallow water where the boat couldn't submerge, surrounded on all sides by hostile land. It made him very claustrophobic. *Sitting ducks,* he thought. But there was no choice. They couldn't risk a bad connection; the ship-to-shore data link had to work. And the target had to be within walking distance. Xombies didn't drive, though Langhorne would probably have them doing that next.

He climbed the ladder to the bridge cockpit and accepted a pair of binoculars from Dan Robles.

"Can you still see it?"

"Yes, sir, it's still there all right." Lieutenant Robles sighed, nursing untold grievances, the lids of his eyes heavy with the weight of injustice. "Dead ahead."

Coombs wasn't bothered by his quartermaster's attitude, it was nothing personal. He knew that Dan Robles was not affronted by him but by the world at large. Dan had once been a funny guy with a droll Latin sensibility, who could make you laugh with the slightest flex of his pencil-thin mustache, but the Xombie apocalypse had deeply offended him, and now he simply had no more patience for such nonsense. Not that Robles would ever complain or fail to follow the strictest definition of duty—that was a matter of honor. Coombs couldn't imagine what kind of crisis it would take to crack the man's haughty composure (he was the only officer willing to act as liaison to Dr. Langhorne, undeterred by her ghouls), but thus far nothing had, and that was saying something. That was saying a lot. Dan was one of the loyal ones, the steady few, and the captain trusted him completely.

The sun had set. The water was glassy-still, reflecting the acrylic pinks and blues of dusk, and the dark city skyline. The three huge smokestacks of Narragansett Electric loomed to port. At once Coombs could see what Robles was talking about—even without the binoculars.

Through the raised gates of the city's hurricane barrier and under the highway overpasses, less than a mile upriver, there were fires burning. Deliberate bonfires, a neat line of them. Coombs felt a wave of childish nausea at the sight, adrenaline curdling his blood: *Who's there?* The fires appeared to rise right out of the canal, reflecting orange in its black surface. What could it mean? A chain of floating crucibles in the heart of Providence? He could smell acrid smoke.

"The natives are restless," Robles said.

"Jesus. You think Xombies could do that?"

"I doubt it. Set fires like that? Langhorne's tame ones, maybe. Not the ones out in the wild. Why would they?"

"Then who? Who else could survive out there?"

"Somebody who's eager for attention, obviously."

"From us, you think?"

"Or about us. Broadcasting our position. I'm thinking of the Moguls."

"They can't dig up a radio?"

Robles squinted thoughtfully. "Then maybe an invitation: Coast is clear, no Xombies. Welcome ashore."

"Funny. How about an SOS?"

"Possibly an SOS, yes."

"Or a trap."

"Could be a trap, yes."

Coombs sighed in frustration. This was getting them nowhere. The question was whether to stay or leave, and if they left, where to? He knew what Kranuski would say: Norfolk. But Norfolk was dead, everywhere was dead . . . except here. Coombs watched the distant flames for a moment, blood thumping like voodoo drums in his head.

"One way to find out," he said.

Coombs was surprised at his own recklessness—as an inspector for the Naval Sea Systems Command, or NavSea, his job had been to eliminate risk, to take new submarines on shakedown cruises and rid them of bugs. He administered the SubSafe program, and was ruthless in implementing its strict requirements through all aspects of submarine construction and testing. Not everyone appreciated the job that he and his team did; he often sensed resentment from civilian techs who didn't like their work scrutinized and critiqued, and especially didn't like having to do it over if it didn't pass muster the first time. Or the second. Or the third . . .

Now many of those same civilians were part of his crew, and here he was, endangering the boat in a hundred different ways, putting all their lives at risk for some ridiculous plan that could only come to grief. Why? That was the sticking point, the quandary of quandaries for which there was no good answer anymore. Why indeed? Why do anything? Coombs knew Robles would have the simple answer to that one; he was always game.

Robles would say, *Why not?*

"That's WaterFire!" Alice Langhorne said, sounding bemused but also amused.

"It's what?"

"*WaterFire.* It's a festival they hold in Providence. That's why those braziers are in the river. It's kind of a big street carnival—I've been to it. On summer nights they play music, and people stroll along the riverbanks to watch the fire."

"I think I've heard of that," said Robles.

"Watch the fire, huh? That's it?" Coombs said.

"That's it. It's a big tourist draw."

"Why is it happening *now*?" Kranuski demanded.

Langhorne lowered the binoculars, shaking her head. "You got me. Maybe we look like tourists."

Coombs asked her, "Do you still want to go through with your operation?"

"Hmm." She raised the binoculars to her eyes again. "Well . . . I don't think we have any choice, do we? We're here. What else are we gonna do?"

"We sure as hell *do* have a choice," erupted Kranuski. "Captain, those fires could be a beacon opening us up to aerial attack. We know the Moguls have planes, and there may be others. I advise we leave while we still can."

"Rich, if someone wants to call in an air strike on us, we're already dead ducks. The tide's against us; it would take us all night to get back out to deep water. In the meantime, we'll be wallowing in the bay like a beached whale. Besides, nobody's going to try and sink us, especially not the Moguls. If anything, they'd try to capture the boat—it's too valuable a prize to destroy."

"I agree," Kranuski said sharply. "So maybe while we're going on this wild-goose chase, they're setting up a blockade, fencing us in. It wouldn't be hard. Are you willing to let that happen?"

Coombs heard the unspoken accusation: *Like you did before?* "We're not going to gain anything by hiding at the bottom of the ocean, Rich. Our supplies are low, time is running out. At some point, we have to roll the dice, and I say that time is now." Coombs awkwardly turned to Dr. Langhorne, all three of them squeezed together in the bridge cockpit. "Alice, are your . . . uh, people ready to disembark?"

"Anytime."

"Then for God's sake, let's do it."

CHAPTER **FOUR**

NANTUCKET SLEIGH RIDE

AP—Thursday, December 16—According to government scientists, contamination by the mysterious substance known as "Agent X" or "Blue Rust" is much more widespread than previously supposed.

"We are finding it throughout the environment, including inside the human body, where it forms a weak bond with anaerobic hemoglobin," said Cary Welks, Director of the National Science Foundation. "But I want to stress that so far we have not seen any adverse effects in humans."

Agent X was first discovered in October by researchers at NASA's Ames Research Center, who noted an unexplained increase in malfunctions involving highly sensitive, vacuum-sealed electronic equipment. Since then, similar effects have been reported around the globe.

—**The Maenad Project**

Lt. Cmdr. Dan Robles was never a "team player" in the sense of being blindly loyal to senior authority—he never had much use for that particular military mentality. A child of illegal immigrants who went through hell to get their citizenship, he always had the deepest regard for the

American Dream, if not necessarily the American reality. "My country right or wrong" did not sit well with him; you couldn't trust an institution with your soul. Though eager to serve, Dan never believed it was in his country's best interest that he be a robot who just followed orders. He did what he did because he thought it was right, or because it didn't matter one way or the other. Plenty of things in life didn't matter much, and he was content to toe the line. Why not? You couldn't very well have everybody making up their own rules. Thus, most of his nineteen-year naval career had been relatively uneventful, though his flippancy toward officialdom and mindless patriotic bromides had probably cost him at least a grade in rank—some senior officers didn't appreciate the philosophy that true patriotism included a deep sense of skepticism and a healthy dose of the absurd. That was why he quickly washed out of the Marines.

No, Dan Robles always hoped that if the official version didn't cut it, he would go his own way, no matter the consequences. But this ideal of his had never been truly tested until Agent X.

He would never forget the night that civilian mob arrived at the submarine pen, threatening to sink the boat unless they were let aboard—and the crew's anger and confusion at being ordered to risk their necks helping the hijackers. Officers like Rich Kranuski and Alton Webb would never forgive Harvey Coombs for caving in to pressure, but as far as Robles was concerned, the commander did the only sensible thing. Fred Cowper was not bluffing; he would have sunk the boat. Furthermore, those people had an absolute right to be there—they had been promised a ride to safety, and it was only because of their marathon refit that the vessel was seaworthy in the first place. They had been swindled.

If guys like Webb and Kranuski thought he was a traitor

for going along with it, Robles took that as a sign that he must be doing something right.

These were things he had learned about himself since the end of the world.

"Wait a second," Robles said, tethered to the rail and standing above them on the sail's crest. "Captain, there's something else out there. Drifting toward us."

They all trained their binoculars up the river.

"What now?" It was too dark to see properly, but Coombs could make out a long, black object moving downstream with the outgoing tide. A boat of some kind. It lazily floated toward them under the hurricane barrier. *What the hell . . . ?* As it emerged into the moonlight, it began to resemble a strange canoe, with a shiny silver blade rising like a figurehead from its prow. "What *is* that?" he asked. "Hiawatha?"

"It's a *gondola*," Langhorne said. "Wow."

"A gondola? Like in Venice?"

"Yeah. It's because of—"

"It *is* a gondola," said Coombs queasily. "What the hell is a gondola doing here? Don't tell me: It's because of Firewater."

"WaterFire."

"Dan, can you see anybody in it?"

"No. It's too dark."

"We better throw some light on that, then."

"Or blow it out of the water."

"Either way, it'll make us conspicuous."

Kranuski snapped, "Are you kidding? Nothing's gonna make us more conspicuous than we already are. We can't let it near the hull—it could have a bomb in it . . . or worse."

Coombs thought about it, then said, "Rig the spotlight, quick. And pass up that carbine."

As Kranuski and Robles handled this, Coombs asked

Langhorne, "In your opinion, could Xombies be tending those fires?"

"I don't know. Not ordinary ones, I would say."

"That's what I thought."

"But there's always the possibility . . ."

"What?"

"That Miska's out there."

Robles turned on the spotlight and swept its beam across the water. The eerie, drifting gondola suddenly stood out starkly from the surrounding darkness, as if pinned under a microscope. With its lacquered black hull and red velvet seats, it looked to Coombs like some kind of funeral barge, a weird, medieval specter lost in time and place. Discordant as those torches.

"There's somebody in there," Robles said urgently.

"Shit." They all raised their weapons and took aim, ready to pour fire down.

"Wait!" Robles said. "It looks like a little kid. He's not moving."

"Who gives a crap?" said Kranuski, wielding the rifle. "Let's sink the bastard before he does move."

"Hold up," Coombs said. "Can you tell if he's blue?"

"I don't think so, sir."

"You don't think you can tell, or you don't think he's blue?"

"He's not blue. He's definitely not blue. I can see him breathing."

"Try hailing him," Langhorne said.

To Kranuski's disgust, Coombs switched on the microphone, and said, "HEY, KID. CAN YOU HEAR ME?" His amplified voice echoed across the water. "LET US KNOW YOU'RE ALIVE, SO WE CAN HELP YOU."

For a moment, nothing happened. Then a small, shivering

hand rose into the light, and everyone on the bridge heard a
deeply reassuring sound, a noise more welcome in its pure
humanity than any words could be. A sound no Xombie
would utter:

It was the high, thin whimper of a child.

Exercising extreme caution and a long hook, they wrangled
the gondola alongside and took the boy aboard. Alice Langhorne gave him a sedative to calm him down. He was in
shock, practically catatonic, and instantly fell into a deep
sleep. All she had gotten out of him was that his name was
Bobby. He looked about ten years old, filthy, and half-
starved. *You think this is our firebug?* Coombs had asked
her. Alice could only shrug—the poor kid didn't look capable of striking a match. It would be interesting to find out
how he could have survived all these months, but in the
meantime she thought it best to let him sleep.

After cleaning Bobby off, then treating all his minor cuts
and contusions, Langhorne hooked the unconscious kid up
to an IV drip and relegated his care to the other minors on
board, the older boys in the Big Room. One of Phil Tran's
medical trainees got the duty, a scraggly kid named Sal
DeLuca—teenage son of the late Gus DeLuca. Tran assured
her he was smart. Anyway, they had more than enough
space back there, a regular Boys Town. And Alice had other
things to think about.

"All hands prepare for exiting shore party, logistics
hatch two."

Coombs's terse command rang through the ship, and everyone knew exactly what to do—Kranuski had drilled
them on it, and Alton Webb made damn sure there were no

mistakes. All doorways in the control section were sealed off and tightly dogged, leaving only a single passage leading from the quarantined third level to the open topside hatch. In that way, the crew would be insulated from any threat, and the unleashed Xombies had nowhere to go but up . . . and out.

Alice Langhorne was posted forward in the communications suite, the "radio shack," a tiny compartment in the far bow. Though she regretted not being able personally to escort her fellows topside, she knew it was more important that they begin to function alone—she wouldn't be there to hold their hands when they went ashore. She was seated at a computer console, wearing a radio headset and intently watching live video from the third deck. It was a split-screen image broadcast from two tiny digital cameras bolted to the late Ed Albemarle's blue skull—what Langhorne dubbed her "Xombiecams"—one facing forward and the other back.

When all was in readiness, Coombs called down to her from the bridge. "This is it, Alice. Proceed to move them out."

"Gotcha." Switching on her audio feed, she said, "Guys? Guys, listen to me. It's time to go up. Ed, open the aft door and move them out." She had tested this and was confident it would work, but it was still a relief to see the picture on the screen lurch into motion. "They're moving."

The gondola had been salvaged—there was no point in risking a raft if they didn't have to—and was secured to a cleat at the far stern, where the deck sloped underwater toward the boat's great rudder fin. Now Commander Coombs watched from his perch atop the sail as Xombies began to emerge from the logistics hatch and move aft down that long, long stretch of deck.

Though he was thirty feet above them, the sight of those things still made him uneasy. Surely it was utter madness to imagine they could be set loose like this and come back of their own volition. That they could be made to go on some kind of complicated scavenger hunt and even obediently return to the ship laden with groceries. Langhorne made it all sound so feasible . . . but she was crazy. And if she was crazy, that meant he was crazy, too, for listening to her—a zombie himself.

Coombs could never get over how they moved. There was something bizarre about it, a jerky precision like a windup toy. Buglike, that's what it was, like ants or flies, flickering so you couldn't quite take them in except in blinks. Yet at the same time they could be boneless as an octopus, fluid as wisps of smoke

It was fully dark now; Coombs couldn't see as well as he would have liked, but things seemed to be going as planned—far better than he'd expected, actually. *So far so good.* There were forty of them, all strung together on a cable, and he tried to keep count as they emerged: . . . *twelve, thirteen, fourteen . . .*

There was Albemarle, unmistakable from his size, an alarming, naked behemoth still clutching his big hammer from the factory. With his hammer and his video headgear, he looked almost human. Coombs watched as he loped to the gondola and swept aboard with barely a ripple. Several other Xombies also boarded the boat. They were the ones strapped with spare batteries, lights, and other devices that had to stay dry. As the gondola cast off, those left behind began slipping into the water, ducking under its forbidding black surface as easily as crocodiles from a riverbank.

Then, as if by magic, the gondola began to move. It glided away without any visible means of propulsion, and Coombs knew the creatures down there were pulling it, towing it as they walked along the murky bottom like some perverse Nantucket sleigh ride. He shook his head in sickly wonder.

He was interrupted in his reverie by a yelling from his headset. It was Alice Langhorne.

"What was that, Alice? I didn't copy."

"I said Lulu's gone!"

"She's what?" Coombs felt an icy rush down his spine.

"Lulu broke out of her case and escaped! Do you understand? She's going with them!"

CHAPTER **FIVE**

BLUE MAN GROUP

In attempting to chronicle the Maenad epidemic, we are like
archaeologists trying to re-create an ancient civilization from a
few potsherds. The available record seems to be nothing but
a catalogue of loose ends, the timeline of human history having been clipped like a cheap length of twine. But the unraveling
was not so total. Throughout America and the world, there were
refuges, havens, isolated pockets of relative security that continued to survive long after the initial outbreak. Most of these were
militaristic in nature—bases and other fortified compounds—but
others were due to geographical or cultural factors: islands, prisons, work camps, heavy industries such as oil drilling or mining,
religious retreats. What they all had in common was a lack of
women. For wherever women went, there followed doom.

—**The Maenad Project**

New Year's Day, 6:29 A.M.

Downtown Providence is deserted, all the office buildings
and banks, the immense Providence Place Mall, the arena
and the convention center, closed for the holiday, closed forever, and the boy skitters antlike through its brick canyons,

heedless of either the harsh, wind-driven sleet or his own harsh tears mingling with it.

"No, no, no . . ." he whimpers as he runs.

Occasional cars shoosh past, taillights gleaming fire-alarm red off the wet pavement. Church bells are ringing, and not far away he can hear sirens and the blaring drone of car horns from I-95—it sounds like the world's biggest traffic jam. But Bobby Rubio barely takes notice of the din, or of any of his surroundings. All his thoughts whirlpool around one frantic goal: to find his father.

A big car pulls up alongside Bobby, dousing his sneakers with slush, and its driver leans across the passenger seat, yelling, "Get in, son!"

Bobby's heart leaps with the impossible hope that it is his dad, but realizes at once it's just a stranger, a red-faced old man with a cockatoo crest of white hair and the leering urgency of a drive-by pervert. Disgusted, Bobby peels away with a snarl.

The car matches his pace, the man calling out, "Listen! It's an emergency! Do you hear me? I'm trying to help you! You have to get off the street!"

Ignoring the voice, Bobby cuts sharply up a narrow one-way alley so the man can't follow. Why did everything bad have to happen at once?

"Good!" the man's voice shouts at his back. "I hope they get you!" The car spurts away.

Bobby emerges on Washington Street and breaks left, making for the massive brick edifice of the Biltmore Hotel at the end. It's not the hotel he wants, but the multistory parking garage behind the hotel, the Parkade, where his dad works. Beyond the hotel, the buildings open up in front of City Hall, and he can see others running. There's some kind of ugly riot in Kennedy Plaza: people breaking the windows of blocked cars to drag out screaming passengers, and other people fleeing their vehicles and being chased across the park. He can't see much of what's going on, but even from a distance he can tell that the ones causing all the trouble look crazy, weird—they look like his mom looked. They look . . . *blue.*

No—don't look at it! Bobby shudders in fear and turns away, gratefully ducking out of sight into a corner entrance of the garage.

Sheltered from the freezing wind and rain, he is suddenly aware of the frantic speed of his body, its manic clockwork spinning out of control to some kind of explosion or collapse. He yearns to start shrieking and never stop, or just curl up in a corner of the piss-smelling concrete stairwell and vomit up deep wracking sobs until he is empty inside. *Oh God, to be empty, to be blank.* He's shaking so hard he can barely think or stand. But he can't stop now; he's almost there.

At the far back of the garage, at the base of the steeply twining exit ramp, he can make out the familiar, bearlike figure of his father behind the fogged glass of the lighted cashier's booth.

Bobby whimpers, "Dad, Dad," as he shambles forward, nearly swooning in anticipation of laying down his horrific burden, of relinquishing it to his father's easygoing strength. His dad will know what to do. His dad will have to know . . .

Pain woke him up—something piercing the back of his hand. Bobby opened his eyes to an amazing, inexplicable vision. He was in an enormous tunnel of some sort, a windowless atrium four stories high, with rope ladders scaling the balconies and a strange ceiling of numbered white domes. Laundry was strung from one side to the other, giving it the look of a tenement courtyard, and makeshift structures of wood, fabric, plastic sheeting, and cardboard cluttered the steel-grated tiers. But the most amazing thing was that there were *people*—not blue-skinned monsters, but real human beings. Boys, all boys. The place smelled like a locker room and sounded like one, too, the scores of teenagers roosting in that metal cavern like so many pigeons, clambering up and down the scaffolds, sprawling in hammocks, chattering and calling to one another across the echoing subterranean galleries.

Ow—there was that pain again. It was from a big fat IV needle—a bag of clear fluid was dripping into his hand from above. Bobby had nearly yanked it out trying to sit up.

"Hey, you're awake," said a hoarse teenage voice, speaking from behind the glare of a hanging lamp. "Whoa, just chill, lie back, you're safe here." The voice spoke into a microphone: "Uh, Mr. Tran? He's awake."

"How's he look?" squawked an intercom. "Is he lucid?"

"I don't know." To Bobby: "Are you lucid?"

"What?"

"He seems okay to me."

"Keep an eye on him. Talk to him. I'm tied up here at the moment. Can you handle it a while longer?"

"Yes, sir, I guess."

"Good man. I'll be down as quick as I can. Just make sure he's comfortable. Remember what I've shown you, Sal. This is just like our first-aid drills, no different."

"I'm on it, sir. Over."

"Who are you?" Bobby asked, squinting into the light.

"I'm Sal DeLuca." He moved the lamp so that Bobby

could see him. Sal Deluca was tall and thin, almost gaunt, with large, intense eyes that studied Bobby through long hanks of unwashed brown hair. "What's your name?" he asked.

"Bobby. Bobby Rubio."

"Bobby Rubio," Sal repeated, writing it down. "Age?"

"I'm ten . . . I think."

"You think? You don't know your own age?"

"I don't know . . . How long has it been? What month is it?" Bobby was suddenly seized with panic.

"April."

Slumping with relief, he said, "I'm ten, I'm still ten. My birthday isn't until July."

"And how are you feeling, Bobby? Any pain or discomfort?"

"My hand hurts."

"Sorry, we had to do that; you were very dehydrated when you came in. Any other problems?"

"Uh-uh. I don't think."

"Good. Well, pleased to meet you, Bobby." Sal shook the smaller boy's limp hand. "Welcome to the Big Room. You want some bug juice? It's like Hawaiian Punch." He handed over a straw cup full of red liquid.

Bobby accepted it eagerly, draining the sweet drink in one gulp. Catching his breath, he asked, "Where is this place?"

"What, the Big Room? It's the middle section of the hull, where all the Trident missile silos used to be—my dad helped pull 'em out. Now it's Crib City, one big slumber party. It's minorly out of control right now. Nobody wants to be in charge since the last Youth Liaison Officer, Lulu, got Exed. She thought she had something wrong with her that kept her from going Smurf, but it still got her in the

end, and all her friends. I heard she got my dad killed, too."
A shadow passed over Sal's face, cleared.

"Anyway, this is juvie country all in here—the adults pretty much bunk forward or aft of us. We've got the best deal on the boat, don't you think?"

Bobby could hardly follow any of this, except for one word: "Boat? What boat?"

"What boat do you think, dude? *This* boat."

"We're on a . . . boat?"

"Not a *boat*, dipwad, a *submarine*."

"A *summarine*? No way."

"Yes way. *This* is a submarine, all this. Didn't you know that?"

Bobby recoiled. "You're crazy. There's no summarine." He looked past the older boy at the steel catacomb beyond, his eyes welling with furious tears. "You're lying."

"Dude, I swear to God. Ohio-class FBM—biggest one they make. We're about thirty feet below the waterline."

Eyes overflowing, Bobby cried, "You're *lying*! You're trying to trick me! We're not underwater! We're *not*! Let me *go*! I want my dad! *Dad!* I have to find my mom and dad! *Dad! Mommeee!*" The boy began to thrash wildly against his restraints.

Oh man, Sal thought. *Here we go.* Ignoring the stares from above, he hurriedly squirted a precious cc of Demerol solution into the kid's IV line, wishing Lieutenant Tran were there to supervise. "Take it easy. There you go . . . there you go. Don't worry, everything's gonna be okay. I miss my dad, too, man." Brightening, he said, "Hey, how 'bout some pancakes? I've been saving some for you, for when you woke up."

Bobby stopped struggling. "Pancakes?" he sniffled.

"Yeah, I got 'em right here." Sal held up a covered

tray. "But you can't have any unless you promise to be cool."

"I will," Bobby said desperately, starting to cry again. "I will, I swear."

"Hey, it's all good." Sal passed him the tray and helped him sit up. Bobby trembled with eagerness at the sight of the food—not only pancakes, but dabs of applesauce and scrambled eggs. Everything was cold, but he didn't care. Wolfing it down, he scarcely noticed the rapt, hungry eyes following his every mouthful, nor did he realize that all activity in the vast chamber had paused to watch him eat.

Nearly drooling himself, Sal said, "Make it last, kid."

"How could she have gotten off the boat without you seeing her?" Kranuski said accusingly. "That girl was critical; her body is the only existing reservoir of Miska's serum! Without her, we have nothing."

Coombs shook his head. "I realize that, Rich. She's small, it was dark. She must have just slipped out with the others. I wasn't looking for her."

"Are you sure you were looking at all?"

"You're out of order, Lieutenant. Yes, I was looking. I didn't see anything. Apparently no one else on watch did, either. All I can think is that Albemarle must have shielded her with his body."

"Well, what happens now? If she's gone, that means we lose the Xombies, right? I mean, without her blood to control them, we can't take them back on board. So the mission is effectively over." Kranuski sounded eager for this to be so.

"Not necessarily," said Alice Langhorne, intently watching her video monitor. The image was a blurred green jumble of infrared. There would be little to see until dawn. "All it means is that she left with them. Whether she'll *stay* with them is another matter, but there is clearly some residual bond there. Maybe that's a hopeful thing—she's obviously much more capable of independent reasoning than they are. In fact, her faculties ought to be perfectly intact. Unlike the rest of them, she's been vaccinated with the actual enzyme, the pure concentrate, which should have preserved all her higher brain functions. If she's at all sane, they could probably use her help, and so could we. I mean *look* at this." Langhorne pointed at the poor picture quality. "How am I supposed conduct them under these conditions?"

"Come *on*," blurted Kranuski. "She saw the opportunity to escape and took it. Like any caged animal. We're never going to see her again."

Dr. Langhorne said patiently, "I can't predict what she's liable to do. All we know for sure is that so far they are still on task, and until that changes, there is no reason to jump to conclusions. Lulu led them when she was alive, why not now?"

"Give me a break. You're just stalling."

"You heard her, Rich," said the captain. "We're going to stick to plan . . . for now. In the meantime, I want you and Mr. Robles to develop some contingencies for resupplying our provisions in case Langhorne's expedition doesn't return—food stores are at rock bottom, and those kids are going to start crashing if we don't do something fast. I don't need to tell you what will happen if we have any deaths on board, if that room back there becomes a nest of Xombies. The whole city is at our doorstep: restaurants, shops, warehouses—there must be something we can do in reasonable safety, even without the Blue Man Group at our disposal. Make this your top priority. I want at least three serious options on my desk by 0600. Don't be afraid to be bold."

"Be bold . . ." Kranuski wasn't listening anymore. Gesturing at someone out the doorway, he said, "Captain, I'm afraid I have a very different priority right now. If you order us to stay here, against all reasonable expectation of success, and in complete disregard for ship's safety, I must advise you I intend to follow regulations."

Everyone froze. Suddenly the hum of the electronics seemed very loud.

"Don't do it, Rich. This is not the time." Coombs felt the hulking presence of Alton Webb crowding into the radio shack behind him. He was alarmed to realize that except for Dr. Langhorne, he was surrounded by Kranuski's gang: Webb, Jack Kraus, and even a civilian, Henry Bartholomew, who blamed Coombs for the death of his nephew Jake. None of Coombs's faithful was in sight. He said, "If I don't need a security detail to protect me from Xombies, are you saying I need one to protect me from my own crew?"

"It's not your crew anymore." Richard Kranuski took a deep breath, and announced, "Commander Harvey Coombs, I hereby relieve you of command and confine you to quarters, pending charges of incompetence and gross dereliction of duty. Mr. Webb, please escort the captain to his new quarters."

"Rich, I'm telling you to consider what you're—" Coombs tried to leap for the intercom. There was a brief, ugly scuffle, Webb overpowering the captain and taking him in a choke hold.

"Don't fight, you're just making it worse for yourself," Webb grunted.

"Oh that's great," said Langhorne in disgust. She turned to Kranuski: "That's just great. Brilliant move, Caligula. What comes next? Public executions?"

Richard Kranuski turned and leaned into her face, their

profiles strikingly alike, one black-haired, one white, both icily handsome and equally contemptuous of the other. "You've got exactly until the next tide to prove to me that you're not a waste of space on my vessel," he said. "Then we sail—with or without you."

CHAPTER **SIX**

X GAMES

Although most representatives of the federal government and armed services acted heroically in the face of the crisis—and indeed died at their posts—there is substantial evidence that major resources were diverted to private interests at the time they were needed most to shore up the collapsing national infrastructure. Classified military records, preserved as part of the SPAM initiative, reveal hundreds of examples of elite forces providing extraordinary security and logistical support for private individuals and their families, while more vital emergency personnel were left exposed to be killed or infected in droves. While it is tempting to assume that these were merely random incidences of corruption amid the greater chaos, a pattern emerges that suggests an organized, methodical, and highly secretive program to abandon the existing government and establish an alternate one.

—**The Maenad Project**

"Hey, guys, guess what!" shouted Kyle Hancock from the rafters. "Captain Coombs has just been arrested! Kranuski's in charge now!"

There was an eruption of activity in the great compartment. Some of it was cursing and complaining, some was cheering, but most of it was eager chatter of the wait-and-see variety. None of the boys had much love for Harvey Coombs—they had pretty consistently starved under his watch. The only time they had eaten well, in fact, was for the few weeks they had been in the service of the Moguls . . . and that had had its own drawbacks.

Sal DeLuca looked up from his chessboard and felt a twinge of anxiety: *Not again.* No wonder Tran was too busy to come aft, with another mutiny going on. How many captains were they going to run through on this boat? This made three so far. He looked across at his younger opponent, the new kid, and said, "Don't worry about it. It's probably not going to make much difference to us."

"Check," said Bobby, intent on the game. Sal's plan to distract the boy from his trauma was proving almost too successful—the kid had moves.

"No you don't," Sal said. He skated his queen to the king's defense, and instantly realized she would have to be sacrificed. *Damn.* He might as well resign right now—you couldn't do anything without a queen. Trying to stall, he asked, "So, how'd you make it out there?"

Bobby grunted, "Huh?"

"How'd you survive so long?"

The boy pointedly ignored him. It was clear he wasn't ready to talk about it; the force of his attention had been honed to a thin wedge, a fragile tool unsuited to other uses. Push too hard, and it would break.

"You don't have to talk about it if you don't want to," said Sal. "You want to know how I made it through? I rode my bike."

Bobby grunted again.

"Seriously. You want to hear about it?" Sal didn't wait

for a reply. "I don't know how they knew something was gonna happen, but on the day before New Year's, all of us were supposed to get picked up by buses and taken under escort to the submarine plant where our dads worked. Or uncles or brothers or whatever—only immediate family. Just get on a bus with no explanation and *no girls allowed*. But I missed the bus! My dad and I were kind of living our separate lives, and I wasn't home a lot. We had different schedules and really didn't meet up much, especially over vacation. I never even got his message. I was heavy into BMX, and used to ride my bike a lot between East Greenwich and Wickford to visit my girlfriend. The terrain there is *excellent*—there's a lot of rugged country. I was training for the freestyle event at this year's X Games. Anyway, we went to a New Year's Eve party down around Narragansett, but then Wendy got a headache and wanted to go home, so we left early, even before the countdown. I was kind of pissed, but it was her car, you know? She didn't even want to stay over at my place, even though we would have had the whole house to ourselves.

"Wendy hardly said anything all the way home. That's what sucks—I didn't know it was the last time I'd ever see her, so I didn't even kiss her good night, just got my bike out of her car and that was it. Last thing I saw was her taillights going down the hill, with the sound of people yelling and horns honking and fireworks all over the place. I remember thinking, 'Happy New Year—yeah right.'

"I went in the house, nuked a frozen burrito, and turned on the TV. It was only a few minutes after midnight, so I figured I could still catch some of the celebrations—New Year's Rockin' Eve or whatever. But that was the first sign that something was messed up: Most channels were either dead air or 'experiencing technical difficulties.' The rest were showing old reruns. I could *not* believe it. Dude, it was like, 'Is this the worst New Year's Eve *ever*?' I thought about calling Wendy on her cell but just went to bed instead. I was pretty wasted.

"The next morning I woke up with a pillow over my head and a *wicked* headache. I don't know if it was more from the hangover or from the noise—there were car horns and sirens and car alarms going off all night. It was *still* going on. And we live in a pretty quiet area usually, a lot of officer housing. I got cleaned up and took some ibuprofin, then I noticed there were about ten messages on the answering machine, so I hit the button. It was my dad."

All at once, Sal couldn't speak. It was maddening. He wanted so bad to be over this, but he knew that if he said one more word, he would start crying again. *Come on,* he thought, pinching the back of his hand hard enough to leave a welt. *You can't keep doing this, it's ridiculous. He's better off dead—handle it!*

But Sal couldn't help it. It was the memory of his father's scared voice on that answering machine, saying, *Sal, are you there? If you're there, pick up—it's an emergency. Did you get my note about the bus? There's going to be a company bus coming to pick you up tomorrow to bring you to the plant. It is very important that you be on it, all right? Very, very important. You'll find out why when you get here. Do not miss this bus, son, whatever you do.*

Before Sal could begin to wrap his mind around that, the next message started: *Sal, pick up. Pick up! Shit. Shit, shit, shit. You're still not there. Okay, listen, this is important: You missed the bus, but you still have to get to the plant. I don't care how you do it, but come here as quick as you can. This is no joke! Whatever you do, avoid other people— there's some kind of murder epidemic going on, and a lot of crazy psychos are running around killing people. I know what you're thinking, but it's true. Watch out for women especially—they're all contagious. I'm not allowed to leave, or I'd come get you. I'm serious, Sal, take your bike and get out, now. Stay off the roads. Go as fast as you can, and don't stop for anything. My God, I hope you get this message.*

All the other messages were pretty much the same, though increasingly desperate. His father was crying by the end. Sal had never heard his father cry before.

Standing amid the familiar clutter of his kitchen, holding a box of cornflakes, Sal couldn't process the information—it was like he was still dreaming, or stoned. Sal's father Gus DeLuca was probably the most infuriatingly hardheaded person he had ever met, a man who had zero tolerance for anything he deemed "fantasyland," so *something* was seriously wrong. Worrying that his dad had snapped, he went to his father's room. The drawers were pulled out and the old man's Samsonite suitcase was missing. Returning to the kitchen, Sal found the note about the bus taped to the fridge calendar. It had been there a couple of days. He picked up the phone to call the plant, but the line was dead. In a daze, he turned on the TV. Snow—all snow. Pondering, searching for anything that would make sense, Sal opened the window and leaned out.

Wow.

The air was full of smoke. He could see cars backed up along the road, and there were alarms going off far into the distance, an insane multitude of alarms—the most he'd ever heard at once. But he couldn't see any people. That was the weird thing. With all the noise and disturbance, neighbors should have been standing in the road checking it out, but Sal couldn't see a single person.

And then he did. Just as he was about to shut the window, he caught sight of a group of people charging up the street. Three women leading five or six men. They were half-naked and running like maniacs, but the main thing was, they were *blue*. Really *blue* blue, like zombies in a cheesy horror movie. It was sick. Their mouths were wide open, and their eyes were black and bugging out of their heads.

At first Sal couldn't move, frozen in shock, but as they crossed his driveway he snapped out of it and shut the window. They saw him then, and he would never forget the sensation of being spotted, like prey—it was as if they *locked on* to him. *Holy shit!* Everything his dad had said was still spinning in his head, so he didn't have to think long about what to do. He just did it.

On the fly, Sal grabbed his helmet, his jacket, and his BMX bike, and plowed through the back door. If there had been a Xombie lurking out there, he would have been toast. Sal knew exactly where he was going. His backyard overlooked the train tracks, and past that it was all swampland and miles of rugged trails he knew by heart, so he jumped on his bike and took off toward the back fence. Out of the corner of his visor he saw something nasty come rushing around the porch, but before it reached him, he hit the ramp he used for practice jumps and popped over the fence. Just like he did every day.

After that he never stopped pedaling. In a straight line it was only about eight miles between his house and the submarine works, but navigating through the rough terrain made it a lot longer. At some point it started sleeting, making the icy trails even more slippery. Tiring, he followed the railroad tracks as long as he could, until blue maniacs started coming down the embankment ahead of him, then he made for the woods again. Aside from crazy blue people, there were other obstacles to avoid: blind gullies, dense brush, ponds, houses, roads, and a lot of fenced government property. At least it was winter, and the ground was hard; in springtime, he often got bogged down in the mud.

But there was a problem. Sal was gathering *followers*. It was becoming a regular entourage—he hardly dared look back. Even though the freaks were naked and barefoot, they never quit or got tired, just kept chasing him. Every time he had to backtrack or change direction, they drew closer . . . and all the time more and more were accumulating. At first he had barely noticed them, they were so few and far away, but the longer he went, the more he began to see rows of them in the distance, fanning out like hellish search parties, waiting for him to hit a wall or a dead end or the limits of his own endurance—anything that would hold him up long enough for them to close their noose. It was just a matter of time.

Then it happened. Out of nowhere he was completely blocked, cut off by an impenetrable woodfall and forced back to the railroad culvert. In that moment, Sal feared he was done. They were all around him, sweeping in for the kill.

That's when he heard the train.

It was the high-speed Acela Express—one of the same trains that killed his old dog, Banjo. His dad had had to scrape the poor hound up in a bucket. Those trains were so fast that by the time you saw them coming, it was already too late—everyone who lived along the tracks had a story to tell. But right now Sal wasn't afraid of being killed by a train. He was more concerned with it blocking his escape so the crazies could do the job. They were all around him now, forcing him toward the railroad tracks as if they knew this was their chance. Compared to those horrible, gaping faces, the train didn't seem so scary, which was how Sal managed to do what he did.

Leaping into motion, he rode his bike straight at the railroad ditch. As several maniacal women threw themselves in his path, Sal head-butted the nearest one with his helmet and jumped down the steep gravel embankment. It was almost too late—the hurtling locomotive was *right there*, roaring up to meet him at 150 miles an hour, and the psychos on his back clinging fiercely as he crossed the tracks—

WHOOOOOM!—

—and then their weight was *gone*, jerked loose by a violent shock wave that almost spun Sal off his bike. The rest of the train roared by, barely inches away. Before it completely passed, he was already on the move again, climbing the far embankment.

Looking back, he could see a mess of busted meat and bone flopping along the tracks like wet laundry: twitching arms and legs and tumbled-out guts and cracked heads bouncing through the air like hairy coconuts.

Trancelike, Sal said, "Worst thing I ever saw . . . and also the best, you know? I sometimes wonder if there was even anybody alive on that train, you know? I think God sent that train! But more Xombies were still coming, still trying to catch me, and I had to move."

"*Make* your move," said Bobby impatiently, fidgeting.

Sal suddenly realized he had been thinking aloud for some time. Telling Bobby the whole story. The crisis had passed.

"In a second, dude," he said. "Don't you want to hear how I got to the factory compound? It was like a fortress, man—they almost didn't let me in! Or how, after all our work refitting this tub, the Navy crew was just going to bail and leave us behind? Leave us for the Xombies?"

"Make your *move*."

"All right, I *will*!" Sal slammed down his queen.

"Checkmate."

"I know!"

CHAPTER **SEVEN**

XIBALBA

This report represents the last official document commissioned by the combined agencies of the federal government of the United States of America, or by emergency representatives of those agencies. All such agencies and personnel are declared to be in recess for the remaining duration of the crisis. They are furthermore ordered as a matter of national security to take shelter at secure locations and remain there until such time as it becomes possible to resume their official duties. The purpose of this report is to create a factual account of the Maenad Epidemic, collating all available documents into a single reference. It is not exhaustive, representing only "found" materials—no research in the ordinary sense was possible. Nevertheless, this volume represents a heroic effort on the part of all involved, many of whom gave their lives in the course of its creation. It stands as their epitaph. Let it not be America's.

—The Maenad Project

Smoke was on the water. Dawn showed through the black teeth of the city. Out of the haze, a long, dark shape drifted into view, barely disturbing the mist or the river's glassy surface: a gondola. There was a pale figure standing in the bow, a young girl in a periwinkle blue nightgown, with black hair and blacker eyes. Not real—she could have been a statue. An exotic, ethereal creature, blue-skinned as Shiva, lifeless as a painted figurehead. Larger figures hulked behind her, grim blue footmen frozen in her thrall.

And now, from the water, other beings began to rise. Slowly, ponderously, like mosquitoes being birthed from the husks of their aquatic larvae. First just eyes gleaming wetly, then whole gaping faces, mouths and noses streaming sea-water, then rubbery-slick shoulders, trunks and gangling arms, finally naked blue feet treading indifferently through the polluted muck of the shallows, turning up rusty nails and broken glass secreted in the silt. The wire connecting them to the boat and each other was draped with slime— was it threaded through their bodies?

Lulu and her landing party passed the first of the still-glimmering braziers, a steel grate rising on a pedestal from the water, its contents now burnt down to a smoldering toxic slag of tires and plastic and crackling human bones. Black leaves of charred debris twirled slowly in the current.

The gondola scraped ashore at the foot of a concrete ramp, and Lulu stepped off without getting her feet wet. Ed Albemarle took the lead, all the rest trailing him in a loose V formation, their bodies strung along a high-tensile braided steel cable that was threaded through their spines and rib cages. The Moguls had wired them so for ease of handling, and the submarine's skittish crew had demanded they remain that way. Lulu was the only one able to walk freely.

She followed as they emerged on a waterfront path, a strip of parkland bordering a road, with quaint old buildings of brick and quarried stone on the far side. There was a little debris on the ground—broken glass, loose shoes, windswept paper, and other trash. The windows regarded them blankly.

"You're doing fine," said the disembodied voice of Alice Langhorne, piping from a tiny portable speaker. *"Cross the street and keep going up. You're looking for Benefit Street."*

They entered the city. The way was narrow and increasingly steep, archaic and picturesque, with Colonial-era structures all around: residential houses, taverns, lawyers' offices. An art-house cinema advertising a Chinese love story. Lulu could see a number of steeples ranged along the hill and a golden dome. Some windows and doors had been broken open, and there was weather damage—wires down, broken tree limbs—but with the budding spring foliage, the scene was peaceful, nearly pleasant.

Continuing up two blocks, they found Benefit Street. *"Now turn left,"* Langhorne instructed. *"It's a few blocks down, on the left-hand side—you're looking for a red house, number 182. The Lazarus Speake House."*

As the sun came up, they passed the Greek-columned Athenaeum Library (its chiseled inscription: COME HITHER EVERYONE THAT THIRSTETH), then crossed above the white edifice of the First Baptist Church. Cars were sitting abandoned in the intersection, their doors hanging open. A few buildings farther down, they found the address they were looking for, a small, steep-roofed red cottage teetering on the brink of a cliff overlooking downtown. It had tiny windows, built for a time when people couldn't afford the luxuries of light and fresh air, when they huddled close together for warmth. It was nothing, little more than a shack. *This* was Uri Miska's infamous laboratory?

"Go inside," Langhorne said.

The front door was already open, a trail of soggy personal debris scattered along the walk, mostly books and artwork, a trampled Klimt print—glints of gold amid the trash. They crowded in. It was just as cramped as it appeared, with a low ceiling and several small rooms. The rear ones were brighter, facing the sunrise. The furniture had all been torn apart with ruthless efficiency; the place had clearly been searched, stripped. And it hadn't been an easy job, judging from the number of bullet holes riddling the plaster.

As they kicked their way through the wreckage, there were weird rustlings underfoot. Something scuttled crablike into the corner, and Lulu could see it was a disembodied hand. There were a number of hands loose in the room, some with partial arms. There were also legs and feet, as well as squirming organs of all types. The heads had mostly been blown to bits, but they were around, too, eyeballs creeping like snails. Clearly a lot of Xombies had been blasted to pieces by whoever sacked this place.

It meant nothing to Lulu. Her interest was purely abstract as they checked the attic, then the basement, beginning to realize that there was nothing here. No Miska and certainly no laboratory—Dr. Langhorne was wrong, or deliberately lying, as the living were prone to do. To uselessly prolong their dwindling span of life. They would do anything for that. Lulu remembered well.

"Look under the furnace," Langhorne said. *"Move it aside. I'm pretty sure there's some trick to it."*

There was an ancient, rusty furnace in the middle of the basement floor, a heavy contraption set on a huge stone slab. It looked impregnable. Albemarle and Lemuel—the biggest guys—were about to try tearing it loose, when Lulu noticed four massive iron bolts anchoring it in place. They looked like they had been there for hundreds of years, but suddenly Lulu sensed an odd dampness about them, a wispy condensation like swamp gas. Breath from a tomb. *Wait— see?* Without exchanging any words, she set her boys prying up the bolts. Once they discovered that the threads were backward, it was simple. In moments, the whole furnace and slab slid easily aside as if on casters.

There were stairs underneath, descending into darkness. *"Xibalba,"* Langhorne breathed.

"All right, gentlemen. I want you to know that I do not relish taking command in this way. In fact, if there were any other alternative, I would gladly pursue it, even to the extent of resigning my commission. But we have no legal recourse here, no grievance committee, no avenue of escape whatsoever. We are all in the same boat, so to speak. What I want you all to know is that I am here to represent *you*, the ship's officers and able seamen. That includes those of you who may disagree with my present actions. But I think it safe to say that most of us here have become increasingly unsatisfied with command decisions that reflect neither the legitimate concerns of this crew nor any ordinary military protocol. Of course this is not an *ordinary* situation, but that makes it all the more crucial that we act with uncompromising rigor in approaching this new set of realities. That we acknowledge that *we* are a priceless national asset and must act accordingly to ensure our survival. That the preservation of this vessel and its functional crew must now trump any other consideration—at least until such time as we receive orders to the contrary from whatever senior authority may still exist. We are privileged to have the means to seek out such authority, and I intend to do so. Until then, this submarine is our sacred trust, which we are sworn to deliver; these decks represent American soil. That means this boat *is* America, gentlemen. Therefore, I say to you: Anything that is incompatible with the smooth functioning of this vessel must be rejected. Swiftly and with extreme prejudice. Any questions?" Kranuski searched the crowded mess hall for doubters.

"All right, *Captain*," said Dan Robles, standing by the juice machine. He could feel Webb's murderous stare. "What do you propose to do about the provisions? Those kids back there are starving."

"I'm glad you asked that, Lieutenant. That's my first order of business. We can no longer afford to consider ourselves a refugee ship. Everyone on board has to bring something to the table—it's a simple matter of fairness. We all have to earn our keep. Out of eighty-eight boys back there, only about half are working on qual cards. The rest are just taking up space. That can't continue—we can't afford it. So I propose we kill two birds with one stone: Send the unskilled out on a foraging run. We're stuck here until the next tide anyway. Might as well get those kids earning their keep."

"They'll be wiped out!"

"Not necessarily. We don't know exactly what conditions are like ashore, but so far there hasn't been a single Xombie sighting. The only excitement has come from the living: those fires and that survivor kid—another refugee, just what we need. Even Langhorne admits the streets are clear. The only creeps out there are hers."

Phil Tran stepped forward. "Some of those kids can barely stand up, much less go on a raiding party. They're undernourished, half-sick."

"Is that your *professional* opinion, Doctor?" said Kranuski, baldly scornful. Phil Tran had some slight medical training, a couple of years, but he was really a sonar expert. Their original medical officer had bought it two months ago, when out of Harvey Coombs's stupidity Xombies briefly got loose in the boat. Since then, Tran was accorded the role of corpsman—everybody was doing double and triple duty on this cruise. That didn't give him the right to act like Dr. House.

Kranuski continued, "Anyway, that's the whole *point*—they're not going to get any fatter if the food runs out.

Should we send essential personnel out there? Is that what you're suggesting? Or should we just wait in this boat until we *all* starve? I think not. So, Phil, because you're so concerned with those kids' welfare, I'm making it your duty to choose up a shore party and organize the field trip. Map out a location, brief them, and send them on their way. You have thirty minutes. Anything you need, talk to Mr. Webb— he's acting XO. Just make sure to have them back by 0900. That's when we sail."

CHAPTER **EIGHT**

FIELD TRIP

Crisis management was an oxymoron. Virtually every relevant government entity succumbed in the first few minutes: The Federal Emergency Management Agency, the Department of Homeland Security, the National Guard—all folded instantly. Before midnight, there was a functioning body known as the Pentagon—after midnight, there simply wasn't. The building was still there, just as imposing, but within it was a chamber of horrors—a thousand-room death trap. There is evidence that a number of male employees locked themselves into offices, restrooms, closets, or any other hiding places they could find, desperately attempting to call out. As we have seen, this was as ineffectual as the popguns wielded by security personnel. The phone lines were jammed, no help was forthcoming. A voice believed to be that of Army Chief of Staff Bernard Tate recorded this phone message: "All the women staff are (unintelligible)—they're taking over the building! Send troops, send (unintelligible)! We're trapped in the utility room behind the General's Mess, but they know we're here. Oh my God . . . oh my God—(unintelligible)—mania of some kind, chemical warfare. It's spreading like wildfire, infecting the men. They don't stay down! Get away from the door! Get back, get back, shit—(unintelligible screams)."

—**The Maenad Project**

Three hours, that was all they had. Squinting out at the clear light of dawn, they knew it wouldn't be long enough. Not nearly long enough.

Emerging on deck, pale and thin as convicts from a dungeon, the boys wept at their first glimpse of daylight in months. Not since they had first taken refuge in the factory had they felt actual sun. Or the touch of a gentle breeze. Or seen green grass and trees on the shores of a beautiful shining city, close enough to make out the red word BILTMORE on one of the buildings. They were home again. It was a wonderful morning to be out on the water, a wonderful time to be alive. Whatever happened, they were glad to be going ashore.

While the rafts were being inflated, Sal DeLuca had a vivid memory of looking out over this bay with his father at the final company picnic. It was the last meal they ever shared together.

Barbecue grills made from steel barrels, flickering and smoking, the stiff breeze wafting the smell of sizzling chicken and steak across rows of crowded picnic tables. Whitecaps surging up Narragansett Bay like runs of bluefish. The sun had set on the land, but a cruciform black monolith rose high enough out of the water to be transmuted to gold under the purpling sky. It was the fairwater or sail—what laymen would call the conning tower—of an Ohio-class nuclear submarine.

Cries of seagulls and blustering wind were the only sounds as all in attendance had watched a bearded man in a baseball cap climb the hastily erected dais. The man gripped the podium in both hands as if drawing support from either the wooden stand or the dynamic company logo on its face. Those closest to him could also make out the dolphin crest on his hat.

First of all, he began, *I'd like you all to give yourselves a hand for continuing to work and serve your country under the most difficult conditions imaginable. You are all American heroes, and will surely be honored as such by posterity.*

The crowd applauded, though not as one. There were islands of stony discord.

What's going on? Sal whispered to his father, sensing trouble.

Ssh!—just pay attention.

The speaker continued: *When we got the contract to refurbish this decommissioned vessel from ballistic capability to tactical uses, all of us were relieved: It meant our jobs were safe.* People chuckled. *We never imagined that this boat might be the only cradle of whatever hope is left to us in this world.*

Gloom descended, and the man paused a long time, the bill of his baseball cap hiding downcast eyes. When he continued, it was in a somber tone. *So many things could have made this chance impossible. Imagine if instead of being refurbished, the boat had been scrapped. Or if the harbor had never been dredged deep enough to float a boat this size, and we still had to barge them to Groton piecemeal. Or if the OEM's SPAM mission hadn't come along, providing us with everything we've needed to remain operational behind these gates, including fuel for the boat's reactor—we couldn't have done anything without that power. We have Chairman Sandoval to thank for these things, and I hope you'll all join me in giving him a round of applause.*

There was a wary smattering of applause.

I know how hard you've all worked, pulling out those old missile tubes and launch systems, retrofitting that compartment for cargo, going over every system on the boat with a fine-tooth comb. And I know what you've been hoping to get in return—it's the same thing we've all been hoping for: safe passage out of here for ourselves and our families. The boat seems ideal for the purpose: a big, empty submarine with a reactor good for twenty years. Who could blame us for thinking—

Noah's Ark, a man yelled. Scattered *amens* were heard.

The speaker smiled wanly. *Exactly, Bob. Noah's ark. I hear you, believe me. And I know a number of you folks have been determined to launch her with that very name. Unfortunately, she is still the province of the U.S. Navy, and as they have not granted us official license to rechristen her, she will remain nameless for the time being.*

Some people made muted resentful sounds. The one named Bob, a burly man with white hair and a yellowed beard, said, *It's okay to steal it, but not to name it? Come on, the Navy's out of business—they don't care how we use this thing.*

Nobody's stealing anything, Bob. In fact, that's why we've assembled you all here this evening. As many of you may know, the supply barges have stopped coming. We suspected something was wrong in New London last week, when our tug couldn't raise anyone on the ship-to-shore. We've also lost radio contact with COMSUBLANT, with Secretary Clark at Norfolk, with Admiral Stillson at NavShip, and with the USS McNabb, which means the Coast Guard is effectively out of commission. We've had no substantive communication with any military or government authority for eight days now; the lines are all down.

Damn, said Gus DeLuca, Sal's father, as a ripple of anxiety swept the crowd.

Raising his voice, the speaker admonished them not to panic. When they had subsided a little, he said, *Now I know a lot of us had high hopes that we could use this vessel as a means to secure our families until the crisis stabilizes. Listen to me. But because of the loss of outside support, we are simply not going to have the provisions that we thought we would. Listen, please! The contingency plan now is to*

*move the boat offshore with a minimal Navy crew and to
have her remain at a classified blue-water station until otherwise ordered . . . as a matter of national security—* He
had to shout above the sudden, furious din. *Listen, please—
as a matter of national security! Please, there is no sense in
all of us starving at sea! Not when we have a secure compound and everything we need right here—*

Better we should starve on land? someone yelled. *Or
worse?*

Oh my God, that's it, said Mr. DeLuca, eyes welling
with tears. *It's all over.*

I knew it, said Sal.

The bearded man, Bob Martino, stood up in the encroach-
ing twilight, and shouted, *Are we gonna take this, people?
We busted our asses for the last month making that tub into
a safe haven for our sons, so they wouldn't have to end up
the way our wives and daughters did. And these bastards
have known all along that empty promises were the only
leverage they had to keep us working here. And now they
think they're gonna take that hope away from us, buy us out
for the price of a chicken dinner! Well, we got news for them,
don't we? They got another think comin'! They got—*

There was a sharp little *crack*—just a twig snapping,
barely audible over the hubbub—and Bob Martino abruptly
toppled backward, falling between the benches. A few men
and boys cried out or cursed; the rest went dead silent. It
was far from the first sudden death they had witnessed.

Gentlemen, said the ashen-faced speaker, *I am so terribly sorry. It's a horrible thing . . . a horrible thing to have
to do. But Bob knew, as we all do, that the security of this
compound depends upon our complete cooperation. The
security personnel seated among you are trained profes-
sionals who are under strict orders to prevent this facility
from falling into chaos. Try to remember that it's for our*

own safety. Please let us respect and thank these men for their courage in . . . executing this most difficult of duties. Thank you, Officer Reynolds.

Officer Beau Reynolds nodded grimly, still brandishing his pistol. The other ex–Special Forces men at his table cast hard looks back at the crowd, searching for defiance. Two of them wasted no time trussing Bob Martino's limbs and dragging him away in a plastic bag—to be burned, Sal knew. It was the only way. He had heard of the same thing being done with stray refugees who tried to enter the compound; a matter of blunt pragmatism—you never knew who was going to come back. As the bag started to bounce wildly, Sal felt his father grip him by the arm. *Don't look at it, Sal.* His dad choked out the words. *I'm so sorry to put you through this.*

It's okay, Dad, it's okay, Sal said. *I've seen worse.*

Later that evening, back in the hangar, things were unusually quiet. There hadn't been much talking since the shooting, and no more work was getting done. For once the boys had all the time in the world to goof off . . . but nobody was in any mood for the usual teenage horseplay.

That's it, isn't it, Dad? We're all going to die.

Everybody dies sometime, Sal. And if they're lucky, they stay dead.

I bet they're planning on running out on us. The white hats. They know this place is going to turn into some kind of feeding frenzy, and they're not gonna want to stick around and wait for it to happen. They're taking that sub and all their people and guns and all the food and—

Sal, stop!—it's no use.

Well, are we just gonna sit here and let it happen?

You saw what they did to Bob Martino. As long as they needed us to work, we had some bargaining leverage . . . or thought we did. But now the job is done; we're disposable.

*I don't expect we'll see or hear from management ever
again. We'll be lucky to see daylight ever again.*

Well, we have to fight back!

*How? Fight who? We're locked in, son, and I'm not ex-
pecting any more lawn parties in the near future. Best we
can hope for now is that they all pull out and leave us in
peace. Then we can use the tools we've got and break out
of here—survive as best we can. It's not much of a hope, but
it's better than nothing.*

Why not bust out now and fight them?

*With Beau Reynolds and his people guarding the gate?
We'd get about two feet before they mowed us down.*

What about Uncle Sammy? He wouldn't shoot us.

*Your uncle can't help us, Sal. He's out there, and we're
in here, end of story.*

*So that's it, then. That's the plan? Just let them aban-
don us.*

*Unless you can think of something better. I'm afraid I'm
shit out of ideas. I tried, Sal. I'm really sorry.*

*It's fine, it's okay, Pop —you did great. Don't worry. Lis-
ten, I gotta head over to the john, maybe see how the guys
are doing. I'll be back before lights-out.*

Sal left their small, curtained space and walked across the
concrete floor, his steps echoing in the cavernous assembly
building. Nestled among gigantic submarine components
was a maze of crisscrossed tarps and drying laundry, damp
sheets glowing with light and the flicker of cookstoves—a
hobo jungle beneath a soaring ceiling of I-beams and corrugated steel.

As he traversed the alleys and flaps of this indoor bazaar,
Sal thought, *It looks like a refugee camp.* And then: *You're
a refugee, stupid—it is a refugee camp.*

People paid no attention as he intruded briefly on their

private spaces, even stepping over their legs or belongings as he went. Whatever modesty had not been expunged by a month in these close quarters was now stone dead from despair, killed along with Bob Martino.

Men and boys sat staring into space or either wept or consoled the weeping. This place, which had up to now been a clamorous hive of industry, was now hushed as a cathedral during funeral services. Instead of studying, as the boys had been accustomed to doing since they first arrived here on New Year's Eve, they were feeding sheaves of submarine blueprints and technical manuals into pyres, burning their homework. Their fathers, grandfathers, uncles, older brothers—all dedicated employees of the company—did nothing to stop them. Black flakes floated down like snow.

They think they're already dead, Sal thought.

As he waited his turn to take a leak, he noticed he was standing beside the one person likely to help him take his mind off all this crap: Tyrell Banks.

Yo, Tyrell, he said. *How you doing, man?*

It's all good, Sal. Scored me my cup of Jonestown Kool-Aid—gonna be rockin' that Grape Ape like a motherfucker. Better than drag-assin' around here waiting for the fucked-up Donner Party shit that's gonna go down.

Yeah, it sucks.

Phew, you the king of understatement tonight, Sal—next you be tellin' me that Armageddon is bogus, go ahead.

No, seriously, man, I was thinking we gotta do something to snap everybody out of this. I'm not ready to lie down and die.

What you got in mind, man? Hey, I know! You into that extreme sports shit—why don't you hook us up with a little postapocalyptic BMX exhibition? Fuckin' Agent X Games.

Tyrell was joking, and Sal laughed along, but something

in the corner caught his eye: a rack of granny bikes used for
light deliveries around the plant.

Why not?

It was time to go ashore. Officers Phil Tran, Dan Robles,
and Alton Webb organized them into two teams, twenty
boys to a team, and assigned each team a raft—a large,
semirigid inflatable boat. The rafts were designed to carry
as many as forty men apiece, plenty of room for the loot
they were expected to bring back. The boys would have to
paddle out, but lines would connect the rafts to the submarine so that they could be quickly retrieved.

"There's no time for speeches," Lieutenant Tran said
brusquely, ushering them aboard.

Out of Webb's earshot, Robles pulled Sal DeLuca aside,
saying softly, "Bring them back in one piece."

"Yes, sir."

Tran said, "We *know* you, Sal—you're the smartest kid
we have. I shouldn't even be sending you, but *somebody's*
gotta have their shit together out there. I'm sorry."

Sal's teeth chattered with excitement. "That's okay. I
want to go."

"I know." Tran sighed. He gripped the boy's shoulder as
if reluctant to let go, then pushed him away. "Your dad
would have been proud of you. Don't waste any time, all
right? In and out."

Sal was already gone, clambering aboard the boat to join
all the other yellow life vests. *Looks like a damn summer
camp,* Tran thought furiously. Then they were pushing off
with their paddles, awkwardly scudding away. "Watch the
time!" he shouted after.

"Bon voyage, kiddies," Webb said smugly, paying out
line.

Phil Tran could only shake his head, too angry to speak. The asshole hadn't even let them take a radio or a gun. "Mission-essential, too valuable to risk," he had said. Unlike those kids' lives? *You just better hope they come back,* Tran thought. *Otherwise, we are going to have a serious problem, Webb. You and your bogus captain.*

At his shoulder, Dan Robles said, "It's okay, Phil. We've done everything we can for them. We just have to trust in God."

Tran nodded, red-eyed. "Praise the Lord and pass the ammunition," he said.

CHAPTER NINE

NUBS

Cut 'em loose—that was Lieutenant Alton Webb's opinion of those kids and all their would-be adult benefactors . . . including a few fellow officers he could think of.

Civilian refugees didn't belong on the boat. He for one had been furious to learn that Harvey Coombs ever let them aboard. Webb witnessed firsthand the nightmare that had been unleashed belowdecks as a direct result of Fred Cowper's treachery, and neither he nor any other man who had lost friends and fellow officers in that fight could think of these people as anything other than hijackers. And then to let that filthy traitor declare himself acting commander while Coombs was down, filling the control section with armed thugs like Gus DeLuca and Ed Albemarle, forcing good NavSea officers like Rich Kranuski to kiss his ass—it was just incomprehensible.

Then there were the collaborators: Dan Robles, Philip Tran, at least a dozen others. Webb could think of a few choice things he'd like to do to them. If they hadn't lined up behind Cowper instead of Kranuski, the takeover wouldn't have been possible in the first place. Couldn't they see that even if that retired son of a bitch was the most senior officer on board, he was no better than a terrorist? His actions had cost the lives of a dozen crewmen and two Marines, not to mention fatally compromising the mission. Better the boat should have been scuttled than put him in charge. By the time Coombs recovered and arrested the old coot, it was too late. The damage had been done.

Webb could still hear the old man's infuriating Rhode Island accent, so folksy and misleading: *We're gonna have to let 'em below soona or later. Might as well be soona.*

He should have killed the man himself, that first night, but like everyone else, Webb was in shock, clinging for dear life to obsolete notions of military discipline. Focusing on the task at hand. Helping fish those two injured Marines out of the water and carrying them below, where they were laid out on the wardroom table. He thought they were more stunned than anything, having been knocked overboard when Cowper crashed a huge truck into the brow, plunging the whole gangway into the water. But when Corpsman Lennox opened their clothes to check their vitals, it was instantly clear that something was wrong. *This man's not breathing,* Doc said urgently, and began administering CPR. Those were the last words Webb ever heard out of Pete Lennox. Then the shooting began topside, and all available hands were ordered to assist up there.

The sight that greeted him on deck was something beyond his wildest nightmares:

There was a riot. Not on the boat itself, but just above it on the wharf. A thousand murderous hooligans fighting, choking, whacking at each other with hammers. Hundreds of teenage boys were fleeing the melee, swarming over the edge of the quay and dropping from the pier to the dock below, where armed Navy crewmen were helping them cross a plank to the boat's stern. *Helping* them! Several officers appeared to be shooting into the crowd, and it took Webb a second to realize there were Xombies in the mix.

Holy God, he thought, a jet of ice water freezing his guts. *There they are.*

They were the first Xombies he or any of the crew had ever seen, having been sheltered from the plague in their windowless steel cocoon all these weeks. It was a shock actually to be in the presence of the blue devils they had heard so much about: unstoppable, ghoulish berserkers, the women worse than the men. He had to admire the way the rebellious shipyard workers were fending them off with nothing more than hammers and crowbars, holding the line even as skull-cracked creatures bounced back for more. The crew's bullets were not much better—Webb overheard one frustrated officer, popping a spent clip, mutter, *Weebles wobble, but they don't fall down.*

What the hell's going on up here? he demanded of the OOD, Tim Shaye.

Captain's orders! We're to assist in boarding the refugees! The man was sweating and half-crazed.

Are you kidding me? Webb couldn't believe Coombs could be so stupid as to give in to these people's extortion. *What are we supposed to do with them? They're not coming below!*

I don't know, you'll have to ask the skipper. Shaye's radio squawked the order to cast off. *Excuse me, I have to tend the lines.*

Incredibly, the boat managed to get under way and clear of the submarine pen without losing a single crewman. This miracle was accomplished by Webb's simple expedient of ordering the crew below and shutting the hatch, letting the massed refugees fend for themselves topside. No telling how many of *them* were lost before the last Xombie was finally expelled, but of the hundreds remaining, only a handful were adults. The rest were shell-shocked teenage boys . . . and one girl. Everyone, above and below, thought the worst was over.

That was when the real trouble began.

Webb was in Navigation, conferring with Rich Kranuski and Artie Gunderson about the best offshore anchorage, when the general alarm sounded.

Armed detail to the mess! someone shouted over the 1MC. *Xombies on board!*

What now? Gunderson groaned, and was suddenly knocked out of his seat by a hurtling blue body. It was the machinist's mate, Donald Selby, all wild hair and grinning bared teeth. Tackling Artie against the console, Selby forced his gaping wet maw on him, covering the other man's mouth and bending his neck so far backward it cracked, then in one grotesque slurp seemed to suck the very life from Gunderson's wilting corpse.

As Webb and Kranusky fought to pull the men apart, Alton saw Doc Lennox attacking Chip Stanaman in the control center. Chip's family had welcomed Webb into their home one Christmas when he was on break from nuclear power school, and still sent him cards every year with pictures of the kids. *Fuck!* Webb bellowed, unable to break Selby's grip— Gunderson already looked as dead and purple-faced as his attacker, eyes bloodshot and hugely dilated. Webb was on the verge of losing it. He was not a tremendously social guy, but these were his poker buddies, his friends, the only family he knew, and he was failing them.

Forget him! Kranuski barked. *Damage control's not reporting any trouble amidships—we can still contain it right here! I need you to guard that hatch and make sure nothing gets aft!* As Webb obeyed, Rich jumped for the emergency intercom, and said, *Attention all hands. This is the XO: Evacuate CCSM and secure forward bulkhead. Repeat: All decks, secure forward bulkhead.*

Things abruptly settled; the eye of the storm. The command section, which had been a bedlam of shouts and violent scuffles, was now silent. As Kranuski finished what he was doing and leaped for the aft hatch, Gunderson and Selby jerked upright like two fright puppets, lunging for him. It was close. With an assist from Webb, Rich cleared the heavy watertight door just as several more demonic faces came bounding up the companionway at his heels.

The hatch clanged shut with the finality of a tomb.

Game over, Alton Webb thought. If the boat's entire command-and-control section was infested with these things, and at least a dozen vital crewmen were down, including the captain, then they were lost. They had already been desperately shorthanded, with barely a third their normal crew complement; now they not only had to rig for auxiliary control and stabilize the boat but fight Xombies in the bargain. It was physically impossible.

Executive Officer Kranuski was not ready to give up. He had assumed the mantle of acting captain and was busily fielding situation reports. For want of anything better to do, Webb went along with it, pretending that Kranuski knew what he was doing even though the man had never commanded a sub in his life. At least his initial hunch had been right: Just about everything aft of the forward bulkhead appeared to be clear of Xombies. This was confirmed by the two other bridge officers who survived, Lieutenants Dan Robles and Phil Tran, who had already posted a lookout topside and transferred helm control to the aft maneuvering panel. But without some further miracle, they were just treading water until the ebb tide stranded them in the mud. Without proper soundings, they couldn't even drop anchor; its chain would swing them around the rocks and shoals like an immense wrecking ball.

It was Robles who made the suggestion, *What about Fred Cowper?*

What about him?

We have to recruit him, and anybody else he's got up there who can help.

That asshole's the cause of all this!

He's also got more experience than anybody else on board.

That's what makes him so dangerous! Forget it—we have enough on our hands without entrusting the boat to a guy who just threatened to sink it.

Okay, he's a ruthless old bastard, but we can probably trust him to pull his own fat out of the fire. You can always hang him later. Right now we need every available hand.

But what about that girl he's got with him?

You can hang her, too.

"Aim for that dock there," Sal said, consulting his printed-out map.

"What do you think we're doing?" Kyle Hancock said. "It's the current; it's wicked."

"Well, paddle harder—it's going to take us underneath the hurricane barrier."

"No shit."

"Paddle! Paddle!"

The paddlers paddled, putting their shoulders into it, trying to find a rhythm. Sal watched the great, gray barrier loom above them, its open gates like massive steel jaws and the river beyond a yawning gullet, eager to swallow them whole. It was so shallow in there at low tide that Xombies could wade right up and grab them at will. "All together!" he shouted. "Stroke, stroke, stroke . . ."

Then they were clearing the worst of the current, moving into calmer eddies near shore. "Okay, we're good, we're gonna make it," Sal said, heart still racing. "Don't stop, we're almost there."

"Shut *up*," Kyle said. "Damn."

"Yeah, man," agreed Russell. "We don't need you to tell us what to do. We know you're Officer Tran's little bitch, but just try to chill, a'ight? We on it."

Russell and Kyle Hancock were brothers, the only surviving pair of siblings on the ship, and their mutual strength made them de facto rulers of the Big Room. Russell was one year older than Kyle, with a corrected cleft lip and a resulting lisp that made him sound like Mike Tyson. Kids had learned not to rag him about it. His brother Kyle was lighter built, less touchy, with the easy confidence of a born player. As they liked to say, Russell was the muscle, and Kyle was the style. The brothers were not overt troublemakers, they simply used their power to do as little as possible, making needier kids like the Freddies—Freddy Fisk and Freddy Gonzales, or just Freddy F and G, Tweedledum and Tweedledee—do their work for them. Why shouldn't they? There were no extra rations in doing it yourself—the privilege of not starving was reserved for "essential personnel" only. As far as Kyle and Russell were concerned, Sal DeLuca and all the other overworked ship's apprentices were suckers.

"Dude, don't even start," Sal said. "I'm just trying to help us stay alive, okay?"

"We don't need your help—*dude*."

"Yeah, give it a rest. You ain't no ship's officer."

"No, but I'm responsible for *your* ass."

"Leave my ass be. And you best watch your own, bike boy."

They all snickered.

Sal shook his head, grinning in spite of himself. This had been going on for months, part of the friction between the ship's apprentices and the "nubs"—nonuseful bodies. Nubs were often the guys who were having the worst time of it, the true orphans, whose adult sponsors—their dads—had been killed, and who could barely hold it together enough to function, their shock and despair manifesting as attitude. He knew Russell's gibes were a response to the helplessness of the situation, a survival mechanism. A thin wedge against panic, which Sal could totally relate to, having lost his own father at Thule. Hey, to laugh was better than to cry . . . or to scream. Once you started screaming, you might never stop.

The screams came at night, in their sleep.

Now they were below the high dock, fending off its barnacled pilings with their paddles. "Okay, everybody be quiet," Sal said. If there were Xombies up there, they could just jump right into the boats. He tied up to a rusted ladder, and whispered, "I'm just gonna take a look, okay? Nobody move unless I give the all clear."

"What is this squad leader bullshit?" Kyle hissed, getting up. "This ain't no video game, dumb-ass."

"Fine, *you* go first." Sal made room for him to pass.

Kyle hesitated, sudden doubt flashing across his face, so that Russell said, "Sit your ass down. Let a real man go up."

"*Fuck* you."

Russell belligerently mounted the ladder. They watched in nervous silence as he paused at the top, peeking over the edge at first with trembling caution, then visibly relaxing and raising his whole head above. "Come on, chicken shits," he called down. "Ain't nothin' to—"

A blue hand seized him by the throat.

Fighting the thing, Russell lost his grip and plummeted backward onto the raft. The disembodied hand was still on him—not just a hand but an entire arm, ripped off at the shoulder socket, its round bone nakedly visible, hideously flailing and jerking at the elbow joint as it strangled him.

The other boys quailed back, screaming, but Sal lunged for the thing, trying to pry its fingers loose. It was a young girl's hand, its dainty nails painted pink, but it was cold and rubbery, impossibly strong.

"Help me!" he shouted.

Kyle jumped forward to pitch in, then two other boys, his poker buddies, Ray and Rick. As they grappled with it, the naked stump punched Sal in the cheek so hard it cracked a filling. Tasting blood, he braced his knee on Russell's chest, and, with a supreme effort, they managed to wrench the thing loose. It immediately went wild, flexing and bucking in their hands, trying to get at them. "All together now," Sal said. "One, two . . ." On three, they hurled it far out into the water.

"Holy craaap," Russell wheezed, retching over the side.

"Let's get *outta* here!" Kyle shouted.

"Wait!" Sal said. "We can't just go back."

"Why not? I'm not waitin' for the rest of that chick to show up!"

"We got to expect shit like this to happen. We handled it! We can't just give up now."

"We sure as hell can!" Others chimed in: *"Hell* yeah," "We're gone!" "This shit is suicide!"

"Hold up," said a ragged voice. It was Russell. He shakily sat up, and croaked, "Don't nobody do a goddamned thing. I ain't—*hem*—goin' back to that submarine empty-handed. Just so they can lock us in jail again? How many days we already been sitting there dreaming we had someplace else to go, some kinda free choice? Screw that shit. I'm *hungry*." He got up and climbed the ladder again, wobbly but without hesitation. In seconds, he was over the top and out of sight.

For a long moment there was silence, then Russell's face

reappeared. "Come on!" he called down impatiently. "Let's *do* this shit. You wanna eat or don't you?"

Sal started to follow, but Kyle and the other boys shoved past, nearly knocking him into the water. Whether empowered by Russell's confidence, the prospect of food, or the thought of that arm lurking in the water below, suddenly they couldn't get up fast enough. "One at a *time*," Sal said. But they weren't listening to him at all—the old ladder was almost coming to pieces from their combined weight. *Stupid jerks.* "Everybody stay together," he called after them as he tested the rungs.

Sal emerged to find the boys standing at the edge of a weedy lot, reveling in the glorious, slightly queasy sensation of dry land. It looked like no-man's-land—the vacant area beneath a highway bridge. On one side was the flood-control berm—a high rock dam separating them from the city—and on the other a fenced tugboat landing and some condemned-looking buildings. Huge concrete pylons rose above them to Interstate 195. It was all reassuringly deserted.

As Sal joined them, Russell asked him, "Where to now?"

"Well, we gotta cross under the highway and follow the road here through the floodgate. There should be businesses and things on the other side."

"Let's do it."

Following Russell, who was following Sal, the boys trooped quickly and quietly down the road, picking up any likely-looking weapons they happened to find—mostly rocks and chunks of brick. *Sticks and stones can break my bones, but names can never hurt me.* Sal wished he could find a good stick. He looked up at the highway bridge, imagining that the little girl's arm must have fallen from there, picturing the awful scene: the girl in the backseat of her parents' car, the Xombie lunging in and grabbing her arm, Dad hitting the gas—nasty.

They found the tremendous open doors of the flood barrier and cautiously followed the road through. On the far side was a waterfront area of chic clubs and condos, and across the river an immense Gothic cathedral that was the electric company, webbed to the rest of the city by flowing skeins of wire. It was all dead, all out of commission, yet almost perfectly preserved, as if loyally awaiting the future return of humankind. Everything had gone down so fast, there was no time for looting and destruction.

Dodging from one shadow to the next, the boys did what they could to keep a low profile. "I don't get it," Kyle said, eyes wide with tension. "Why aren't there any Xombies?"

"Be glad there ain't," said Russell, gingerly touching his bruised neck.

"It could be that viral thing they talked about—viral progression," Sal said. "The cities got so full of Xombies, they reached critical mass. Once there was nobody left to infect, there was no reason to stay, so they scattered outward across the country. Maybe there aren't any left here."

The boys' chests swelled with hope. "Is that *true*?"

"I don't know. It's just what I heard."

"God, I hope you right, man."

Staying off the exposed waterfront, they followed a shaded inner street with fewer doorways. This led them to a second highway underpass, one older and darker than the first, a sunken hollow, its corroded iron girders busy with roosting pigeons. There were peeling psychedelic murals on the walls, ads for funky-sounding businesses: Café Zog, Olga's Cup and Saucer, Acme Video, Z-Bar. Cars sat dead in the road, their windows broken and doors wide open to the elements. Pigeons were roosting in them, too. This was not a good place to be, it didn't feel safe. The boys could be

cornered here in the dripping wetness, trapped amid the rust
and rank birdshit. "We shouldn't a gone this way, man,"
said Kyle. They walked faster and faster, trying not to panic,
not to run . . .

    . . . and emerged in the light of spring. Before them was
a tiny hillside park with a veterans' memorial, benches, and
maple trees. Dew glistened on the grass. But the boys hardly
noticed any of that. They were more interested in what lay
just beyond: a bright red-and-yellow gas station with a sign
reading FOOD MART.

    Now they ran.

The coolers were dead, the ice cream melted, the milk
curdled, but nearly everything else in the place was edible,
and the forty boys made a valiant attempt to eat it all. It was
a treasure trove more welcome to them than King Tut's
tomb, and as perfectly preserved, not in natron but sodium
benzoate.

    Snack cakes and pies, puddings, nuts, cookies, crackers,
canned meats and cheeses, beef sticks, jerky, pickles, salsa,
pretzels and potato chips galore. Candy! Whole cases of
chocolate bars, chews, sours, mints, gum. And drinks: bottled beverages of every kind—energy drinks, soda pop,
fancy sweetened teas and cappuccino, Yoo-hoo, or just
plain water—all free for the taking. It was a teenage dream
come true, an all-you-can-eat paradise of junk food. All the
cigarettes they could smoke, too, if they wanted them, and
a few other vices besides.

    "Can this stuff make us sick?" Freddy Fisk asked through
a mouthful of minidonuts. "It must be pretty old by now."

    "I doubt it," Sal said, munching Fritos. "There's enough
chemicals in this stuff to last until doomsday."

"Then it's *definitely* expired."

What they didn't eat, they stuffed into ditty bags they had brought from the sub. They sacked the store until all that was left was money and auto accessories. Sated, idly scratching lottery tickets, some of them were already starting to feel that perhaps it had been a mistake to eat so much, so fast. Of that junk. *Damn.*

"I don't feel so good, man."

Sal was consulting the selection of maps. "Well, don't croak yet—we still have a ways to go to get back."

"You guys go ahead, I'm staying here—*urp.*"

"I think we all staying here," Russell said. Something in his voice made them turn around to see what he was looking at. The front windows of the minimart overlooked the little memorial park and the elevated highway just beyond. Until now, the boys had not been in a position to really see Interstate 195—it had been an abstract concept, no more alarming than the underside of a bridge. Now they had a good view of it. Freddy G vomited—*whulp!*

The highway was a river of death, a glacier of stalled metal, curving away as far as the eye could see. Thousands upon thousands of cars and trucks jammed bumper to bumper, all dead silent, the diamond bits of their smashed windows glittering in the morning sun. The interstate had become a colossal junkyard, a graveyard for humanity's mobile aspirations . . . when graveyards no longer stayed filled.

Silent, dead, but not entirely still. There was darting movement there. Not the movement of cars, but of bodies—naked blue bodies. Caught in glimpses: the wink of shadows scurrying between the lanes, a flash of scary Zuni-doll faces. And darker shapes looming beneath the overpass—jumpy silhouettes blocking the light, flushing out the pigeons. Rushing down the on-ramp. They were *everywhere*.

Feeling his insides turn to water, Sal's thoughts raced. *No way, no way, dude. Nuh-uh, no way, oh, no, no, no, please, no . . .*

What he said was, "Guys? Can we, uh, get moving?"

CHAPTER **TEN**

THE UNDERGROUND

As usual, first responders charged into the fire. In the early moments of the outbreak, most EMTs and other rescue personnel simply vanished off the face of the Earth. Radio transcripts and dashboard cameras from police sources provide some of the earliest glimpses into the tragedy. A good example is the video log of 1A86, a patrol car with the LAPD, driven by Officer Mike McGuinness. Responding at 9:04 P.M. PST to reported "rioting" at Torrance General Hospital, the car's camera shows several police cruisers converging on the hospital's emergency entrance. Frantic medics run up to the cars yelling for help, as in the background a number of people can be seen on the ground being straddled and assaulted by crazed-looking women, some dressed in hospital scrubs. In the headlights, their faces appear bright blue. Using loudspeakers, the arriving officers command the aggressors to stop, then jump from their cars to intervene. They first attempt to break the grip of the attackers, then Mace and stun them repeatedly, then finally club them with nightsticks, all to little effect. They seem to have trouble getting handcuffs to stay on. First one and then another officer is attacked as more crazed rioters begin to appear. Shots ring out as officers realize they are overwhelmed—they can be heard screaming for backup. Officer McGuinness retreats to his vehicle and grabs his riot shotgun. At the same time, a K-9 unit pulls up, and the officers try to coax their cowering dog out of the car. As they are doing this, female rioters drag them down. McGuinness tries using the butt of his shotgun to knock one of the aggressors off, but others seize him around the neck, seemingly trying to kiss him as he goes down. As he struggles, his shotgun discharges at point-blank range into the open mouth of one female attacker, blasting most of her head off, but in an instant her body springs right back to join the others now piling onto him. At this point there is no one visible except squirming clusters of blue-skinned people. For a few moments they are all we see. Then they begin to get up, to move on, blowing away like leaves. But where are the bodies of their victims? It isn't until we notice that the dead cops have risen to join their killers, eyes glittering black in the headlights, that the full horror is revealed.

— The Maenad Project

"Uri Miska worked in a hole in the ground," said Langhorne's disembodied voice, echoing in the vault. "So that's where Agent X came from."

The wrought-iron spiral staircase descended into perfect darkness, as if down a well. Certainly there was water somewhere down there—water dripping into water. The air was rank with the stench of mildew.

"Now watch out. He may still be down there."

Lulu went first, then Albemarle and the rest. They hardly needed light to see—the newly independent cells of their bodies were not only photosensitive, but receptive to every other stimulus as well. They moved through a kaleidoscopic world of visible, liquid sensation: sound as strobing colors, temperature viscid as oil. It was only Langhorne who was blind—despite the boat's powerful mast array, reception at her end was sketchy. Broadband was a thing of the past. At her command, the light-boys clicked on, flooding the stone passage with xenon-bright glare.

They were in the terminal end of a large tunnel, its arched stone ceiling at least twenty feet high, its floor a stagnant, tea-colored pond several feet deep. Black trickles of seepage sheened the walls. To Lulu's immediate left was a massive steel door, welded shut, which must have once opened onto the street below Miska's house. The water was full of sunken machinery: generators, dehumidifiers, heaters, sump pumps. But strangest of all were the mummies. Hundreds of blurred bodies lay under the water, row after row of them, all uniformly white as if encased in plaster. Human cocoons.

Lulu knew exactly what she was looking at; she had seen something like this before.

They were Moguls. Not mummies but Moguls. Wealthy, dying men who had deliberately infected themselves with Agent X in order to stave off death—a controlled infection that preserved their higher brain functions. Now they littered the bottom of this flooded cavern like so many discarded beer cans. Human time capsules.

Lulu climbed the rest of the way down the stairs, passing through a metal turnstile onto a raised concrete landing. It resembled a dock, the gateway to a strange, subterranean river. All that was required to complete the image was a ghostly barge, the brooding specter of a gondola like the one that had brought them ashore. *Tunnel of Love or River Styx?*—either way, Lulu didn't have the fare.

The thought of that gondola resonated in her frozen heart like a plucked string: There had been a boy in that gondola—Langhorne said so. Set adrift upon the river like a note in a bottle. But by whom? And from where?

Not from here, certainly. The waters of this secret mausoleum led nowhere; they seeped out of the walls and back into the ground. It wasn't a sewer, or a cistern, or a dock on a river. It only looked that way because the pumps had stopped, had run out of gas and allowed water to start creeping in. Covering the train tracks.

They were on some kind of subway platform, a facsimile of an old-time railroad station, with ornate gilded benches, artificial potted palms, and mock ads for patent medicine on the walls. As the boys' light rigs shone far down the cavern, Lulu could read, DR. MISKA'S MIRACLE TONIC! INVIGORATES THE BLOOD! RESTORES YOUTH AND VITALITY! The place looked like something from an amusement park, but there was nothing faux about the *train*—a row of actual Pullman cars, four of them, their undercarriages wholly submerged, looming deep within that fathomless, dripping tunnel.

Langhorn's voice hissed with static: *"It's an old condemned train tunnel—it runs underneath the whole East Side, right under Brown University, from one end of College Hill to the other. Uri learned about it back in the eighties, when he first started doing research for Brown. Back then, protein indexing was a highly speculative field, and he needed more specialized lab space than they were willing to give him, so he raised the funds to refurbish an old mill in the Jewelry District. That was his 'official' laboratory, the public showcase for his mainstream research. But he needed something a little more discreet for his long-term pet project. Something completely private. So he bribed a few city officials, bought this house, knocked a hole in the basement, and developed the tunnel for his own use."*

Lulu started walking toward the train as Langhorne continued: *"Xibalba is the Mayan underworld, the 'place of fright.' Miska was interested in things like that. That doesn't mean he didn't take his research seriously, any more than when he joked about being some mad scientist out of an*

H. P. Lovecraft story—Lovecraft was from Providence, too. It was his Russian sense of humor. Ukrainian, actually. He was also crazy about fondue. In retrospect, maybe I should have been more worried. I was just grateful to be able to work with someone like him, you know? A shot at the Nobel Prize? Kicking AIDS?—come on." She paused, showers of static filling the gap. *"The sky was the limit with that man . . . right up until the day it fell.*

"Look *at this place,"* Langhorne suddenly blurted out. *"Looks like no one's been here—what an unholy mess. But this is just what I was hoping for: Everything should still be in place."* Her amplified voice was husky with excitement.

"This is where it began," she said. *"Where it got loose. Right here. We tried to take every precaution, but it still got away from us. Got into the water table, into the soil. That was a bad strain, a preliminary strain; we knew that. It still needed essential modifications to preserve cognitive function and . . . other qualities. But in the meantime, we had been deploying it on a limited basis, administering it to investors who were in critical health, just to preserve their bodies until the Tonic could be perfected. We were testing a number of promising enzymatic agents, but there was one in particular that Miska said he was having spectacular results with. That was his exact word: 'spectacular.' He said it completely reversed the negative effects."*

Lulu looked into the murky brownish depths, contemplating the invisible thing that was in there—was in *her*. This entity that had contaminated the Earth and every person on it, spreading for years, bonding to iron and hemoglobin, gestating in women's wombs like the spawn of some incubus, finally to be born as a bastard angel of destruction.

"Lulu? Honey? Why don't you go into the lab first." Langhorne wheedled, cautiously testing the waters.

From her flickering console on the submarine, the doctor

had been watching Lulu with deep fascination, reluctant to address her directly, worrying that the girl would suddenly spook like a deer in the forest. That was partly why she was talking so much—to accustom Lulu to the sound of her voice. The girl was free to go as she pleased, yet she stayed. Why? This world held no dangers for her; she owed them nothing. So what was holding her here? Loyalty? Love? Fear? Habit? Whatever it was, the longer she hung around, the more Langhorne began to think that maybe they had lucked out, that poor little Lulu Pangloss could be more useful than anyone, including Alice herself, had dared hope.

That's a good girl, Alice thought, eyes brimming with tears. *You're doing so good!* Voice steady, she said, *"There's a large liquid-nitrogen tank at the back of the train—it's used for storing blood specimens. There are racks of test tubes inside. Some of them will be labeled PMS for positive mutagenic serum. That's the stuff."*

As the girl obediently complied, Langhorne ordered, *"Boys, don't crowd her, but keep those lights on her. Stay out of the way of the camera."*

Lulu entered the open doorway of the first train car. It was full of deep, wavering shadows from their portable lights. Computer workstations, office furniture, and bulkier equipment crowded the long compartment. There were human knickknacks here and there: family pictures, silly coffee mugs, dead potted plants. Lulu saw a picture of Langhorne pushing a little girl in a swing. Moving on, the next car was full of sterilizing equipment and a row of chemical showers. There were warning signs posted in stages along the way and illustrated instructions for all the proper decontamination procedures. The third car was full of high-tech medical equipment—it had the look of a hospital operating theater, with tiers of benches looking in from outside on the platform. Within the car were several beds with elaborate metal restraints, and three large white tanks with glass viewports. Two of the tanks had Xombies in them.

Lulu remembered almost drowning in a tank like that as she was being interrogated at Thule. Two of her friends had died right next to her as she climbed their bodies to survive. They were both here now, Jake and Julian, serenely bearing lights and batteries. The memory held no terror for them or for Lulu. It was all just very . . . interesting.

The fourth and last car was shrouded in layers of heavy plastic sheeting. At one time the baffles had obviously been pumped up with air, now they hung limp. Lulu and the others tore carelessly through the seals to enter. It was a "clean room," containing air locks, biohazard suits, vacuum tanks, and all manner of UV lamps and microscopes, as well as more arcane scientific gear. Stainless-steel cabinets and refrigerators lined the walls. Like the compartments before it, the place didn't appear ransacked.

"I knew it," Langhorne said. *"They went after our facilities downtown, where the spectrometer and the X-ray diffraction labs are. They didn't even touch this place. Very few people knew about it, and to those who did, it was totally taboo—the secret Mogul burial chamber. Hallowed ground. No one belonged here unless they were dead. But this is where we collated and stored all our information. This is where Miska tied the threads together."*

Lulu approached the back of the car. Something was off there; something didn't fit. Amid all the wildly redundant human safety precautions, a door had been left open. It faced down the tunnel, a gaping window of black void. Beside the doorway was a large, stainless-steel vat. It was almost as tall as she was, plastered with bright yellow and orange warning signs: LIQUID NITROGEN—HANDLE WITH CAUTION. HAZARDOUS MATERIALS. BIOHAZARD. MUTAGEN.

"Cellular aging is associated with patterns of phosphorylation—proteins breaking down—so we developed a fast, synthetic delivery agent that could rewire each cell's nucleus to correct these patterns. The ideal was a hardy, self-replicating cell doctor that would never let the cells die—for any reason. And that's exactly what we came up with: a viral mechanism that enabled each cell to function independently and self-sufficiently. This thing . . . this thing—it was bigger than penicillin, bigger than the invention of fire!"

Lulu unclamped the heavy lid and peered inside. The tank was empty.

"Well?" said Langhorne eagerly, unable to see what was wrong. *"Get it and let's go!"*

There was a distant splashing. Lulu turned and stared blankly out the back of the carriage, her slight body framed by the doorway. From the echoes in that hollow gulf of air, she could sense the tunnel's length: a mile-long river sealed at both ends. A flooded crypt. Its temperature matched that of Lulu's own inner sea: fifty-five degrees. The light from the doorway cast a brown swath across the blackness, out of which loomed her own elongated shadow. Directly below her feet, she could make out the sepia glimmer of submerged railroad tracks receding into the murk.

Her attention followed the line of the tracks to the vanishing point, fixating on something deep in the darkness, a ghostly, lurking presence she could not quite pin down. The unfamiliar sensation caused a ripple of gooseflesh, bristled her hair. Her own reaction shocked and amused her: *How interesting.* She hadn't known she was still capable of fear.

But what am I afraid of? she thought. *I'm the boogey-man here.*

Summoning the awkward instrument of speech, she said, *"Big."* Her voice sounded alien to her, rusty and shrill. It repulsed her. She cleared her throat and tried again: *"There's something big out there."*

Listening from the sub, Langhorne wasn't sure who had spoken. She knew it couldn't be one of the boys, and certainly not Ed Albemarle. The raw, high-pitched sound paralyzed her for a second, because she knew from experience it could only be the voice of an articulate Xombie, but none of her Xombies had ever said a word. With dawning excitement, she realized it had to be Lulu—Lulu was talking! While Alice was absorbing this development, she also scrambled to make sense of what the girl was trying to tell her.

"Something big? Out—out where?" she asked.

Just then the ceiling came down.

Above the tunnel there was an explosion—a series of explosions. Demolition charges had been planted in Miska's basement and along the secret stairwell, detonating in sequence to amplify their effect. Xombies trailing at the end of the cable were first shredded by the blasts, then pulverized by the collapsing mass of the structures above, first the stone ceiling, then the iron scrollwork, then centuries-old timbers, bricks, and lead pipes. Above, Miska's house folded in upon itself, three stories compacting into one, then none, as walls and floorboards buckled, windows coughed out glass, and heavy enameled bath fixtures were sucked downward as if swallowed by a leviathan. In an instant, it all vanished in a billow of smoke, leaving a gap in Benefit Street like a yanked tooth.

In the tunnel beneath, the avalanche of rubble crashed to the bottom, burying the concrete platform and hitting the water with enough force to create sea waves that actually lifted the first Pullman car off its tracks. Dust, smoke, and hundreds of tons of debris roared down as if through a chute, perforating the train like volleys of grapeshot, pelting the Xombies within.

Then, all at once, it was done.

As dust and silence settled, all who were not buried or blown to bits climbed indifferently to their feet. They were filthy and dinged, but unperturbed. Lulu, at the far rear of the train, was one of the least damaged. The shock wave had blown her out the doorway, and she now stood up in sloshing, chest-deep water, sensing the silvery spray of glass and shrapnel embedded in her back. There was no blood or pain; all it took was a serpentine ripple to dislodge the shards, the clean wounds pursing shut like dozens of freakish eyelids.

Lulu's senses were clouded, her body still ringing from the physical shock, but she knew that she was not alone in that water. There was someone else out there with her— someone or something that was both alive and dead, both Xombie and human, the pale shine of its life force eclipsed by the shadow of death, yet not any kind of Xombie she had ever encountered. *Who's there?*

Now a light appeared at the far end of the tunnel, getting brighter and brighter as it came around the bend. As it hove into view, Lulu could see an enormous plunging silhouette wreathed in spray. If she didn't know better, she would have sworn it was a train. She was clear on one point, though: Whatever it was, it had no fear of her and was coming fast.

The memory of her mother—her mummy—rose like a phantom out of Lulu's amorphous mind, that familiar carping voice that in life she so loved and reviled:

What is this, Mummy squawked, *Grand Central Station?*

* * *

"Everybody move!" Russell barked. "You heard the man! Everybody off your ass!"

"Where you think we goin'?" demanded Kyle, frozen in place. He was not only terrified, but angry that his brother Russell was suddenly so eager to throw in with a loser like Sal DeLuca—especially at a time like this. After all they'd been through together, he was gonna start taking orders from *that* guy? No way, uh-uh. What did that fool have that they didn't? Except maybe the map.

"In here!" Sal shouted. He was standing behind the counter, pointing through the doorway of the minimart's utility room. It stank from the boys all having used the employee toilet even though there was no water pressure for flushing.

The boys looked doubtfully at the dark, stinking little cell. "Can we all fit in there?" Freddy asked.

Kyle yelled, "That's a death trap, man!"

"Not there!" Sal impatiently pointed through the room to a door marked EMERGENCY EXIT ONLY—ALARM WILL SOUND. *"There!"*

The Xombies were coming fast; if the boys didn't move quickly, they were going to be trapped in that glass box of a convenience store.

They moved. In an explosion of panic, they trampled each other to reach the back door, the lucky ones bursting outside into an alley. Sal had the advantage of a head start, then Russell and Kyle and the rest of the stronger boys.

"Which way now?" Russell gasped.

"Why you askin' *him* for?" Kyle said. "Just go!"

There didn't seem to be much choice. They were walled in on three sides by several buildings—a church, the rear of the minimart, and a hardware store. Directly ahead, the alley opened onto a back street. Sal went that way, the others following close behind.

Meanwhile, the boys at the rear, who were still trying to get out the exit door, found themselves trapped.

"Hurry up!" they screamed, trying to crush through as leering blue Xombies entered the store.

Micah Franklin, the last kid in line, whose nickname on the boat was Sleepy because he walked around in a trance all the time, perpetually in shock because of the loss of his family, suddenly felt a hard, cold arm around his throat. *Ah, damn,* he thought, unsurprised. Then he was jerked backward off his feet and was gone. The same thing happened to Carl and Scott and Elijah, all snatched up as they climbed over one another to get out. With naked Xombies crashing through the windows, some guys broke and ran, trying to dodge or fight their attackers, and were picked off like rabbits. The last boy to leave the store, Aram Fischer, the boat's resident cardsharp, the con artist, could see Xombies coming up fast as he slammed the exit door. But there was no lock from outside, no way to secure it.

"Oh God oh God," he cried, trapped there with the door shuddering against his back. He could hear a hideous whinnying sound from the other side. *"Somebody help me!"* But the other boys were running away as fast as they could and not looking back. As he strained with all his might, the door popped open an inch, and a long arm slithered through the crack. It seized Aram by the face, thick fingers rooting in his eyes, going all the way up his nose. Before he had time to scream, it yanked him back inside, his legs kicking furiously.

Now Sal and the others were running down the street, trying to stay low as they scurried behind rows of cars piled up at the intersection. They didn't speak, but Sal could hear their gasps and sobbed curses as they caught glimpses of

Xombies converging on the gas station, heard the sound of breaking glass. He hoped everybody got out. Any second now, those things were going to spot them, and it would be all over. They had to get off the street, out of sight, but anyplace they went would be another trap.

Face it, dude, we're screwed.

Even as he thought this, Sal felt that odd peace that always came over him during a race. Running, ducking, jumping obstacles, his attention streamlined into a familiar tunnel vision, everything focusing laserlike on a single goal. It was his training kicking in; he was conditioned to think under pressure. As an aspiring stunt rider, he had cultivated the mind-set of a kamikaze: In the heat of competition, you didn't have time to dwell on what was behind you, or the risks of the next jump—you just went. Fuck the law of gravity. You had to ride balls-out into the teeth of pain, grievous injury, possibly even death. Because that was the game. If you couldn't do that, you couldn't win.

They were emerging into a neighborhood of hip-looking shops and restaurants, past a futon store, an upscale bar. Nothing that looked very promising as a hiding place. Continuing up Brook Street, they passed a small market and a liquor store. *"Liquor store!"* Sal heard Freddy hiss at his back. Sal ignored him, kept running. That was all they needed—access to free beer. On the next block was a hole-in-the-wall video joint, then something that almost caused Sal to jump out of his skin:

A bike shop.

CHAPTER **ELEVEN**

RIDERS ON THE STORM

Q: Does everyone who dies come back to life, like in a zombie movie?

A: This is a hard question. Not because we don't know the answer, but because it is so vital that we treat all those who are about to die as an imminent threat. But the truth is no, most people who die from causes other than direct Maenad infection—which means a Xombie attack—remain dead. The reasons for this are twofold: One, the person's tissues may be insufficiently saturated with the Maenad morphocyte to permit revival; two, a level of cellular degradation has occurred that makes revival impossible. Dead is dead—Agent X can't infect a body with any degree of decay. The only absolutely predictable danger is from those who have become infected spontaneously while still alive, such as menstruating women, and anyone who has been "expired" by them.

Q: So the dead are not returning to life?

A: If a body has not revived within a few minutes of clinical death, it will not revive. This is not Hollywood.

—The Maenad Project

Xibalba . . .

They didn't waste any time arresting her, once it was clear she couldn't regain contact with her shore party. Dr. Langhorne didn't give a damn now that Lulu was lost.

Sitting with ex-skipper Harvey Coombs in the goat locker, unable to do anything but wait, she drifted in and out of the trance state that now constituted a good part of her waking life. Alice wasn't the only one. Nearly everyone on the boat was haunted by the past, visited by dreams and visions that came on so strong it was sometimes difficult to return to reality—the dead world refusing to let go, gripping tight as a Xombie. But Langhorne was a bit different in that the past was as loathsome to her as the present:

Alice! Help me—my legs are broken. That insistent voice, so hard to ignore, harder still to forget. Almost as bad as the actual sight of him had been, smashed and bleeding on the red-stained ice, pitiful as a dog maimed by a car. Helpless in a way that was alien to both of them; she could hear the disgust in his voice—the new and awkward experience of having to beg for help. Alice Langhorne understood perfectly; it was shocking to her as well, after all this time, at long last. But she kept moving, made herself keep moving. Toward the submarine.

Alice! What are you doing? Help me!

I'm sorry, Jim.

You can't leave me like this. Then, to her escaping back, *I saved your life!*

It was true. He had saved her life. Not out of love, though—God forbid. Their marriage, never about love or romance, had always been more of a business arrangement, a limited partnership with emphasis on the limited: Jim & Alice Enterprises. And she had been the silent partner, the spy, working as Jim Sandoval's personal mole into Uri

Miska's organization, serving as a direct link to Mogul Research Division, a subsidiary of MoCo.

Had he ever loved her? Alice wasn't sure if Jim was even capable of such an emotion. She was *useful* to him; he *valued* her. Then again, she wasn't the most warm and fuzzy person herself, and the street ran both ways. Jim funded her research and provided the business and political connections that enabled the ASR project to be carried on without government interference—even if it was only so he could glean a hefty tax write-off—and she provided the product. But there was no denying that neither her work nor Miska's . . . nor Agent X itself . . . could have existed without the contributions of Chairman James Sandoval.

When the ASR prototype, the artificial microorganism that would come to be known as Agent X, got loose in the environment, Alice couldn't help but feel that it had been inevitable, a form of cosmic justice. Looking at those contaminated soil and water samples, she had to laugh: Why not add failure and professional disgrace to her catalogue of sins? And when both Miska and Sandoval had downplayed the threat, advising her to sweep it under the rug, she had no energy left to resist. Nor did she resist much when her ex approached her at the company Christmas party, just one short week before the epidemic.

They were on the top floor of the Biltmore Hotel, with a beautiful view of Providence, when he started blathering some nonsense about the installation of a research laboratory at a military base somewhere in the frozen Arctic—a place she'd never heard of, called Thule.

Air Force base? she asked, only half-listening to him. It was her third drink. Laboratory where? Arctic what?

There's an old Air Force base up there, left over from the Cold War. It's in Greenland. The government's converting

*part of the site into a storage depot for sensitive materials
and personnel in case of a pandemic. Homeland Security
stuff, all very hush-hush. We got the contract*—mucho
dinero. *The downside is that they want it done yesterday.*

I can't go to Greenland.

Why not?

*Why not? Are you trying to be funny? With all this crap
going on?*

*I know you're burned-out; we've all been under tremen-
dous stress lately. That's why I think a change of scenery
could do you some good—not just you, but your whole division. Miska's already agreed to hold the fort. Get away
from here for a little while, a paid vacation out of that
dungeon.*

Why? Are indictments coming down?

*I could think of nicer places if that were the case. This
isn't Acapulco.*

When would I have to leave?

*That's the catch: You have to report by next weekend,
preferably sooner.*

*Well, it's out of the question then. You know I can't go
anywhere until after New Year's.*

Sure you can.

Lowering her voice, she said, *Idiot—I have to be present
in the lab when that morphocyte degrades. What do you
think I've been waiting for all these months? Singing "Auld
Lang Syne" with Regis? I can't rest easy until this thing
elapses and returns to its constituents.*

*You can track it just as easily in Greenland. You said it
was everywhere.*

Are you serious? All my equipment is here.

Not anymore. It's been shipped.

What?

He nodded slowly, the cat that swallowed the canary.

Jim, you better be joking.

Sorry to spring it on you like this.

Since when? she demanded.

Since early this morning. The whole kit 'n' kaboodle, on a C-130 transport out of T.F. Green. Your friend Dr. Stevens rode along to make sure it all went smoothly.

Chandra's in on this? Are you all out of your fucking minds?

I would have told you yesterday, but you were kind of out of it. Hey, it's just for a couple of months. I may even drop in on you guys up there later.

I can't believe this. This is all too weird right now.

Come on—weird is good. Weird is just what the doctor ordered.

Yeah, but which doctor? Witch doctor—I made a funny. Which doctor's the witch doctor?

Alice, you're drunk.

She leaned in close, breathing gin fumes into his face. *And you're a bastard. But I'll be sober in the morning.*

"Well, this is another fine mess you've gotten me into."

Alice Langhorne was sitting on one of the brown Naugahyde couches in the goat locker, playing solitaire. Not looking up from her cards, she said, "What do you suppose happens now? They make us walk the plank?"

Pacing, Coombs said, "There's no plank on a submarine."

"The screen door, then."

"I just don't understand what Kranuski thinks he's going to get out of this."

"You don't? He already sold out the boat once before, didn't he?"

"Not deliberately. I can't believe he did that deliberately.

He didn't know about the Moguls, and as soon as we all realized what was going on, Rich stopped cooperating with them . . . even under torture. I saw it. The man's a walking recruiting poster—his sense of duty is sincere, if misguided."

"You mean he's got a major stick up his butt."

"He has good reason to be that way. There's no margin for error on a submarine. If you heard the tape of the *Thresher* going down, you'd know what I mean. And let me tell you something about Richard Kranuski: He has more reason than most to want to stick to protocol. He had a bad hazing experience at the Academy—a couple of drunk midshipmen hung him off a second-floor balcony by his ankles and dropped him. Ended their careers, and it's only a miracle Kranuski wasn't killed or paralyzed. Since then, he hasn't had much tolerance for games."

"Well, that explains it."

"What?"

"He fell on his head."

"I'm just worried he's being manipulated by Webb."

"That meathead?"

"Alton Webb's been developing a regular little following by playing on the men's fears and telling them what they want to hear. At first I thought it was a useful tool to keep morale up and maintain order, but now I realize he obviously had other ambitions. Webb's second-in-command now; all he has to do is remove Rich, and he'll be running the show."

"I hate to tell you, Chief, but he's already running the show."

"Yeah . . . yeah, but why? For what purpose?"

"Who knows? Demigod of the seas isn't enough?"

"Webb used to be a good officer. Kranuski, too. We all were."

"Those were the days, my friend. The question is, what do we do now?"

"Hold up!" Sal called softly, waving the boys to stop. Still no sign of Xombies. Through the window he could see hundreds of bikes filling every inch of the store. Better still, it was a repair shop, which meant that a lot of the bikes should be good to go, tires all pumped up and waiting for their owners to come get them. He checked the door. It was locked, of course. *Damn!* They didn't dare break in—it would make too much of a racket. What now?

Sensing Sal's indecision, Russell shoved past him and stuffed his coat over a windowpane in the door. As Sal started to say, "No, don't—!" the bigger boy gave it a sharp tap with a rock. The glass tinkled inward, barely audible.

"I done this before," he said, reaching through to unlock it. They quickly filed inside.

As the last of them came in, Sal said, "Wait, where are the others?"

"They gone, man."

"What?"

"They didn't never make it outta the minimart."

"Are you *kidding*? And you just *left* them there?" Sal was almost yelling.

"You left 'em, bro. We were all following you."

"But I didn't *know*! I was counting on you guys to—"

"To what? To die like them? Ain't nobody could help them, man. Come on, what the fuck we here for?"

Trying to gather his wits, shaken by the magnitude of his failure—ten, no, *eleven* guys gone!—Sal said dully, "Uh, yeah . . . just grab whatever you think you can ride. Shit, dude. Keep it simple—no crazy junk with eighty-eight gears. These are good up here. Pull 'em down, check the tires for air . . ." He could feel his eyes watering, wanting to cry.

Something flashed by outside the window. A blurred human shape, bright in the daylight, its eyes and mouth three gaping black pits. Then another rushed by. And another and another. The last one stopped short, peering into the dark shop. There was an electric jolt of eye contact—and every boy in the room felt his bowels turn to water.

The thing staring at them was a teenage girl, or once had been. Now it was a naked blue banshee, deathly savage, with long, curved fingernails, nipples like tarnished iron spikes, and hair a black nest of brambles. Sal was reminded of the cover of an old picture book that had given him nightmares as a child: *Struwwelpeter*—the grotesque boy who never cut his hair or nails. It whirled and came at them.

"Damn," Derrick croaked. "Here she comes."

There was nowhere they could hide; the store was wide open, all glass. As most of the boys scrambled backward, Sal jumped forward and opened the front door.

"Hell you doin'?" Kyle yelled, leaping to stop him.

Sal hissed back, "If it has to break in, it'll give us away!"

Russell rammed Kyle clear of the doorway as the Xombie came hurtling through. "Nail it!" he cried to the others, jumping for cover. They shrank backward, tumbling over bikes and each other to escape.

As the ferocious gargoyle plunged after them, Sal dove to shut the door, then grabbed the first thing at hand, the frame of a little girl's bike, and swung it around by its glittery, pink-tasseled handlebars, hoping to use the sharp ends of the bike's front fork as a weapon.

The Xombie was much too quick. Before Sal could strike, it whirled at him, knocking him onto his back with the bicycle crushing his chest. Powerful blue arms snaked for his throat. As he tried to fend them off with the handle-bars, he realized he was inadvertently twisting the Xom-bie's head—its neck was lodged between the prongs of the fork. In desperation he wrenched the handlebars all the way around and heard the creature's neck snap with a sickening, cartilaginous *crack*. The force of its fury weakened for an instant, long enough for him to kick it off him and pin it to the floor by the fork. "Help me!" he shouted.

"Here!" Derrick said, handing him a bike chain.

Are you kidding? As Sal whipped the thrashing thing, feeling like a circus lion-tamer, some of the other boys found the nerve to join in. Immediately it became a hyper-caffeinated, junk-food-fueled frenzy, all of them fighting each other to get a lick in. Tools were located and put to use—crowbars and tin snips and hacksaws. A bunch of old golf clubs turned up. In less than a minute, the Xombie was chopped and pounded to quivering purple hamburger, its severed joints kicked around the room.

While this was going on, Sal had a moment to step back and wipe his brow. He knew they didn't have long—more of those things could show up any second. It was a miracle they hadn't already. He looked up at the row of used BMX bikes hanging from a rack. There were some okay ones there. Nothing as cherry as his custom Diamondback stumpjumper, but not bad. Choosing a metallic blue Trek, he took it down and checked the feel. It would have to do.

Wheeling the bike to the door, he said, "Guys. I'm going."

The others were shaky from their bloodlust, some puk-ing, the rest shocked and not quite in their right minds. "What . . . ?"

"Listen to me. You see that cross street out there—Transit? I'm gonna ride up that and make as much noise as I can. Give me a minute to draw them off, then you go the opposite way. Go fast, but stick together and don't stop for anything. I'll loop back around and meet you on the other side, where Transit meets Gano. On the map there's another highway underpass down there that we can use to get back to the docks."

"Say *what*?" They were sobering quickly, realizing what he was saying. "You gotta be—"

"I'm gone. Don't wait too long!"

Then he was out the door and riding hard. As he turned the corner, they heard him singing at the top of his lungs: *"Riders of the storm!—Riders of the storm!—Into this world we're born!—Out of this world we're torn!—ner, na-nyer ner ner . . ."*

"Damn," said Russell.

Kyle scoffed, astonished, "Boy be trippin'."

"Trippin' or not, he's clearing the way for us to get out this shithole. I ain't about to waste it." He grabbed a silver Peugeot mountain bike. "Move ass, all of you! Grab a bike and follow me!"

"Dog, where you think you *goin'*?"

"You heard what the man said: Gano Street! That's all I need to know—I been here before. Hurry up! Once I go, everybody else gotta be ready to follow, one after another like clockwork! We ain't slowin' down for nobody."

There was no shortage of bikes; in a few minutes all twenty-nine boys were poised to go, crushing into the doorway. Though the coast looked clear, no one wanted to be first. The Xombie was fresh in their minds.

"Fine. Everybody back the fuck up," Russell said. "If I'm taking point, I gotta have room for a running start, least be a movin' target."

As the others jockeyed for position behind him, a fight broke out: "No way, man!" "*I* ain't bringin' up the rear!" "Yeah, why don't *you* go last?"

"Hell, *I'll* go last." The squawk of Russell's strained throat shut them up. "Get in front, whichever one of you wants to be first. You, Freddy? Derrick? Come on up, dog— I'm savin' the best place for you. I already had one of them things on my neck, I'll let you have the next one. I'll gladly kick back at the *end* of the line, watch everybody else take the heat." Nobody moved. "We straight, then? A'ight, back up, motherfucker."

Kyle, who had been wavering between standing by his brother or defecting to the naysayers, now said, "Get back, fools!" As they cleared away, he gestured for silence, then cautiously opened the door and peeked both ways. Satisfied, he whispered, "Go."

Russell nodded and kicked off into the sunlight. As he raced across the street, he could still hear the receding echo of Sal's singing . . . and something else: a deep, rushing sound as of the wind through autumn leaves, comprised of rapid footsteps and ghastly massed voices. He shuddered, nerves wilting with horror. *Don't let 'em catch you, man.*

Kyle went next, flubbing his pedals as he jumped the curb, followed in quick succession by all the others. Getting their rhythm, they formed a ragged line, zipping unobstructed along the narrow side street. There were no dead cars here, only parked ones, and they made good speed. All that prevented them from going even faster was the incline—they were pedaling uphill. None of the boys had had any cardiovascular exercise in months, trapped on that submarine, and as they forced their bikes up the rise— emaciated bodies already starting to crash from the sugar binge—it became abundantly clear that they were in truly *terrible* shape. Their lungs were on fire, their wasted legs flimsy as rubber bands. Many of the boys had been athletes; it shocked and dismayed them to be so weak.

"Damn, man, I got no game," Kyle said, struggling to keep pace.

"Me either," Freddy Gonzales said. "Slow down, I am *dying*."

"Shut up, you guys!" Russell hissed back.

Turning to face forward again, Russell found himself staring into the face of an onrushing Xombie. It was a big woman with flaming red hair, her open mouth a black grotto that seemed big enough to swallow him and his bike whole. Heart exploding, he instinctively ducked, trying to swerve, but the thing hooked him around the neck, and they spun together in a horrible pas de deux before crashing to the ground.

Seeing Russell in trouble, Kyle made a flying leap from his bike, trying to knock the creature off his brother with a large crescent wrench. Freddy came next, with a claw hammer, followed one after another by the rest of the boys. Having so quickly dispatched the Xombie in the bike shop, they were now much more willing to jump in.

But no matter what they did, they couldn't seem to pry the hideous thing off Russell. Its body was practically fused to him, arms and legs wrapped whipcord tight around his limbs, mouth mashed against his face as it sucked the breath from his lungs. Worse, their mouths were joined together from within by a rootlike mass of flesh. The boys could hear the sickening, hopeless sound of Russell's rib cage crumpling.

"Cut it off him!" Kyle cried tearfully, but some of them were already doing that, dismembering it and hacking at the tough, slippery umbilical as best they could. They just weren't doing it fast enough—Russell's popping eyes were already glazed over, staring blankly through them. He had stopped struggling.

A sudden eruption sent the ring of boys scattering:

"Look out!" someone screamed. *"Heads up!"* There was another Xombie in their midst. It was a boy about their own age, a feral thing still wearing a tattered Patriots shirt. Flying after them, it plucked Nate off his feet, taking the boy in a headlock and capering away with his thrashing body slung over its back. Several boys gave chase, but almost immediately two *more* Xombies appeared, striking like spiders at them as they left the main group. In an instant, Rick and Carlos were down.

Now things dissolved into panicky confusion, people tripping over bikes trying to escape. How could they fight these things and watch their own backs at the same time? Russell was beyond saving; Kyle miserably knew that unless they did something fast, his own brother would bounce back as a demonic Xombie. So would the other three boys, meaning the number of unstoppable monsters they had to deal with would effectively double. Meanwhile, more Exes were popping out of the woodwork like cockroaches. Roy Almeida was hit as he watched, limbs flailing. Kyle was stunned to be so suddenly helpless and alone—there was no one in charge! Without Russell or even that goody-goody Sal, he felt completely lost.

"We gotta get indoors!" Freddy shouted.

"We gotta make a run for it!" yelled someone else.

Kyle roused himself. Abandoning the mess of body parts that were still inextricably clutching his older brother— his soul brother, his best friend and last living family member—he cried, "Everybody on your bikes, let's go!"

That's it, isn't it, Dad? We're all going to die?

Everybody dies sometime, Sal. And if they're lucky, they stay dead.

Once again, Sal DeLuca was riding for his life. It was

literally an uphill battle. When he'd rashly conceived this
plan, he had no idea how soon his legs would start giving
out, but he took strength in knowing that every inch he
climbed would at least be rewarded with an effortless downhill glide on the return journey. He was sweating and dizzy
from carb and caffeine overload—he *never* ate that kind of
stuff.

Transit Street was shady and tree-lined, narrow as an
old cart path, with quaint, pastel-colored historical houses
arrayed on either side. The road was not particularly
steep, but Sal might as well have been pedaling up Mount
Washington—this was the first time he realized how much
of a wreck he'd become. Had he been able to weigh himself, or look in a mirror, he would have been shocked at the
sunken-eyed wraith staring back at him. Since the end of
the world, he had lost nearly a third of his body mass.

Sal didn't know the College Hill district very well, having grown up miles away in South County, but he had been
to Providence enough times to have some sense of its geog-
raphy. This was the hilly part—he knew that much. Beyond
that, he had to rely on the map and his own sense of direction. East, west, north, south—those he could handle. Up
and down he was learning as he went along.

His intuition (and the map) told him that heading west
up Transit was a smart move: Xombies were drawn to population centers, so it made sense to get off the main drag
and into quieter neighborhoods. He could lure the creatures
in after him and use the cobblestone maze of Colonial-era
city planning to confuse them, slow them down—*they*
didn't have maps to find their way out.

Sal knew he didn't dare head too far in that direction,
though, because Phil Tran had told him that Lulu and the
rest of Dr. Langhorne's "subjects" were foraging somewhere around here. Benefit Street was highlighted in red on

his map, with the scrawled warning, TO AVOID. Sal was in full agreement with Phil on this point. The last thing he needed was to run into those things, however harmless they were said to be.

His plan was simply to pull a Pied Piper routine, clear the road for Russell and the other guys to get a head start in the opposite direction, then ditch the deadheads and loop back around to rendezvous with his team at India Point. From there they could follow bike paths along the waterfront all the way back to the rafts.

Easy as pie . . . in *theory*. What his map didn't show was that Brook Street was in a trough, a former creek bottom from which it had derived its name, and that by turning up Transit he would be hill-climbing at the same time as he was acting as live bait for hordes of the undead. *Nice going, Scout,* Sal thought ruefully. *So much for that merit badge.* He could only hope the other guys were having an easier time of it.

At least one part of Sal's plan was an unqualified success: The Xombies were coming. They had heard his singing and were swarming out after him like hornets from a disturbed nest, following hard on his wheels. He didn't dare look back, but he could hear them behind him, a gathering roar like the tide.

The Xombies are coming!—that was the crazed thought that ran through his mind like the ravings of a demented Paul Revere. *The Xombies are coming, the Xombies are coming!*

Then the sight that he had been expecting and dreading: more Xombies in front of him, trying to cut him off—half a dozen jittering blue monstrosities coming over the crest of the hill.

But Sal had prepared an exit strategy. Riding straight at them, he cut right up a cobblestone alleyway—and found

himself on an even *steeper* hill. *Oh, man!* It had looked so
good on paper! As he gunned forward, standing on his pedals, he barely had time to react as a small Xombie with only
half a head lunged out of a driveway at him. *Oh no you
don't!* Swerving hard to avoid its grasp, boosted by a
screaming rush of adrenaline, Sal darted willy-nilly between houses and yards, jumping his bike up and down
curbs and porch steps as the grotesque thing skittered close
behind.

Suddenly he was cornered. It was going to get him; he
had no choice. A veteran trespasser, Sal had been in similar circumstances before, chased not by Xombies but by
vicious dogs or irate homeowners, and in his everyday life
had taken to carrying a can of pepper spray when he went
riding on private property. He didn't have his trusty spray
can now, but Phil Tran had smuggled him something even
better.

Don't use it unless you absolutely have to, Phil had
whispered, slipping the cloth-wrapped package into Sal's
coat pocket. *The sound will give you away, so it's only to be
used as a last resort. It might buy you a couple of extra
seconds.*

It was Lieutenant Tran's personal sidearm: a Navy-issue
.45-caliber automatic pistol, loaded for bear with explosive
dumdum bullets. *Don't forget to release the safety,* Tran had
added. *And don't shoot your own foot off.*

I won't, Sal had said. *Thanks, man.*

As the creature's flailing blue hand caught the back of
Sal's jacket, yanking him up short, he twisted around and
rammed the gun into the center of its chest. The revolting,
half-faced thing pushed right back against the muzzle,
heedless, headless, its cratered skull healed over and
smoothly misshapen as some abstract Modernist sculpture,

with a dirty blond pigtail on one side. A weird tentacle of raw flesh lashed out of its open gullet at him.

BANG! Having never fired a gun in his life, Sal wasn't quite prepared for the recoil, which sent a painful shock up his whole arm. The force of the concussion knocked him and the Xombie apart, blasting a fist-sized hole through the creature and bowling it backward to the ground. Without waiting to see if it would rise again—he knew it would—Sal shot it again, then unloaded on the next nearest attackers before leaping his bike into motion.

All of a sudden another loud bang rang out—a string of echoing bangs, rattling the house windows and shaking the ground. Not gunshots, but explosions. A fast sequence of blasts, powerful as thunderclaps, coming from over the hill—from the direction of Benefit Street. *Whoa,* Sal thought, feeling that he had triggered the explosions somehow, that something was answering his shots.

No time to think about it. The pursuing Xombies froze in their tracks to listen, bodies cocked like alert dogs, and Sal didn't waste the opportunity. In an instant, he was through the alley and over the hump, turning right onto the next street and blazing downhill with the wind cooling his sweat.

CHAPTER **TWELVE**

GANO STREET

Q: What makes them look so bad?
A: Well, the grisly complexion is because their bodies have been deprived of oxygen. They're cyanotic. That's a precondition for Maenad infection—it can't work in the presence of oxygen, which is why Xombies must strangle or otherwise suffocate their victims. We think that's part of why they behave as they do, because their brains are damaged from lack of oxygen in the few minutes prior to the disease taking over. After that, nothing can hurt them, but whatever brain function they lose in those first minutes is critical.

Q: Then how did living women become infected in the first place?
A: That's the big mystery. Tests show that most women's hemoglobin has a far greater susceptibility to Agent X infiltration than men's, which means the disease has been spreading longer, perhaps building up in their systems until it reached a kind of critical mass. But why the disease should have become virulent all at once, worldwide, is something we don't understand. It may be connected to the lunar cycle, or it might suggest that it was deliberate, like a timer going off.

Q: Are you suggesting it was an act of terrorism?

A: Anything's possible. One of the worst tragedies of this thing is how every female, whether infected or not, was immediately declared a menace—we'll never know how many millions of them were needlessly quarantined, driven from their homes, or killed outright. In this way, we exacerbated the Xombie crisis far beyond the problem of the plague itself, which could not destroy us as long as there was one immune female somewhere out there—and there may have been many. In condemning them all, we abetted our own extinction.

Q: What do you say to those who think it was God's judgment?

A: I'd say God acts in mysterious ways.

—**The Maenad Project**

"Mr. Kranuski."

"Mr. Coombs."

"To what do we owe the honor of this visit?"

"Cut the bullshit. You know as well as I do. Where are the spare command keys?"

"They've been missing since Fred Cowper was in charge."

"Why don't you ask *him*?" Langhorne said brightly.

Kranuski ignored her. "Don't bullshit me. I know somebody's been using those keys to gain access to restricted areas of the boat and tamper with the system. That's mutiny, sabotage. Do you still have any honor left? Is that what you want? To scuttle the boat? Kill us all?"

"Of course not," said Coombs, offended. "I have no idea who could be doing that. How could I? It's not like I had time to talk to anyone before you locked us in here."

Rich Kranuski said, "I knew you were incompetent, but I never thought you'd stoop to something like this out of sheer spite. I am not your enemy, Harvey. I know I fucked up at Thule, but now I'm just trying to preserve what few military regulations still apply, and which we are both duty-bound to observe. This is still a Navy vessel."

"I understand that."

"Then don't you understand that whoever's fucking around with the safety sensors is fucking with your sworn mission as a Navy officer? False alarms in the coolant valves are not my idea of a joke."

Langhorne piped in. "Tell it to Cowper."

"Shut the hell up."

"Oooh, tough guy. Mister macho. I heard how you treat little girls."

"Shut up, or you're gonna make me shut you up."

"Oh no, am I in for a spanking?"

"I think you better hear her out, Rich," said Coombs,

"What the hell are you talking about?"

"Ask *her*."

"Ask her what?" He turned to Langhorne. "What is it you're supposed to know?"

Alice Langhorne didn't seem to be listening, suddenly more absorbed in pouring herself a cup of coffee and stirring in a packet of sweetener.

"I'm waiting, Doctor. And if you don't wipe that smug expression off your face, I'll do it for you."

Taking a sip, she said, "Give me a break. Of the three useless captains on this ship, you're the worst."

"What are you talking about, three captains? I don't have time for this."

"I'm *say*ing, genius, that with Coombs under arrest, some of the men are taking their orders from another captain, and it's not you."

"What the hell are you—are you insane or something? Fred Cowper's long gone, and you know it. We saw the last of him up around the Arctic Circle."

"He's not gone. The orders you gave to dispose of his head were never followed—it didn't get dumped down the TDU. It's still here."

"Oh, really? Where? Hidden in the fruit bin?"

"It was in a locker on the third deck until we sent out the shore party. It disappeared after that, and I thought maybe my Xombies had taken it. But now I don't think so. I believe Fred Cowper's still on board."

"*Bullshit!* I can't listen to any more of this." To Coombs, he said, "I suppose you're going to stand there and swear to me she's telling the truth."

"I have no idea. But I will tell you what you already know, that there have been some strange things happening on board. You've heard the chatter about the boat being haunted, and it's not just the kids doing the talking."

"That's just sailor superstition. Everybody's on edge. It doesn't mean there's a fucking head rolling around loose."

"You're probably right. I don't know."

Kranuski steadied himself. "You know, according to strict ship's protocol, I am authorized to use lethal force if it is necessary to maintain operational integrity. I could execute you both, right here, right now. And I would . . . except that it would only create a worse hazard for me to deal with. I know you both know that—you know I don't dare kill you. Not with a gun. But fortunately there's another way of handling traitors and saboteurs on this boat. You're familiar with the trash-disposal unit. It's the way I thought we got rid of Fred Cowper, and if I find out you're lying to me, it's the way we're going to dispose of you."

Langhorne waited until he was finished, her face flushing bright red, then broke into laughter. "I'm sorry," she said, wiping her eyes. "I have a weakness for dumb jokes."

One by one, the boys were being taken—grabbed off their bikes like cattle culled from a herd. Kyle counted down the sounds of crashing bicycles as each one fell: fifteen, fourteen, thirteen, *twelve*—two-thirds of the guys who had started out were gone. But he was numb to it, in shock from the loss of his brother. If this went on much longer, there wouldn't be anybody left to meet Sal. If Sal was even still alive. Their mission was a joke, a ruse to get rid of them, just as Russell had said. A plot cooked up by Kranuski and Webb and the rest of the Navy men to conserve the food supply. To save a few pounds of grits.

Far behind them, he heard the crack of a gunshot. Before the sound could fully register, there followed a series of booms like Fourth of July fireworks. In the distance, a plume of black smoke rose into the sky.

"Holy shit," said Freddy, gasping for breath. "What's that?"

"I don't know," Kyle said. "Keep pedaling."

"Sounds like a war."

"Don't matter what it is; it's way the hell back there."

"Maybe it's a rescue party from the sub!"

"Then they in a world of shit like we are. Ain't no rescue party. Shut up and keep moving—we're almost there."

The street had leveled off, and the end was in sight: They were coming to a T-intersection that Kyle supposed must be Gano Street. He expected to see a highway underpass—a clear route back to the waterfront. But when they got there, there was no underpass, just more houses, and the street sign said GOVERNOR.

Where the hell are we?

The boys were piling up behind him, faces agog with panic, wondering why he was hesitating. "Don't stop!" they shouted, blue death clawing at their backs. Kyle didn't know what to do—he couldn't very well tell them they were lost. It was that damn Sal DeLuca's fault!

"Over there!" Freddy cried in his ear, pointing up the street.

There it was: another sign for Transit Street, half a block over. So they hadn't yet reached the end after all. Transit continued on after Governor. Kyle gratefully kicked off, relinquishing his lead as other bikes swept past. Most of them probably knew this part of town better than he did anyway. He was suddenly shaking so hard he could barely grip the handlebars.

Now the street was wider, beginning to dip downhill. The twelve remaining boys had all caught up with each other and were riding clumped together like a school of bait fish. Nobody wanted to be on the outside. Another block down, and they could see water—a river or an arm of the bay—bordered by green fields.

"That has to be the Seekonk," Todd called. "Which means Gano Street is straight ahead!"

With this news there was no stopping them. Legs spinning, hearts surging with wild hope, the pack spread out a little, swarming downhill as fast as they could, faster than even Xombies could run. As speed and momentum increased, so did their sense of power: Boys carrying crowbars, hammers, and makeshift lances took the lead, jousting down the few Xombies that blocked their path, clearing the road.

At the bottom lay Gano Street. A few blocks to the right was the passage to India Point Park—and the bay. All they had to do now was zip through there before the Xombies got wind of them. Then they would be back on the waterfront, fenced off from the rest of the city, within spitting distance of the rafts. Practically home free.

It was all just as Sal had said . . . but where was *he*?

Kyle slowed at the bottom of the hill, brakes squeaking.

"What are you doing, man?" said Freddy, wobbling up short beside him. "We gotta go!"

"You go ahead," said Kyle. "I'm gonna wait a few minutes."

Freddy was dumbfounded. "Wait? Wait for what?"

"In case Sal shows up."

"*Sal?* Are you kidding, bro? He's *dead*, come on!"

"No doubt. You guys go—*go!* I'll come in a couple minutes."

"Don't be stupid, man," said Todd Holmes. He was a slight but wiry boy, with a faint mustache and ropy blond dreadlocks. He had learned tattooing while in juvie for felony tagging (he was the infamous TH, whose initials graced every corner of Providence), and his forearms were covered with bluish black runes. Todd was the boat's artist-in-residence and, probably because he didn't speak much, was something of a guru among the nubs. "Once we go under that bridge, it's gonna bring all those things down after us. Nobody else is gonna be able to get through there. That's why we all have to go together, *now*."

"That's why *you* have to go! So go! Get the fuck out of here!"

"Why are you *doin'* this, man?" Todd said softly, urgently. "Because of Russell?"

"*Shut* up."

"I understand, man; he was like a brother to me, too . . ."

"Shut *up*."

"If he wants to stay, leave him," said Derrick Agostino, wild-eyed with fear. "Sorry, man, but we can't waste any more time."

"I didn't ask you to," said Kyle.

Freddy said, "But he's just—"

"*Leave* him! We gotta *go*, do you get it?" Derrick pointed down the street. "Dumb shit, look!"

"Oh my God."

All of a sudden their escape route was rotten with Xombies, hordes of blue figures pouring down the highway on-ramp and out of the side streets.

"Too late," said Todd, "they've seen us. What do we do now?"

"Whatever we're gonna do, just do it," said Derrick. "Here they come."

Kyle looked up the hill. More Xombies were coming down Transit Street, a whole pack of raving "blue meanies." That was a name some of the boys had picked up on the ship because it softened the terror. But nothing could disguise the awfulness of seeing his own brother skittering among them. *No, Russell.* He grieved. *Not you, man.* "We gotta do what Sal was trying to do," Kyle croaked, forcing himself to look away. "Lead 'em off, then ditch them and circle back around. Come on."

The lowest concentration of Xombies looked to be in the open fields right across the road, so Kyle went that way, cutting across the parking lot of a Dunkin' Donuts. The other boys followed eagerly, grateful just to be moving. Riding as hard as their weakened conditions allowed, they raced for green lawns. A Xombie in their path was caught up in a gauntlet of vengeful blows, clubbed down and quickly pulverized, its head impatiently struck from its body and batted away like a polo ball. They knew the drill now: Get them before they got you. Don't flinch. Teamwork. Leaving the broken thing flailing in their wake like a defective toy, they left the pavement for soft grass.

They were on an athletic field, with basketball courts

and a baseball diamond, bisected by a dirt track. A high, mowed berm rose along the edge of the field, to prevent balls from escaping into the surrounding marsh, and tall brush bordered the sides. Just up the shore was an ancient railroad drawbridge, an overgrown, rusty colossus jutting permanently into the sky.

They took down another Xombie on the grass—it was getting easier. But there was also a lot of room here to maneuver, to overwhelm with force, and Kyle knew that unless there was also a way out, these same advantages would soon favor the Xombies. The boys were already very tired and could only ride in circles for so long. In a few minutes, it was going to be a hellish playground, the ultimate game of tag.

"We need a back door," Kyle called, resting his heavy monkey wrench on the handlebars. "Somewhere we can retreat to when the time comes. Where's this road go? Anybody know?"

The others shook their heads. Todd asked, "Don't *you*?"

"I never been here before."

"Well, what the—" Before Todd could register his incredulity, a whoop rose up from far in the rear. All of them turned in amazement.

It was Sal DeLuca. Riding his bike like a daredevil, Sal was *flying*, thrusting all out down the hill, whipping between Xombies right and left. The creatures hardly had time to see him before he shot past. As he reached the bottom, momentum peaking, he barreled toward a converging mass of them in the donut-shop parking lot. It looked hopeless for him, his way blocked. *Look out, man!* Kyle thought, scalp prickling.

Sal didn't stop; he charged right into them at top speed. A dozen maniacal blue devils leaped to tackle him, but suddenly Sal hit a beveled parking bumper, bouncing his bike straight up and over as the Xombies violently cracked heads below.

Now he was away and clear, cruising onto the grass as if just having broken the victory tape, his face flushed with relief and exertion. But as he drew near, his expression flattened with concern.

"Where is everybody?" he demanded, pulling up alongside.

"They dead," said Kyle. "Where *you* been?"

"*Dead*, are you kidding? How?"

"Same way we gonna be if we don't do something quick." A Xombie approached, and the bigger boys clubbed it down. "How do we get out of here, dammit?"

"Under the highway!" Sal said.

"That road is *closed*—look!" Xombies were now covering Gano Street from one end to the other, swarming like enraged ants.

"Oh. Shit . . ." Blanching at the sight, Sal fumbled out his map. He had to stop reading as it became necessary to flee.

Riding for their lives, Kyle said, *"Well?"*

"I don't know! The only way is to go under the highway to India Point!"

"Well, we obviously can't *do* that!"

"It's either that or jump in the river!"

"That's bullshit, man! There's gotta be another way!"

Sal shook his head. He didn't say what he was thinking: *Dream on, dude. You took too long to reach the underpass. You were too slow, and you blew your chance to ever leave this park. You shouldn't have let yourselves get surrounded like this—that was dumb, wicked dumb. I did my part, risked my ass to draw them off, and what do I get? Bunch of dumb nubs, that's what I get. Now I get to die with you—thanks. Thanks a lot.*

"What about that smoke? What's that?"

"What smoke?"

Kyle pointed it out to him, a small puff of gray rising above the tree line.

"That wasn't there before," said Todd.

"Maybe there's somebody there!" Freddy cried hopefully.

"Yeah, maybe somebody's trying to signal us," Derrick said.

Scanning the USGS map, Sal said, "This says there's nothing back there but some old train tracks. Mr. Tran specifically marked it off-limits, see? It's in Lulu's area of operation."

"I thought they were supposed to be way the hell over on the opposite side of town."

Sal shrugged helplessly. "Looks like there's a tunnel or something. All I know is, it says not to go this way."

Kyle said, "Well, maybe we need Lulu's help at this point, you ever think of that?"

"How can Langhorne's pet Xombies help us? They're just a bunch of . . . Xombies!"

"Idiot! Those Smurfs of hers are hooked up directly to the boat—at least we can let Langhorne know we're in trouble."

It was an incredible idea, running to Xombies for help, but Sal couldn't think of any argument. They had no choice. And there was no time to debate it anyway. "All right, let's go."

The road became a rough path through the sticks. Now they had to pick their way more carefully, agonizingly aware of hideous goons flooding across the field behind them, hemming them in. Sal alone could possibly make a break for it, a last-ditch effort to lead the Xombies away, but he couldn't bring himself to try. He was exhausted, they all were. Subconsciously preparing to quit—just to let go.

Far from getting out of the park, the boys were becoming ever more deeply cornered in it, forcing their bikes down a muddy hollow littered with beer cans and plastic jugs and dirty diapers, junk tires and box springs. It stank of rotten eggs—the brackish nearness of the marsh. The path became uneven, rolling upward, hemmed in by scarlet sumac and walls of reeds—once they got into that brush and had to start running on foot, it would be all over.

They came to a set of ancient railroad tracks, leading eastward toward the monolithic, upraised trestle, and west down a tunnel of dense foliage. There was a flattened car across the tracks. Sal entered the leafy passage. He didn't know how far they would get before the Xombies caught up, but it was worth a try.

"Where does this lead to?" asked Freddy Fisk from behind.

"A train tunnel, I think. It goes under the whole East Side. If we can sneak back under cover like this, maybe we can pull an end run to the rafts," Sal said hopefully. "Nice call, Kyle."

"My pleasure, man—can we just go?"

Now they were able to pick up the pace though they could only ride single file, and at times the greenery was so thick that they had to push their way through.

"You think there are ticks in here?" asked Freddy G. People hissed at him to shut up. "Haven't you guys ever heard of Lyme disease?"

"Shut the hell *up*, man."

Freddy decided not to ask about poison ivy.

Bumping along the old railway ties, the boys were hyperalert to any sound or movement in the surrounding woods, but all was silence. It became swampy, the ground a soggy mulch of dead leaves and trash and black mud, the rank material clinging to their tires and flying up behind them in greasy clods. The mulch gave way to puddles, then a continuous oily pool that gradually rose to cover the tracks.

Sal stopped, hanging on to a branch rather than put his feet down. As Kyle pulled up alongside him, he whispered, "Yo. Check it out."

Ahead of them was a yawning black cavern flanked by graffiti-ridden concrete buttresses—an old train tunnel. This was the source of the smoke they had seen. A lazy gray plume still wafted from the darkness. Though obviously condemned and shut up for many years, the tunnel's steel doors had been breached and now stood wide open, like a gateway to some infernal kingdom.

"Should we try calling down there?" Sal asked.

"I don't know," said Todd.

"Well, I ain't goin' in there," said Kyle.

"I know," Sal readily agreed. "It's too bad, though. If we could use this tunnel, we might be able to cross right under the hill without the Xombies ever seeing us. Take a shortcut back to the boats."

"Yeah, but if there are some of them in there . . ."

"I know. Plus, we have no lights, and we don't even know if it's open on the other end."

"Not to mention it's flooded."

"That too."

"So what now?"

"We have to climb up there to the street." Sal indicated the steep wooded bank.

Kyle looked at the thick underbrush. "With our bikes?" The other boys, who had been gathering behind, looked shell-shocked and utterly whipped—they could barely keep their bikes upright. "It'll take forever for all of us to get up there. The Xombies are comin' *now*, man. And bet your ass there gonna be more up top."

Sal erupted, "What the hell do you want me to say? We gotta do *something*! You're the one who—"

As he spoke, he became aware of a hollow rushing sound like the echo from a storm drain. Kyle's eyes flicked past him and suddenly grew wide, fixing on something, their dilating pupils vivid with a pale light of terror. Freddy and the other boys gaped as well, all of them rocked with the same unspeakable fright. Sal turned his head.

It was the tunnel. The thunderous noise was coming from deep within it—the sound of a roaring cataract. It was growing louder every second: some great mass rushing up like a dark tsunami.

"Xombies!" Freddy shouted

The boys broke and ran. Abandoning their bikes, slipping and sliding all over the place, trampling one another into the muck, most of them had no idea where they were going—as long as it was anywhere but there. Only Sal stayed with his bike, dragging it a little way up the bank. "Up here!" he shouted to them. "We have to go this way!"

Then he froze, suddenly aware that something was standing next to him in the bushes. It was something very big, a shadowy human figure half-hidden by the leaves. Alarming enough if it was a Xombie lurking there . . . but then the thing stepped into a bar of sunlight. The sight of it caused Sal to reel backward on his ass, legs entangled in the bike.

It was not a mindless Xombie—a Xombie would have attacked by now. This was something else, something even more preposterous: a nightmarish hulk assembled from surplus Xombie parts. A hideous Frankenstein's monster crudely patched together with steel stitches. In what he thought was the final second of his life, Sal DeLuca gaped up at the monster's seething form, a crazy quilt of bristling scalps, mottled blue skins, veinous bodily nets and sinews, and, worst of all, a living cuirass of animate human faces, all held together with what appeared to be metal staples. They *were* staples—what Sal at first took to be a huge, holstered pistol was in fact an industrial-sized staple gun.

"CHEW DUNE, BOA?" the thing roared at him.

Sal fainted.

CHAPTER **THIRTEEN**

THE FOUNDING FATHER

There was no food, or news. No one came around at all; trash and filth thrown in the corridors just stayed there. The prisoners who had televisions and radios kept them turned way up so everyone could hear, but all the channels were off the air except one, and that one just kept playing a tape loop from the Emergency Broadcast System—some vague warning about a disease causing women to go berserk, which the men already knew. Then the electricity went out. When the cell toilets went dry, the prisoners became very nervous. Sometime in the early morning of the third day, a voice came over the prison loudspeakers:

"Gentlemen, attention. Attention, gentlemen. Wake up, please."

The inmates stirred. Some began to yell. "Who's that? Hey, we need water in here! Who's there? Help! Help us!"

"Attention. I ask for everyone's attention. My name is Bendis, Major Kasim Bendis. I am a professional soldier, and I've come to save your lives."

A gabble of voices echoed down the cellblock: "I *told* you!" "Get us outta here, then!" "I demand to speak to my attorney!"

Bendis said, *"The judges are gone, the attorneys are*

*gone, the guards and police are gone. Everyone you knew
on the outside is gone, and you have been left here to die.
But I've come to offer you a choice in the matter."*

"Just let us out, motherfucker!"

*"I can do that. I can do that, and will, if that is your ul-
timate choice. But if I do that, you will be choosing death.
Since my team and I were airdropped here and are now
trapped with you, I would prefer that we all survive."*

"Airdropped? Who the fuck are you, man, James Bond?
Where's the rest of the damn cavalry?"

*"There is no cavalry, no National Guard. No rescue—all
that is over. Forget your former persecutors and think of
yourselves as the rulers of your own destiny. Your own*
country. *Yes, this is your country now. I'm a private contractor working for the company that owns this facility, and
I've been sent to help you rescue yourselves. And to do that
you have to listen to me. I didn't come here to get us killed,
or to make us into more of* them—*the infected. There are
already enough of* them *out there. And be assured that if I
just release you all from your cells, that is what will happen. You are hungry and scared, you are desperate to make
some sense of what's happening, so you will try to leave—
it's not unreasonable. You will open the gate and expose us
to Agent X infection: the Maenad psychosis. They are waiting out there, trust me, and once it starts spreading in here,
it will be too late. That would be a terrible waste since you
are the lucky ones. You won the biggest lottery of all time,
being within these walls, being men, and it's my job to help
you make the most of it.*

*"But I'm not here to make that decision for you. I'm just
here to help you make it for yourselves—to advise you.
What I need you to do now is pick a representative. Pick
someone among yourselves to speak to me, one-on-one, and
I will release him. Once he has been fully briefed on the*

situation, he will pick a council representing the dominant factions among you, and together they will assume full control of the penitentiary. As I said, I am only here in an advisory role—you are in charge. So choose your government."

After an hour of rancorous debate, they arrived at a consensus. Their leader was a man they all knew, a jailhouse celebrity who did not put on airs or demand special treatment, a humble and private man. He was Joe Angel, aka Angel Suarez, aka El Abrigo, aka El Dopa—this last being the name he was best known by, as it was the name he recorded under. In his two years in the joint, El Dopa had somehow managed to be a jailhouse musician, a convict-rights advocate, and a crusader for world peace through the healing power of transcendental meditation. He was a uniter, not a divider. This had served him well not only in the joint but on the outside, where record executives were falling all over themselves to sign the next big crossover star.

The truth was, El Dopa had never been a criminal, and his teenage years had been characterized less by drive-by shootings than by drive-thru cheeseburgers. He was a suburban kid from a solidly middle-class family; there were no ties to gangs and crime syndicates, not even any crimes to speak of. His conviction on illegal firearms possession was a calculated PR stunt arranged by his agent and record company to boost his street cred upon the release of his debut studio album, *El Dopa Represents*. As a first offender, he'd expected to get off with time served, probation, and a stint of community service that he could use to push his album in schools, but his arrest coincided with an election year, the War on Terror, and the governor's tough-on-crime campaign. Joseph Xavier Angel, twenty-nine, small-town boy, small-time crook, Vedanta Yoga enthusiast, was blindsided with five years hard labor.

Marcus Washington—Voodooman—had no objection to El Dopa's election as spokesman—*Why not?* He didn't know the man personally, and frankly he didn't much care. Like all the inmates, Marcus had sat in his cell for the last three days staring at his three hungry cellmates and grimly contemplating the future. They were all doing it, in every cell of the prison: sizing each other up, assessing each other's weaknesses, coming to a consensus. No tortuous discussion was required; the process of elimination was subliminal and automatic, as if on some level they had always known they were going to eat each other. Only the victims were unsure—that was what identified them as victims.

Marcus was everything El Dopa pretended to be: Born into backwoods poverty in the wilds of Texarkana, he had run away from home at twelve and started making deliveries for drug dealers in New Orleans. He graduated to gang membership at thirteen, dropped out of school at fourteen, and wound up in the system at fifteen, convicted for killing three rival gang members. Then it was years in juvenile detention, followed by more years at the ACI—medium security—where he was convicted a second time for murdering another inmate before finally being transferred to the private supermax facility at Huntsville.

At first, the whole business about Agent X had seemed pretty promising—any lifer serving six consecutive terms for capital murder had to be interested in any change in the status quo. It was like the bull in the card game: Without some kind of major intervention, Marcus had no hope of ever again tasting freedom. He barely remembered its flavor.

El Dopa met with Major Bendis for several hours, then came out and freed the leaders of every major prison faction, holding a private discussion with them for more long hours. Water was provided. Finally, the council emerged, and El Dopa addressed the rest of the population:

"Those with the most power bear the most responsibility—how could it be otherwise? They're the ones most capable of doing anything. In our society, money equals power. Thus it follows that those with the least money should bear the least responsibility. The poor should be given the most slack. And yet we here have borne not only the least opportunity but the harshest punishment. Most of us have never known the benefits of civilization; how could we be expected to uphold its laws? Especially when the rich and powerful are exempt. It isn't us who profit off war, or religion, or political corruption, or the rape of the environment. Those crimes, which cause misery and death to billions, go unpunished, or are in fact *rewarded*, while the corporate media demonize our petty crimes of poverty, our acts of human desperation, our very *survival*, and we are sentenced to lifetimes of slavery.

"Well, we have finally been freed. We are in charge of not only our own destinies but the destiny of the country as a whole. The reins of power have been handed to us, and we must act accordingly—responsibly. If we just leave and scatter in all directions, we will end up like everybody else out there: crazy or dead. We gotta stick together, work as a team, as an army, to build a new society. Everything we need is out there, free for the taking, but in order to get at it, we need technical assistance, and that's where Major Bendis comes in. He's been sent not only to help us but to ask for our help. He says there's a new world government being formed out there, a government we can help create, which will correct the mistakes of the past. A government in which we will all have shares."

El Dopa held up a certificate resembling a treasury bond. It read, ONE MOBUCK, and in smaller print, *This Mobuck*

entitles the bearer to 1/125,000 share of all benefits accru-
ing from membership in the entity known as the Mogul
Cooperative or MoCo, redeemable in gold or services.
"You see this? Money's no good anymore—this is the
official currency of your new country. This is power. It represents a percentage of the total wealth—the more you
contribute, the more it's worth. The more *you're* worth.
That makes us all major stockholders. People, this is like
having a share of McDonald's back when it was just one
restaurant—priceless.

"But we gotta move. There are other groups like us, other
prisons all over the world, and if we don't get on board
quick, the shares will be divided into smaller and smaller
fractions, sold and resold until they're watered down to
nothing. Right now we have the early-bird advantage—
we're the Founding Fathers." He waited for this to sink in,
then said, "Okay, then. Go ahead, Smitty."

The chairman of the Prisoners' Rights Committee stepped
forward. "Y'all been waiting long enough, so we are going
to open the cellblocks and let you out, but that don't mean
you can up and leave. That would be suicide. There's a plan
for how to do it right, and we're respecting you enough to
trust that you'll assemble in the main hall and listen to the
rest of what we have to say. It's very important—all our lives
depend on it. Give me a shout-out if you agree."

Everyone shouted yes, and the cellblock doors were
rolled back.

There was a stampede for the exit, like the ringing of a
school bell.

The prisoners were scared, they were hungry, they were
thirsty, and they were pissed off to have been kept waiting
here one minute longer than they had to be when they could
already be seeing to their mothers, their wives, their children, or otherwise making the most of this Get Out of Jail

Free card. They had more important things to do than sit
here listening to bullshit speeches.

Of the five thousand men in camp, only a few hundred
had actually witnessed what happened the night of the
rodeo; the rest could barely make sense of the garbled reports coming over the airwaves or the goofy horror stories
circulating by word of mouth: *Crazy blue bitches? Maenad
what? Agent X? What the hell is that?* Many of the men
were in the joint for crimes against women—assault, rape,
murder—and were accustomed to forcing their will upon
the opposite sex, making women cry and plead, using them,
breaking them, then turning them out to earn pocket money
to spend on fresh bitches. The thought of a female being
dangerous was laughable: Women were generally weak and
gullible, suckers for any man with a sweet line of patter;
they needed a firm hand to control them. Scrape away the
clothing and makeup and high-ass attitude, and they were
helpless as baby chicks: holes that begged to be filled. Their
only purpose was to serve men, and if they talked back or
got out of line, it was a simple matter of laying down some
tough love . . . which was where the police, and the judges,
and the prison system came in.

But if there *were* no police . . .

Hence the men smiled and nodded and patiently sat
through those whole long speeches, but as soon as the doors
rolled back, they shook off the unsolicited advice like a
long-winded sermon in the prison chapel when all they
wanted was free wine—they didn't need El Dopa, they didn't
need no funny money, and they certainly didn't need any
half-assed Rambo motherfuckers telling them what to do.

Marcus himself held back, as did all the boys who had
been at the rodeo that night. No one who had seen that, who
had those sounds and pictures playing in his mind day and
night, was in any big hurry to dash outside, however hungry

or thirsty he might be. They tried to impress this upon the men around them, but the momentum to leave was too great . . . until the jackhammer sound of a modified AK-47 caused everyone to fall back in panic. Bits of concrete and ceiling insulation rained down on their heads.

It was Major Bendis. He and his men were sitting in the shadows, blocking the passage to the main guard station, barring the exit. They were dangerous men, men with a philosophy of violence, all five of them heavily laden with weapons and belts of ammunition. Despite their smoking guns, they appeared perfectly at ease, lounging back in plastic kiddy desks from the visiting area.

Speaking into a megaphone, Bendis said in his odd foreign accent, "As I said before, you are free to go. Just not all at once. We'll let you go in your elected groups, starting with the smallest. Will the smallest group please to come forward? Everyone else stay where you are."

The sixteen representatives of ILL—the Incarcerated Libertarian League—pushed through the crowd. They were all paunchy, red-faced NRA supporters and militant anti-government types who had been convicted of weapons charges and tax evasion, or who had killed bosses, coworkers, and ex-wives in suburban shooting rampages. Because of the latter, high-profile atrocities, most of them were on Death Row, where they shared a dormitory and were kept on permanent suicide watch: intrusive searches, twenty-four-hour video monitoring, and bright lights all night long. The thought that they were about to just waltz out of here scot-free was incredible to these men—they were all too familiar with betrayal, it had to be a trick of some kind—so they came forward hesitantly, upper lips sweating, pudgy nail-bitten hands trembling in disbelief.

Bendis nodded at El Dopa, who waved the men through, saying, "Go on, you're free."

Two of the soldiers led them through the various gated
levels of the security station, the processing room, and the
outer waiting area, to the heavy exit door. The outside video
monitors were all dead. Directing them to wait, the lead
mercenary peered through the security glass, then popped
the latch. Jerking his bearded chin toward the exit, he
hissed, "Run! Now!"

The men ran. Barging through the door into bright
daylight, the first thing they saw was the surreal sight of
the warden's white stallion nibbling the grassy verge of the
inner keep. The huge animal huffed and tossed its head,
rearing away as the group headed down the enclosed path
between fenced exercise yards to the outer compound. Beyond that was the secure parking and the driveway to the
main gatepost, a fortified checkpoint through steel jungles
of chain link and concertina wire, sandwiching a perimeter-
long dog run and great thick brambles of razor ribbon.

Those brambles were full of naked dead people, scare-
crows of raw meat, their clothes and flesh torn off and hanging in rags from the wire, their mangled bodies bent in
impossible contortions, limbs all but torn off trying to swim
through the steel thicket, finally stuck fast.

Horrific as this sight was, the convicts had already either
seen it themselves or heard about it from others with
outward-facing windows. They were focused more on the
peaceful vista just beyond: the rolling green landscape of
the prison farm, thousands of acres surrounded by a single
outer fence that bordered the service road. From what they
could tell, the plague had run its course; the landscape was
deserted. No guards to stop them, no crazy women running
wild, just clear sailing all the way. Basking in the sunshine,
they jogged anxiously toward freedom.

They made it as far as the parking lot before the Xombies
hit. First there was just one—a creature so torn from its

passage through the wire that it was practically skinless, all purplish muscle and yellow fat, its torn belly an empty cavity. It was a woman.

The men shouted to each other as the thing came around the building, skittering as though hyped-up on meth or PCP, much faster than they could run and open the gate—they were already out of breath. Fleeing wasn't an option; the only choice was to stand and fight. Even though they had no weapons, the men weren't overly alarmed at the prospect—they were comfortable with their sixteen-to-one advantage. One torn-up madwoman didn't stand a chance.

First, they tried to just shoo her off, waving their fists and yelling, "Fuck off! Get out of here! Beat it!" but she kept coming. As she drew closer, and they really got a look at her—that flayed face with its hugely exposed black eyeballs rimmed in yellow—some of the men became more doubtful, but the ringleader, an ex-Marine named Sherman Oakes, said, "Holy Jesus, she's already got both feet in the grave! Probably drop dead from a stiff breeze." He wrapped his jacket around his fist, and the others did likewise, forming a defensive half circle to meet her.

Then another Xombie appeared from behind them. It was a guard, a young guy named Cyril Shaklee, who was blue in the face but otherwise intact except for one of his legs having been ripped off at the hip. He scrambled forward on his three remaining limbs, crablike, freakishly fast, and was followed by two more creatures rounding the east wing of the building. Furthermore, the dead ones caught between the fences suddenly came back to life, barbed coils twanging as they bucked and wriggled through, leaving dangling gobbets of flesh.

The convicts' line began to fray, trying to keep all the spastic creatures in view. As the woman charged among them, Sherman Oakes swung at her with a royal haymaker, hoping to take her out with one punch, but she dodged inside his fist and hooked him around the neck, toppling the big man backward and clamping on. The others kicked at her as viciously as they could, trying to knock her off without having to actually touch her, but she was grafted to her man, legs around his chest, arms around his neck, and the lower half of her face buried deep in his mouth as though trying to crawl down his throat, cracking his jaw as she sucked his lungs inside out. She couldn't be budged.

"God*damm*it," someone said, realizing they were in over their heads. Resolve buckling, first one man, then another and another and finally all of them broke off the fight, half of them running for the gatepost, the other half scattering senselessly the way they had come. The gatehouse was the nearest hope of shelter, but it was a losing race: Several creatures were emerging from the wire right beside the gate, and those already running free were at the men's heels.

The first man to run, a forty-year-old former postal worker named Ted Kleinmetz, made it. Arriving at the open door, he cried to the others, "Come on, come on!" But a lightning-quick monstrosity lunged at him from the fence, and Ted had no choice but to slide the metal door shut against it. The demon hit the door with a crash, cracking the wire-reinforced window and leaving an inky smudge.

There were gun ports in the walls, and Kleinmetz frantically scanned the office for firearms, but the guards had obviously taken everything when they left. He could hear the other men's muffled screaming outside, and things banging against the doors and windows that might or might not have been human—he couldn't bear to look. *Oh God oh shit . . .* Searching the drawers, he found a police baton and some pepper spray, clutching them to his chest as he sought a hole to curl up in and wait out this nightmare.

He found one: a tiny, windowless closet in the back, with a toilet and sink. But as he stepped inside the dark cubby, his right foot fell down a gap in the floorboards, and something grabbed his leg from underneath, twisting and pulling with inhuman strength. His hip joint ruptured with an audible *crack*.

Screaming in agony, he realized the impossibility of his entire body fitting down that crevice, the incomprehensible ramifications of that, and the last thought Ted Kleinmetz had as he blacked out from the pain of his leg being ripped off was a memory of something one of his victims had said to him right before he pulled the trigger:

Uncle, dammit, uncle!

CHAPTER **FOURTEEN**

HOPALONG CASSIDY PHALANX

"**C**HEW DUNE, BOA?" the monster roared again.

Sal awoke, confused, then recoiled and squeezed his eyes shut, hoping to die quickly. He couldn't bear to look. Every inch of the thing held a new horror: cancerous growths of ears, nipples, belly buttons, genitals—a cannibal collage of misplaced organs. And on top of it all a head like a spiny leather cactus, with three blackened holes for a face. It reminded him of something out of a comic book he had once read, about a swamp monster called the Man-Thing, whose tagline was *Whatever knows fear BURNS at the Man-Thing's touch.*

Sal was speechless, unable to think. Deafened by the blood rushing in his ears, he was yet able to sense that the other boys had gone equally silent and still. And he knew why: They were surrounded, the wood taken over by dozens of these horrific things, rising amid the swamp brush like ghastly sentinels.

The monster leaned closer. "Ahmo ask yew once mo: What the hail you all doin' heah? Ah-bla Inglays?"

Its heavy Southern drawl suddenly clicked.

"Nothing!" Sal cried, relieved to understand, to at least be able barely to comprehend what this appalling vision was saying to him. To know that it was in some way human. This hopeful possibility triggered a domino effect in his mind: Of *course* it was human! Yes, he could see it now, a face through the eyeholes—there was some kind of man in there. The Xombie flesh was only skin deep, a grisly living *costume*. He was not a Xombie at all but *dressed* in Xombies. Armored from head to toe in living Xombie flesh.

Weeping, Sal cried, "We're running away from Xombies! They're coming! Help us, please!"

"Xombies, *hell*. You ain't—"

Just then the churning, rumbling noise within the tunnel became very loud. Waves lapped out from its mouth, fanning across the mired boys, then a single high, resounding voice: *"Yeeeeehaaaaaaaw!"*

And out came the boat.

It was a large amphibious truck, a converted military landing craft of the type called a duck boat, familiar to Sal from preapocalypse days as a tourist ride. The aft end of it was covered with a peculiar, fleshy canopy resembling a Conestoga wagon, Xombie skins stretched over aluminum ribs like the translucent webbing of a bat's wing. On its hull, painted in ornate letters, were the words PRAIRIE SCHOONER. The vehicle's open front appeared shaggy, its high gunwales festooned with an odd, rippling mass of bluish fronds, opening and closing like blooming flower petals. Not flowers—arms. A thousand clutching, severed arms, nailed down like blossoms on a Rose Parade float.

"We found one of Miska's!" the truck's driver shouted. Upon seeing the boys, he pulled up short, and called down, "Well, well! Looks like we ain't the only ones to bag us a prize. What we got here?"

In their ghoulish second skins, the vehicle's crew were no less unspeakably awful than the men on the ground, each one's costume arranged differently according to personal idiosyncrasy, each one with a large black number scorched—branded—on the front of his leathery helmet. But there was no question now that there were ordinary men underneath. Aside from the massive vehicle, the proof was in the axes, spears, guns, lights, and sophisticated night-vision equipment they carried—Xombies traveled much lighter. But with their Xombie armor and medieval weaponry, they resembled nothing so much as a boatload of hideously deformed goblins. Aliens. Mutants. It was not such fanciful monstrosities that sprang foremost to Sal's mind, however. The whoops, ropes, drawling banter, and holstered staple guns were indicative of a slightly more reassuring archetype.

Cowboys, he thought crazily. *Rednecks. Shit, that's all we need: a bunch of sadistic backwoods shitkickers— probably necrophiliacs, too. Necrophiliacs and cannibals. They'll rape us, then kill us, then rape us again, then eat us, then wear our skins as hats.*

Somehow that still wasn't as scary to him as Xombies.

"Who—who are you guys?" he asked shrilly.

"Ain't that funny," said the monstrous vision. "I was about to ask you the same thing. But I guess we both have to wait—trouble's nigh."

"Harpies bazaar!" someone whooped.

The Xombies were upon them.

First there was the sound, a rushing commotion in the dense underbrush, crackling like wildfire. Then, far down the glade, Sal saw a solid wave of manic blue bodies sprinting toward them. Swarming up the railroad tracks, the river of trampling ghouls gathered force as it approached, secondary streams of Xombies merging with it out of the trees.

Sal barely had time to think before a blue hand seized him by the front of his jacket. The hand was not attached to a person, but to the end of a long pole wielded by a man on the duck boat. The man shouted, "Hang on!" and in one dizzying swoop Sal was swung over the high rail of the truck—its frilled arms following him like iron filings after a magnet—and dumped hard onto its rubberized foredeck. Someone planted his bootheel on Sal's chest, using a crowbar to pry the hand loose. It *hurt*.

Knocked flat on his back, Sal rolled aside just as another boy tumbled in, crying *"Hey!"*—it was Kyle Hancock. Two other boys followed in quick succession, Todd Holmes and Freddy Fisk, boated like flopping tuna, then finally Ray Despineau. No sign of the rest; they had scattered, fleeing into the trees. Sal tried to get up, but one of the grisly men pinned him with a spear handle, and barked, "Stay still!"

Suddenly, they could hear Xombies all around the vehicle, the terrifying wash of sound filling the air. Sal's body tensed in expectation of blue demons pouring over the rails—the duck boat was wide open. But the creatures did not come in. As the truck lurched into motion, the men on foot calmly hoisted themselves up the rear step, piling in with practiced ease. The Xombies weren't touching them.

"Phew, that's a peck of 'em," one said, voice muffled beneath his spiny meat helmet.

"You have to help the others!" Sal cried. "Please!"

"We would if'n we could, but they already gone. Ain't nobody can he'p them now."

A flurry of Xombies boiled up against the rail, threatening to spill over.

Freddy screamed, "Why don't you shoot! They're coming in!"

"We don't waste good ammo on Harpies."

Another said, "Don't do no good."

"Fact it makes things worse. Just more bits and pieces to contend with."

Their resolve on this point was demonstrated when a

feral blue infant leaped from a tree toward the huddled boys. Instead of shooting it, the crew deftly speared the flailing thing in midair and pitched it overboard. They all had such lances; the craft's topside bristled with them, every one unique as though for a specialized purpose, or perhaps just customized to suit the user. The basic design was long wooden handles tipped with variously shaped iron spikes, blades, and sharp-pronged hooks, though a few also had severed Xombie hands affixed to them. The choice of such a tool, and the skill with which it was being wielded, evinced a level of casual use that Sal found both alarming and wildly reassuring.

The boys could hear Xombie skulls thwacking against the hull as the truck plowed through. Its angled bow was particularly well suited to this purpose, rafting atop the slippery living cataract.

Prairie Schooner, Sal thought. *Injun country.*

Heedless of the six-wheeled juggernaut, Xombies were squashed into the mud by the dozens, by the hundreds, their ribs collapsing like crates and inky blood jetting from every orifice. It was a temporary condition; they would be back. Over the rail Sal could see blue arms flailing as more Xombies lunged against the sides, but they weren't coming aboard. Something seemed to be preventing them from hanging on.

As he watched, a particularly eager female crested the railing only to be stopped short by contact with that garden of disembodied limbs nailed to the gunwales. The effect was immediate: Hundreds of undead arms, themselves intent on the boys, jerked like a mass of disturbed snakes and hurled the attacking Xombie against a tree.

"Why aren't they coming in?" Freddie whimpered.

"The hands," Sal said. "The hands aren't letting them. I don't think they like being grabbed."

"You got that right," said the leader. "They strongly object to bein' manhandled by one of they own. You ever see how magnets repel each other? That's what it's like. Them Harpies spook to each other's touch—it's like an electric shock or something. Maybe it reminds 'em a what they is."

Another man said, "Nah, that ain't it. They just a hindrance to each other, that's all, an obstacle to be avoided—ain't no feeling about it. All they can see is us, like as if we got a damn neon sign over our heads."

"Don't make no damn difference why it works," said the first man, "long as it works." To the boys, he said, "They won't even fight over us. They got this system for keeping things polite: first come, first served. One to a customer. Ain't you never noticed how when a Harpy grabs someone, the rest of 'em just shy off? We call it the Solomon Principle. Otherwise, they'd tear each other to pieces, and us, too. By wearing their doodads, we give off that vibe of being spoken for; our dance card is full."

"Damn," said Sal, awestruck. This was like discovering fire. "It's like the ultimate camouflage!"

Kyle said, "I wish we'd known about this shit sooner. Get me a Xombie-skin jacket."

The man nodded. "Damn straight. It's like a protective membrane, like them Nemo fish that can live in a poisonous sea flower. We just goin' back to nature."

"How'd you figure all this out?" Sal asked.

"*We* didn't. It come down from the man upstairs—part of our shareholder benefits. But your boys on the sub must get the tech updates, too. Ain't you got no company rep?"

"Oh . . . sure. Definitely."

Still dumbfounded, Freddy asked, "But can't it get at you? Their skins, I mean? Aren't you scared of it touching you? Hurting you somehow?"

"It wants to—that's what holds 'em on so tight. That, and some staples. But we figured out that by using pelts from different Harpies it causes friction between 'em, and the aversion keeps 'em on their own little territories, like countries on a map. That's what we got goin' here on each of us: a little model of détente."

It did look like a map. A hairy, pulsating relief map. "But how can you stand it touching you?" Kyle asked.

"Oh, it don't touch us, trust me. We're all wearing protective duds underneath this. You gotta: Once it latches on, it's very hard to remove unless you tempt it off with bare skin, which is why we been makin' you boys keep your distance. Don't get in reach of them hands, neither. Harpy hide is tricky stuff. It can be sticky or slippery, depending, and you cain't never forget that it wants to get at you. Because *it* surely won't."

"Then how do you ever get it off again?"

"Oxygen. Pure oxygen neutralizes Agent X—puts the meat right to sleep."

Freddy piped up. "Carbon monoxide works, too."

The man looked at him strangely, said, "That's true, but that'd also put *us* to sleep. Forever."

The truck left the densest concentration of Xombies, and the ride became smoother. The only sounds now were the engine and the slash of foliage against the sides. They lurched left, turning sharply up a marshy path and trundling over a downed chain-link fence. Bumping over a curb, they were suddenly back in civilization, the parking lot of a small shopping center. EASTSIDE MARKET said the anchor store, and adjoining it were a chain video outlet and a drive-thru bank. Across the parking lot stood a large pharmacy.

The leader announced, "Last stop! Ever'body off the bus." When the boys started to get up, he said, "Not you. You boys need to stay down, out of sight."

Men had been hard at work here already. Every shopping cart in the place was lined up outside the market, fifty or more, all laden with groceries. There were also rolling pallets covered with larger bulk items: huge bags of rice, beans, flour, sugar, and hand trucks stacked with more cases of goods. They had cleaned the place out. A second duck boat was parked across the lot, its crew busily raiding the drugstore.

"Daaamn," whispered Kyle. "They got a major operation goin' here."

"Yeah," said Sal.

"If they can walk around out in the open, what they need all this food for? And where they takin' this stuff? They got enough here for an army."

"I think you answered your own question."

The leader shouted, "All right, load 'em up."

The truck's fleshy canopy was pulled back, and a small crane was deployed, winching the goods up onto the deck. Not everything would fit. There would obviously have to be several more trips. The men didn't seem to be in any hurry. It took half an hour just to stow this one load and make sure its weight was distributed evenly.

Though it appeared that they had dodged the main body of Xombies, every now and then a straggler or two wandered in, sensing the boys and running across the parking lot. The first time this happened, they flipped out, pointing and shouting hysterically: *Ohmygodlookout!* By the third time, they just watched mesmerized as the terrifying fiends out of their worst nightmares, unkillable demons that had terrorized them and destroyed the world, were methodically harpooned and dragged by an electric reel to the back of the vehicle, where a bunch of them already hung, flopping helplessly.

"Like a string a catfish, ain't it?" One of the men laughed.

Freddy asked, "What happens if a lot of them come all at once, like before?"

"We'd just have to drive you boys around the block and lead 'em off. They're pretty dumb. Normally, we don't even see 'em—it's you they after."

Then the loading was finished, and they all took seats as best they could amid all the sacks and cartons. The boys felt strange to be surrounded by so much food when they had been hungry for so long. *If the guys on the sub could see this!* The thought reminded them that it was becoming late; they were overdue. Would Kranuski sail without them?

The engine rumbled to life, and they drove back down the embankment the way they had come, back to the train tracks. In a moment, they were out of the trees and in sight of the big railroad trestle. Turning aside, the driver eased them down the steep bank of the river and straight into the water. Plunging heavily downward, the truck settled deep, bobbed upward, and became a true boat.

Sal suddenly had the crazy thought that perhaps they were being returned to the submarine. Could it possibly be that all this food was for them? Was there some alliance between these men and those on the sub? He didn't dare say anything, not wanting to jinx his wildest hope that the terror of the last few hours was finally over. That they were safe.

As the amphibious truck scudded downriver toward the bay, its ugly-masked captain asked, "Now, what you boys doin' here?"

Another man said, "They come off'n that submarine, Marcus, I told you."

"Shut up and let them tell it. We know you boys come off that sub; the question is why?"

Sal hesitated. He thought it might be dangerous to mention that they were refugees from MoCo—the Mogul Cooperative. The place up north from which they had all barely escaped and which had left them all with grim souvenirs of their brush with corporate governance: permanent scars on their foreheads . . . and deeper scars on their psyches. It was more than likely that these men worked for the Moguls. He stumbled for words, but before he could speak, Kyle answered, "Hunger, dude. Provisions."

"Provisions?" The man spoke the word as if it was a foreign language. "What do you think we been doin' here for the past week but gathering trade goods? You don't but have to load 'em on board."

I knew it! Sal thought. He had no idea who this man thought they were, but he nodded, and said, "Oh, okay. Cool."

"But they just set you ashore, anyway? To play tag with them blue monkeys?"

"We needed food."

"Son, food's about ninety percent of what we *do*. They's already near on two hunnerd tons of it sitting on the *Mobile Bay* just waitin' to be picked up. I don't get it. Somebody's confused here, and it ain't me. Now, let's try this again real slow: Did they really send you out in your shirtsleeves on a little shopping trip, or is it that you was lookin' for something else? Down that tunnel back yonder, maybe?"

"I'm really not sure, sir. We have a new commander, and things have been a little . . . confused lately, so I guess maybe they forgot to tell us something."

The men shook their heads and made sounds of contempt. "So you're just out here rustlin' up some grub? Some bacon and eggs, maybe? Some Malt-O-Meal? Shit, son, I guess they don't like you much. What'd you think them signal fires was for? I suppose you don't know nothing about that tunnel back there."

"We don't."

"That look like a Piggly Wiggly to you?"

"No, sir. We—"

The man jerked his chin up at a Xombie jutting from the vehicle's saw-toothed bowsprit. Sal was shocked to realize that it was Lulu. "Or this little cutie right here—ain't she about the tamest Harpy you ever seen? Now why is that? See, that tunnel was booby-trapped eight ways to Sunday—anybody goin' in the front door would get flushed right out the back. We done had it staked out for three days now, just in case some person or nonperson of interest might happen along and trip the switch. Like this 'un here."

Sal now had a pretty good suspicion of who these men were, upon whose mercy they were depending, and it didn't look good. These had to be the foragers, the worker ants at the bottom of the Mogul pyramid, the ground troops in the war for groceries. Slaves to the machine just as he and the other boys had briefly been slaves.

"Don't *tail* me you don't know what I'm talkin' about, boy."

Before Sal could stop him, Freddy Fisk piped in. "We know *her*. That's Lulu Pangloss. We had a bunch of Xombies like her on board. They're different because they all get shots of Lulu's blood, and it acts on them sort of like, like Ritalin or something."

"Her *blood*?" the awful face asked, leaning in. "Run that by me again, son."

"Dr. Langhorne gave her something—I don't know much about it, but they call it the Tonic. Ow!—lay off! She and the other Xombies were sent ashore separate from us because nobody knew what they would do on their own. If they came back, I think Dr. Langhorne was hoping to use them as a foraging squad."

The men's eyebrows rose at this; they looked at each

other. One of them mouthed the word *Tonic*, and another, *Langhorne*. Freddy sensed the heightened interest and suddenly wondered if he should have spoken so freely, rubbing his arm where Kyle had pinched it.

Trying to limit the damage, Sal cut in. "But we don't know anything about that tunnel—we were just on the run from Xombies." He became choked up. "Most of our party's been wiped out."

The circle of gruesome helmets stared silently at them for a long minute, eerie as witch-doctor masks, then one of the men asked, "Why you boys on that submarine in the first place? Since when does the Navy give out free kiddie rides?"

Sal replied, "We helped fix it up for a refugee ship. Our dads worked for the submarine company."

"You the leader?"

Sal hesitated, but when none of the other boys spoke up, he said, "I guess."

"I figured, 'cuz you seem to be doin' most of the talkin'. What about the rest of y'all? Why you got them scabs on your foreheads? Look like a bunch of damn Hare Krishnas. And I still don't understand how come they sent you out like this, pedaling damn *bicycles*! Just don't make no damn sense. Something ain't right, and I mean to find out what."

Kyle replied, "It's the first time we've gone ashore, sir. The city looked empty. I guess we just weren't expecting so many Xombies."

Ray Despineau spoke for the first time all day. He was a quiet, shy boy, made quieter and more introverted by the loss of his family. On the boat he rarely spoke to anyone but Sal, and only in the gloomiest tones. This had become something of a running joke among the other boys, which had caused Ray to retreat even further inward. In monotone, he said, "You bump your head a lot on a submarine."

The men burst into gales of laughter.

Helmet bobbing, the Texarkanan said, "Shit, son, you made my day. Well, all right, then. Don't you worry none about it. Don't make a lick a sense, but I suppose it'll all come out in the wash. In the meantime we-all gone be buckaroos. Shee-it, boys! Where the *hail* are my manners? We ain't even been properly introduced. Name's Marcus Amos Washington, but they call me Voodooman. You'll have to excuse us if we don't shake your hands, but it might be a little hard to turn loose again. My second-in-command here is Mr. Righteous Weeks."

"Greetings, boys," said Weeks. "Marcus won't tell you how he got his name, but I will: It's from the prize bull he rode to win his first championship belt—one mean mo'fuckin' steer name of Voodoo. Nobody else ever went the full eight seconds on that devil, not even in the professional circuit. That was goin' on twenty years ago, when Marcus warn't much older'n you boys and green as grass, so you can take that as proof that anything's possible in this here world—hell, look at us now. Lemme hear you shout: *Yee*-haa!"

Looking at each other, the boys feebly replied, "Yee-haa."

"Come on now," Weeks prompted. "YEE-HAA!"

"Yee-haa!"

"That's just pitiful. Let's show 'em how to do it: YEEEE-HAAA!"

"YEEEE-HAAA!" all the men whooped, shooting pistols in the air and outwhooping each other.

While this was going on, Sal happened to notice that the tide was running at its peak. If Mr. Kranuski's plan still held, the sub would likely be on the move. But since it couldn't submerge until it reached the open sea, they could probably still catch it if they tried. He had to yell to be heard above the din: "Sir? Could you just tell me, are we going back to the boat now?"

"The boat?"

"The submarine."

"What's your hurry, son?"

"Well, they told us they were going to sail with the tide, and we're running pretty late."

As though reassuring a small child, Voodooman said, "Now, don't you worry none, we gone get you to your boat . . . all in good time. Meantime, you just set a spell."

Sal didn't like the way he said it.

"Here are your new quarters," Kranuski said, opening the door to the executive-officer suite. "Don't ever say I never did anything for you."

Alton Webb went inside, nodding appreciatively. It was nothing he hadn't seen before, but it was finally *his*. Quite a leap for a guy who never expected to be promoted above senior chief, much less become a commissioned officer, lieutenant grade—and now the ship's XO, no less. It would have been a dream come true if it all wasn't just more proof that everything had gone to shit. That devalued the achievement somewhat.

Webb looked around the little cabin, cozy as a first-class train compartment with its fake wood paneling, personal desk, bunk, and cleverly stowable sink. His whole body was tense with anticipation.

"Ah, my old room." Kranuski sighed jokingly. He had been in there less than three months. "So many memories . . ." He tapped the bulkhead as though petting a loyal old horse, then ran his hand down to the handle of an adjoining door. It opened onto a tiny shower compartment that connected the XO quarters with his new command stateroom on the opposite side.

Looking at the floor, Kranuski jerked back with a start.

"That head's been in here."

"What head?" asked Webb.

"What head? The head! That fucking head! Fred Cowper's head!"

"I thought it went down the TDU."

"That's what Langhorne originally said she did with it. Now I'm not so sure." Kranuski fidgeted for a moment, scanning the nooks of his quarters. He could barely look at Webb; suddenly he felt dangerously vulnerable, as though he had made a critical error in chess. Gathering his composure, he asked, "How are the preparations coming along for getting under way?"

Webb was studying him closely. "Everything looks shipshape. We ran a test on the A induction valve but couldn't trace the glitch—probably a bad sensor. The tube itself seems to be working all right. Other than that, all critical systems are in the green. The tide's just hitting peak. If we pull anchor now, we can run right out on the current."

"Good. No word on those shore parties?"

Alton Webb's broad face remained blank. "No, sir."

"All right." Kranuski sighed. "Prepare the bridge for surface maneuvers. Get everyone on station. Let's get the hell out of here."

CHAPTER **FIFTEEN**

BOBBY RUBIO

"**D**ad, Dad . . ." Bobby cries, panting as he approaches the exit booth. He can hear a tinny radio voice saying, "*—the public is instructed to wait in their homes for the duration of the emergency, with the exception of essential medical, law-enforcement, and military personnel. To maintain critical lines of communication, phone usage is restricted to—*"

Behind the fogged windows, his dad is bent out of sight, only the humped back of his brown garage uniform showing as he fiddles with something on the floor. Bobby opens the metal sliding door with a crash. "Dad—"

A silver-haired, steel blue mummy stares out at him. The ghoulish creature is wearing his dad's brown coat and stooping over the big man's lifeless body to remove the key ring from his trousers.

Bobby starts to scream, but the grim specter lunges at him and claps a long, rough hand over his mouth, pinning the boy's frantic body in a painfully tight bear hug.

"Shhh," admonishes the monster. In a voice that is slow and deep and oddly gentle, it says, "Don't worry, I'm not one of *them*. I didn't kill him; he killed himself. I just found him this way."

Now Bobby notices that his dad's shirtsleeve is rolled up and there is a blood-filled syringe hanging out of his arm. Bobby knows all too well what that means, knows it is the reason his parents had been through counseling and finally gotten divorced, but this final cop-out is not something he is prepared to accept.

Kicking wildly, Bobby tries to bite, to escape, to scream, *He didn't kill himself! He didn't! He never would!*

Out the back of the garage, across the exit driveway and beyond the overflow parking lot, Bobby can see a man riding a sputtering motorcycle down Fountain Street. The man is being pursued by dozens of crazy, half-naked blue people, mostly women—the street is full of them. The motorcycle's engine keeps coughing and dying, and its rider keeps kick-starting it, barely keeping ahead of the pack. But the running stalemate can't last. Finally, the man realizes it's hopeless and ditches the bike, trying to dodge his attackers on foot. In final desperation he pulls a handgun out of his jacket and fires at the nearest one, popping away uselessly as it tackles him. A hurtling police cruiser swerves hard around the trouble and keeps right on going. There will be no help coming.

The terrible blue man releases Bobby and stands back. "We have to go up," he says, indicating the concrete ramp. "Up top. It's the only place."

Shattered by shock and grief, Bobby moans, "Why? Why is this happening?"

"Don't you know? Ask yourself what the King of Kings has in common with a monarch butterfly, then provide the means of mass production. But wait, you say: Where is our crucifix, our chrysalis? Do we weave a cocoon around our heart . . . or cast it in Portland cement?" He lurches out of the booth and starts up the ramp.

"How come you're not like the rest of them?"

"Argyria—silver toxicity. Occupational hazard. I was blue before blue became the new black."

The man is clearly nuts, but Bobby is still alarmed to see him go. "I can't just leave my dad here!" he cries.

Without a backward glance, the man says, "Then you'll join the millions of other satisfied customers."

Bobby falls on top of his dad and weeps: "I'm sorry . . . I'm so sorry, Dad. Why did you do this? How could you leave me here?"

The voice on the radio continues to drone. *"—BBC World Service reports that a similar crisis is sweeping Europe and Asia, and that the UN Security Council is convening an emergency session—just a moment . . . just a moment, please. I have just received word that due to technical difficulties we will be going off the air in five minutes—"*

Then Bobby kisses his father's cool, bristly cheek and gets up. "I'll come back as soon as I can," he promises tearfully. He goes out and gently shuts the door.

Out in the rain and sleet, those other blue people are approaching, pouring out of doorways and becoming an insane mob, a whirling, insectlike swarm that overwhelms everything in its path. Stragglers at the outer fringes are nearing the garage—any second now, they'll see him.

Bobby still doesn't understand why the old man's skin is blue—blue like *them*—and yet he obviously doesn't want to be caught by those things any more than Bobby does. That's what prompts the boy to follow.

Trying to be as inconspicuous as possible, Bobby ducks low and scuttles up the ramp, relaxing a bit as he rounds the first turn and is out of view of the street. He still can't see the old man—where does the weirdo think he's going? The roof? Bobby has been all over this garage from top to bottom, and he knows it's a dead end. The only refuge up there would be in the stairwells or the elevators—dismal places where drunks piss and women occasionally get raped. Is that it? Is the man luring him up there to kill him . . . or worse? Somehow Bobby doesn't think so. For one thing, if the strange man had wanted to murder him, he could have done it right in the garage booth, and for another, Bobby hardly cares anymore.

From outside, Bobby hears echoes of the chaos engulfing the city. He hurries up. At the top of the ramp, where it opens to the sky, Bobby can see the man standing atop the huge concrete cylinder that supports the spiral exit ramp. "In here," he says, offering Bobby a hand up.

In where? Bobby thinks dully, taking the boost and finding himself precariously balanced on the edge of a deep chasm. *Whoa.* The pillar is hollow inside, a vertical concrete tube thirty feet wide and three stories tall, with rusty rungs protruding from the wall. It shocks him out of his lethargy.

"The Green Heart," the man says, starting down.

Clinging to the narrow ledge with both hands, Bobby stares at the top of a small tree. He doesn't like this, but the city outside is hardly more promising: There are fires everywhere and sounds of mass panic. He has already been out there and doesn't want to go back. Following the old man's lead, he straddles the curved wall and lowers himself to the first rung. It's a long drop if he slips. Hanging on for dear life, hugging the concrete, he makes his way down. At one point he almost screams, thinking sharp claws are digging into his back, but it's only the bare branches of the tree. There is grass below, and clumps of weeds. The cylinder wall is covered with velvety green moss. Hurrying down the last icy rungs, he drops to the

ground. The noise and chaos seem far away, softened by the
patter of drizzle.

The place is an overgrown garden, just thirty feet in di-
ameter, with several small trees and a grassy hummock in
the center.

"Over here," the man says.

The hummock is actually a dugout shack, little more
than a jumble of construction debris under a turf ceiling. It
reminds Bobby of forts he and Felix built: plywood and
cinder blocks and waste lumber, all covered with plastic
tarp.

"Give me a hand," the man says, pulling up a heavy slab
of plywood to reveal an opening down into the ground.
Bobby pitches in, and in a second he's looking at a roomy
bunker at least six feet deep, its walls shored up with dirt-
packed stones. Cookware, tools, and personal articles are
stuffed into cubbyholes. A stepladder leads down to a dry
wooden platform on which there are rugs, a chair, a steamer
trunk serving as a table, a gas lamp, a bookshelf, a bedroll,
and a rusty filing cabinet. To one side is a small niche containing a camp stove, quantities of canned and dry goods, a
washbasin, and a barrel of water. Altogether a regular little
den—a Hobbit house with all its cozy bric-a-brac. Dim
daylight filters in through plastic water bottles.

The man picks up a garbage bag and offers it to Bobby.
"Want a donut?"

Bobby shakes his head.

"Still fresh—they just tossed 'em last night."

"I'm not really hungry."

"Suit yourself."

While the man heats a pot of water for tea, Bobby looks
up at that remote circle of sky. From here he can't hear
anything that's going on in the city—Providence seems

very far away. Does that mean he's safe? Maybe it's over for now, the running and terror. Maybe the worst of it is done with, and soon everything can go back to normal. Some things never will, of course, not anymore, but maybe some things can.

Bobby Rubio sits down to wait.

CHAPTER **SIXTEEN**

XMAS

"**S**ir, I've got traffic. Very close—under a thousand yards, bearing three one oh."

"That's *inland*!" Kranuski bolted from his stateroom and rushed to the sonar suite. "What's their heading?" he demanded, buttoning his shirt. On the flat-panel monitors, he could see the familiar saw-toothed waves of different small-craft signatures.

"They're upriver," Phil Tran said. "Reception's bad in these shallows, but I'd say they're idling or moving away. At least four—no, five contacts: three light diesels, low rpms, and now two high-speed impellers—probably Jet Skis or something similar. I'm catching a lot of support activity, too. Sounds like heavy machinery and general deck noise. Somebody's got a regular little marina going out there. I guess we know who set those fires."

"Sir?" Jack Kraus called. "Topside watch reports smoke and sounds of organized activity, bearing three one oh."

Kranuski went to the control room and raised the periscope. The mouths of two rivers opened into this uppermost arm of the bay: the Providence River, immediately astern, which passed through downtown and was where they had seen the signal fires, and the Seekonk River, which lay half a mile east. Getting his bearings, he followed the contours of the nearby shore eastward to where it cut inland at the mouth of the Seekonk. Around that bend, rising above a line of trees, he could see a thin plume of smoke.

"Goddammit," he said. "All right, let's be ready for them. All hands to battle stations. Mr. Robles, muster an armed detail and post them on deck. Make sure they look as intimidating as possible."

"Yes, sir. Uh, sir, the Moguls cleaned us out good. Except for those ceremonial carbines and a few personal side-arms, we're down to slingshots."

"I know that! I said try to *look* intimidating! Make more rifles out of broomsticks if you have to. And don't knock slingshots—remember Davy and Goliath. Here, take my gun. Mr. Webb, you rig the outboard and organize a quick recon patrol around the point so we at least know what we're up against."

They didn't go to the submarine.

At the mouth of the river, just beyond the interstate highway bridge, was a flotilla of two massive cargo barges, each one half the length of a football field, each with its own tugboat. One was a junkyard pyramid assembled from big metal shipping containers—tractor trailers stacked in colorful tiers like so many Legos, with labels like MAERSK and SEA LAND, sharing deck space with the enormous crane that had put them there. The other barge was more striking, its tall white superstructure resembling that of an old-time riverboat, including smokestacks and paddle wheel, though the latter appeared to be purely ornamental; it didn't touch the water. Other amphibious vehicles were there, too, as well as small watercraft of all kinds.

As the duck boat drew closer, Sal could see that holes

had been cut into some of the cargo boxes, making jack-o'-lantern-crude windows, and that there were lights inside and fuming stovepipes on top. Some of these perforated containers were homes for people, not cargo. And there were other, weirder shantytown structures: faulty towers banged together out of plywood and corrugated metal, with blue plastic port-a-johns jutting on planks over the water.

Yes, people were living out here by the hundreds, per-haps thousands, packed together like junkyard bees in a rusty hive. Sal could smell them: mingled odors of raw sew-age, trash, and fryer grease. He could see and hear them, too. Some shot hoops while others called out bets from windows and still others hooted down from rooftop deck chairs, cracking beers. A better life than that aboard the submarine, clearly—this was a well-functioning caravan, a whole floating village, a Mongol horde. A Mogul horde.

As they passed under the bridge, and the view opened up, Sal was startled to see two more duck boats plowing toward them, heading inland. The crews catcalled and made crude gestures at each other as they passed. The sudden sense of relative normalcy, of routine human traffic, was overwhelming. Sal hadn't felt this way since first catching sight of . . . of . . .

Thule, he thought apprehensively. The Mogul base.

"So who do you guys work for?" he asked.

"*Work for?* We work for ourselves, son. We're indepen-dent contractors." Marcus seemed offended at the very thought.

Sal held his tongue. Could it be they weren't connected to the Moguls after all? Or maybe they just didn't know they were. Coombs and the Navy men hadn't known—not until they got to Thule. Feeling a buzz of possibility, Sal asked, "Are you all refugees?"

"Lifers, boy! Reapers! Skinwalker Platoon, Rodeo Zulu

Tango! The one and only Hopalong Cassidy Phalanx out of Huntsville, Alabama."

"Is that the Army?"

"Is that the Army? Shee-it! That's the Army, Navy, Air Force, and Marines, rolled into one! That's the full and complete membership of the Huntsville Prison Rodeo Association! We're George Washington, brother! We're Thomas fuckin' Jefferson, Abraham Lincoln, Napoleon Bonaparte, Alexander the Great, Julius Caesar, and Lewis and Clark! We're Paul Bunyan, Wild Bill Hickok, and John Henry! We're the Founding Fathers, y'unnerstan? Forget your dead white men, *we* the dudes they gonna write history books about, the ones who redraw the maps and make up the laws. While everybody else just accepts the way things are, we make up reality to suit us. This is *our* country now, and we its new hee-roes! When men get back around to building monuments, they'll be dedicating them to us. When they name all the new states and territories, they'll be naming them after us! Naw, they won't even have to name them, because we already done it. Look around you, boy— you ain't in New England no more. On that side of the river is the great state of Shaka Zulu, New Africa, granted by solemn treaty to the Mau-Mau Brotherhood. On the eastern shore you got the Mexican paradise of Aztlan, laid claim to by our brothers in La Raza. And we ain't leavin' out the white folk: White Pride staked out some sweet reservations for y'all down around Connecticut and Long Island—the Aryan Evangelical Co-Prosperity Sphere. And this here's the People's Expedition of the New United States! Uncle Spam has granted us charter to all the lands we can claim . . . so long as we keep up our end of the bargain."

"And what's that?"

"Shit, boy, work with me! Don't you even know why you're here? To gather weekly shipments of supplies and

deliver them up to you folks for pickup. SPAM, it's called—
hell, we only been doin' it all up and down the whole damn
eastern seaboard. Government handles the rest, using cargo
planes, submarines, ships, and whatnot. It ain't no damn
secret. What did you think them signal fires were for, a
weenie roast? When we saw that big-ass submarine come
humpin' up the channel, we damn sure figured that's what
y'all was here for—'less there's some other submarine we
don't know about."

Sal shrugged, heart pounding.

"Then you folks take it all up north somewhere, Valhalla, God knows where that is—we just call it the North
Pole. Whatever they're using as the provisional capital until
they can come back, jump-start the country again." He lowered his voice to a stage whisper. "I hear tell they got
women up there to use as breeding stock. Must be right
nice, considering all the goodies we send 'em."

Sal couldn't help asking, "Why do you do it?"

"Yeah," Kyle said. "What do you get out of it?"

"Same as you. Manifest destiny! We the new colonials,
man—we building a new nation, all pulling together. And
it ain't just a one-way street: They provide us with logistical
support, mapping out the best pickings, updatin' us on the
latest research—that's how come we here at all. Couldn't
hardly set foot on dry land before. Now we got free run of
the place, and it's only gonna get better. Soon they'll have
a vaccine for Agent X, then everything will start up again . . .
with the deck reshuffled in our favor."

Sal thought Voodooman's mythologizing had the sound
of something predigested and regurgitated whole, a canned
pep talk like those self-help tapes his mom used to listen to
in the car. A mantra to ward off dread. But perhaps he was
wrong about the dread—these men all seemed to be having
the time of their lives. And why wouldn't they be? Unex-

pectedly freed from prison, given the run of this all-you-can-grab Armageddon—it was like hitting the jackpot.

He blurted, "Doesn't it scare you, though?"

"What?"

"That it might never happen. That all this might be just pie in the sky?"

"Pie *hail*. It's our cut of the American pie, boy—the American dream. Forty million acres and a mule. Property is power. Power of ownership—that's the story of the human race. People come and go, but real estate is forever. We're taking ownership of these new territories so that when Agent X runs its course, and the scientists hand down their cure, we'll have staked our claims. Australia was founded by prisoners; this'll be *our* homeland, our Botany Bay."

But how do you know you can trust them? Sal wanted to ask.

The duck boat approached the nearest barge, the cargo carrier, its flank looming above like a rust-streaked cliff topped with barbed wire. One of the men shouted, "Boat Three with fresh fish. Open up!" and a door cranked open, lowering on chains like a drawbridge. When it was at the level of their gunwales, the crew tied up as though to a dock, and the boys were ushered up the ramp. Looking inside, Sal felt as if he was entering fantasyland.

First, he and the boys were greeted by an equal number of dour-faced, heavily armed men—men who nevertheless were dressed in the most outlandish pimp costumes, tricked out from head to foot in garish formalwear usually reserved for Broadway musicals and Mardi Gras parades, all feathers, spangles, glitter, and glitz.

"What the hell is this?" Sal said under his breath.

Kyle replied, "Looks like a Halloween party."

Ostentatiously decorated sombreros and chaps, tuxedoes and tails, maroon top hats, Dick Tracy fedoras, fancy cowboy hats with bands of silver skulls, toreador suits in blinding colors and patterns—plush purple and green velvet with linings of ruffled silk, snow leopard and zebra patterns—striped zoot suits and bolo ties, bloodred snakeskin boots inlaid with turquoise. And bling!—massive jewel-encrusted rings and gold chains, Cartier studs, sapphire pendants belonging to the czars, priceless museum pieces from Aztec coffers or Egyptian tombs.

The men themselves were not as fancy as their couture, resembling a post-office billboard's worth of sketchy characters and ugly mugs, FBI's Most Wanted, their thick necks and bald heads marked with scars and thug tattoos. Beneath their expensive clothes and cologne they reeked of sweat and machine oil. But they were well fed, and at least they weren't dressed in pulsating Xombie flesh—for the moment Sal was grateful for any trace of civilization.

"I don't think we gonna meet the dress code," whispered Kyle, dazzled in spite of himself. He had always been vain about his appearance, shoplifting designer clothes and primping in front of the mirror so long that his brother Russell used to joke, *You worse than having a sister, man.* The thought of his lost brother was like a sucker punch to the gut.

"You guys always dress this way?" Sal asked.

"Pert much ever night, after work," said Voodooman.

"Why's that?" asked Todd.

"Naught else to do . . . and because we can. Keeps the blues away. Out here, we like to make every night a party."

Freddy asked, "There's gonna be a party?"

"Hail yes! We observe all the formalities in this organization—gotta keep up all them good old traditions.

This here's Big Rock Candy Mountain! You boys ain't never been to a party till you been to a lockup hoedown. Ain't a lot of fun left in this world, but one thing us saddle pimps know how to do is party!"

Sal said, "Uh, sorry, sir, I'm not sure we're really up for a party. We're pretty beat. We lost some friends, and it's been a rough day."

"That's when you need to get likkered-up the most! But don't you fellas worry, the party ain't gonna get goin' till after sundown. You got a few hours to rest up yet."

Working up his nerve, Sal said firmly, "Well, that's just it—we were thinking we need to get back to the boat. We're way overdue, and they have to be wondering what happened to us by now. If they think we didn't make it, they might sail without us."

"Don't you worry, son—your rust bucket ain't goin' nowhere."

"It's not?"

"*Hail* no! We got 'em in the sack. Ain't but one way in and out of this bay, and we control the out. Trust me. Now come on, let's get you squared away."

The boys were directed to wait while the crew from the duck boat went into a clear plastic tent. Once they were inside, the enclosure was flooded with purified oxygen from a large tank, and immediately their Xombie leathers began to relax, turning pink and bloody, sagging off them like so much raw meat.

"Ohhh, sick, dude," Todd remarked under his breath.

The men effortlessly stepped free, scooping the shed hides into steel drums. Removing the limp sacks of their helmets, they revealed gleefully sweaty faces marked with numerous gang markings: scars, brands, purplish prison tattoos. Having seen the deckhands, the boys were less surprised than they would otherwise have been, no longer expecting from the men's country twang to see a bunch of redneck hillbillies. For the most part, these were ghetto warriors, pimped-up *vaqueros* and part-time buffalo soldiers—convicts before they were ever cowboys.

The lids were cinched down tight, and the men emerged to be hosed off, gratefully shedding layers of protective gear and sweaty hazmat coveralls.

Suddenly someone shouted, *"Duck!"* and Sal spun to see several wet Xombies leaping onto the ramp. They had been clinging like leeches beneath the duck boat.

He and the other boys scattered, screaming, but the men on the barge were ready. In an instant the creatures were roped, gaffed, and pinned to the deck, then their limbs and heads hewn from their bodies. The loose parts were bagged and tied off as if for some future purpose.

Carpet remnants, Sal thought. *Scrap leather.* He watched, revolted, as those bags—as well as Lulu and the captive Xombies at the stern—were hoisted away by crane.

"Fun's over, gentlemen," said Voodooman. Out of his flesh suit, wearing shorts and flip-flops, he was revealed to be a knobby-kneed older black man with gray in his beard. "Go on up."

They were led around the deck to where a rope ladder dangled from the mountain of shipping containers. There were more ladders up to the higher tiers. It reminded Sal of pictures he'd seen of an Indian pueblo in New Mexico.

Voodooman said, "We pull these ladders up after dark, so you don't need to worry none about Harpies kissin' on you in the night."

The boys climbed to the next level, following as the man briskly walked them around the first shelf of the pyramid. It was like the sundeck of a very unruly cruise ship, littered with deck chairs and sun umbrellas and just plain litter. They passed a port-a-john on a plank and were told to remember its location. At intervals there were holes cut in the metal floor, and at one of these the boys were directed to go below.

"Just like on the submarine," Kyle said, climbing down the ladder.

"Yeah."

It wasn't quite the same as the sub though, didn't have that subterranean heaviness, that density that always made Sal feel like he was locked inside a bank vault. This felt more like a barn: stinky but well ventilated, and not nearly as claustrophobic.

First they descended into a long shipping container loaded to the ceiling with cases of soda pop. Open at one end, it faced into a fluorescent-lit corridor under the pyramid, and they were taken down this narrow passage to another container—a bare box about the size of a bus and nearly as comfortable, with dozens of hammocks and folding cots, a hundred-gallon barrel of water, soap, rolls of paper towels, and a washtub. The perforated walls rang with raucous sounds of men.

"This is my crew's bunkhouse here," said Voodooman. "We'll let you use it for now, just until you get fixed up. All I ask is that you don't bring any food in, on account of the rats."

"Rats?" squeaked Freddy.

"What food?" asked Kyle.

"*What* food?" The man seemed to find this amusing. "When you get hungry, just head on down the passage— I'm sure you'll find something."

He left them alone, and the boys considered their situation. It was all so overwhelming, and they were so exhausted after the long, terrifying, tragic day, that they barely had the energy to discuss the situation.

"What do you think?" Sal asked softly.

"I don't know," said Todd, yawning. "Looks like they don't know much about us or the sub, which is good."

"I agree. They obviously think the boat's here to hook up with thcm and get supplies for some kind of bogus 'provisional government.' Sounds a lot like MoCo to me."

"Maybe it's true," Kyle offered. "Did you ever think of that? That would explain why Coombs brought us here in the first place, and why the crew mutinied."

The boys lay stunned as this possibility sank in.

"Shit, man, you're right."

As they were mulling this over, one by one, the exhausted boys fell asleep.

On one level, Lulu was aware of her body being rudely stripped from the jagged spike upon which it had been impaled, her gaping, shredded body cavity huge and drafty as a hollow tree. She felt herself being bound up with baling wire and bagged in coarse burlap, then tossed and banged around like a sack of bulk mail. While this was going on, she remained perfectly inert, as immune to rough handling as a rag doll, her consciousness dwelling elsewhere, out there, up where the stars pooled, carried along on tides of gravity and time. But it was not the immensely distant phenomena that held her attention. There was something else going on up there, something much closer to home, close and drawing nearer every minute—an amorphous paisley shape in the void, white on black, fuzzy as smudged chalk on a blackboard and crude as a child's drawing of a tadpole: a bulbous head with a long, trailing tail. Invisible to the naked eye, and insignificantly miniscule by astronomical standards, this eyeless object seemed to stare right back into Lulu's mind as though shining a spotlight on

the back of her skull—no, not on *her*, but on Earth itself,
the whole planet. Fixing upon it with the obsessive fertility
of a sperm contemplating an egg. It was coming, this thing,
not directly but on a wide, looping intercept, using the giant
planets Saturn and Jupiter as slings to multiply its force. It
was coming. How she knew this she didn't know, nor why.
The knowledge came unsought, delivered upon her like an
unsigned threat. What did it mean? It occupied the space
of dreams, but whether this was dream, vision, sheer figment of her imagination, or impending truth, Lulu didn't
know . . . or care. She was barely capable of caring. To
her it was merely interesting—an abstraction like everything else.

Punish Mint, said a voice in her head. *Punish Mint Gum.*
The sound of that voice had more of an effect on her than
being skewered on a pike, more than having her skull fractured through burlap; it actually caused her to wince. Within
the stifling bag, a blue tear ran down Lulu's dusty dead
cheek, shed by a tear duct that instantly closed up shop,
withering like a dried flower and being sucked up in her
head. The last tear of her residual humanity.

Mummy, she thought.

They opened a trapdoor, opened the neck of her sack,
and dumped her down the well. From one darkness to
another, deeper, Lulu landed headfirst in a sump of cold
grease, a gummy tank of artificial amniotic fluid that
enfolded and encased her, making the least movement
arduously slow . . . had she wanted to move. But she didn't.
She was content to float, to feel. And she wasn't alone.
There were hundreds of others buried around her, bodies
entwined every which way like fossils in a tar pit, or flies in
amber.

And one of them was her mother.

* * *

They woke to the sound of music. Not music, actually, just a *beat*, a powerful stomping of feet that caused the metal walls to vibrate. It was the middle of the night.

"Sounds like a party," Sal said grimly.

"Rock the house," said Kyle, rubbing his eyes. "Where's it coming from?"

"One way to find out."

They woke Todd, Ray, and Freddy and left the room, heading down the corridor. There was no one around. Some of the truck trailers had been set a few feet apart, creating a maze of narrow passages deeper into the stack, and the boys ventured down one of these. Following the music, they entered a crevice that got narrower and narrower before suddenly opening on a much larger space.

"Daaaamn."

A kind of courtyard spread out before them, an open-topped hall perhaps a hundred feet long, with sheer walls of stacked shipping containers and the night sky visible through a web of rope netting. The place was bright with laughter and the yellow flames of torches, dense with voices and music and the aromas of marijuana and hot popcorn. Half the people were making music of one kind or another—a lush cacophony of mismatched instruments and voices that sounded like the world's biggest jug band—and the rest were stomping and singing along. The song was "O-O-H Child," by The Five Stairsteps.

"I guess this is the party," Kyle said.

"No duh."

"Well, howdy, boys!" It was Voodooman. They hardly recognized him now, a blinding apparition in a hot pink suit and ten-gallon hat. He looked like a Nashville novelty act. "Glad you could make it! How do you like our little pleasure dome? Feel free to mingle, and help yourselves to the grub!"

Help yourselves—that was the invitation of a lifetime.

The room was a hoard of treasure, a moveable feast heaped high with vast quantities of luxury goods and non-perishable goodies of every kind, amid which the crowd milled freely, sampling at will. It was like an all-you-can-eat buffet in a bulk food warehouse. But Sal felt too conspicuous, too vulnerable to join the free-for-all. He and the other boys were still sick from the convenience-store splurge, sick from losing friends and brothers, sick with worry and confusion over what to do next. They couldn't relax, much less enjoy themselves.

Sensing their hesitation, Voodooman said, "Don't be shy, boys. Listen, we're all family here. Things ain't like they used to be, with folks all fired up at one another, steppin' on each other's toes. Them days are over. What reason do we have to fight? There's enough here for everybody! Look yonder, you'll see Bloods dancing with Crips, Muslims with Mormons, Latin Kings chillin' with White Pride. Those labels don't matter like they used to in the joint. We're all brothers now, and we got us a whole world to carve up, like the Twelve Tribes of Israel. Here, let me take you to meet El Dopa."

Dragged through the room like starstruck peasants, the boys gaped at truckloads of wine and champagne, cigarettes and cigars, whole hams, sides of bacon, sausages and other cured meats, every kind of canned and dry goods, imported chocolates and cheeses, a huge trove of prescription pharmaceuticals, enough designer clothing to stock a Fifth Avenue department store, and endless cases of cheap beer and expensive liquor. There was also a huge arsenal of military weapons and ammunition. But what really caught the boys' eyes were the Christmas decorations everywhere they

looked: a large street display made of lights spelling MERRY
XMAS as well as ivylike profusions of red and green bulbs,
giant glowing candy canes, fake Christmas trees covered
with flock and silver and gold tinsel, images of angels, rein-
deer, bells, gold stars, gold ornaments—gold everywhere
they looked, even hanging overhead. *Real* gold: golden
lamps and chandeliers, gold jewelry, gold goblets and table-
ware, gold eggs, gold coins, gold bricks. Several Oscar
statuettes. At the center of it all, a massive golden crucifix
with a bloody, tortured Christ.

Sal noticed other gory Christ images as well, valuable-
looking paintings and museum pieces, and asked, "Are you
guys Catholic or something?"

"Some are, not me. We don't trouble much about each
other's religions since El Dopa turned us on to Bhakti-
Yoga."

"Yoga?"

"I know what you're thinking. But it ain't like that; it's
a kind of philosophy—the spiritual glue that's held all us
different groups together and carried us through a lot of bad
shit. It was invented hundreds of years ago by a dude in
India, man by the name of Ramakrishna. He basically said
that it don't matter what religion you are—all religions are
paths to God. He said, 'All rivers flow to the ocean.' That's
what's helped us get along so well up to now. Which ain't
to say Jesus Christ don't have a special significance. As
someone who was raised from the dead hisself, he reminds
us what it's all about."

"What's that?"

"The promise of eternal life."

"Like a Xombie?"

"Whoa, now. Jesus wasn't no Xombie. Xombies are
devils; we want to be angels. That's what Uncle Spam has

promised us as the reward for our labors, and I've seen enough to know it's true. There are angels roaming the Earth again, folks immune not only to Agent X but to the rigors of sickness and death. They're out there, and if we serve them faithfully, we may even earn a place at their table. In Valhalla."

Working up his nerve, Sal asked, "What do you guys know about Valhalla?"

"I expect you boys would know better than we would. It's the last capital—the New Jerusalem. The City of Angels, and I ain't talking about no damn Los Angeles." Voodooman eyed him intently. "Why? You been there?"

Rushing to cover his tracks, Sal said, "No! Just . . . curious, I guess."

"I hear that. It's the only paradise left in this world, the last and most ideal government. It's where all of man's wisdom is being kept safe, in preparation for the Savior's return. And it's the place we send our dead, so that someday they can live again."

"So you believe Christ is coming back."

"Some folks do. Personally, I don't know if it'll necessarily be Christ himself, or some other redeemer. I never been religious, but I believe that something is coming. Some higher power. We've all heard tell about it from the Harpies we catch: a glowing light in the sky, getting bigger and bigger. We call it the Big Enchilada. It's comin' all right." Suddenly the electric lights flickered off, and a brilliant spotlight winked on over their heads. "Oh shit, hold up—the Thuggees are on."

The boys had arrived at the center of the room. At the front, rising above a wall of truck batteries, was a platform in front of a blue velvet stage curtain. A carpeted ramp rose to the dais, which was empty except for a fancy wingback chair and a microphone, both gleaming in the spotlight. The crowd cheered as a fur-coated man mounted the ramp. "Welcome to the Thug House!" he called.

Speakers on the walls began throbbing with a familiar beat.

"Is that 'Funky Cold Medina'?" asked Sal.

"Seriously, dude," Kyle said, rolling his eyes. "Learn your history. It's 'Going Back to Cali,' by LL Cool J."

Making up his own lyrics, the man onstage mumbled along to the beat, listlessly punching the air. *"I'm singin' 'bout Vedanta, Vedanta, Vedanta—I'm singin' 'bout Vedanta—Kill your ego—"*

Kyle whispered in Sal's ear, "Yo, it's the Grinch."

Sal shushed him . . . but the man *did* resemble the Grinch: a prune-faced faux Santa, prematurely old, with bad teeth and jaundiced eyes. He was dressed in a fur-collared red cape over a red velvet suit, with gleaming black platform boots and a peculiar furry cap that was more Attila the Hun than Kris Kringle. In his rich brocades, the man was a strange fusion of Hollywood hustler and Russian Orthodox priest—half pope, half pimp.

One by one, as at a beauty contest, a line of extraordinary figures began to sashay out from the wings, making strange shapes with their arms and singing a high-pitched chorus. The room erupted in cheers and wolf whistles.

Oh my God, Sal thought, heart pounding. The boys around him gasped.

Women. Women of every shape and size, only their stage costumes identical. All were barefoot and bare-limbed, bodies painted coal black from head to toe, with peculiar skirts of gnarled roots or sticks, beaded breastplates, and great quantities of gold bangles and other jewelry, including jewel-encrusted crowns or tiaras that held back tremendous manes of wild black hair. In their hands they carried wicked-looking curved blades and objects that resembled withered fruit. It took Sal a second to realize that their disturbing black faces—red eyes popping, red tongues protruding—were only masks.

It didn't matter that they were weird-looking; what mattered was that they were *women*. The boys were rapt, drunk on music and incense, their frozen hearts thawed with childish yearning for this impossible bounty from a dead world. Some of them started to cry, reminded of what they had been missing, keeping buried in their hearts: every woman they had ever known. The sight of these unearthly black goddesses dredged it all up.

Hearing the other four sniffling, Kyle leaned over and hissed, "Hey! Assholes! They're dudes!"

Freddy Fisk physically recoiled, blinking tears. "What? No, their voices—"

"It's a recording. Just look, stupid!"

It was true. As soon as Kyle spoke, the illusion fractured and their wistful soft focus sharpened to a painful resolution: These were not women at all, but frightening *caricatures* of women. Under their masks, ebony body paint, and fake boobs, they were nothing but transvestites.

Parading above the boys was the unlikeliest female of them all, a gangly, chicken-necked character, his face disguised but his leathery Adam's apple bobbing as he lip-synched along. Like the others, he was wearing a necklace of shrunken heads and skeins of teeth that swayed like rosaries as he danced languidly to the beat. A separate blackened head dangled from his fist, leaving a trail of perfumed smoke as he waved it around by its long hair. The tuberlike objects that made up his skirt were desiccated arms—children's arms. Viewed closely, they were every bit as real as the shrunken heads.

Unable to bear it, Freddie cracked, whimpering, "Oh no, no, no! Please, not again!"

The boys had been through this before, far up north at
Thule, and were still traumatized from the experience. This
same heinous charade. They remembered all too well the
shame of being tarted up in wigs and makeup, fodder for
elderly Moguls seeking a female substitute. Even though
there had been no choice—it had been either give in or die
horribly as a guinea pig for the Mogul Research Division—
they bitterly regretted having allowed themselves to be so
abused . . . and would gladly die before they'd ever let it
happen again.

Falling to his knees, crying, Freddy begged, "Oh God
no . . . nooo . . . they can't *do* this to us! They can't make
us do it—"

"Shut *up*, bitch," said the gawky dancer, jarred out of his
mellowness by Freddy's outburst. "Joo so *stu*pid! Nobody's
making nobody do nothing—this ain't no fucking *Scared
Straight*. Who are these punks, anyway?" Still dancing, he
turned to Marcus Washington, demanding, "Voodooman,
why you do me like this in the middle of my rumba? Joo
know how I hate to be disturb."

Marcus said, "Sorry, Chiquita—I just need two seconds
with El Dopa, you don't mind. It's kinda important."

El Dopa—the Grinch—overheard and nodded from his
perch, dismissing the dancer and beckoning the boys with
a flaccid wave.

"Shit, go ahead," Chiquita said. "Why not? Just because
it's a fucking lost art." He flounced offstage and sat down
in a huff. To the boys, he said, "Joo have to shut up and
listen when he speaks, okay? He's the boss around here, so
give him some damn respeck. He's also a fucking recording
star, *entiendes*?"

"Oh shit, man," hissed Kyle. "That's really El Dopa!"

"Who's El Dopa?" asked Sal, unnerved.

"Are you kidding me? You never heard of El Dopa? He

did all those pirate tracks from prison—dude had some mad beats. He was heavy into Eastern religion. He did that chanting thing: *'Como Se Lama'*!"

Chiquita nodded. "He's a bad motherfucker, so don't mess with him."

"Thass right," El Dopa slurred. "Ain't nobody better fuck with me. I got karma on my side, baby—I have mastered Mahasamadhi and passed beyond birth and death. Everybody said my career was gonna blow up as soon as I got out of the joint, but Agent X beat me to it: Was the damn world that blew up. But it's cool—I finally got me a headlining gig, hey! Yo, Marcus! Rise and come forth."

"What up, El?" said Voodooman. "How you doing, brother?"

"It's all good, man. I see you starting your own Boys' Club. Who these cats?"

"They from that big mother sub off downtown. We picked 'em up goin' into Miska's tunnel, along with a real interesting Harpy, regular damn Kewpie doll, tame as a kitten. They claim her blood has some kinda magical effect on other Harpies, chills 'em right out. They also mentioned the name Langhorne."

El Dopa's eyelids drooped to mere slits. "Well, ain't that nice. Friends in need. Chiquita! Put out some milk and cookies for our young guests, would you? These boys look hungry." He clapped his hands.

The dancer scoffed, "Fuck you, I ain't putting out shit."

"How nice to know that in this vast, deserted wasteland, it's still possible to run across folks with mutual interests," El Dopa said lazily, waving at them to dig in to his pharmaceutical tray: candy-colored pills and capsules of every type. "Small world!"

The man's hooded eyes bored directly into Sal's, and the boy felt the skin prickle at the nape of his neck. There was

an absence behind those eyes, a vacuum as harshly unfor-
giving as a black hole in deep space. Perhaps El Dopa had
been a whole person once, but now he was damaged, shut
down inside from having witnessed one too many unthink-
ables. Sal knew plenty of people like that, ghosts living in
a ghost world, and one thing he knew was you didn't want
them calling the shots.

"There's just one thing I don't understand," the wizened
man said. "The *timing*. See, things have gone a little funny
with our sponsor. We've had a slight . . . *communications*
breakdown. I assume your people on that submarine must
have a direct line to Valhalla, all that high-tech gear you got
out there. Right? Can you also jam radio signals? Suddenly
here you come along, and what's the first thing you do?
Start poaching on our turf."

Sal jumped in, "No!—I mean, I don't think so, sir. The
Navy officers don't really tell us anything, but I know the
boat maintains radio silence almost all the time, so—"

El Dopa wasn't even listening. "I hope they don't think
we're going to renegotiate our contract," he said. "Is that
why you're here? Give us a little wake-up call? Introduce
some healthy competition, a little competitive bidding? Are
they unhappy with what we've been sending them? Think
somebody else could do the job better? I'd like to see them
try. Or maybe you're with a rival agency? Come into our
territory and try to muscle us just because you think you so
bad with that big-ass submarine? Is that it?"

"No, sir. At least, I don't think so."

"Boy don't *think* so. Well, there must be SOME explanation!" El Dopa flung his beer bottle at the floor, then
subsided and pondered them for a moment. Shaking his
head, he sighed, "I guess there's nothing for it but to call up
Uncle Spam."

Eavesdropping, Chiquita said, "Why you gotta do that?

I had enough of that creepy spider. He don't say shit no more."

"Now, baby, he is still our esteemed company agent—the only one we have. Don't worry, I'm not sending you." He clapped his hands. "So let it be written, so let it be done." Abruptly dismissing the visitors, he took up the mike and started singing again: *"Cortez was a gangsta, a measure of thanks ta, conquistador killa in the biblical mold . . . bust a cap in the Az-tecs, dust the map what he did nex', and played Montezuma for a room of pure gold . . ."*

The dancer's leering mask was fixed on them, something out of a nightmare. "The audience is over," Chiquita said. "Get out before somebody carry you out."

"Oops," said Voodooman. Hustling the boys away, he said, "I guess he'll call for you in the morning. For now, you guys just enjoy the party. That's what it's for. If anybody mess with you, tell 'em you're under the special protection of the Skins."

The boys nodded agreeably, but as soon as Voodooman was out of sight, they felt scores of predatory eyes on them. Kyle, feeling particularly ogled, said, "Let's beat it the hell out of here, please," and they began to move back toward the exit, huddling close together. The faster they moved, the more unwanted attention snowballed around them:

"Hey, baby, how you doin'?" "You stepped on my foot, bitch." "Shit, you fine, girl." "Oooh, honey, come on over here, show me that ass." "Lookee here, bitch, lookee here . . ."

"Hey now, what's your hurry?" It was another one of the heinous dancers—one of the more convincing ones. He planted himself in their path, his buttery-soft voice cutting through the gauntlet of cruder remarks. The boys were forced to stop in their tracks.

Taking out a cigarette and accepting a light from the

crowd, the dancer took a puff through his mask's leering bloody mouth, and said, "You boys won't let a few hardened criminals chase you away, I hope. As you can see, they're harmless. We have a strict hands-off policy."

Fending off a rough grope from the mob, Sal said, "We're—*hey!*—under the protection of the Skins—"

A brutal voice drooled in his ear, "I don't care who you under, bitch! You under me now, punk."

"Shut up, Carl," the dancer said, his muffled voice suddenly dropping an octave, "unless you want me to use your boiled skull for an ashtray." The other man retreated under a gale of jeering laughter. Resuming his composure, the dancer purred, "How do you boys feel about flaming Zombies?"

"Excuse me?"

"The house drink." Not waiting for their reply, he said, "Get these lads some drinks." A dozen men ran for the liquor. The other convicts immediately lost interest and drifted away.

Desperately hopeful, Freddy said, "You can control them?"

"It's the feminine mystique, what can I say."

"But you're not a real woman," Kyle said contemptuously.

"Shh!—don't tell anybody."

"Then how come you let them do you like this?"

"*Do* me? Who's doing who? Listen and listen good: I'm not some punk gal-boy from the joint, I'm a straight-up K-Thug Original, a Kali Dolly after the Black One herself. Old school, baby—the *oldest*. In case you hadn't noticed, women are synonymous with scary shit nowadays, and us Tarbabies are the scariest motherfuckers of all. Put on this uniform, and it's like the red on a black widow spider: Nobody better fuck with you, not unless they want to take on the whole Dollhouse."

Sal asked, "I don't understand. What are you supposed to be?"

"I told you: Kali—goddess of destruction. Mother of the Thug cult. That's where the word comes from, son."

"Like Lassie, you mean?" Freddy asked.

"Not *collie*, stupid," said Todd. "Kali—K-A-L-I."

"How'd you guys come up with this?" Kyle asked.

"Originally some of us started dressing in drag because Major Bendis told us it might act as camouflage against the Harpies. Didn't work, but it gave us a certain social clout, which was nice, and also a sense of power—fighting fire with fire. As anti-X defenses improved, we incorporated them, so that we're running pretty state-of-the-art right now. Those bulky skinsuits the Reapers wear are old technology, strictly 1.0, but they had trouble enough getting used to that; they're not about to change. The Kali thing came after—it was El Dopa's vision, his way of unifying us."

"So you guys believe in all this?"

"Ain't a matter of belief, honey—it's pure survival. Rule number one is that the best defense is to protect your airway, don't give 'em an opening, so face masks are a no-brainer. We started with hockey masks, but learned pretty quick that Harpies play rough; a few straps are no deterrent. So some of us volunteered to make the mask permanent."

"Permanent?" The boys' hackles went up.

"Absolutely. Drill a few anchor bolts in the back of your head, nothing to it. Valhalla sent us kits with all the instructions. Really, everybody should do it—it's a matter of public safety. But try getting a lot of these guys to agree on anything, much less wearing a muzzle. That's the problem with democracy. Likewise, not everybody can stand to cover themselves with ichor. It sticks permanent, but there's no better repellent."

"Ichor? You mean that body paint?"

"It's not paint. It's not ink, either. It's blood—Harpy blood."

The boys got their drinks—huge flaming rum cocktails that looked inordinately delicious. Under pressure to keep things polite, they guzzled the fruity concoctions and immediately got a pleasant buzz. More rounds of drinks arrived, and with the alcohol came relief from worry. Feeling safer, they began to accept the finger food that was being passed around: enormous trays of oily pickled peppers, sausages, meats and cheeses, tinned cookies and fruitcake. Some of them also accepted smokes from a bounty of hand-rolled cigarettes, though Sal bitched about this. Meanwhile, the drinks kept coming. Helpful people guided them to truckloads of designer clothing, amazing stuff, and invited them to take anything they wanted. There was a curtained nook for changing, and the boys gratefully shed the filthy clothes they had been wearing for months and replaced them with whole new wardrobes of exotic finery.

Modeling a Matsuda jacket, Kyle said tearfully, "Dude, I have been hurting for some phat threads." He emerged to great applause.

"I think I'm wasted," burped Freddy, swaying a little.

"Yeah," Sal said, head swimming. He was breaking out in cold sweats. "We gotta get out of here."

"No way, man," slurred Kyle. "I ain't nearly done."

"Me neither," said Freddy.

"Yes you are. We gotta go while we can still walk."

Kyle turned on him. "Fuck you, Sal, *fuck* you. You ain't tellin' me what to do. Don't you fuckin' lay hands on me, bitch. This ain't the fuckin' boat—ain't nobody gonna tell me what to do. I had enough."

"You've had enough all right," Sal said. The men around them were starting to take an interest, smirking. He tried to nudge Kyle along, whispering, "Don't do this, man. Not now, not here."

"No! I said no! You got my brother killed—I don't know why we ever listened to you in the first place. You can have that fuckin' submarine, I'm stayin' right here. I like it better here."

Suddenly all the attention shifted away from them to a commotion nearby, an explosion of shouting and cheering. Sal was trying to use the diversion to usher the others out of the room, when Todd said, "It's Lulu."

Freddy stopped. "Lulu? Where?"

Ray mumbled, "They got her nailed to a board."

"They can have her," Sal said. "Come on!"

"I thought you dug her."

"Maybe when she was alive. Shut up and move!"

Across the room, Sal could see several men carrying an X-shaped wooden frame through the crowd, stirring up a hornet's nest of excitement. There was a naked blue body affixed to the planks—Lulu's body. She had a jeweled tiara jammed onto her head. Groping hands swarmed over her as she passed.

Sal's guts churned. He had gotten off to a bad start with Lulu Pangloss, refusing to acknowledge her authority over the boys on the boat—who did she think she was?— and then holding her at least partially responsible for everything that had happened since, including the death of his father. But in his heart of hearts Sal knew that Lulu was just a convenient target: The Last Girl on Earth. He resented her because it was safer than admitting he might like her—that would have been too pathetically hopeless, joining her goofy clique of admirers. So he had avoided her . . . and thereby avoided her fate.

Craning to see, Todd said, "What the hell are they doing with her?"

"I'm not sure I want to know," Sal replied, running out of steam. The alcohol was starting to really hit hard now, and he could barely see straight.

The boys stopped their unsteady flight, sensing that they were no longer the main attraction. As they watched, the men laid Lulu on the floor and were pushing back the clamoring mob.

"Back off!" a huge man yelled, firing a pistol into the air. He was wearing a wizard's outfit, complete with pointed hat. "You'll all get your chance!" He held up a roll of tickets and began handing them out. "One to a customer! Everybody gets one who wants one! Pass 'em around!" One of the tickets filtered back to the boys. It was numbered and looked like an ordinary raffle ticket.

Lulu still looked dead, or perhaps unconscious; in any case she seemed very small and harmless, her pale blue skin luminous as Krishna, with the black crescent of her forehead scar making a sleeping third eye—the antithesis of a raving, feral Xombie. She looked like a fairy princess. Still, the men weren't taking chances: They had nailed her down good and sewn her mouth shut to prevent any possibility of the dreaded Xombie kiss.

Now the wizard mounted the stage, and said, "Gents, we've all seen this little sleeping beauty since she come in this evening. Some of you been wondering why she's so meek and mild. How come she looks like a china doll instead of a bat-faced freak like all the others? The answer is, she ain't no ordinary Harpy. She's special. We found her in Miska's hidey-hole, and I got it on good authority that she's had a touch of his secret dope. She been living in harmony with regular folks, crowded together in a damn submarine, and they're none the worse for it. Look at those boys over yonder—they're the proof! Out riding bikes in the world as if they got some special gift. They'll tell you that just today

she was out fetching kindling with them like a good Girl
Scout. Point is, she ain't neither dead nor alive, but she's the
best of both worlds . . . at least for our purposes."

A raucous cheer went up, and a few loud objections:
"She's just another damned Harpy, preacher!"

"Yeah, what kind of stunt you trying to pull?"

The preacher replied, "She's more than a Harpy, for one
thing. She's one of the Anointed from Miska's own test bed,
a vessel into which he poured his elixir. Don't you understand? Fools!—that makes her body a font in which we
may anoint ourselves. Look at her! Can anyone here deny
she's different from the rest of that cursed society out
there—all the people that judged us, and were judged in
turn? This may be God's will that delivered her to us, and
who are we to question His judgment? We been given do-
minion over this Earth and all the creatures on it, or did you
forget? Her unclean loins have been sanctified, purified,
and may be our path to salvation. Manna from heaven!"

Other men tried to argue further, but were booed down.
This was a rare amusement.

Businesslike, the preacher said, "Now I got here a box
with all your numbers in it. We gonna pick as many as
we can fit in a night. If your number ain't picked, don't
worry—we'll get to you tomorrow night, or the next. Put
some mileage on this filly before the Man wants her back!"

The crowd erupted in thunderous applause.

"Okay, here we go: Number 13886!"

A huge, goateed man who looked like a TV wrestler
threw up his fists and roared, "Yes! Yes! *Fuck* yeah!" He
pushed through the cheering crowd, accepting their con-
gratulations, then stood over Lulu and shouted, "This one's
for the balcony!"

All eyes turned upward to see an odd figure peering
down from a caged window in the topmost tier: a hooded

man in dark sunglasses and a ski mask. The crowd fell silent, and the boys could hear people muttering, *the Major, the Major*.

"Who the hell's that?" Kyle asked.

A bystander replied, "That's Major Bendis—we call him Uncle Spam. He's our military advisor, our company rep: Everything comes through him. Only we ain't seen him since he got quarantined."

"Quarantined for what?"

"He almost got killed a couple days ago when we first got here—I guess it fucked him up pretty bad. Led an assault on a building where he thought Miska was hiding and just about got his ass blowed off. Anybody else, they would have left him ashore—you can't take chances with that shit—but he's our only link to Valhalla, so his men patched him up and brought him back. You don't argue with those boys on the B Team, not if you like your skin. Luckily, we don't see them much. Bendis was the one who sprung us from the joint and trained us to survive like we doin'—a hard motherfucker. Used to be some kind of mercenary commando, ex–Special Forces. We all figured him for a basket case, but maybe he's starting to heal up. Oh shit, look at Joe Earl."

The raffle winner was making a show of stripping off his snakeskin boots, swinging them around his head, and tossing them into the crowd to gales of wolf whistles. Then he got down to business. Snapping the kinks out of his joints, he had started to unbuckle his belt when suddenly there was a loud burst of gunfire. Everyone turned.

"Get the fuck off her," Kyle Hancock said soberly. He was holding a gold-plated Tec-9 machine gun with a banana clip, part of the Xmas display. "Unless you want to lose yo dick."

Kyle stepped forward, the crowd parting before him.

"I'm asserting my prerogative as an official representative of MoCo," the boy said. "That girl's Mogul property, and she's part of our mission, whatever it is. I don't know her purpose for being here; they don't tell us those things. But whatever it is, it's got nothing to do with being molested by you motherfuckers. So put her back in the hold or the brig or wherever the hell you got her from, or I swear to God I will empty this clip on y'all's Dolce and Gabbanas."

Men stood frozen, as if waiting for a signal. They weren't afraid, just fascinated by the turn of events. This was a new one. Suddenly there was a sound of applause from above—Uncle Spam's black-gloved hands were slowly clapping.

El Dopa nodded from the stage, and whoops of jeering amusement rose from the crowd as Joe Earl skulked away. The tension collapsed. Without a word of protest, the preacher's men hustled Lulu out of sight, and the party resumed in full force. All at once, the boys found themselves totally ignored.

Kyle hesitated, unsure of what to do next. The gun was too heavy to keep holding up. "So is that it?" he asked shakily.

"Yeah . . . I think so," said Sal. "Nice going. You ready to leave now?"

"Hell yes."

They dropped the gun and ran.

By early dawn, the party was over. Except for a lot of snoring, the barge had gone still. Sal and the other boys were sprawled in the bunks with their clothes and shoes still on, dressed for a quick getaway, squinting in their sleep against the painfully bright pinholes of daylight from outside. Freddy's pillow had a damp crust where he had vomited. There was a loud knock at the door.

WHAMWHAMWHAM!

"Huh?" Sal came half-awake, head throbbing miserably. "Hello?"

"Get up, punk!" It was the crabby Kali impersonator, Chiquita. He banged on the door again, then kicked it open, knocking aside their makeshift barricade. His neck was unshaven under his black mask, and his shaggy headdress was up in curlers. "What the fuck is this shit? Joo been summon to have breakfast with El Dopa. Hurry!"

Sal shook the others awake, and they all followed Chiquita down the corridors and up on deck, now morning-bright under a dome of blue sky. Looking at a passing wisp of cloud, Sal woozily remembered something his mother used to say to him: that the Earth was a big spaceship, and when you looked at the sky, you were really just looking out a window.

Walking around the barge, shielding his eyes from the sun, Sal was struck again by the ingenuity of using something like this as a floating fortress. First, the whole thing was compartmentalized, so that a Xombie outbreak in any one area could be contained quickly without spreading through the whole complex. Second, all the living modules were on the upper tiers, reachable by a series of rope ladders that were only lowered on request. Furthermore, the whole place was locked down tight at night, offering only an impregnable metal wall. Windows were little more than saw-toothed gun ports, all high up and meshed over; mooring lines had manhole-sized discs on them to discourage rats as well as larger pests; and the barge's gunwales were alarmed and thickly barb-wired. None of this could totally prevent Xombies from coming on board, but once they were there, they didn't leave again . . . or at least not in one piece. The men joked that it was like a Roach Motel, *Xombies get in, but they don't get out.*

Ushered aboard a small motor launch, the five boys were taken the short distance across the water to the casino barge, its upper tiers beaming white in the sun, the lower part sunk in deep blue shade. Climbing the gangplank, they passed through a utility tunnel and entered the main room of the vessel: the gambling floor. It was clean, elegant, and empty—everything the other barge was not. Here all was mirrored and Greek-columned splendor, with trickling water fountains, crystal chandeliers, a glass elevator, and gold fixtures reflected into infinity. Most of the gaming tables and slots had been thrown overboard, leaving a vast expanse of plush blue carpeting surrounding a raised island in the middle, on which stood a lonely-looking unmade bed. That was a little peculiar.

El Dopa was waiting at the bar, wearing silk pajamas. Several Kalis were there, too, black hair pinned back and their leering masks weirdly inconsistent with their posture as they slumped over cigarettes and coffee. They had to drink through straws—did they have to eat that way, too? A silver tea service was set up separately on a rolling cart, and El Dopa sipped from a dainty cup. The bar's entire length was loaded with cheese and bacon and smoked salmon and canned and dry fruit and cereal and reconstituted dry milk and butter and jam and chocolate nougat and ten different kinds of bread and crackers to spread them on.

As the boys queasily approached, El Dopa pressed the button on an intercom. "Mr. Bendis!" he said. "You have a visitor."

There was a hiss of static, then a whispery voice: *"Send him up."*

"Chiquita, will you send up Mr. Eagle Scout here so that he may consult the oracle?"

"You go ahead on up," said the hideous mask to Sal. "The rest of you stay here."

"If one of us goes, we all go," said Kyle.

"It's okay, Kyle," Sal said. "I'm cool with it."

Kyle replied, "Oh, he cool with it. Well, fuck you, man, *I'm* not cool with it. You been acting like King Shit around here ever since we started out, and it ain't like you done such a fucking great job that you deserve to be spokesman for the few of us that's left." To El Dopa, he said, "He don't call the shots for us, and he sure as shit don't speak for *me*."

"Kyle, come *on*," said Sal.

"*No*, man, it's about fucking time somebody else took the lead. If anybody's going, I'm going. *I'm* going."

"Joo don't do shit unless I say so."

"It's okay, Chiquita," El Dopa said. "Boy wants to go, let him go."

"Up where?" Kyle asked.

"The elevator," Chiquita said sharply, pissed off at having been overruled. "Are you blind? Move, bitch! Ain't no fucking request!"

"Fuck you," Kyle said, too tired for this bullshit—he was trying to be reasonable here. Suddenly his head was yanked back by its braids and a sharp steel point pressed to his throat. A whole arsenal of scary metal syringes had appeared from under the dancers' robes as if by magic, weird weapons resembling chrome-plated caulk guns, their injector tips resting on the boys' ripe jugulars and eager to stab. The boys stood frozen at needle point, afraid to breathe.

"*Say something now, punk,*" snarled Chiquita behind his leering plastic face.

"Sorry! I'm sorry!"

"*Joo wan' me to shove this needle up in your skull? You want I should cook your stinkin' brain in your head so it sizzles out your nose like hot lava?*"

"No!"

"Then *do* like you been tol' to *do*!" He contemptuously shoved Kyle up the steps to the elevator platform. "Next time I flick you like a fuckin' Bic, except there ain't gonna *be* no next time, unnerstan'?"

"Okay, *okay*, I'm going," he said. Hemmed in by another ominous Kali, he said, "Can I go, please?"

They stood aside. Kyle traded a grim look with the other guys, hating to be separated from them. Sal shook his head no, ready to lay it all on the line right then and there, but Kyle's expression was fierce—it said, *Don't*.

He went into the elevator. Something somewhere was making a loud, repetitive grinding noise, a noise like a hundred squeaky shopping carts, which to Kyle sounded like the rusty clockwork of El Dopa's brain.

"Top button," called the shriveled leader. "Go all the way up to the roof." Then, as the door closed: "And say hello to Satan's little helpers for me—I mean, Santa's. Damn, I always *do* that."

CHAPTER **SEVENTEEN**

THE INFERNAL MACHINE

"**R**ich, we have a problem."

Kranuski didn't need Alton Webb to tell him they had a problem. For the last two days, he had been trying to get an all clear to raise anchor, and every time they were on the verge of doing so, some critical system went haywire: more red lights on the Christmas tree. Now, once again, the tide was too low to do anything; they had missed their chance. Worse than that, someone was tampering with the guts of the ship, no question. It was brazen sabotage.

"Al, did you know that a wooden clog used to be called a sabot?" he said wearily, studying the crew manifest. "People used to wear wooden shoes to work, and when they were unhappy with management, they'd throw their clogs into the machinery, 'clogging' it up—hence, sabotage."

"That's fascinating, Rich." Lieutenant Webb was holding a piece of wiring that looked as though it had been chewed through. "Well, I didn't find any wooden shoes," he said, "but this came from the turbine generator fuse box. Looks like somebody doesn't want us to leave."

"Really? Thank you for that brilliant observation. Who's responsible for that department now?"

"Fletcher. He's one of ours."

"Who else could have had access to it?"

Webb shook his head. "It's a loose ship. Robles, maybe. Emilio Monte. Or Fisk—his son was one of the ones we sent out. But Fisk is essential."

"They're all essential. Coombs has too many friends on board; I can't confine them all."

"No, but you can make an example of one or two."

"What would you suggest? Flogging? That's only gonna piss off our gremlins even more. And I'm not even sure it's any of the men we're dealing with."

His eyes flicked to all the dark crevices in the ceiling.

Okay now, keep your shit together, Kyle thought, going up. As he stepped off the glass elevator, the rhythmic churning sound he had heard from below was much louder. It was clearly not the elevator mechanism. The third and top floor of the casino had a balustrade overlooking the gaming pit, running alongside suites of administrative offices, private gambling rooms, and signs pointing the way to a rooftop restaurant and cocktail lounge, all dark and deserted. Looking down over the railing, he could see the brightly lit bar area where El Dopa and the boys were, and also into the curtained stage just above them where bands had once played. The sight caught him up short.

That raised platform was definitely where the sound was emanating from, but what the hell was going on there? Kyle's first thought was a gym: He could see a lot of movement—what appeared to be people exercising— sweaty bodies spinning and pistoning up and down, with a sound like the sawings of a weird, tuneless orchestra.

It took him a moment to make sense of it. For his eyes . . . and his mind . . . to adjust.

Filling the whole stage deck of the casino was something

that Kyle could only liken to a grotesque modern art installation. But it wasn't art; it was a functioning machine—a machine comprised of wheels and hinges and moving Xombie parts.

What the fuck?

Hundreds of headless, limbless, or otherwise partial Xombies dangled from greasy axles like so many rows of foosball players, skewered through the ribs and joined side by side, their remaining arms or legs bolted to rotating cam shafts and pumping away as fleshy pistons in a giant engine. Rubber IV tubes, or rather hoses, ran from the Xombies to plastic jugs full of cloudy yellow liquid. The combined effort of all those bodies caused the whole mechanism to vibrate, risen flesh and car parts rocking on rusty springs, creating a weirdly musical rhythm—it *was* an orchestra, or a hideous calliope.

Kyle caught his breath—Lulu Pangloss was there. They had wasted no time. Her body was too short to reach the cams, so they had left her intact and rammed the axle bar through her skull, ear to ear, instead of her chest. But she was not madly pedaling like the others. Her body just flopped in place, going with the motions like a corpse.

Suddenly her dark eyes flicked upward, meeting his and dilating like two bubbles of black tar. Kyle was struck by a powerful sense of connection, strong as raw electric current—his whole body stiffened, and he jerked his eyes away, heart pounding. She *recognized* him.

He was ashamed, sickened—what was the point of this sadistic bullshit? Just to torture them? Then he saw the insulated cables connecting the gearboxes to banks of truck batteries, and he realized there was a purpose.

Generators, he thought. *Are you serious? They're using them to generate power!*

As disgusted as he was, he had to admit the awful genius

of it. Not everybody had his own nuclear submarine. It had never occurred to him to wonder what was keeping the drinks cold and the lights on around here. Now he knew: *Pedal* power—store it up all day, tap the free electricity all night. Diesel generators would be noisy and smelly and attract attention, not to mention wasteful to fuel. Between the duck boats and the demands of the Moguls, there was probably not much gas to spare.

He remembered something Voodooman had said to them the night before—something Kyle had failed to fully comprehend at the time, but which rose in his thoughts now like a wave of nausea: *'Stead a horsepower, we got Harpy power—you're looking at five hunnerd Xp right here. It's a Xombie-based economy, son. Your tax dollars at work.*

The whole infernal machine was arranged so that it faced the group of guys blithely munching toast at the bar. Clearly they were the objects that galvanized the Xombies' manic activity, like a carrot dangled before a mule, or the electric bunny at the dog track. They were bait. There was something incredibly dangerous and perverse about it: that sweatshop of captive demons flailing away while El Dopa's people yawned and sipped coffee.

Kyle could see Sal and the other boys staring anxiously up at him from the lit floor of the hall, completely oblivious to the hideous Xombie contraption churning away just above them—two irreconcilable realities separated by nothing more than a heavy stage curtain. Yin and yang. He wanted to warn them, to shout, *Look out—Xombies!* But when they waved tentatively up at him, faces questioning, he just nodded back.

That bed—the unmade bed on the platform below. Kyle suddenly realized that El Dopa was a lot smarter than he looked and also why the man was probably crazy:

It was El Dopa's job to sit here all day as a magnet for

the Xombies, using his own living presence to encourage them—that was *his* bed down there. For doing so he had a drone's privilege of being waited on hand and foot and being excused from all other duties. He was both goat and pharaoh—the living deity not of the men on this barge but of its Xombie slaves. Sure, maybe he was allowed brief respites, a few hours here and there to socialize, but when the party was over and everybody else was safe asleep on the other barge, he was the one who came back here to his gilded cage, the canary in the coal mine. For this they made him king. Kyle wondered: Was El Dopa the highest man in the Reaper hierarchy . . . or the lowest?

Kyle tore himself away from the balcony. *Get a grip,* he thought. Peering into the dim cocktail lounge, he saw a spiral staircase. Go all the way up to the roof, they had told him. Fine. Climbing the narrow stairs, he entered a dark, leather-padded corridor. Tiny cubicles with massage tables branched off to either side. Squeezing along the passage, he headed for a circle of reddish lamplight at the end. It was coming through a smeary porthole in a swinging door, and as he pushed through, he could hear a gruff murmur of conversation on the other side. The talking ceased as he poked his head in.

An arsenal of weapons was pointed at his face. Kyle held very still, feeling sweat pop across his forehead.

"I'm supposed to talk to somebody," he said, the words hanging awkwardly, as if tangled in the haze of cigar smoke. "Somebody named Bendis?"

Four heavily armed men just stared dully at him, their shaved heads gleaming like planets orbiting a Sterno-powered sun. Kyle knew these must be the dreaded mercenaries sent by MoCo, the much-whispered-about "B Team." To him they looked more like punk rockers or carnival geeks than soldiers: tribal pain fetishists covered with scars, tattoos, and extreme piercings, skinny and scruffy-bearded, with steel teeth and spiked dog collars. There was something wrong with them; their eyes were not so much cold as blank, not quite focused. They looked drugged . . . or insane.

This was obviously their room, a dim red bachelor pad full of beds, booze, a bench press, dirty laundry, dirtier pictures, and about a hundred guns. There were blackout curtains on the windows, and a girl-shaped target full of tomahawks against one wall. Beneath all the cigar smoke, the place reeked of death, and Kyle could see why: Weird altars of charred skulls and other human bones filled every corner like grotesque floral arrangements. Dried scalps on wig stands. Hunks of dark-cured meat dangling from hooks, marbled purple and white where pieces had been sliced off—Kyle shied from looking too closely.

Not saying a word, barely moving at all, one of the men inclined his head toward the rear door, the fire exit.

"Thank you," Kyle said, trying not to hurry, fearing to turn his back on them.

The door opened onto a rooftop patio—a pleasant place to dance or have a luau under a canopy of Japanese lanterns. It was deserted, just a few empty chairs and tables, two barbecue grills made from fifty-five-gallon oil drums, and a hanging bird feeder that creaked slightly in the breeze. Kyle stood at the rail and breathed deep, taking in the view of green shoreline. *What the fuck am I doing here? Next time keep your damn mouth shut, fool!* Seeing those men had cleared his hangover like magic.

There didn't seem to be anyplace else to go. He thought he was expected to wait, but after a moment, he noticed a higher structure—the highest point on the barge:

It was a portable radio shack: a weatherproof canopy stretched over an aluminum frame, resembling an igloo. A steel cable ran from there to the top of the other barge, with a basket seat that could be pulled across the water by ropes.

Oscillations of white noise emanated from the tent. A shortwave aerial sprouted from its top, and greenish light shone from its low doorway. Kyle glimpsed a man in a wide-brimmed hat, just a brief silhouette, then it was gone.

There didn't seem to be any way up there, no ladder or stairs. "Hello?" he called up. "El Dopa sent me?"

The paper lanterns bounced, and Kyle felt a breeze on the back of his neck, balls shriveling with the sudden itchy sense that someone was behind him.

He turned to see a man curled up on one of the patio chairs. The man was perfectly still, sitting hunched under a tattered black poncho as if hugging his knees to his chest, face hidden by the brim of a floppy bush hat. The sight reminded Kyle of Clint Eastwood in one of those old spaghetti Westerns: The Man with No Name.

A voice seeped out from under the hat, a voice both slippery and bone-dry—and not unlike Clint Eastwood's: *"Do you see it?"*

"Excuse me?"

"Up there." The man raised a long, knobby finger to the sky.

"No, what?"

"Wormwood. The Big Enchilada. It's right there, plain as day. You don't see it?"

"Um . . . maybe. What does it look like?"

"Don't humor me. You don't know me well enough. Nor I you."

"No . . . uh, my name's Kyle Hancock." He started to offer his hand and immediately stopped himself. "I'm with the shore party from the submarine? Sir, we need to get back, or they're gonna leave without us—if they haven't already. We're way, way overdue."

"Leave? They have nowhere to go . . . any more than we do."

"What do you mean?"

"You know what I mean. The temple of the Moguls is gone, as are the Moguls themselves. They evaporated, like all organic life must evaporate."

"What do you mean, evaporate?"

"Gone. Burned. Scattered upon the waters, same as dousing the coals of a campfire. Such is life. Only a few embers remain, but they, too, will soon go cold."

"How do you know that?"

"From the quiet. No more transmissions, no more signals. The last ones made it clear enough: There was a struggle, and while the doctors were fighting, the patient died."

"The Mogul doctors, you mean?"

"It's a figure of speech. What I mean is, you are lying. You know exactly what happened because you helped bring it about."

"I didn't do anything, I swear."

"You did it trying to preserve your own feeble lives."

"Hey, we didn't do shit. Doesn't everybody have a right to live?"

Quick glimpse of black teeth in an odd, leathery grin. The voice said, *"How did you get that scar?"*

"I bumped my head."

"That was the site of a Mogul implant—the badge of Thule. You removed it. There are very few places on Earth where such technology is still employed. You've been to the forbidden city. You know where it is . . . and why it's gone silent."

Kyle decided to lay his cards on the table: "Mister, we're just trying to survive, same as you. All I know is, we had to get away, or they would have killed us. What happened after that, I don't know."

"*Well, I do. Because I listen. I hear. I hear when the gods speak . . . and sometimes when they croak.*" He set a small digital recorder on the table and pressed PLAY. A thin, halting voice, captured off fuzzy radio airwaves, spoke as if reading a prepared statement:

"*To all American service members, MoCo affiliates, and interested parties. This is Colonel Brad Lowenthal speaking. I and my fellow Air Force officers hereby declare our independence from the tyranny of the Mogul Cooperative. We have been used, abused, and lied to: MoCo is not America, and we are not sworn to support or defend it. The Moguls developed Agent X for the express purpose of creating a permanent ruling class, a master race, and as loyal Americans, we can no longer stand by and allow this to happen. Thus we reject Mogul authority and advocate open rebellion against its agents, both at home and abroad. This is a call for immediate action. If the ideal of democracy still means anything to you, join us in freeing ourselves and our nation from Mogul tyranny. It is time to take back what is ours. God bless America. Lowenthal out.*"

Kyle shrugged, uncomprehending. "Sorry, I don't really get it. What's it mean?"

"*It means I'm out of a job. Without a mouth, there can be no mouthpiece. My days here are numbered. As soon as they learn the truth, I will be fired—quite literally.*"

Kyle lowered his voice. "What? Them Reaper dudes don't know about this?"

"*Oh no. Only you . . . so far.*"

"Why tell me?"

"*Because you and I both share the same secret: We are*

obsolete. Both existing here under false pretenses. Straw men, destined to burn."

Sensing an opportunity, Kyle said, "We don't have to. Not if you help us get back to the boat. You can come with us."

"Where is there to go?"

"Anywhere!"

That grin again. *"And nowhere. I once had hope, too. Believe me, when I received the information that Uri Miska was still alive here in Providence, I wanted nothing more than to find him. You may not be surprised to know that my men and I are experts at interrogation—if Miska was hiding a cure, I was confident we could pry it out of him."*

Kyle felt they were getting off topic. "Miska again. What is it about that dude?"

"Are you joking?"

"I'm not! Who the fuck is he?"

"Uraeus Miska is the most wanted man on Earth . . . what's left of it."

"Okay. That still don't tell me why I should give a shit."

"You don't know about Uri Miska . . . and yet you were looking for him as well."

"We weren't, though. It was all a mistake."

"Some mistakes can be deliberate. Dr. Miska is the man behind Agent X—author of both the disease and the cure, and one of the founders of the Mogul Cooperative . . . as well as its betrayer. He gave the disease but kept the cure. I was a mercenary soldier and military advisor for MoCo; it was my job to train and equip nineteen thousand prison convicts held in MoCo-owned penitentiaries. We were to conduct salvage operations for the Moguls, and had rigged up seven river barges for that purpose. We burned through ten thousand convicts the first month out, five thousand the second. By the third month after the Agent X epidemic, with

*experience and technical support from MoCo, we started to
become more adept at our work, plundering the Gulf Coast
and the cities up along the Inland Waterway. We were sack-
ing Baltimore when I got the assignment to catch Miska.
The Moguls had already failed to catch him during the
initial outbreak and assumed he was dead. Now there were
reports that he was active in Providence again, and they
wanted me and my forces to find him. What I found instead
was an errant grenade. Fortunately, we were near Miska's
research facilities, and I was able to be saved."*

"What happened to you?"

*"Oh, I had a bit of a turn. But after the initial shock, I
was saved, just as all may be saved—hallelujah. Saved by
Him. I was born again."*

"You're a Baptist? Me too!"

This seemed to amuse him deeply. *"No. Not quite.
There's only one who could save me, who can save any of
us: Uri Miska himself. Yes, Miska saved me. He gave me his
message of salvation and undying love, that I should carry
it to my people here. Save them, too, before it's too late—
before the ball drops and this great opportunity is lost
forever. But I am not the man I used to be, Kyle. I know that
if I attempt to pass on Miska's gift, they will in their igno-
rance try to stop me, and I am far from confident that I can
overcome their resistance. Even my own men will prevent
me. There's too much at stake for us to let that happen. I
need your help."*

With a feeling like soft mallets beating a minor chord on
the xylophone of his spine, Kyle asked, "What do you
mean? My help in what way?"

*"Come here and I'll show you. I told you before that
all organic life must evaporate, but there is life that is not
organic. There is a form of life that is as stable and as un-
yielding as stone—permanent as death. Let me show you."*

Kyle began backpedaling. "Cool—listen, I really have to go to the bathroom—"

"You are lying to preserve your life, but didn't your mother ever tell you that lies, like death, will eventually catch up with you?"

"Screw you. My mother's dead."

"Exactly. Fortunately for us, there is an alternative . . ."

Uncle Spam pushed back his deck chair, its metal legs screaming against the metal floor, and tipped his head up to reveal his face in the lamplight. It was the face of a skull—eyeless, noseless, denuded of most of its flesh. What meat there was clung to the bones like lichen on a rock, grayish and rubbery, tenaciously spreading new shoots. He stood up, though he had no legs to stand on—only a cleaved mass of bone and tissue from the chest down, splaying open like a nest of snakes as he rested his weight on it, all the separate strands and slabs of gristle, the exposed blue innards and rickety splintered bones, acting in concert with his arms to hoist him up and carry him along on his back, groin first, crablike, an uncanny death's-head and torso gliding on a forest of fleshy roots. He looked like a grotesque mollusk—a human gastropod with a second mouth at his crotch, a gaping vertical maw lined with sharp ridges of splintered pelvic bone, wide enough to reveal the writhing, vestigial heart deep within, straining in that damp nest of ribs like a baby chick eager to be gorged.

Oh shit! Kyle thought frantically, spinning for the door. *Oh shit oh shit oh shit—*

He didn't make it.

CHAPTER **EIGHTEEN**

SNAIL TRAILS

Rich Kranuski lay awkwardly in his new stateroom—the captain's quarters—and tried to steal a few minutes' sleep. He was bone-tired from being on station for the last forty-eight hours, coping with the crisis of traffic in their near vicinity—a ghost fleet of small engines puttering in and out of a ghostly marina, with all the sounds of routine human activity that went with it, even music. XO Webb had finally been able to confirm visually that the sounds came from no phantom but from a veritable floating *city*: Two enormous barges with attending tugboats and a host of lighter vessels, like mother ships with a litter of pups, all tucked into the mouth of the Seekonk River. Scum, sea gypsies, human trash from the squalid look of them, but whether pirates, refugees, or MoCo, it didn't much matter: Whoever they were, they were bound to be frightened, sick, and hungry. If they were anything like the crew of the sub, they would also be dangerous . . . and there were a lot more of them.

The only question was: Why hadn't they attacked yet?

The presence of potential hostiles in such close proximity lent great urgency to his efforts at trying to chase down the source of all the recent vandalism—or at least put a scare into whoever was behind the snafus. No doubt it had something to do with the failure of those kids to return from shore—Dan Robles and Phil Tran had certainly made their feelings known, but the unspoken resentment was even worse: It was as if the entire crew had suddenly turned against him. He could sense the angry whispering, the ill-concealed loathing everywhere he went: *You sent those boys to their deaths.* Even Webb had started subtly to distance himself as though from a bad smell, when the whole thing had been his idea in the first place! Kranuski silently railed, *Why can't they understand that I'm as frustrated as anyone, but that someone had to start making the hard calls.* And hard calls were all that was left now—no matter who commanded the ship. Let *them* try to lead under these conditions.

Come on, come on, come on! It wasn't going to get any better the longer they stayed here; Kranuski was desperate to get under way, if they could just patch things together long enough to clear out. But whoever it was, the mystery bandit was still at large, jacking one key system after another.

Worse still, Rich couldn't shake the feeling that the perpetrator was watching *him*—that no matter where he went, he was being discreetly followed by some lurking presence. Gremlins. At first he thought it was paranoia, but several times now he had heard strange noises and turned around to find himself facing an empty passage . . . except for that one time when he caught the briefest peripheral flash of something round and pale disappearing into the ventilation bay—an indistinct balloon shape that his imagination filled in with Fred Cowper's gnomish features. *I'm just tired,* Kranuski thought, which he was, but it still disturbed him deeply. He badly wanted to believe it was his imagination, an optical illusion or maybe a trick of the light. Anything.

Rich was not prone to superstition or flights of fancy. He

didn't believe in vengeful ghosts or other such Halloween nonsense—God knew it had taken him long enough to wrap his mind around the concept of Xombies, but his threshold of absurdity had been pushed far beyond its limit in these past three months, and he was determined to be realistic: He couldn't ignore any threat just because it clashed with his former sense of reality.

Certainly he couldn't think of any reasonable explanation for the weird, glistening trails he kept finding in the least-accessible parts of the ship, as though someone or something had dragged a slimy mop everywhere he, or it, went. It reminded him of a joke he once liked to tell, but which now kept running through his pounding head like a broken record: *Why did God give women legs? So they wouldn't leave snail trails.* It wasn't so funny now.

Then there was the business with the safe.

The captain's safe was supposed to be sacrosanct. He was the only one with its combination, and in ordinary times that responsibility would have represented a degree of military privilege that was far beyond merely commanding a warship. Within that tiny Pandora's box was all the awesome potential of a Trident nuclear submarine: code books, missile coordinates, mission profiles, classified technical specs, all the mission-critical logistical data needed to independently carry out a full-blown nuclear exchange.

Of course, all that stuff was long gone, removed by STRATCOM, along with the missiles themselves, when the boat was decommissioned. Except for a few Navy-surplus torpedoes, she was more or less toothless now, little more than a refugee scow, her mission reduced to carting around a valuable reactor until they could find someone in authority to give it to. If the ship's safe was in large measure what made the captain the captain, then what was he anymore but a petty bureaucrat? A school bus driver.

And it wasn't even so much that Kranuski's safe was empty. It was that it had been violated, scorched, with a big black hole where the combination lock should have been. The sight of that hole galled him no end, affronting his sense of military order. It was a constant reminder of the kind of undisciplined individuals he was dealing with now.

The empty safe was Fred Cowper's doing. That damned old man had broken into the safe during the brief few hours that he and his gang were in charge of the boat after Harvey Coombs was incapacitated. Captain Coombs had quickly recovered and relieved Cowper of duty, arresting him for mutiny, but not soon enough to safeguard the safe—Fred had wasted no time cutting that baby open and making free with its contents.

The safe had not been empty then. Aside from some reasonably current military intelligence and the only complete SPAM manifest, it had also contained a sample of an experimental Agent X antidote, salvaged from Miska's research lab and brought aboard by James Sandoval—*Chairman* Sandoval. Cowper must have instantly grasped the serum's hostage value. He squirreled it away and never gave it up, even under some pretty heavy interrogation, knowing he and his daughter Lulu were safe only as long as he held that secret in his head.

A lot of good it had done him, or that big-mouthed girl Lulu. From what Kranuski had seen, Miska's mysterious Tonic was no antidote at all but merely a kind of Xombie Prozac. Valuable enough in its way, he supposed, as a limited means of keeping small numbers of Xombies in check (although even that had not been borne out by Langhorne's shore party), but far from the grand hope for humanity he had been led to expect. Clearly, there was no such hope.

Looking at that black hole in the safe, Commander

Kranuski had the creeping sensation that something inside was looking back at him. At times he even thought he heard things from it: ratlike scritchings in the night, an odd flibbery-flubbery noise, and, once, even a loud, metal slam that jarred him out of a fitful sleep. Or was that just a dream? Increasingly, he was having trouble distinguishing dreams from reality.

Stupid, he thought impatiently. And yet . . . for some reason, he couldn't bring himself to open the safe anymore. It was right there in his quarters, staring him in the face, but he just couldn't do it. He almost thought of asking Webb to take a look inside for him, make it seem like a casual thing. He would have if only Webb weren't already treating him like some kind of convalescent-home patient, going behind his back. Webb was a loose cannon, and Kranuski didn't want to cede to the man any more authority than he already had.

Strangely enough, Kranuski almost wished Fred Cowper *was* somewhere on board—he would have liked to consult with a more-experienced man about some of these issues. Someone other than Harvey Coombs. Someone who understood the terrible burden of ordering innocent people to their deaths so that the less innocent might survive . . . or the essential problem of captaining a doomed ship to its fate.

Of course, the rational part of him knew there was no such assistance to be found, not from Cowper's head or any other quarter. He was all alone.

"We have to get the hell out of here," Sal said, dabbing his split lip with a towel. "We got away from the Moguls; we can get away from these bozos, too."

They were back on the crane barge, their second evening as guests of the Reapers. Kyle had not come back with them from the casino, and the other four boys were nearly in a state of hysteria, compounded by injuries to their bodies as well as their pride: Refusing to return to the cargo barge without Kyle, they had been beaten, kicked, and all but dragged back by El Dopa's black-masked goons. Something had to be done.

"I agree with Sal," said Todd. "We need to get out of here before the shit hits the fan. Something big is going on, something they don't want us to know about. The ship's gotten so quiet, did you notice?"

The four boys sat in their box and listened to the sounds of hectic activity reverberating through the metal walls. *Quiet?* Sal thought. The thing rattled like a tin drum, with men returning from the day's foraging mission. But Todd was right—the commotion seemed unusually furtive. There wasn't the level of profane banter they had heard the day before, just murmurs of intense conversation. Already they had begun to learn the basic rhythms of life in this floating ark, and the near silence wasn't usual. Certainly it wasn't like the submarine, where people worked around the clock in shifts, and the Navy officers might turn up at any moment to make sure they were keeping busy.

On the barge, it was much more loose. An endless cycle of long siestas and longer fiestas, punctuated by short bursts of hard physical labor. More or less everyone stayed up late into the night and slept late into the morning, which was one of the prime luxuries the convicts had been denied in prison. Nevertheless, certain routines from incarcerated life continued to hold true: Domestic chores were relegated to the "gal-boys"—male hausfraus and pot-watchers—who provided sexual gratification and never went ashore. These were not the same as the Kalis, also known as the K-Thugs or Tarbabies—the fearsome transvestite junta responsible for home defense, whose cultish authority was nearly equal to El Dopa's. Then there were Skinwalkers or just Skins, Voodooman's clique, former rodeo hands and other such daredevil types who executed the foraging missions in return for the choicest pickings.

It was a fairly open system. Any man who questioned his role was welcome to switch, but from what the boys gathered, this was a very uncommon occurrence—not everyone could handle the extreme commitment of joining the Kalis, or the radical requirements of the Skins. Easier to mop floors as someone's bitch.

The shore missions left every afternoon, a fleet of four duck boats and support vessels gathering tons of supplies and depositing them on the crane barge. At the end of a week, most of this enormous quantity of goods (whatever the barge crews didn't take themselves) would be transferred to a prearranged shore depot, where they were marked with a large, Day-Glo X and left there for pickup at the convenience of their Mogul overlords. Once the goods had been claimed, there was always a sealed package left in their place, containing shares of Mobucks and the latest news and science updates direct from Valhalla. Airmail, the Reapers called it. It was a matter of some concern to them that in recent days the airmail had mysteriously stopped . . . almost as peculiar as that submarine just sitting out there, ignoring its load of tribute. Why didn't the thing take its cargo and leave? Company policy strictly forbade the Reapers from contacting the ship directly (the official reason for this was that security of trade routes would be jeopardized if the different transportation branches were allowed to mingle—a tactful way of saying that the military crews refused all truck with looters and thugs), but it felt like they were all holding their breath until the sub went away. Yet Uncle Spam kept telling them that everything was under control.

Whether the Reapers believed this or not, the boys could sense tension and scuttlebutt, dark secrets on the wind—unpleasant schemes that would require their attendance whether they liked it or not.

"What about Kyle?" asked Sal.

"What about him?"

"We can't just leave without him."

"It's not like we have a choice," said Todd. "Who the hell knows what they're doing to him over there? Longer we stick around, the more likely it is that it'll be our turn to find out."

"He's probably dead," said Ray Despineau in his Eeyore-like monotone.

"Which is what we'll be, too, as soon as they contact the boat," Todd said. "It's only a matter of time before they realize we're fugitives from their precious Valhalla. I can't wait to find out whatever it is they'll do with us then. Guaranteed it'll suck."

"You guys are crazy," said Freddy, becoming more nervous by the second. "How do you think we're gonna get out of here?"

Sal looked thoughtful. "I don't think it should be too hard to escape if we do it in the early morning when they're all asleep and hungover. It's not like they keep guards posted on deck."

"They don't need guards," Freddie argued. "I've heard those outer decks gather Xombies every night—they have to mop them up every day as the first order of business."

"We can handle a couple of Xombies with the weapons they have lying around loose. The whole place is a damn armory."

Todd said, "Maybe, maybe not, but we'd wake up half the barge doing it. All it takes is one guy blowing the whistle, and you can kiss our asses good-bye—somehow I don't think they'd look kindly on us declining their hospitality, much less stealing their shit."

"So what do you suggest? Stay here?"

Freddy shook his head. For the first time in his life, he realized he had an opinion that didn't square with the dominant majority—these guys didn't have a clue what they were saying. As far as he was concerned, Kyle Hancock had been their last voice of reason, and without him, there were no clear options. "I don't know, man. I mean, even if we could escape and make it back to the boat, what is there to look forward to? Getting stuck in that dungeon until they starve us to death? Whole time I was in there, I felt like Pinocchio in the belly of the whale—I ain't down with that no more."

"Are you down with staying here and being somebody's house elf?" asked Sal. "Because that's how it works, Freddy, you know that. They talk a lot about freedom of choice, but it's all based on survival of the fittest, law of the jungle. Sure, there's no rules here as such, but haven't you noticed that there's a really strict social code? The amount of freedom you get depends on what caste you belong to. From each according to his ability, to each according to his need . . . just so long as you accept your rightful place in the dogpile. They look outrageous, but they're a bunch of conformists sticking to a script because that's what's worked for them up to this point, kept them alive. There are no rebels here—the real rugged individualists probably all got killed off the first week."

Freddy said, "They eat good, though."

"They do eat good. But I think if we can get back to the boat with what we now know about Xombie protection, our supply problems might be over."

"That's a big *if*. We don't even know if the boat's still there."

"It's there, it's gotta be there. Kranuski and Webb might be assholes, but the rest of the crew wouldn't just bail on us like that. Plus, this whole place is freaking out about something, haven't you noticed? Guarantee you it's because of the boat. Look, I say the time to move is tomorrow morning. We just act like we know what we're doing and slip out right under their noses. Anybody asks what we're doing, we say that Voodooman dude told us it was okay."

"Yeah? And what then? Jump overboard and swim back?"

"I was wondering about that myself," said Todd.

"I knew it," groaned Ray. "We might as well forget about it—we're dead."

Ignoring him, Sal replied, "I was thinking more along the lines of those water scooters they've got tied up alongside."

"Are you kidding? Steal a boat? Talk about pissing them off, plus we'll be sitting ducks in those—I've ridden a Jet Ski before, but I'm no daredevil like you. They'll chase us down and blow us out of the water before we can get five feet."

"I'm betting more like five hundred. Just enough of a head start to get out of sight."

"Out of sight of what? Dude, try a mile—the sub's at least that far. We'll have targets on our backs halfway across the bay."

"That's why we don't head downriver to the bay—we don't go to the sub at all. We run *up*river, duck under the highway overpass, and break for shore using the bridge pylons as cover. Then we cut overland back to the tug docks, where we started out."

"*Overland?* I hate to tell you this, Sal, but aren't you forgetting something? Something that's blue and fucked-up and starts with the letter X?"

"*No*, that's the best part . . ."

The door flew open with a bang, causing the boys to jump.

"Hey, got a minute? I want to talk to you fellas."

It was Marcus Washington—the genial Reaper captain known as Voodooman. They froze at the sight of him, terrified at what he might have overheard.

"Am I interrupting something?" he asked, looking around inquisitively. The night's fiesta was going strong, and he was wearing an entirely different party getup—gone was the pink suit, replaced by a gaudy Hawaiian shirt, golf slacks, and shiny Italian loafers.

"No," said Sal, as the others tried to look casual. "What's up?"

"I think you know what's up."

"What do you mean?"

He checked the booming corridor and shut the door. "It's time you dudes got out of here."

The boys were silent, the hair standing up on the back of their necks. Was this a trap?

Voodooman continued in a low voice, "Things have been cockeyed ever since Uncle Spam come back, but he and his posse ain't never taken no one prisoner before. Can't say as I like the sound of that—just rubs me the wrong way. Far as I knew, you boys was to be offered every courtesy as citizens of the U.S. of A.—ain't no call for takin' hostages or torturin' nobody. Problem is, that big old submarine of yours done got folks spooked. We don't know what it's waitin' for, and neither you or Uncle Spam done give us a straight answer. Long as it sits there, we're sewed up tight in this river. I don't think El Dopa's got a damn clue what he's doin' with y'all—he's just tryin' to cover his butt.

"Fact is, some of us been getting real tired of sending all these goods up north, wishin' we could go our own way.

Can't see as how we even need Uncle Spam all that much anymore. These last couple weeks have proved we can get along perfectly well by ourselves. Sure, we needed a leg up at first, but lately it's gettin' so that we're doing it by habit rather than for any actual ree-ward. Maybe there's others feel the same on that submarine of your'n."

"There are. We've told you everything we know," Sal said.

"Maybe you have, maybe you ain't—point is I don't give a tinker's damn. I think as long as we hold you boys, we're just draggin' this thing out, whatever it is. Obviously, your people won't leave without you, which means we gotta send you back, pronto. You all are about the same age my sons woulda been, and it ain't right to hold you against your will. This ain't no fuckin' jailhouse strike. You got a right to your freedom, same as us."

The boys nodded hopefully, hearts thrumming.

"Here's my problem: I can't let you go without authority from either El Dopa or the major hisself, and they ain't talkin'. So here's what I'm gonna do . . ."

The four boys left their quarters before dawn and went down the puke-smelling corridor to the Coca-Cola van, where they fortified themselves with caffeine and sugar, then proceeded to the ceiling hatch at the end. There was a thick plywood cap screwed on it, and they quickly removed the wing nuts, trying to be as quiet as possible as they opened the lid.

Dim pinkish light came in, along with cool morning air that smelled like low tide and lilacs—a smell oddly like the funeral parlor where Sal's mother had been shown. The boys climbed single file onto the roof of the first tier, taking with them the rolled-up rope ladder to access the outside deck of the barge. Before lowering it, they scanned the area for Xombies. They could only see one side, but it looked clear. Voodooman had promised them it would be.

Every one of them was well armed. Under cover of the party last night, Marcus Washington had crept around the deserted passageways and empty dorms, taking anything that he thought might be of use to the boys, returning with the goods as well as detailed instructions. After he was gone, they smoked cigars and got plastered on peppermint schnapps, tearfully saying their good-byes to each other and the world—it was an emotional night, and quite likely their last.

Now they all had throbbing headaches, dry mouths, and a revolting aftertaste—as well as four samurai swords, three fire axes, two machetes, a couple of crowbars, and two military-grade Taser weapons of Israeli manufacture. These were all items that had just been lying around loose amid mounds of other clutter, so Voodooman wasn't expecting the loss to be immediately noticed. For that matter, he could have given them anything from machine guns to light artillery to rocket-propelled grenades . . . except that it was wiser if they didn't wake up the whole barge.

Lowering themselves to the deck, the four boys crept to the bow ramp, where they had first come on board. Everything was in deep shadow, and they moved carefully to avoid tripping over anything. There was a lot of equipment here, stuff for the shore patrols, but they were mainly interested in one particular item: the oxygen tent.

There it was, deflated, heaped against the wall like a tarp-covered pile of junk. Racks of full-body coveralls and other protective gear were set out to dry, stinking of bleach. A large air tank was connected to the tent's gasket, and Sal cautiously opened the valve by increments. It hissed, but hopefully not loudly enough to be noticed.

For a moment nothing happened, and Todd said, "Turn it up some more," but Sal said, "Wait." Creases in the clear vinyl began to pop out as the tent inflated.

It was all too reminiscent of the inflatable fortress of the Moguls—the bubble of bloated excess that was Valhalla—swelling bigger and bigger like a physical manifestation of the boys' growing anxiety.

Swallowing his fear, Sal said, "Ray, Freddy, scope out the boats down there, will you? Make sure Voodooman cut the wires, and we can get down without any hassle. While we're waiting, we should also put on these coveralls."

"Fuck that," said Freddy. "They'll mess up the crease on my new threads."

"So will the Xombie that kills your ass."

Freddy and Ray reluctantly complied, grumbling that they were digging themselves a deeper and deeper hole. They still weren't sure that this wasn't just an elaborate trap. But they were committed now, there was no backing out. If it wasn't quite the first daring escape they had ever taken part in (that would have to be the hijacking of the submarine, followed by the exodus from Thule), it was by far the most nerve-wracking. Not to mention they felt stupid in hooded plastic jumpsuits.

Returning, Freddy said breathlessly, "Boats are no problem—the keys are in the ignition, just like he said. Maybe we should forget this and just take one now."

"No, you said it yourself: They'll blow us out of the water. Our only chance is a fast dash to shore before they can get their bearings."

"Well, you look like a bunch of Oompa-Loompas."

Todd tossed him a suit. "Join the club."

"What about this stuff?" asked Ray, glumly referring to all the strange protective equipment littering the deck: wire helmets resembling weird birdcages, shoulder and knee pads, chest and back plates, gauntlets made of light, flexible steel mesh.

"We have to put that on, too. And be quick—sun's coming up."

"*Everything?* We'll barely be able to move in all that junk."

"Everything. You heard Voodooman—if they do it, we do it."

They covered themselves with mesh armor from head to toe, checking each other over and cinching hard-to-reach straps. Fortunately, most of the fastenings were Velcro and very simple to figure out. Inflating the tent proceeded apace, until at last the thing stood rigid before them, a lot bigger than they remembered—big as a house. It looked like one of those bouncy kiddy rooms at the fair.

Sal shut off the valve, and they crowded through the air lock, stiff and clumsy as astronauts. It smelled like plastic inside, like a new beach ball. The steel drums were all on a wooden pallet in the center of the main chamber, and beside them was a compressor and a bundle of tall gas cylinders marked OXYGEN—FLAMMABLE—DO NOT EXPOSE TO OPEN FLAME.

With trepidation, the boys examined the sturdy lid clamps on the barrels.

"You sure you wanna try this?" asked Todd.

"No," said Freddy.

"This is stupid," said Ray. "We're all gonna die."

"Shut up," Sal said. "It's the only way. Come on, you saw how they did it."

"Go ahead, then."

Using a crowbar as a lever, Sal sprang the first clamp . . . then the second. The lid was free. As the other boys stood well back, he worked the crowbar's tip under the lid and prized it off.

Gross.

Underneath was a slimy mass of naked flesh, looking for all the world like raw turkey skin, except there was too much of it—a whole barrelful. It was bluish gray, shot through with tiny capillaries of a brighter, almost violet hue. The flesh was wrinkly as wet laundry, and even showed a zipperlike seam where two patches had been stapled together. It made Sal sick to look at it, queasy; his eyes were playing tricks, making the Xombie flesh appear to be bulging upward, swelling like rising dough. Heaving toward him.

"Shit, man, look out!" Todd shouted, knocking Sal backward as a great flap of translucent flesh fanned up out of the barrel like a huge sail. Falling in slow motion, Sal was reminded of a magic trick he had learned as a kid—the scarf from the hat that just keeps coming and coming. Todd dove clear as the thing batted wildly in the air, a gigantic webbed hand seeking something to grab, a six-foot-tall bat wing that even made a weird chittering noise.

The oxygen!

Lying on the floor amid tumbled oxygen cylinders, Sal suddenly realized what was wrong: They had inflated only the outer envelope of the tent, the part that supported the structure, without flushing the inner chamber with pure oxygen. They had opened the stupid can in plain, ordinary air!

Feeling like a complete fool, and probably a dead one, he grabbed the valve on the nearest oxygen tank and gave it a spin, blasting a stream of gas at the shimmering quilted membrane that was just then breaking on him like a veiny, steel-stitched wave.

The force of the oxygen filled the thing like a billowing sheet . . . and all at once it was collapsing, blushing, retreating into a shriveled pile in the corner, attached by a rag of pink meat to the open drum.

"Fuck," Todd said. He and the other boys were tangled together on the floor, having tripped over each other trying to get out. "You *got* the bitch."

"Yeah," Sal said, getting up and retrieving his face mask. "Sorry—I didn't realize there were separate tanks for the O_2."

"Hey, better late than never."

"Ain't like *we* knew what was goin' on. I thought we were toast."

"Yeah, good job, dude."

Sal shrugged, turning the valve low. He already felt a little giddy from breathing pure oxygen. Determined not to make any more fatal mistakes, he said, "Okay, we gotta move fast before we pass out in here. Everybody come over here and let's see what we can do with this stuff . . ."

It was disgusting, like handling flayed human skin that had been sewn into grotesque sheets—which is exactly what it was. Fumigating everything with fresh oxygen before they touched it, the boys were appalled at what twisted things they had been driven to: They were wearing human body parts!—something only the most disgusting psychopath would do. Nauseated and retching, they pretended it was rubber and tried not to breathe through their noses, making sounds of revulsion as they squeamishly draped themselves with slimy tissue of every kind. The stuff had been sewn together into crude overlapping ponchos and skirts that hung slackly to the ground, threatening to rip and fall off at any moment. More stapling was required to make it stay on, but the dragging hems were still collecting bits of dirt.

"Okay, you—you all ready?" Sal asked, shivering as if from a chill.

"No," Freddy said. Ray echoed him, and Todd said, "Not really, dude . . . but there's no turning back now."

Standing ready at the oxygen tank, Sal said, "Open the tent."

Freddy and Todd spread the tent flaps wide and let the outside air in.

Only a small percentage of the atmosphere is oxygen—the four boys were well drilled in this from living aboard the sub—most is nitrogen and other gases. But oxygen is the only one vital to animal life, the only hedge humankind had against Agent X. This was by design: The blood-oxygen bond interfered with Agent X absorption, which was why Xombies suffocated their victims. But oxygen was only effective against Xombies at artificially high concentrations (toxic carbon monoxide worked even better, as Lulu Pangloss had proved) such as those found in hospital ICUs, decompression chambers, and other such rarefied environments. Dilute it even a little, and the Maenad cells came back with a vengeance.

Waiting for the unthinkable to happen, Sal had a little revelation: If the atmosphere was comprised of pure oxygen, Xombies couldn't exist. Then again, neither could any vegetation—damn. Nerves jangling, he wondered how long it would take for the effect of pure O_2 to wear off in Xombie tissues. *Should have a stopwatch* . . .

"Think of it as a s-science experiment," he said, trying to make light.

"Yeah, we're the guinea pigs," Todd said.

It was fast. The tent walls wobbled as a fresh ocean breeze swirled in and replaced the funk of four sweaty, unwashed boys occupying a big plastic bag. In a few minutes, they would have used up all the oxygen anyway, just by breathing—Sal couldn't help thinking they were fools to rush it.

Nothing's going to happen, he thought, as an odd crackling force began spreading across the surface of his body.

At first it felt like a stiffening blood-pressure cuff . . . except all over. The tension spread unequally, so that some patches expanded faster than others and were answered by slower pressures elsewhere, creating an odd kneading sensation, a give-and-take as warring cellular kingdoms strained to achieve equilibrium.

Weird—it was *alive*. Sal's real skin crawled as those hanging meat skirts retracted, tightening and hugging the contours of his legs and lower torso, while the flesh cape and hood embraced his chest, arms, and head. The graying undead skin expanded and webbed outward to cover every inch of him, probing for chinks in his armor with the rippling delicacy of a predatory mollusk enveloping a clam. It was disturbingly like being caressed sexually, squeezed in alarming places, uncomfortably snug at the groin. He could feel the blood being forced from his thighs into his head as though his body were a toothpaste tube.

For a minute he thought he was suffocating, and he had to force himself to breathe against the pressure. *Oh shit . . .*

Then it let up: The weight on his chest met a counterforce from his back, and the two sides canceled each other out in twisting knots of repulsion, clinging to Sal's mesh panels like limpets sealed fast to a rock, both refusing to give way. The odd patches of hair on it—someone else's hair—bristled menacingly.

I can't do this, I can't do this . . .

Worst of all, the flap of flesh on his head oozed like melting wax down the screened dome of his helmet, threatening to completely block off his vision as well as his air. Panicking, Sal tried pushing it back and stapling it fast, but the skin was muscular and quick, rebellious as a live octopus. He couldn't get a grip—the flesh sheathing his gloves rebelled at handling it, so that Sal's hands kept slipping off, making him feel frustratingly clumsy.

He could hear the other guys going crazy as well, rocking the tent as they spun in circles or thrashed around on the floor trying to rip the weird membranes off their faces. Sal was about ready to start doing that himself, the sound of his trapped breaths booming loud in his mask.

In desperation, he found a machete and slashed at the thing, poking eyeholes and scraping their bleeding edges back. The holes tried to close immediately, grotesque eyelids weeping dark juice, but he kept digging, and suddenly Todd was there with a butane torch, shooting a jet of blue flame at the questing lips until they blistered and charred, searing open. He had done the same thing for himself, his perforated flesh helmet resembling a deformed jack-o'-lantern. Resembling a Reaper.

"Whoa, watch my eyes," Sal said, gagging on the stink of burning flesh. As soon as he could see properly, Todd handed him another minitorch from a box on the floor, and they both set to work helping the others. It went quickly, and in a couple of minutes everyone was out of danger, if slightly hysterical. Voices muffled inside their helmets, they all thanked Todd profusely.

"That was quick thinking, man."

"Yeah. Good call."

Todd shook his head apologetically. "Sorry, guys. I would have done it sooner, but I had to be sure the oxygen count was back to normal before I lit a flame. Otherwise, we'd have been crispy critters in here."

They looked at Todd with dawning respect.

Sal was feeling better. Not just better but strangely euphoric, as though his whole body had become lighter and more compact. The more he moved around, the more the stiffness of the suit seemed to vanish, all its mismatched pieces joined under a pulsating web of Xombie flesh to form a snug body glove that supported him in all the right places. Though it had to weigh at least fifty pounds, the animated skin had a springiness that somehow helped distribute and carry the weight. It even had some kind of heat-exchange property that was keeping him cool. This was better, he thought, than his protective BMX gear.

The others were beginning to notice the effect as well.

"Damn, dude, we *ugly*," said Freddy, rolling his spiky scarecrow head as though snapping out kinks in his neck. "But this shit really works."

"Just so long as we can get it off again," grumbled Ray.

"Don't say that, man. Don't even say that."

"Okay, Sal, what now?" The boy didn't answer, and Todd repeated, "Sal?"

"Quiet," Sal said. He was frozen in place, facing the clear wall of the tent. Suddenly, everyone realized what he was looking at: Dozens of frightful human shapes were standing outside, their black manes and machetes blearily visible through the plastic. There was no mistaking those exaggerated female silhouettes.

It was the K-Thugs—the terrible Kalis.

CHAPTER **NINETEEN**

PHOSPHORYLATION

Rich Kranuski was in the belly of the ship, the "snake pit," looking for the source of a particular glitch that kept cropping up in one of the pressurized hydraulic manifolds, an area classified as a "hazardous system" because its failure could jeopardize the boat. No one else had been able to trace the problem, and he had finally taken it upon himself to have a look. Without being able to dismantle the system, there was not much point to looking except perhaps as an act of self-abasement, a final wallow in the mud before reinstating Coombs and placing himself under arrest.

It was better than being on the bridge with all those eyes on him—anything was better than that. Everyone was so strange all of a sudden, watching him as though he was some kind of monster, and the aft section had become so quiet. The boat felt empty. He couldn't stand it.

Poking around the subflooring, a region called the Yellow Brick Road for its painted blocks of lead ballast, Kranuski shined his flashlight up into the jungle of pipes and braces under the auxiliary machinery room. That was when it would have been really useful to have a crew of experienced chiefs on board. *Unfortunately, I don't.*

Somewhere nearby, he heard a splash. Sweeping his

flashlight aft across rippling puddles of oily bilgewater, he saw something like a blurry white octopus slip out of sight between two swash plates.

Shit, he thought. *There you are.*

"Cowper?" he called, feeling at once terrified and ridiculous. "Come out and show yourself."

For a moment there was nothing. Then, from the shadows came a low moaning sound, like a Siamese cat. It almost sounded like words, but Kranuski couldn't decipher them. Another fluttering splash.

"Hello?" he said. "Come out, or I'll shoot." Feeling his way aft under the low ceiling, he crept toward the source of the noise.

He was beginning to think the thing had disappeared, that he had lost it or it had never been there at all. *Impossible.* Then, in a corner, his flashlight beam picked out a white bulge, half-concealed in the nook beneath a rusty gusset plate. It was pulsating, wet, and slimy. *It can't be,* he thought. *It's fucking absurd.* He cocked his service pistol.

Nearing the spot, Rich could feel his gorge rise. The thing—whatever it was—was in a blind hole; he had it cornered. For better or worse, he was about to come face-to-face with the cause of so much fear and despair over the last three days, the thing that had not only brought the ship to its knees but made him question his very sanity. He aimed the gun, point-blank.

"Fr-Fred?" he croaked softly. His heart was slamming so hard it hurt his chest. "It's all right, I'm not going to hurt you . . ."

Cautiously approaching, keeping the object centered in his flashlight beam, he squeezed into the space with it . . . then stopped. Kranuski's anxious face flushed, collapsing into a frown—*What the hell?* Letting out his breath, head throbbing, he stepped over the intervening steel frame and picked the thing up.

It was a ball of dripping wet rags in a white handker-chief, on which eyes and a mouth had been crudely drawn with grease pencil. The bundle was fastened to a length of nylon fishing line that ran up through an access panel in the floor above.

Incredulous, unable to form a coherent thought, Kranuski followed the line up, sticking his head out the opening in the next deck.

"Sorry, Captain," said XO Webb, and hit him in the head with four feet of galvanized pipe.

"Oh *shit*," Freddy squeaked.

"It's *them*."

Sal nodded, trying to control his drumming heart. His first thought had been Xombies, but Xombies didn't have attitude. These things were posing out there like comic-book characters. Not mindless Harpies then, but the blurred figures of demonic, coal black goddesses . . . or rather, god-dess impersonators: Tarbabies. K-Thugs. Worshippers of the Hindu goddess Kali—the Black One. Pitiless arbiters of their nightmarish New Age religion.

One of them took a last drag from a cigarette and flicked it overboard. "Come on out, babies," he called. "Joo-hoo! Stop comparing dicks and get out here. That chamber ain't no toy—it's off-limits. You done got us outta bed, so you best come out and explain what you think you doin'."

"No way," hissed Sal. "*Fuck* that—fuck it. Everybody take your weapons and get ready to make a run for it."

"Don't be stupid," Todd said, "they'll blow our brains out."

"I don't see any guns, do you?" Sal unsheathed his samurai sword. "They don't *carry* guns." With two great swings,
he hacked an X in the tent wall, nicking the inflated support
columns so that air started whooshing out. Todd tried to
grab him, to hold him back, but their skinsuits bristled at
the contact, folds of flesh ruffling wildly and knocking them
apart. It was like touching a live wire.

"Guys!" Ray shouted. "Something's wrong with Freddy!"

The smaller boy was on the floor having some kind of
seizure, his stumpy legs kicking and his hands clawing at
his throat. There was a gap between his helmet and the rest
of his suit, and Sal realized that he had not fastened the
helmet's mesh cowl down properly: the collar of Freddy's
flesh cape had tightened on his exposed neck like a noose.
The Xombie skin was strangling him.

"He's choking!" Ray cried. Suddenly Freddy leaped to
his feet in panic and dove for the tent flap. "Stop him!"

Sal tried to tackle Freddy around the legs but was unable
to get a handhold because of the repulsion effect. He knew
that if they let the kid get away, he was going to die, but
nailing him was harder than catching a greased pig. Ray
and Todd flung themselves at the boy from both sides, trying to knock him down and rip his helmet off, but Freddy
had the inertia of pure panic, bowling through them and
tumbling to the deck amid the encircling Kalis. Caught off
guard, the convicts leaped back in surprise from the con-
vulsing, flesh-suited figure at their feet.

"Help us!" Sal shouted at them, as he and the other
two boys scrambled clear of the collapsing tent. "It's killing him!"

Ignoring their plight, Chiquita demanded, "Why you
little fuckers dressed like this?"

"We wanted to be Reapers," Sal replied frantically, unable to remove Freddy's helmet. "We thought we could

impress you! Hurry, please help him!" The younger boy was already unconscious, possibly dead, which meant that in a few seconds he was going to become a Xombie.

Chiquita's eyes narrowed to sharpened flints behind the baleful leer of her mask. "Joo lie to me? Oh no, I don't think you wanna lie to me. Peoples that lie to me will never lie again." He removed his massive syringe from its arm clip, squatting down and pressing the tip against Freddy's constricted throat. "It's very inneresting," he said. "If you die inside this suit, what do you think happens?"

"Help him, or I'll kill you!" Sal cried, rearing up with his sword. Suddenly a loop of rope came out of nowhere, dropping over his upper body and yanking him backward to the deck—it was the actual Reapers, standing above on the container stacks. Roused from their beds, they were out of sorts as well as out of costume, plying their rodeo skills in fanciful silk pajamas. More ropes came down over the other boys, the Reapers jumping down to secure them, careful not to touch the twitching flesh of their suits. There was no sign of Voodooman.

"Now watch," said Chiquita.

Hovering over Freddy's lifeless body, the hideous masked figure waited like a vulture for him to suffocate. It wasn't long. Suddenly Freddy's grisly patchwork armor started moving, seething, writhing against its stitches as though trying to rip itself apart. The stitches began to tear, bleeding blue, and all at once the hood flap popped off and skittered away across the planks, revealing Freddy's gaping Xombie face. One of the Tarbabies nailed the escaping skin with the sharp heel of his boot.

Freddy exploded—that's what it looked like. He erupted to manic life, a half-baked gingerbread man, his living armor attempting to tear itself loose from him . . . and he from it. But because every part was simultaneously recoiling from every other part, it had no way of breaking free except to rip loose of the staples and leap into space.

Twisting every which way, Freddy's bones snapped like twigs, his body flailing around the deck in manic convulsions, jerked in fifty directions at once. He rolled into the midst of the K-Thugs, and they went to work on him, trimming Freddy like a side of beef. The tattered remains of the living cloak tried to worm away, dragging pieces of mesh, but the savage Kalis squashed it underfoot like Italian peasants making wine. The other three boys screamed, begged, and finally had to turn away, weeping.

Righteous Weeks came down. Rappelling by his lariat to where Sal lay defeated, the big ex-con kicked the boy's sword away and leaned over him, peering through the scorched eyeholes of Sal's helmet.

"If y'all gonna be honorary Skinwalkers," he said gently, "first thing you gotta do is fetch your own skins. Can't be wearing another man's rig—that is a serious violation of Reaper etiquette."

"Damn straight," said Chiquita. "Every suit gotta be tailor-made; otherwise, it ain't gonna fit right, maybe pinch a little around the neck. Ever heard of pick your own lobster?" He knelt over a hatch in the floor and wrenched a rusty bolt aside. "Here it's pick your own Harpy." He pulled back the heavy lid.

The three boys were dragged over so they could see down inside. The dark space below was filled with a thick gray substance resembling petroleum jelly. Within those murky depths, countless pale blue human shapes slowly tumbled and thrashed, their actions impeded by the dense grease. One of them rose into the light, glistening under a thick layer of translucent goop.

It was Voodooman.

Taking up a long-handled gaff, Righteous said grimly,

"We been through a lot, ain't we, Marcus? Sho nuff is a sorry world." To the boys, he said, "Take this as a lesson to you. This is what you get when you cheat your friends. Least *I* thought we was friends." Planting the pole on Voodooman's forehead, he pushed him deep under the muck. "Consider it an initiation: Every Reaper got to skin and dress they own Harpy. Ain't no ready-to-wear in this outfit, no off-the-rack, not when it comes to a real live ghouly suit. Just like you don't want to trust no fool to pack your parachute, every man gotta take responsibility for dressing his own self. We all strickly custom-tailored. Now, which one of you's gonna be first?"

"First to what?" Todd snarled.

"Why, jump in and fetch one."

"Fuck you," said Sal.

"Hey, looks like we got us a volunteer."

As the Reapers busied themselves maneuvering Sal over the gruesome well, the other two boys' attention was suddenly drawn elsewhere.

From over the barge's high gunwale, through a gap in the barbed wire, a mass of alarming newcomers appeared. Fluidly as serpents, they started spilling down onto the deck. Human yet inhuman, shapeless yet terribly familiar, mottled blue and fluttery-quick, with black smudges for eyes and gaping pits for mouths, they rose up to loom behind the hooded figures of the oblivious Kalis.

Sal saw Chiquita turn his head as if sensing something and found himself literally face-to-face with a hulking great Xombie. It was Big Ed Albemarle, dripping from the sea and still clutching his rusty hammer. Beside Albemarle were men and boys with whom Sal had once been acquainted, all deathly blue and slimy with algae: Julian Noteiro, Lemuel Sanchez, Cole Hayes, at least a dozen others who had died at Thule and been resurrected, recruited to serve Dr. Langhorne aboard the sub. But they were not Langhorne's creatures, they were Lulu's—Lulu's guys, her Dreadnauts. They had not come for Sal. They had come, finally, for her.

"Holy shit," Todd muttered.

"Damn," Ray said.

All hell broke loose.

The Kalis were quick, incredibly fast, and Sal realized why these people had survived for so long. They were the end product of a ruthless process of elimination that had begun months before, weeding out the weak and the reflex-impaired. Anyone who had to think twice was an early casualty. Those remaining were the cream of the crop, the instinctive stone killers, the naturally gifted who could practically kill in their sleep—a veritable Olympiad of murderers.

But the Xombies were quicker.

As a spatter of gunfire rained down from the upper decks, Chiquita swung his machete at Albemarle, slashing the bigger man's throat to the bone, but Albemarle indifferently clocked him with the hammer, shattering his mask and the skull beneath, catching Chiquita's limp body in his huge arms. Face revealed, Chiquita was a chinless man with bad teeth, born Roy Ortiz in La Paz, Mexico, who had invented his female alter ego in homage to his beloved mother Chiquita. Roy was one of the few K-Thugs who had been a cross-dresser even before the Agent X plague, even before jail.

Ed Albemarle opened his mouth wide—a bottomless pit as dark and cold as the vacuum of space—and covered Roy's lower face, sucking the air out of his lungs. The man's bony chest collapsed with a familiar, sickening *crunch*. Absorbing the Xombie's vitalizing infection, Roy's dead body swelled with manic energy, breaking away and landing on all fours like a human tarantula, bugged-out black eyes darting for prey.

In the first skirmish, half the Kalis went down, and the others appeared to be equally doomed, waiting only for their brothers-in-drag to pop back to life for the battle to be over. But they were far from resigned to their fate: Not only were they expert hand-to-hand fighters, armed to the teeth. They were also shielded from Xombie assault by their repellent coating of black ichor—this in addition to their molded carbon-fiber masks, steel neck braces, and twelve-gauge shotgun loads embedded in their Kevlar-padded false breasts. To hug one of them was to trip a Claymore mine.

The short lag time was enough to make it an unexpectedly equal battle: The Xombies were more occupied with subduing their immediate victims than with defending themselves against the remaining K-Thugs, who knew exactly where to strike in order to undo the undead.

One by one, Xombies fell thrashing to the deck, their major tendons severed at the roots and a compound of white phosphorous injected into their chest cavities with gas-powered morgue syringes that the Kalis kept strapped to their forearms for just such an occasion. A potent weapon under any circumstances, white phosphorous had a particularly lethal affinity for Maenad body chemistry: Any ghoul so injected rolled around spewing incandescent foam from its nose, mouth, ears, and other orifices, its body swelling up and erupting like a grade-school science project until it abruptly collapsed into a puddle of burning grease. The deck quickly became a filthy abattoir awash with Xombie gunk and slithering remains. From above, red specks of laser sights darted amid the action, exploding whatever they touched.

But very quickly—shockingly quickly—the Xombies were back on the offensive, their numbers replenished by hordes of new arrivals, as well as all the active severed limbs and body parts squirming underfoot. Such chunks now became a significant hazard, flopping around like rabid squirrels and latching onto passing ankles, scrabbling up under robes. Freddy's revenge. The battle became desperate, a chaotic scrum of flying blades and swearing futility, so that any second the boys expected to wind up alone on deck with an orgy of ghouls.

Momentarily left alone, Sal, Todd, and Ray quickly managed to loose their slipknots—but there was nowhere to go. They were surrounded, trapped in the bottom of the barge with grisly combat raging in front of them, their backs to a sheer, twenty-foot-high wall of shipping boxes that comprised the lowest tier of the pyramid. There was no cover, nowhere to run.

"What the fuck do we do now?" hissed Todd.

"Take a number," Ray said. "They'll call us when it's our turn to die."

Struck with a *duh* moment of inspiration, Sal said, "Wait, I thought these suits were supposed to protect us!"

"Not from Reapers."

"No, that's my point!" Gathering up the slack lariats, he wound them around a cleat and dropped the lassos into the open grease pit.

Trying to stop him, Todd said, "Hey! What do you think you're doing?"

"Leggo!—you're right, it's not Xombies we need to worry about."

"Yeah, but I'm not ready to trust my life to this suit— thing didn't come with no warrantee."

"It's our only chance!" Sal said. "We have to get past them to the boats!"

"Riiight," said Ray, nodding dully. "With those assholes up there shooting everything in sight? Awesome idea."

"Most of them just got out of bed—they don't have a clue what's going on. They're not paying any attention to us because they think we're Reapers. The only ones who know the truth are too busy fighting to do anything about it."

There was a sudden eruption from the bilge—a fountain of splattering grease as Xombies started spurting out like newborn reptiles. Crowding each other, drooling slime, they clambered over the suited boys, shoving past them toward more likely subjects.

Ray freaked out a little as Voodooman crawled over him: "Sick, man—*don't touch me!* Oh my God, oh my God . . ."

"Follow me!" Sal shouted, bolting. Todd shrugged and followed.

Ray thought, *That's crazy*, but if Todd was going, so was he. No way he was staying behind with these nasty things popping up out of the deck like disgusting fetuses. He grabbed his samurai sword and ran.

The deck was a vision of hell, demons alive and dead closing in on every side, and Sal didn't think they were going to make it. The boys hacked wildly, neither knowing nor caring if those they chopped down were human or otherwise. Then they were pushing through incoming Xombies at the rail and vaulting over, Sal's flesh mitts giving excellent purchase as he clung to the rope netting on the opposite side.

Shit—it was a longer drop than he'd thought. But the boats were there: several dozen light watercraft of various types—Jet Skis, Zodiacs, Boston Whalers—all moored around a string of bright yellow pontoons chained to the barge. Todd was already clambering from one pontoon to the next, heading for a pod of Jet Skis at the end.

Jumping down to the wobbly platform, Ray looked at Sal through their cactus-headed helmets, and said, "Whoa. Some grip, huh?"

"Yeah, sticky. Move your ass." Sal glanced up to see armed Reapers descending by nets from the upper decks. The shooting let up while their comrades were in the field of fire. It was now or never. He followed the other two across the bobbing footbridge. Todd had managed to untie the mooring line that held all five Jet Skis together, keeping three while the rest drifted off on the current. Ray got on the second one.

"You better let me on back," Sal said. "I never rode one of these before."

"Are you serious?"

"No—I'm into bikes, not boats. Move over!"

"You can't—our suits can't touch."

"Just let me on, and we'll figure it out!"

Todd snapped, "No! Just get on one and do what I do!"

Sal reluctantly straddled the third craft. "What now?"

"It's like a motorcycle: Turn on the ignition and throttle up." He revved the handle. "Okay?"

Sal tried it, nodded. "Okay."

"Now follow me."

They started forward, accelerating upriver. As soon as they cleared the shadow of the barge's hull, spurts of water began popping up all around them. One banked off the cowling of Sal's Jet Ski, leaving a deep gash. *Oh shit,* he thought, ducking low.

But the shooting was sparse, disorganized, and fell off sharply as they moved out of close range. Obviously, the Xombies were the primary concern. The boys went faster as they got the feel for how the Jet Skis handled, really punching the gas as they passed the bogus paddle wheeler and made for the sheltering arches of the I-195 highway bridge.

Sal stared up at the floating casino's towering super-structure, searching for any sign of Kyle in its upper windows. He knew the boy was probably dead, but the possibility that he was still alive and being tortured for information while they rode away was almost unbearable. If only he would see them and jump out a window, so they could pick him up. *Come on, Kyle, come on . . .*

Then, incredibly, Sal saw something, something that made him slow to a puttering idle. There was a bright reflection on the glass, but for a second he could vaguely make out a face looking down at him from the highest window . . . then it turned away and was gone. Letting out his breath, Sal gunned his water scooter beneath the bridge and around the thick stone abutments to where Todd and Ray were waiting on the far side.

"We made it, man!" Todd shouted as he pulled up. "We really made it! Holy shit!"

Ray asked, "How we ever gonna get these suits off without that oxygen tent?"

"Cross that bridge when we come to it!"

"We did just come to it."

"Oh man! This is excellent!" Todd was beaming, shaking his head in wonder. "So that's it, dude, that's it! We ditch these things and head back across town to the rafts, then hit the boat and tell the skipper everything we know. Should be a cakewalk now . . . long as the boat's still there." There was a hitch in his breathing, and suddenly he started to cry. The suddenness of the meltdown seemed to catch him by surprise. "What the fuck, man," he sobbed.

Sal knew exactly what he was thinking because he had the same thought: *Thirty-seven down, three to go.* Taking a deep breath, he said, "You two go ahead without me. I'm not leaving just yet."

Trying to collect himself, Todd didn't register the words. "What?"

"I'm going back for Kyle."

"You're *what*? He's *dead*, man."

"I thought I saw him just now, when we passed that other barge. I don't know if it was really him or not, but I can't just leave him behind—not when it should have been me up there. I already left everybody else; I don't care about what happens to me anymore. I can't face going back to the boat if I don't at least try."

"Are you crazy, dude? It's suicide! What the hell you think you're gonna do?"

"I don't know."

"Oh, great plan."

"What I do know is that in this suit I might be able to pass for one of those Reaper assholes. They're all tied up fighting Xombies right now, so there won't be any better time. I'll catch them with their pants down."

"So you're just going to sneak back, grab Kyle, and waltz right out of there?"

"Pretty much. You saw that casino—there's only a few guys there with El Dopa."

"That we know about." Dizzy with incomprehension, Todd said, "Don't do it, dude. We need you."

"I have to. I'm sorry. I know it's messed up. You guys go on without me."

"Fine. You know what? You suck. Go ahead—we're leaving."

Suddenly Ray spoke up: "Uh, Todd? I don't think I'm going anywhere." Sheepishly, he held up his gloved hand to show some blood on it. "I think I been hit."

It was true—Ray had been shot in the right side, the bullet passing through his Xombie oversuit and the various layers of material beneath. It was impossible to examine or treat the wound; the Xombie flesh puckered around it like a cat's anus. There was not much blood. "Just leave me here," he said glumly. "I'll only slow you down."

"That's it then," said Todd, unable to hide his relief. "Sal, you have to come ashore with us. I can't carry Ray back by myself."

Sal slumped, knowing he had no choice but to give in, to abandon Kyle just as he had abandoned all the others. He would have preferred to die, but Todd was right: Ray needed medical help. He needed both of them.

"Nobody's carrying anybody anywhere," said Ray, grimacing from the pain. "Sal's right. I'm gonna stay right here, and the two of you are going to go get Kyle."

CHAPTER **TWENTY**

CLASS WARFARE

"This is Alton Webb speaking. Due to Commander Kranuski having abandoned his post, I am taking emergency command of the boat. All senior personnel report to the wardroom."

Webb knew that to certain people on board, these words would be as shocking and unwelcome as a fire alarm. And he knew exactly which ones would come running the fastest: those with the most to fear. The guilty.

They didn't disappoint him. "What happened to Kranuski?" demanded Dan Robles.

Perfectly composed, Webb replied, "I don't know, Dan—he's gone missing. We'll have a full investigation as soon as it becomes feasible. In the meantime, let's focus on the situation at hand."

"You have no authority to command the boat," said Phil Tran. "Half the men outrank you."

"No, they do not. Yesterday, Mr. Kranuski issued me a field promotion to commander. You're out of order, *Lieutenant*—as executive officer, I am next in line. End of story."

Robles said, "I'm afraid we don't accept your authority."

"Is that right? Is this a mutiny, then?"

"No—what *you're* doing is mutiny. We're trying to run a clean ship. Just step aside, Webb, and put a real captain back on deck."

"A real captain. Who would that be, I wonder?"

"The only captain we have, the one who was assigned the duty in the first place: Harvey Coombs."

"Coombs—what a surprise. Sure, let's put the saboteur back in charge. But then, you two are his unofficial representatives, aren't you? Did he tell you to get rid of Kranuski? And I suppose I'm next, is that it? Or am I supposed to conveniently back down and step aside?"

Webb leaned away from the table, revealing his .45 automatic. All the other sidearms had been collected and locked up, he had seen to that. A silence fell over the wardroom.

"Sorry to disappoint you, gentlemen," he said, "but it ain't gonna happen. I know you two have been monkeying around where you don't belong—you've made your contempt for legitimate authority very clear ever since you backed Fred Cowper's little People's Revolution . . . and we've been paying for it ever since. Do you still think you did those folks any favors bringing them on board? Well, the social experiment is over. I'm returning this ship to principles of logic and discipline. Of which the first order of business is to eliminate the sabotage."

"Sorry to tell you," said Tran, "but you've got the wrong guys."

"I don't think so, I really don't. What I *would* like to know is what you thought to accomplish by keeping us here. Did you cut a deal with those river rats out there? Because at least that would make sense. Believe me, I've thought about it myself—I mean, if we're all there is, just us, no more Big Daddy telling us what to do, it's all over. Forget your country, your Navy, and your Uniform Code of Military Justice. Forget all your hopes and dreams. If we're going to survive this shitstorm, we're gonna to have to come up with a new way. Which is why I called you men here."

"I thought it was to shoot us," Robles said.

Webb nodded thoughtfully, bleakly, at them. "I still might," he said. "That depends on you."

He knew this was going to be the hard part—harder even than killing Richard Kranuski had been, or cramming the man's body down the trash-disposal unit. Just as ugly . . . but just as necessary.

"Listen to me," he said. "We can't go on this way. You and I know that. Men like Kranuski and Coombs are the past; they'd get us all killed because they can't cope with the kind of extreme changes that have taken place. There's a harsh new reality, a whole new playbook, and if we don't accept it, we're all going down with the ship. But if we *do* accept it . . ."

"What?"

"The sky's the limit."

"How so?" asked Phil Tran.

"Well, the first thing we have to accept is that our knowledge is a precious commodity in this world. The boat is worthless without us, and there are other nuclear vessels out there, other warships that just need trained crews in order to be functional again. *We* can train them. That means we can pretty much write our own ticket in this new society. Nobody can touch us."

Tran scoffed, "The Moguls didn't seem to have any trouble."

"The Moguls were different. They conquered us by dividing us. Deceiving us. It was Kranuski's mistake to believe them—a mistake I'll never repeat, believe me. Rich was my best friend, but he was stuck in the past, weak, and his weakness made him a danger to all concerned. Phil, I know how you felt about sending those kids ashore. Well, what happened to them is eventually going to happen to all of us if guys like Kranuski and Harvey Coombs call the shots. They're trying to cling to something that's gone. The truth is, we have a lot more to fear from ourselves than we do from scavengers—this boat is a death trap unless we get some outside help. There's no food left. In a matter of days, the rest of those kids are going to start dropping like flies, and that'll be the end of the Good Ship Lollipop. That rogue convoy out there is our only hope. Dammit—we need them. We *need* them. Probably more than they need us."

Suddenly, the men became aware of a new presence in the room. It was Bobby Rubio—the little boy they had found floating in the gondola. He stood at the doorway, staring up at Webb with big, glassy eyes.

"You killed him," he softly.

Startled, Webb said, "What?"

"You killed him."

"Oh for God's sake, this is all we need. Get this kid *out* of here."

"You killed him," the boy repeated. "I saw it."

"Killed who, son?" asked Robles.

"The captain," said Bobby. "I saw you kill the captain."

"Give me a *break*," Webb snapped. "Beat it, kid! I'm warning you."

Robles looked from the kid to Webb. "*Did* you kill him?"

"No! Of course not!"

"You did it, didn't you?" said Tran.

"This is ridiculous." With a feeling of skidding on ice, Webb realized no one was going to intervene for him, not even those who had always backed him up: Jack Kraus, Bartholomew, Tom Nelson. Rather than tossing the brat out, they were just standing there and letting him babble on. The trouble, he realized at once, was that they were all former friends and allies of Rich Kranuski—any loyalty they had to Webb was merely a by-product of his relationship with that much more attractive and dynamic personage. A serious miscalculation.

"You killed him," the kid repeated dully, like a squeaky windup toy.

"I'll be damned." said Jack Kraus, staring at specks of dried blood on Webb's jacket. "You *did* kill him, didn't you, Al? I thought the two of you were like brothers."

Scrambling for ground, Webb conceded, "We were! But there was no choice; he was going to release Coombs. I couldn't let that happen. This is exactly what I'm taking about—I did it for all of you. With Coombs in charge, we'd be right back where we started: with those kids and that Langhorne bitch having the run of the boat."

"You're out of your mind," said Tran.

"No, Rich was out of his mind—total Section Eight. You should have heard him going on about Fred Cowper's head. I only did what was necessary to save the ship."

Robles stood up. "You're under arrest, Mr. Webb," he said.

"Bullshit. You have no power to arrest me."

"You're under arrest on charges of murder and sabotage."

"Sabotage!"

"You're the one who needed the boat to stay here. You're the one who wanted to sell us out to the Moguls."

"Bullshit! *You're* the traitor!"

Tran stood up as well, edging around the table, and saying, "Easy now, Alton. Surrender your weapon before anyone else gets hurt."

Backing away from them, Webb said, "Take one more step, and I'll shoot. I have the authority. One way or another, the sabotage stops here."

Phil didn't stop, and Webb said, "You asked for it," and

fired, hitting him in the chest. The man faltered, then shook his head and kept coming. Webb shot him again in the face, popping a neat round hole in his forehead and blasting a chunk out the back of his scalp. Tran's head jerked from the impact, but still he didn't stop. Wiping oddly colored blood out of his eyes, he came on with infinite patience. Nor did the others seem to find anything unusual about this.

What the fuck?

Retreating out the forward door, Webb cried, "Stay back! All of you!"

Webb grabbed the little boy and carried him up the forward companionway. No one seemed to be following, and when he emerged two flights up at the command deck, there was no one in sight. *So that's it, so that's it,* he thought, not quite knowing what "it" was.

"*You're* the crazy ones," he muttered.

Hauling his unresisting hostage aft through the radio shack, the sonar room, and into the control center, Webb was disconcerted to find the whole first deck deserted. He hit the general alarm and dragged the boy into the CO stateroom, barring the door.

Catching his breath, Webb put the child down and switched on the 1MC. "Attention all hands, attention all hands," he announced breathlessly, voice crackling from speakers throughout the ship, "this is Commander Alton Webb speaking. This is an emergency. I hereby order all security personnel to report to the main deck. There are . . . enemy insurgents aboard." He didn't know how to put it so as not to sound stark raving mad. "They have infiltrated members of the crew and are attempting to take over the ship. Please acknowledge this message."

There was no reply; the speaker remained silent.

Suddenly, he heard a muffled voice in his ear, as if inches away: "C'mon, Al, get with the *program.*"

Webb nearly jumped out of his shoes, spinning in the direction of the voice. There was no one there. Of course—the room was much too small for anyone to hide. Was the kid a ventriloquist? He checked the shower—empty.

"Who the fuck was that?" he demanded.

Moon-eyed, the boy raised his skinny chicken arm and pointed a grubby, accusing finger at the plundered captain's safe. *Webb's* safe now, for what it was worth; Alton Webb's personal keep, with its scorched door from which the lock had been gouged like an offending eye, leaving an ugly black peephole.

"No fuckin' way," Webb said, yanking it open.

"How ya doin', Al?" quacked Fred Cowper's severed head, staring out at him with great black fish eyes. Cowper's mouth yawned open to a grotesque degree, splitting the old man's face from ear to ear like the exaggerated jaws of some primordial sea creature, one of those deep-sea monstrosities with teeth as huge and sharp as a cocked bear trap—a ravenous Pac-Man.

Webb slammed the door on the dreadful specter—*OhGodohmyGod*—and recoiled backward, holding his gun out at arm's length and training it on the safe. Before he could decide whether to scream, cry, or just go raving batshit, he heard a crackling sound beside him and turned to see the kid. What he saw, rising nearly to the ceiling, was beyond all comprehension.

Now Alton Webb did scream.

CHAPTER **TWENTY-ONE**

BLUE SUEDE

The Blue Man's day-to-day routine was simple:

He rolled out of bed when he wanted to, had a leisurely breakfast of tea and stale donuts, then moseyed across the cylinder to his pit latrine, where he did his business while reading a paperback copy of Boswell's *London Journal*. After that he washed up, polished off a chapter of Cellini's autobiography, added several more pages of closely written script to his own extensive notes, and had a light lunch. Then, if he felt like it, he might leave the cylinder to make his rounds of the garage and the wider city. These could consist of something as simple as raiding the Mr. Donut Dumpster in the alley or fetching water from the sink in the employee restroom. Or they might require more stealth, such as making a run across the pedestrian overpass to the Biltmore Hotel. You never knew who might be watching.

The habits born of years of vagrancy served him well. Truly, not much had changed: He had been a fugitive before, and he was still a fugitive.

In bygone days, the man known only as Old Joe Blue had been a familiar figure downtown, and particularly well-known in transient circles, where he was even more an

object of curiosity than he was in the world of "squares"—
homeless society being necessarily insular and mutually
reliant. But Joe wandered in and out of their company with
the same ghostlike detachment as he did everywhere else,
partaking of charity handouts, freebies, and day jobs, then
vanishing back into the ether.

Where did he live? Who was he, and who had he been?
Since Old Joe didn't panhandle or sleep on the street, the
system generally left him alone, but what was wrong with
him? Argyria—an overload of colloidal silver—was the official explanation, but how, when, and why? The man himself was not clear about specifics. One rumor was that he
was a former silversmith from one of the old factories in the
Jewelry District, and had developed metal toxicity from
years of breathing the vapors. When the factory closed its
doors (as so many had, in the age of Kmart, Wal-Mart, and
cheap imports) he was thrown out like an old pair of
shoes—blue suede shoes, they joked. This story was certainly more plausible than Joe's own explanations, which
were rambling diatribes about doomsday and salvation—
the man was a notorious crackpot. But few dared to contra-
dict him, and anyone who did challenge that eerie shambling
figure had an odd way of never being heard from again. So
people left him alone, and the more superstitious ones
crossed themselves in his wake.

"Wormwood," Joe might mutter, standing in a soup line.
"Read your Book of Revelation. Most comets are like dirty
snowballs, just ice and dust. But not that one, no, that comet
there is a Trojan horse. Don't you get it? It shouldn't have
come anywhere near us, it's on a whole different trajectory,
but it *changed*, it *zigged*. Do you understand what that
means?" When people started edging away, he would shake
his head, mumbling, "Dodos—dodo birds."

Old Joe's lifestyle was flexible enough to accommodate

not only the end of human civilization, but a guest to share it with. Noah didn't build the ark just for himself, Joe reasoned. So in his fits of hoarding he stored away enough provisions for at least two people to weather an extended siege—which was exactly what he had been preparing for all these years. The boy didn't eat much. With minor replenishment, Joe figured they were good for at least four months. Plenty of time for the last vestiges of the old world to be scoured away.

For it was only then that his life's work could truly begin.

"Here, look at this, look here," Joe said, showing Bobby his trove of old magazines. Pulling out a moldy issue of *National Geographic*, he said, "Take a look at this cover story about Saturn—the Cassini mission: 'On July 14, 2005, the spacecraft descended to a hundred miles above Enceladus's south polar region. Data indicated that plumes of material were erupting near the south pole. Then, four months later, Cassini made images that showed geyser like eruptions of water vapor and ice particles shooting far out into space.' Unquote."

When Bobby didn't react, he grew impatient. "Do you see what I'm saying? Enceladus! Here we thought it was only Jupiter's moon Europa that had liquid water and the potential for life, but now we learn that Saturn has its own salad bowl—the moon Enceladus. Picture it: an aquatic race living in perpetual darkness, in a hydrothermal ocean under miles of ice. It's a womb down there, a whole damn amniotic planet. They live and grow in that fishbowl for millions of years, competing against one another, developing tools and higher intelligence, until one day one of them starts to wonder what's above that frozen ceiling? Does it go on forever, to infinity? And maybe they kill that guy for heresy, and the next guy and the next guy, but eventually space starts running short—see, it's a very small moon, just three hundred miles wide—and they start thinking seriously about the possibility of other oceans in the ice, other worlds to conquer. Meanwhile, their science develops to the point where they can start drilling boreholes long enough to reach the surface. Eureka."

The old man sat back, nodding. "Do you see now? They send a ship. Not a ship of metal but a ship of ice. Ice! Forging it, smelting it like metal, building it up layer by layer like a beehive. An artificial comet. Maybe their whole race inside, a billion of 'em, who knows? We saw it being launched, we tracked it . . . and then we forgot about it. But not everybody forgot, oh no. Some have been keeping an eye on that thing. We saw when it used Jupiter as a slingshot to accelerate, and when it altered its course. That's when we lost it, but the projections don't lie. Oh yes, it was always aiming for more temperate regions, and one hot spot in particular, the Florida of the solar system, with an ocean that could practically swallow up their whole planet.

"How do you fight something like that?" Joe said. "Even if it is only a regular comet, how do you survive against it—even if nothing else on the surface of the Earth will?"

The man was crazy, but he was all Bobby had. "I don't know," the boy said, uncomprehending.

"You make lemonade."

That night, as Bobby dreamed of running and running, his host sat upright a few feet away, comfortably ensconced in the reclining seat from a Lincoln Town Car. The old man was completely still, unblinking, stolidly inert as a wooden Indian.

Imperceptibly at first, something began to happen.

It was as if Joe was having a seizure of some kind, his back arching and his mouth opening so wide it stretched his jaw past its limits, so that the joints could be heard popping from their sockets.

Now a thing like a weird flowering plant began erupting from his upturned throat, a branching, ribbed stalk, followed by a glossy pink orchid uncurling its petals—no, *two* orchids: a matched pair of unspeakable bromeliads that were the old man's inverted lungs. They swayed in midair at the ends of their bronchial tubes like twin cobras from a snake charmer's basket, seeming to have a life and mind of their own, billowing up with every appearance of unutterable bliss. Not just lungs, but the whole glistening contents of the man's body cavity were flowering up and spreading forth like a blooming bouquet. His carcass turned inside out, bones and musculature rolling back like a thick foreskin. Bobby didn't awaken even as the grisly mass arched over him, its nodules and clusters and veiny membranes trembling with excitement.

Grotesquely slow as it would have seemed to the perception of an appalled onlooker, the ghastly efflorescence was over in a matter of seconds. Before Bobby could awaken or react, the thing was upon him, enfolding his face in its violent moistness, prying him open with velvet pliers, gently gulping the boy's life breath in one heaving spasm, a miraculous convulsion that transformed the boy and restored the old man to his seat. An instant later, there was no sign that anything unusual had occurred.

CHAPTER **TWENTY-TWO**

THE WHOLE ENCHILADA

Todd and Sal crossed back under the bridge, using the grandiose floating casino to screen themselves from the cargo barge. They could still hear gunfire and shouts of battle over there.

"Doesn't look like anybody's coming after us at least," Sal called across the water.

"Not yet, anyway."

Gliding under the shadow of the casino's superstructure, the boys felt slightly safer, less visible. The problem was getting on board: The gangplank was raised, and there was no other obvious means of entry. Todd took that as reason to quit right there, but Sal thought the big red paddle wheel looked climbable and persuaded the other boy to hold his Jet Ski steady while he stood on its seat and reached as high as he could—*there!* Once he had a handhold, the Xombie glove gripped tight, and he was able to swing his legs up. What he had not anticipated was how to get Todd up without also losing both Jet Skis. They had no rope to tie them with.

Making a snap decision, Sal hissed down, "Just wait for me here."

"No way, man. I came this far, I'm not letting you go in there alone."

"You have to. It's better this way—if anything happens to me, you can get back to Ray." He didn't wait for argument, climbing over the rail and hurrying across the deck. The main-entrance door was open, black as a cave.

There was no chance to scope out the situation properly, so Sal steeled himself and ducked into the open hatch, hugging the wall. All the lights were out. Remembering the layout from before, he knew he was in an antechamber before the main gambling room—a lobby and coat-check area with benches, potted trees, and a service counter. Hiding behind the plants, he peered deeper inside.

The place was deserted, dim and shuttered as an empty convention hall. El Dopa was nowhere to be seen, nor were any of those Kali goons. Muted sounds of shooting and other commotion filtered down through the open skylights, but otherwise there was no noise of any kind.

Keeping a low profile, Sal slowly made his way to the center of the room. The bed was still there, still unmade. It was actually an entire bedroom set, with a night table, a lamp, and a comfortable sitting chair. There was a thick book on the table: *The Tibetan Book of the Dead*. Once again, he thought the furniture looked like some kind of weird museum exhibit, set up on its pedestal in the middle of the room.

The deeper he went, the more convinced he was that the entire casino was abandoned, and this conviction was only reinforced when he tried the elevator and found its buttons dead. The power was out. There was a stairwell in the back corner, and he climbed up to the next level, a curtained platform that had once served as a lounge area and cabaret stage. Now it was half in shadow, and Sal could make out row upon row of silent machines—frozen gears and wheels and springs, power cables and truck batteries, all with no readily discernible purpose. It reminded him of the old textile mills he had seen during a school field trip to Lowell, Massachusetts—monuments to unsafe labor. The floor beneath was wet and stained black, and there was an odd smell that the boy associated with the submarine's forbidden third deck—Dr. Langhorne's section. It made his hair stand on end.

Continuing up, he found himself on the highest balcony, the last place they had seen Kyle. Feeling an intense need to pee, Sal scanned the offices and restaurant, the restrooms and kitchen, then cautiously made his way up the spiral staircase in the back. Had that face been a figment of his imagination? He was trembling uncontrollably—this was the only place left to look.

Emerging in a pitch-dark corridor with padded leather walls, he worked his way toward a cracked circle of dim red light. It was a broken window, a round porthole in a heavily padded door. No sounds from within, but something smelled really bad. *Okay now, okay . . .*

Working up his nerve, taking a deep breath, Sal pushed through and was struck with the full putrid stench, like burnt hair, burnt flesh. It was worse than when his mother used oven cleaner on the ancient crusts under the broiler, a foul, musky animal stench—the funk of pure, concentrated death. The walls and ceiling were full of bullet holes, like stars, and these bright constellations were the only source of light. In the red gloom, Sal could make out piles of blackened bones, human skulls, and possibly worse—he didn't stay long enough to find out. There was no need to: That charnel pit was all he needed to understand that everyone on this barge was gone. Surely and most importantly, the boy he was looking for was gone.

Gagging, weeping for Kyle, for himself, for all of them, Sal covered his mouth and rushed to the next door—the last door—

—and broke through into blinding daylight.

Sobbing, dashing across the breezy sunlight of the top deck under a canopy of paper lanterns, Sal vomited over the rail, hacking up his guts into the sea far below, then stood back and stopped in amazement. Shielding his eyes from the sun, he squinted across the water at a sight so astonishing and terrible that it shocked him out of his own grief.

A hundred yards away, the other barge was still at war, still fighting the Xombie invasion. Only by now its deck was literally covered with human remains, great crawling heaps of blasted, smoldering offal, an unkillable killing field. With hordes of fresh meat still coming over the side.

Hundreds of Reapers were lined up on the bottom tier of the cargo pyramid, twenty feet above the carnage and pouring gunfire down on the swarming invaders. The men had an arsenal of firearms laid out behind them, and gun caddies running back and forth, replacing weapons that jammed or got too hot to hold. The shooters had gone through an extraordinary quantity of ammunition, but apparently there was plenty more where that came from. The only danger seemed to be that the pile of creeping flesh would get so high that Xombies could use it as a ramp to reach the upper decks.

"Oh my God," Sal said.

The number of Xombies coming on board was nothing short of amazing—the riverbed must be packed with them. Scanning the whole panorama, his eyes were drawn to the highway bridge just a few hundred feet away, and he stared in amazement at thousands of Xombies choking the span and toppling over the railing into the water. Others were walking into the river from shore, running in like strange, spastic bathers and vanishing from view only to emerge minutes later over the barge gunwales.

Both tugboats had come alongside the embattled barge,

and their crews were trying to cut the rope netting hanging over the side, which was the Xombies' point of ingress. In order to avoid being attacked themselves, they had to clear the gunwales with high-pressure fire hoses. A man had managed to barricade himself inside the crane cockpit and was transporting others by sling to the tugboats and a dozen other vessels. Everyone was shouting advice and encouragement. It was also, Sal noticed, a beautiful spring morning.

Sal heard a metal scraping sound.

"Peekaboo, I see you," said a girl's voice.

He turned. It was Lulu Pangloss.

The Ex-girl was dressed in a sailor suit with the casino's gold logo embroidered over the breast pocket. She sat casually in a deck chair, her doll-like face preposterously blue, and her black eyes twice as large as life.

Sal faltered, his back pressed against the rail. "Lulu. Shit. What's . . . goin' on?"

Voice bright and bottomless, Lulu said, *"Quite a view, don't you think?"*

"What are you doing here?"

"Think of it as a humanitarian mission," she said. *"Free inoculations. Bring the kiddies."*

"I thought they . . . killed you."

"They wish." A smoky giggle.

"I'm looking for Kyle—do you know where he is?"

"I'm right here, bro."

Glancing up to the roof above the patio, Sal was struck dumb in the literal sense—he suddenly found it difficult to form words.

No, he thought. *No—hell no!*

Perched up there like a parade spectator, with his legs dangling over the side, was Kyle Hancock. The boy was not blue . . . but he was not human, either. Aside from the half-healed bullet holes in his head, there was an unsettling emptiness about him, a vacuum. Something in his X-ray gaze made Sal feel nakedly exposed, even in that Xombie suit. He couldn't make himself meet those eyes, but those thirsty eyes met *him*, and he could actually *feel* them probing and prodding like invisible fingers.

"What happened, Kyle?" Sal asked, mouth dry. "Where's El Dopa and all them?"

"We handled them." Tilting his head toward the other barge, he said, *"They over there now."*

"Why are you both here?"

"Waiting for you, brother."

"Me? Why?"

"Because I knew you'd come."

"Yes, to save you," Sal said bitterly. "But it's too late."

"I've already been saved, Sal."

"Looks more like the exact opposite."

"I know. It looks strange, but the crawl from darkness is always difficult. Birth pangs are painful."

"You're not Kyle—Kyle didn't talk like that."

"I'm still here, there's just more of me. Kyle was a dot; now he's a line. Yesterday, I was standing where you are, trapped in that point of time, full of the same thoughts and fears. I remember the feeling: It was like being blind and helpless . . . a tiny flame in a wind tunnel. Scary. I wish you could just trust me, but I know it doesn't work that way."

"Is that supposed to make me feel better?"

Lulu cut in: *"Feeling better isn't the point. The point is surviving. Going on. That's what what Agent X was invented for: saving your stupid ass from the end of the world."*

"Don't you mean *causing* the end of the world?"

"No. The end of the world is coming from up there." She pointed her dainty blue finger at the sky. *"I know you can't see it yet—neither could we. But it's there, like a white*

ball of dust, getting brighter. Closer every second. Soon it will be brighter than the full moon, and when it hits Earth, it will scour the planet's surface like a billion atom bombs. Nothing will live, nothing will survive it . . . except maybe us."

"What the hell are you talking about?"

"The Big Enchilada. Uncle Miska knew about it. A few others did, too, but were forced to keep it a secret. They called it Wormwood. It's a comet, a huge body of ice and debris blasted off one of Saturn's moons, Enceladus, in a volcanic explosion."

"The Big Enchilada—oh my God," Sal muttered, shaking his head. "You people are crazy."

"Miska found out about it years ago and dedicated his longevity research to preventing it. He knew no higher life-forms would survive the impact but that certain primitive bacteria could—the same bacteria that seeded the early Earth. If human cells could be engineered to resemble these bacteria, then mankind might survive—hence, Agent X. He calls it the galactic prophylactic."

"How the hell do you know all this?"

The question seemed to catch them up short. They looked at each other, Lulu cranking her bulbous doll's head completely around, a cherubic nightmare with pigtails.

"I don't know," she said finally. *"We just do."*

"When's this huge disaster supposed to happen?"

"It could be at any time."

Sal didn't have a clue what to think anymore, his whole foundation of reality having come unstuck. It wasn't just the shock of hearing Xombies speak intelligently, or of learning that Kyle had joined that deathless horde, or even of seeing daylight through the shrinking cavity in Kyle's chest—everything was wrong, ever since Agent X. God had gone wrong, the whole world was inside out, desecrated beyond redemption, and Sal couldn't handle it anymore. He was done playing, he quit, and in quitting, something in him broke loose; the adrenaline drained from his spine like quicksilver, leaving numbness and exhaustion. All he knew for sure anymore was that he wanted no part of this.

Across the water, someone with a megaphone yelled, "Fire! Fire!" At first the men there must have misunderstood, because the shooting increased, but then people started pointing up at the smoke pouring from the container stacks. "Ship's on fire!" the megaphone squawked. "Fire in the hold, fire in the hold! Abandon ship!"

The defensive line collapsed as men started running around like ants, barking orders and screaming that everyone had to reach the boats. This was no small challenge: the Xombie-infested deck had been a rather abstract menace before, an annoying but purely technical problem to be dealt with in good time. Now suddenly it was a moat that they had to ford before they burned to death. And the barge was full of flammable, toxic, explosive cargo—there was no time to lose.

Black smoke began pouring out of the deck hatches and windows. There was a series of metallic bangs from within the pyramid that caused the whole thing to jump, and a hundred smoking holes magically appeared in the metal. Schrapnel *whanged* like bullets off the deck, and the sea was sprinkled with tiny white splashes. But threaded among those splashes was a white ribbon—the wake of a Jet Ski.

It was Todd. Todd was coming for him.

Sal took a deep breath, closed his eyes, and took a running leap over the railing.

He was just off his feet when something hooked him around the arm and neck and yanked him backward, upward, carrying him into the rope canopy. A cold, hard cheek pressed against his, and a sardonic skull's mouth lined with black teeth whispered in his ear:

"Haven't you always wondered what it would be like?"

Choking, trying to break free, Sal found his free arm tangling with the disordered mass of flesh and bone that was Uncle Spam's lower body. Its branching, animated nest of gristle was clinging to the overhanging netting like a spider to its web, upper torso dangling, arms carrying the boy as it scrambled up toward its lair in the radio shack.

Sal's own strength was insufficient but that of his Xombie oversuit more than made up the difference: It flexed violently, every fiber rolling like a fleshy wave—a wave comprised of individual Maenad cells popping upward like coral polyps, or spectators in a microscopic football stadium. Starting at Sal's feet, it gained force as it rose to his neck, finally converging to whipcrack against Uncle Spam's clutching arms. The result was explosive, breaking the headlock and dropping Sal's body to the top deck.

Stunned, he tumbled, got up, tried to run—and dove straight into the ropes. Something scuttled toward him, knocking him down, sitting on him like a ton of rank-smelling wet kindling. Pinned, Sal fumbled in his utility bag for the butane torch, then shoved his arm deep inside the chomping, slimy maw and flicked it on. With a bleating sound, the crushing weight vanished.

He barely had time to think, *What the fuck is it?* when Uncle Spam came for him again. Sal had no peripheral vision in his helmet, but he saw the lanterns bob as the thing approached, and his mind raced for what to do. Jump?— Lulu and Kyle were on the patio just below; if he twisted his ankle, they'd have him.

At the last second, he grabbed the metal basket of the

barge-to-barge traverse, freed its anchor hook, and flung himself out into space. At the same instant, the monster pounced on his back, twanging the cable and doubling Sal's downward acceleration.

It was a long, fast glide, their combined weight causing the braided wire to sag steeply, the basket's steel coasters screaming from the strain. "Get off!" Sal shouted, fighting as best he could while hanging on by his arms. It wasn't fair: The nightmarish creature at his back had all the advantage. It was like a big, ghastly tick with a human head, interchangeably using its hands or the meat hooks of its grisly undercarriage to hang on and attack. If not for the protection of Sal's Xombie suit, he would have been dead already.

But suit or no suit, the thing was winning. In free fall, the boy whipped his head from side to side, trying to protect his airway as bunches of fluttery, slippery claws tore the Xombie flesh from his face mask and began punching through the wire mesh. Elsewhere, he could feel them stripping him, sharp pincers worming between the seams, burrowing into his tough blue leather to seek out the warm skin underneath.

The shuttle came to rest at the belly of the cable—the exact midpoint of the hundred-yard span between the barges, less than twenty feet above the water. Swirling smoke from the burning freight barge wafted across, choking him. Nowhere left to go, neither forward nor back.

Sensing Sal's hopelessness, the hideous mouth wheedled in his ear. *"Just relax. There is no need to suffer any longer. Let go, and you can join your friends."*

Let go? Letting out a shuddering, sobbing laugh, Sal said, "Okay." He let go with one hand, swinging in space, and with his free hand reached for the large, three-pronged grappling hook used to secure the basket.

"Nice hanging with you," he said, and jammed the hook's barbed points deep into the corded tendons of Uncle Spam's neck, throwing his full weight on it and dangling there. The monster recoiled, furiously grappling with the hook and chain.

Sal let go.

Shed of his weight, cable and basket jounced upward, catapulting Uncle Spam away like a rubber tarantula on a string.

Hitting the water, Sal plunged deep. Icy salt water dashed him in the face, flooding his mask but otherwise leaving him dry inside. The Xombie flesh contracted instantly, clamping tight and creating a waterproof seal over most of his body. Except for a threadlike trickle down his back, Sal was quite warm although completely unable to see, hear, or breathe.

The air trapped in his clothing made him fairly buoyant, popping him back to the surface with a minimum of effort. Athlete though he was, he had never been a tremendous swimmer. As a young child, he had taken swimming lessons at the YMCA—that was the extent of it.

Shaking the water out of his mask, the boy looked around for some sign of what to do next. His range of vision was not good. The two barges seemed very far away, as did the peaceful-looking green banks of the river. Large things were swirling around his legs, but they didn't touch him.

That leak was starting to worry him, however. The suit had been shredded back there in the fight and couldn't close properly. Freezing-cold water was pooling in his boots, making his toes numb, but worse than the cold was the weight—suddenly he was having to tread water just to keep his head up. Maybe this wasn't such a good idea. On top of that, he could feel the pull of the tide; if he didn't figure out what to do pretty quick, he was going to drift around the point and out into the vastness of Narragansett Bay. While that might get him closer to the submarine, it would also put him far from shore. He'd never make it back alive.

I'm sinking.

Sal's legs were flooded halfway up to his calves now, dragging on him like a pair of loaded buckets. The effort required to stay afloat was becoming exhausting; if he stopped paddling for even a second, he would drop straight to the bottom and join all the others down there. Were his friends down there, too? Maybe looking up at him from the dusky green riverbed? He could hear Todd's voice: *I got you, dude . . .*

Without meaning to, Sal let up on his strokes, and water sloshed into his mouth. Swallowing a big gulp of brine, he vomited in his mask. *No!* Todd was up above, reaching down from his Jet Ski, trying to get ahold of Sal's helmet.

Fighting not to choke, unable to believe he was drowning, Sal flailed for a breath of pure air so he could keep up the struggle for just two more seconds—two seconds! That was all Todd needed. But then all of a sudden it was too much, everything against them, scales overbalancing like the pot of beans in that game he and his mom used to play before she died, and Sal went under.

CHAPTER **TWENTY-THREE**

SNAKE PIT

"You have reached the offices of Mogul Research Associates. The offices are now closed. If you know your party's extension, please enter it now and we will transfer you . . ."

". . . You have reached the office of Dr. Alice Langhorne. Please leave a message after the beep."

"Alice, pick up. It's Chandra Stevens."

"Chandra—what is it?"

"Sorry to call you so late, but I thought you should know we just got the first test results back."

"Go ahead—I'm listening."

"They're positive."

"Which ones?"

"All of them."

"Even—?"

"Yes. It's definitely in the environment, and spreading. You were right. We're gonna have to call in the CDC before someone else does."

"Now slow down. First, you know as well as I do that it's benign—Benign by Design, remember? Second, it has a limited number of generations. It can't replicate forever, and its biological half-life is only a few more months. It will inevitably deteriorate."

"But not before it contaminates the entire biosphere. Which it will soon if it's already in the water table, colonizing iron—and if it's already in us."

"I think we have to accept that there's nothing we or anyone else can do to prevent that."

"We can go to the CDC."

"What good would that do? Just cause a big investigation and a lot of hand-wringing. It won't change anything. Ultimately, this thing just has to run itself out."

"You have reached the home of Dr. Uri Miska. Dr. Miska is not available right now to take your call, but if you leave your name and number, he will get . . ."

"Hello?"

"Dr. Miska, it's me."

"Hello, Alice. What a pleasant surprise. I was just dozing on the couch, watching Ron Popeil demonstrate his rotisserie oven and chanting 'Set It and Forget It' with the studio audience. It was like a sutra. If you're ever suffering from stress-based insomnia, I recommend it."

"I will, Professor. But Dr. Stevens just called me with some disturbing information, and I thought you should know right away."

"Okay, but first let me tell you my theory of infomercials. Here it is, the secret: You know why infomercials are so pleasant to watch? Why they draw you in? Because there are no commercials!"

"That's good, thank you, but please listen: The ASR has escaped. Multiple independent field tests have confirmed it's in ferrous subsoil and spreading like wildfire through groundwater."

"Any idea how the agent could have been released?"

"Not yet. At the moment we're playing catch-up."

"Your people haven't spoken to anyone else about this? The press? The CDC?"

"No."

"That's good. Don't. Because how we deal with this now will entirely determine its public importance. Do you remember the hullabaloo about genetically modified corn finding its way into the marketplace? No one else does, either. Realistically, this a nonproblem, an arcane scientific event of no interest to anyone, which has been anticipated with adequate safeguards. Of course we will track its progress, but I am sure it will eventually resolve itself if we just don't make a mountain out of a mole-hill, yes?"

"That's what I explained to Dr. Stevens."

"Wonderful. Beautiful. So what are you doing calling my house in the middle of the night? Is this an emergency?"

"No. Sorry to bother you, Professor."

"That's all right, that's all right. It's not the end of the world."

—Transcript #874-7732,
The Maenad Project

El Dopa stood on the plunging bridge of his command yacht, a forty-eight-foot Chris Craft Roamer with an aluminum hull and all-mahogany interiors, and surveyed his armada.

Surrounding him were sixty other vessels, the major portion of which was a fleet of thirty-six Williard 10M Utility Boats, taken from the Navy yard in Mobile. These were sturdy open boats, packed to the beams with an assault force of nearly a thousand heavily armed and armored Reapers, all hunkered under tarps. The rest of the convoy, acting as a screen, was an assortment of Coast Guard cutters, various trawlers and pleasure cruisers, four amphibious trucks, two tugs, and a host of smaller craft. They were all flying white flags.

Under cover of heavy smoke from the gutted crane barge, this armada streamed from the mouth of the Seekonk River and banked right, facing the sunset. The uppermost reach of Narragansett Bay spread out before them, bright as a sea of new pennies. To the right was downtown Providence; to the left, tank farms and freight terminals, then the long passage to the Atlantic.

Dominating the view was an ominous black silhouette: the submarine. There was certainly no missing it, that long steel island with its winged tower rising above like a gigantic headstone.

As they neared it, a voice squawked from loudspeakers on the lead Coast Guard vessel:

"HOLD YOUR FIRE. WE COME IN PEACE. WE JUST WANT TO TALK."

There was no reply, no sign of anyone having heard, and no time to repeat the message—they were already there.

Covered by sharpshooters and several deck-mounted Gatling guns, the Williards swept in from the submarine's stern, splitting into two groups and streaming up both sides of its featureless black hull. Weighted lines were heaved across the jettylike expanse, fastening the boats on one side to those opposite. When the hawsers were drawn tight, the fleet closed on the sub's flanks like a row of stitches. It reminded El Dopa of a cartoon he had once seen of *Gulliver's Travels*, where tiny people shot lines over an unconscious giant's limbs to secure them. It was a tricky operation: Without its cleats in place, the submarine was a uniquely featureless object, offering nothing to tie up to and no good purchase on its round sides for any kind of landing. El Dopa was impressed with his men's ingenuity; though few of them had much previous experience handling boats, they had all become quite adept sailors over the past four months.

Now the boatmen swarmed from their vessels, whooping and hollering as they rappelled onto the sub. They all wore the cowboy boots, weirdly decorated helmets, and body armor that distinguished them not only as Reapers but as the elite Hopalong Phalanx, whose new commander, General Righteous Weeks, was eager to prove himself.

Watching from a safe distance, El Dopa said to his second, "They're aboard." He picked up the microphone of his marine radio, and announced, "Attention submarine, I need you folks to listen to me. We don't have much time, so I ask for your full attention. You are under attack. Those sounds you hear are authorized representatives of the People's Expedition of the New United States taking over your ship. We demand your surrender, and will sink you if you don't immediately comply. Trust me, we are capable of doing what we say. If you cooperate, I promise no one will be harmed—you are worth more to us alive than dead; otherwise, we wouldn't bother doing what we're doing. With that in mind, perhaps we can negotiate some sort of mutually beneficial arrangement. Work together. On the other hand, if you refuse to surrender, you simply make yourselves and your vessel useless to us, and we will take you out. So I'm telling you to prepare yourselves for whatever is about to happen. It's up to you. Don't be afraid—it's time we all made our peace with eternity. You have one minute to decide."

Righteous Weeks stood on the deck of the submarine and wondered what to do next. So far it had been much too easy—not a single shot had been fired. Could it be a trap of some kind? Every inch of the sub's five-hundred-foot deck was occupied by his men now, right up to the top of the sail, so he didn't think there was any hiding place from which they could be ambushed. He knew that the harbor was too shallow for the monster to submerge. But he was no expert on submarines, nor were any of his men. He had certainly never seen one this big before, much less set foot on it, so he was very tense. Not for the first time, he regretted the loss of his friend Marcus. Voodooman knew about shit like this.

The leader of the few remaining Kalis came over, the one called Betty Boom, and asked him, "Where do you want us to set the charges?" They had a boatload of plastic explosives and radio detonators, courtesy of Uncle Spam.

"Anywhere—I can't see as it matters much."

"It does, though. I've done a lot of welding, and this HY80 steel is a bitch. Blowing any kind of meaningful hole in this mother is going to take everything we've got."

"Then use everything you've got."

It helped to see that someone had defied and defiled the sub already, laying claim like dogs marking their territory, undermining its awesome power with some choice graffiti. The rubberized black deck and conning tower had been tagged like the sides of a subway train: XOMBOYZ, NUBZ, LULU, the classic skull and crossbones.

"Looks like pirates already been to work on this thing," Weeks said.

His second-in-command, Grover Stix, laughed, "Yeah, somebody done beat us to it."

One of the men came running up. "Hey, Righteous, take a look at this."

"What is it?"

"Somebody left the front door open."

It was a hatch at the far bow, just forward the conning tower. Weeks hustled over and pushed through his gathered men. "Well, damn."

It was open, all right. A round well in the deck, exactly

like a manhole in the street, with rungs leading down to darkness. Taking a megaphone, Weeks leaned over the hole, and said, "ATTENTION SUBMARINE: YOU HAVE THIRTY SECONDS TO SURRENDER."

He didn't know if anyone was listening, and he didn't much care. Fuck a siege—if nobody answered, he was fully prepared to start bombing this motherfucker until somebody cried uncle. He called up El Dopa and briefed him on the situation.

"So the hatch was just sitting there open?"

"That's affirmative, out."

"A little convenient, wouldn't you say?"

"You got that right, El D. Personally, I think we ought to pump a few gallons of fuel oil down there and drop a match."

"I don't think so, at least not yet. Let's try smoking them out first. Over and out."

Righteous gave the order, and a case of olive drab tear-gas canisters was brought up. Taking one and pulling its key, he said, "Stand back," and dropped it down the hole. Immediately, a thick white smoke began roiling in the depths. He dropped another.

Nothing. They waited five minutes, listening intently, but the sub remained utterly silent. The sun disappeared behind the horizon, leaving a reef of vermilion clouds.

El Dopa came over the radio: "Think they could have flown the coop?"

"Well, the sentries had their hands full today—I wouldn't expect they was completely on their game. Wasn't as if we expected these jaybirds to abandon ship. And what for?"

"The whole world's been abandoned, why not this boat?"

"True enough. Your call, hoss."

Considering the situation, El Dopa said, "I know you

guys lost your Bluecoats, and I'm short of Thuggees, but *somebody's* gotta go down there, check it out. If it's possible at all, we need that submarine. Having that thing in our pocket would go a long way toward making up for our losses today."

"It's cool, man. Bendis done drilled us on this commando shit; I got that motherfucker *down*. Trick is to get as many our folks inside as quickly as possible—pile in and overwhelm them with force, so that the fight is over before it can even begin. Won't be no booby traps in here, not unless they want to blow themselves up in the bargain."

"Good. And try not to kill everybody—a submarine without a crew is no good to us."

"Affirmative. Righteous out."

The Reapers on deck looked at him challengingly. "After you, brother."

Weeks didn't hesitate. To lead this army, you couldn't show fear. Donning a hooded gas mask over his steel face guard, he led them below, descending into the undulating layer of smoke as into a milky pool.

To his second, Grover Stix, he said, "If this is an ambush, be ready to haul ass out of here." He lightly tapped the barrel of his sawed-off combat shotgun against his head. The gun had a flashlight, a laser sight, and a drum full of special expanding rounds for use at extraclose range. It could stop a rhino.

At the bottom, Weeks paused, peering around, then waved the others down. They descended into a room full of pipes and ductwork, with a narrow corridor running through it, and other rooms branching off in the thick haze. Every wall was covered with control panels and softly humming banks of electronics—a lot of buttons and colored lights that were meaningless to them. Except for the beige tile floor, which was reminiscent of banal institutional settings the convicts were all too familiar with, it all looked very high-tech and complicated.

Dense white vapor filled the ship, flowing downward in lazy freshets and swirling across the floor, gliding from one compartment to the next, deck after deck, with the insidious flowing grace of a centipede. But the Reapers were unfazed by the smoke, in fact could not see it—their gas masks were equipped with ultrasonic goggles that generated a black-and-white digitized image of their surroundings and rendered the gas invisible. There was a sort of *acoustic* haze, however, a blurring effect caused by sound-damping tiles on the sub's walls and ceiling—it took them a few minutes to figure out the distortion.

At one end was a stairwell leading down, at the other a hatchway opening into a much larger space. Everything appeared to be deserted.

"Shoulda signed up for the guided tour," Grover said. "Where is everybody?"

"Just keep your eyes open."

The line of men filing belowdecks grew longer and longer, a parasitic worm pulsing downward, oozing segment by segment into the ship's belly.

"Goddammit," said Weeks. "What the hell do they think they're up to? Hide-and-go-seek?"

The place was a regular catacomb, riddled with holes and hidden passages. The men kept bumping their heads. Heading downward, they peered into a deserted mess hall, its vacant leatherette booths weirdly cozy, then continued forward through a smaller dining room and a sleeping area. At the end was a locked door marked DO NOT ENTER.

"Open sesame," Weeks said, blasting the lock. There was a scream, and the door swung open on two people wearing oxygen masks.

One of them was a woman.

"Good God a'mighty," said Grover Stix.

"Don't move!" barked Weeks, training his gun on them and making room for the men behind. "Who the fuck are you?"

The man stepped forward. "I'm Captain Harvey Coombs, United States Navy."

"You're the captain of this thing?"

"Uh, no—actually I was relieved of command. That's why I'm locked in here. We're both under arrest."

"Under arrest? You better not be fucking with me! Who's in charge? Where they at?"

"The one you want is Mr. Webb. I'm afraid we don't know where he is—or anyone else for that matter. We've been in here for the last two days."

To Langhorne, Grover said, "You a real woman?"

"How flattering."

"Goddamn. What's your name, then?"

"I'm Dr. Alice Langhorne. Pleased to meet you."

"*Langhorne?* God*damn.* You the one's friends with Uri Miska?"

"That's right."

"Holy shit. You been up at Valhalla, ain't you? What's it like up there? Is the streets really made of gold?"

"Shut up, Grover," said Righteous Weeks. "This ain't no social call—we got business to attend to." To Coombs, he said, "You gonna take us to whoever's in charge of this pig boat, and you gonna tell 'em we demand their immediate surrender. I don't want no killing if I can avoid it. We just want to partner up with y'all."

"Well, if you came this far, I assume you must have already been through the control center. That's where the commander usually is."

"Ain't nobody up there now."

"Wait—nobody at all?"

"We ain't seen one damn soul since we come in."

"That's . . . unusual. I don't know what to tell you. All we can do is keep going down."

"Lead on, chief. And don't you *fuckin'* try anything, I swear to God."

The next deck down looked gutted, all its furniture and electronics pulled out and only capped ends of wire remaining. "Look like somebody done stripped this place good," said Grover. "Reminds me of what I did to my house after the bank foreclosed on it." Coombs and Langhorne could barely see anything through the smoke and had to be helped along. There was a series of bumps from somewhere below, then a loud whooshing sound.

"What's that noise?" Weeks demanded.

Coombs said, "Sounds like the muzzle doors closing and the tubes being drained. The forward torpedo tubes."

"You didn't have to say that—I know what tubes means."

"Then that is the sound of the tubes being blown dry."

"So somebody's down there?"

"Would have to be."

Following the noise, they arrived at the bottom, emerging in a roomful of machinery that led into another space that was obviously the torpedo room.

"I'd avoid doing any shooting in here," Coombs said. "That's the auxiliary machinery room—we call it the Snake Pit. There are a few thousand gallons of reserve diesel in that tank, and those torpedoes up there run on some nasty flammable stuff. Not to mention the explosive warheads themselves."

The Reapers ventured forward, pointing their weapons down the racks of deadly green cylinders until all their sonar beams converged on something odd at the end of the aisle:

several interlocking metal cases the size of coffins, finished matte black and plastered with military inspection certificates. Their lids were open and all the shelves pulled out, as if someone had recently been raiding their contents.

"Where they at?" Righteous demanded.

"They're gone," Coombs said, peering myopically through the haze. "You see those cases? Those are for diving gear—SEAL gear. It was part of our SPAM manifest. Stealth rebreathers, assault weapons, night-vision scopes, satellite uplinks, laser range finders, cameras, cadmium battery packs, covert reconnaissance and communication equipment. Also limpet mines and all kinds of ordnance, you name it."

The Reapers listened like a rapt tribe of Neanderthals to this recitation of state-of-the-art commando stuff: SEAL gear for a SEAL mission that was as cold and dead as every conflict of the old world, relics of an extinct civilization. The very definition of lost treasure in that almost all of it was missing—most frustratingly the guns and ammo.

Popping a skull-like diving mask out of its foam cradle, Harvey Coombs said, "See? Do-it-yourself SEAL team. Just add water."

"Where'd they go?"

"Outside." Coombs indicated the four chrome hatches. "Through these tubes."

"What the fuck they doing out there?"

"Any number of things. Repairs, reconnaissance . . . underwater demolition. We have a few master divers on board who are qualified to work with underwater munitions, so—"

"Munitions? Shit. Grover, tell Betty Boom to keep an eye out for fuckin' frogmen. Ain't *better* be no Navy SEALS out there, or they gonna be dead SEALS. You, too."

"Wait a minute," said Coombs, gesturing for silence.

There was a peculiar squeaking sound coming from within the torpedo tubes.

"What's that?" asked Weeks.

"They're back."

"What? Back?"

"Ssh!" said Coombs. "You hear that? Someone's in there now—that's why the tubes were drained. Probably stuck waiting for whoever is supposed to let them back aboard."

The Reapers leveled their weapons. Righteous Weeks said, "Go ahead and open them doors."

"Only if you give me your word not to harm anyone," Coombs said.

"Open the doors right now, or I'll geld you like a motherfuckin' bull calf! Now do it!"

After a moment's hesitation, Coombs released the four breech doors, starting with starboard tubes one and three, then moving across to tubes two and four. The tubes were at a sideways angle and pitch-dark inside, making it hard to see down their full length.

Righteous Weeks shouted, "All right, everybody out! Don't try any—"

He was cut short by a flesh bomb, an avalanche of briny-cold meat: four twenty-foot tubes of solid-packed offal tumbling into the chamber as if from a grisly cornucopia. Guts! Guts amok! The light strobed with hysterical gunfire as this slippery living bouillabaisse of human parts disgorged onto the floor.

In the tight space, there was nowhere to go, and the front ranks of Reapers were instantly overwhelmed by the frenzied host. Immune to terror or surprise, the men didn't panic but had no defense against such an amorphous attack—a hellish migration of clawing, grasping morgue refuse that clung on and climbed their bodies to cover their masks and clamp tight around their throats. Guns were no good at all. As the first men were engulfed, those nearer the door recognized that they had a brief opportunity to get the hell out of there, cut their losses. And they didn't hesitate—they knew they wouldn't get another chance. The problem was all the guys in the way.

Fighting his way through the pileup, Righteous Weeks realized that he had made a serious mistake bringing so many men down here. Dragging the woman, he barely managed to get out the door before it was shut against the heinous enemy, then he joined the fight to seal it up against other poor fools still trying to jam through. There was no choice: Once this shit got loose, there would be no stopping it.

Grover Stix was buzzing with the thrill of being alive. Though he had been right in the thick of the nightmarish attack, his slight build gave him an advantage over men in luckier spots. With the wave of slurry sweeping toward them, he leaped atop the torpedo racks and shinnied down the tight space right over the others. In a second, he was out the door and helping Righteous close it.

As the door clamped shut, he had a last glimpse of that Navy man, Coombs, standing silent and seemingly calm amid shuddering webs and fronds of viscera.

As soon as the valve was dogged tight, Weeks turned and slapped the woman across the face with his shotgun. She fell back against the wall, banging her head.

"What the fuck was that all about, motherfucker?" Righteous demanded. "What kinda shit you tryin' to pull on us?"

"I beg your pardon," she said, adjusting her cracked oxygen mask. "I never promised you a rose garden."

Before Righteous could hit her again, the big pressure door in the amidships bulkhead clanked open, revealing a hazy black void—the impenetrable vastness of the Big Room.

"What's down there?" Weeks demanded.

Alice smiled and replied, "The rest of the boat."

There was no movement within the lightless depths aft. Through the men's sonic goggles the view had that strobing, stilted quality of a convenience-store security camera. Suddenly, out of a side cranny, the blurred shape of a little boy appeared and dashed through the doorway.

"Hey, stop him!" yelled Weeks, shining his echolocator on the kid's skinny back just as he vanished from view. "Who was that?"

"Bobby Rubio," Alice said. "Kid we picked up when we first got here. I thought maybe he belonged to you."

"Not hardly."

Pondering the situation, the Reapers considered their options:

Grover Stix offered, "I say we clear outta here and drop a thermite canister down the hole. Fuck this shit."

"Yeah," said another man. "What do we need with a submarine anyway? It's like a damn dungeon down here. I like to be in the open, or at least somewhere with a window."

"Damn straight—this thing's worse than being back in the hole."

"Now hold off," said Righteous. "We didn't just risk our necks and sacrifice twenty good men so we could pussy out at the last minute. This is an opportunity we ain't likely to ever get again—a chance to declare our independence. Hell, boys, we already in possession of this shitcan; we own it, lock, stock, and barrel, and now you want to queer the whole deal because of a little fresh meat? Just when we got 'em in a sack? We're holding the strong hand here; it would be a shame to cut and run when we're this close to winning the pot. We got the game, we got the numbers, and we got the grit—now we just got to see their bluff."

Without waiting for the others, he boldly walked down the short passageway and ducked through the aft hatch.

Once inside, Weeks found himself staring up at a room as big and cold as his old cellblock back in Huntsville. He couldn't see much beyond thirty feet—the sonar imager, designed for close-range operation, dissolved into gray murk—but from the hollow sound he could tell it was a very big space. As in the rest of the sub, there was a jungle of pipes and wiring, but here there were no walls or ceiling to contain them, just a steel-grated pier extending into darkness and a dim jumble of machines in the gully below.

The others followed him in, voices hushed as if entering a church. Trying to demystify the place, Righteous rummaged in his pockets until he found something to throw—the first silver dollar he had ever plucked from between the horns of an angry bull. *Fuck it,* he thought, and chucked it high up into the air, smiling as it dinged off the roof, bounced down invisible ledges, rolled, and went still. He was about to say, *Y'all might as well get comfortable—I don't go nowhere without my lucky dollar*, when something small and heavy struck him in the forehead. His lucky coin!

"Holy shit," he said, skull ringing.

"What's wrong?" asked Grover.

"Didn't you see that? Somebody winged my coin back at me. Sucker nailed me good, too; ahmo have a goose egg."

"Shit, man—an inch lower, and you'd be wearing an eye patch for the rest of your life."

"It's more a them damned kids, gotta be." Struck with a notion, Weeks shouted, "Come on out, boys, we ain't gonna hurt you none. We're on your side. I heard tell from your friends that you ain't hardly had a square meal since you first set foot on this barge and that the men here don't treat you no better than damn dogs. That ain't right. If you can help us, we'll put a stop to that. Sooner we can talk turkey with you and the rest of the crew, the sooner we'll get your bellies so full of ham and beans and biscuits and bacon and grits and corn bread and applesauce you won't never even have room for the pecan pie. We know what it means to be prisoners, to be shut up in a hole where you can't even reckon the days. Come out, and you'll be part and parcel of every decision we make—it's a democracy. Come be one of us, and we'll sure be glad to have you. It's a big, beautiful world out there, enough for all."

As Righteous spoke, he began to hear furtive scufflings from above, sounds like many feet pattering along metal ledges, filtering downward with stealthy urgency.

"Shit, there they are," said Grover.

Weeks could see them now: pale, gangly teens loping with unhurried speed along invisible black cliffs, some sliding and leaping down invisible ladders to the lowest balconies, where they spread out along the edge like a jury, while others gathered atop high outcroppings of webbed cargo. They were wraiths, seriously underfed and pale as grubs, with the haunted eyes and starkly jutting collarbones of concentration-camp inmates.

"These dudes been doin' some hard time all right," muttered Grover.

There were quite a few of them, fifty or so, but not nearly enough to present any serious threat to the growing ranks of armed Reapers who now covered the bottom deck from end to end. *Guns, hell,* Righteous thought. *These boys look so sickly you could probably blow them over with a stiff breeze.*

"All right, here's the deal," he called up. "We got no quarrel with you boys, but we just lost some of our best men back there, and we're a mite tired of games, so if you could just lead us to whoever's in charge, we'll be putting this submarine of yours back on a payin' basis."

The boys remained silent, watching the men with the mute fascination of a lost tribe of aborigines.

"What's wrong with you? *No habla ingles?* Come on!" Righteous aimed his weapon up at one of the nearest spectators, and said, "You. Come on down, son, and talk to me."

The boy didn't move; didn't even seem to register the words.

The silence grew awkward . . . then aggravating. Prison had made Righteous and the rest of the men very sensitive about being ignored. Shaking his head, General Weeks said, "What we got us here is a failure to communicate."

"Hey, Righteous," said Grover urgently. "Did you notice something about them kids?"

"What?"

"They ain't wearing no gas masks."

There was a missed beat as Weeks digested this, then suddenly he and all the other men started to hear something underfoot. Sweeping their acoustic beacons down into the machinery, they were taken aback to see movement amid all the tubes and tanks, a whole lot of squirming shapes: slick body parts wriggling forth from the shadows, issuing from channels under the decking, extruding from the deep crevices of the boat's intimate plumbing.

"Holy shit! Pull back! Everyone out!"

As the men tried to retreat they found the exit jammed, the line stalled by an equal and opposite force coming in. Their own rear guard, who had been posted along the upper decks, were now in full flight, pursued downward by the plague of lively human remains.

"What's going on up there?" Righteous shouted furiously. "Go back, go back—ain't no way out but up!" He tried shooting to get their attention, but there were already half a dozen gun battles going on to determine who was coming and who was going. *Shit,* he thought. *What would Voodooman do?* Fighting was no good; somehow he had to get above the Xombie tide, and fast. The narrow deck was becoming a precarious place to be. Some men were leaping across to higher beams and islands of machinery, staking claims above the squirming charnel horde.

To Alice Langhorne, Weeks shouted, "How do we get out of here? Show us the way up, or I'll cap your ass!"

She only smiled that infuriating smug smile.

"Fuck you, bitch," he said, and shot her in the belly.

Langhorne was blasted backward, tumbling into the bilge.

Picking his way over beams and catwalks, Weeks tried to find an opening through to the next level, but all he found were narrowing spaces packed with webbed cargo and machinery—dead ends. And all the while those boys stared down blankly from the mezzanines as though watching a play.

"You little bastards better show us the way up there or so help me God there ain't gonna be one of you left standing by the time I'm through." They ignored him.

Panic began breaking out among the men as crawling remains got among them, swarmed over them: "It's on me, it's on me, *shit!*—"

That was enough. Righteous started shooting, shot boys in the front and boys in the back, his shotgun pellets ripping through their shirts and flaying their translucent skin. The boys faltered, fell . . .

. . . then got up again.

Two specters rose out of the tumultuous gloom. The tall one was Alice Langhorne, glowing unearthly pale like some screen siren from the age of silent film. The other was Lulu Pangloss.

"Come on down, you guys," Lulu called, her unearthly, cool voice echoing across the galleries—not loud, yet pure and clear as a bell amid the screaming chaos. As the boys started coming, she said, *"Don't worry—they don't bite."*

"You," Weeks said in furious despair as he loosed his remaining firepower, shucking the empty shells into space. The soft antipersonnel rounds were as chisels in soft butter, mushrooming and blooming as they passed through the advancing boys, whittling their bodies into modernist sculptures.

Yet still they came, so that Righteous knew this was it: The Big Day. And he was glad.

"What the *hell's* going on down there?"

You been played, brother. Shoulda knowed it was a trap—damn! There had been tumultuous sounds of fighting, then the submarine abruptly fell silent. Without warning or explanation, all contact was broken off; even the men posted directly below the hatch had disappeared and wouldn't answer. It made no sense—a hundred men couldn't just vanish out of the blue like that. Not *these* men. But no reinforcements had been called for, and El Dopa was reluctant to send any more until he knew exactly what they were up against.

He wanted to abandon this cursed submarine at once, but the truth was he couldn't afford to. His forces needed a secure base of operations, at least until they could get their shit together. He sure as hell wasn't going back to that casino in the dark, even if his men had searched it from top to bottom and assured him it was deserted. With the Harpies loose, he wasn't sure he'd ever be able to sleep there again. How could everything have gone so wrong so fast?

First, he had been jarred awake by the shooting upstairs

in the suite occupied by Uncle Spam's bravos. That wasn't
so unusual—those maniacs were always blasting away at
something or other, but usually they did it outside. Then
there had been a spell of calm, followed by sounds of
someone—or some *thing*—skittering across the balcony
and down the stairs. At that point he dispatched his Kali
Thugs to check it out. As they went up, weapons at the
ready, jingling noises could be heard from the vicinity of
the Xombie Generator, or Gen X—what his people called
the Harpy Jukebox.

And that was when all hell broke loose. El Dopa still
didn't know exactly how it happened, but one thing he did
know was that whoever was up there must have pulled the
cotter pins that held all his captive Harpies in place. Free of
those pinions, they slid off their racks with the ease of
greased rotisserie chickens. Terrifying blue chickens.

It was a close thing—much too close. If not for his body-
guards taking the hit, he would never have had the valuable
seconds he needed to escape. But once he was safely in the
raft and paddling away, he realized his troubles were only
beginning: The other barge was at war, besieged by a zillion
more Harpies. It wasn't until hours later, when his surviving troops were safely aboard their lifeboats and trying to
figure out what to do next, that El Dopa learned that the
three Jet Skis he'd seen leaving the scene were those boys
from the submarine. They had stolen Reaper gear and
Reaper boats, and trashed an entire barge just to cover their
escape. Most disturbing of all, the whole plot had been
cooked up by one of his most trusted lieutenants, Marcus
Washington, aka Voodooman.

That was when he and his men came to the conclusion
that there was only one thing to do: trade up.

El Dopa wished he was as confident now—things
weren't playing out quite as he had hoped. An entire pha-

lanx was gone, and the follow-up party he dispatched below had also vanished without a trace, so that now the men were balking at going down there again. Helpless to initiate any action, he felt marooned, as if he had been banished to sit here in limbo, watching his men mill like ants on the endless deck of a haunted submarine, gradually overthrown by the cruciform shadow of its baleful black sail. Night was coming on fast.

All right, this was long enough—if Righteous Weeks was alive, he would have reported by now. *Time to blow the motherfucker wide open.* Charges were wired and ready; all that was required was to move the boats off to a safe distance. Once the submarine was breached—its conning tower ripped clear off and its top deck peeled back and gaping open like a giant Jiffy Pop—he'd take the rest of his men and see if there was anything inside worth salvaging . . . or any survivors worth saving. He didn't expect there would be.

That was when the lid came off all by itself.

Betty Boom was standing directly over the forward hatch, closing it over the shaped charges to amplify their force, when suddenly the whole topside of the sub started popping open. Not with explosions, but mechanically, hydraulically, as all twenty-four enormous Trident missile doors sprang from its flush black surface, flipping outward like thick steel petals and catapulting the men and equipment on them out into the harbor. Mooring lines stretched across the sub's deck were either snapped or yanked out by their cleats, or they jerked entire boats out of the water to smash against the upraised hatches as though spiked by giant Ping-Pong paddles, leaving them dangling brokenly, dripping fuel.

Observing the spectacle from his command yacht, El Dopa was spared either the indignity of being launched into

the sea or the injury of falling down one of those twenty-
four wells that had suddenly opened in the sub's deck. He
did have a moment of acute embarrassment when he
screamed for retreat, expecting any second to be hit with a
barrage of nuclear missiles. But there were no missiles
and not enough boats left to retreat. When, after a few minutes, it became clear that nothing was happening, a Reaper
lieutenant named Bone Voyage radioed him from the sub.

"There's no missiles down there," the man said. "It's
hollow—a big, empty shell. Can't see nothing in the dark,
but we're gonna get some lights on it."

No missiles? So it was a bluff? *The mother of all moth-
erfucking bluffs!* To cover his embarrassment, El Dopa
called his armada back and ordered a wholesale assault.
The sub was wide open now, ripe for invasion. Whatever
was happening, it was imperative he regroup his scattered
forces and get some lines down there, or if not that, a shit-
load of TNT. No more Mr. Nice Guy.

Organizing the few hundred men who hadn't been knocked
unconscious or drowned, El Dopa ordered his cruiser alongside the sub, and shouted, "I'm personally taking charge of
this operation! Everyone who can fight is to follow me! We
need lines and sharpshooters up there, now!"

Loading an extralong clip into his nickel-plated Uzi, he
boarded the sub at its far stern and rallied his people. Cautiously approaching the missile bays, they trained spotlights
on that double row of hazy pits, each one seven feet wide
and vanishing into unknown depths. The lights didn't pen-
etrate far. Watching his footing, El Dopa leaned over the
abyss and peered inside.

"Hello!" he called. "If anyone can hear me down there,
sing out so we can help you."

At first there was nothing, just dense smoke swirling
like on the surface of a polluted well. El Dopa got a whiff of

tear gas and had to retreat, coughing. Then movement—
something rising out of the smoke: an eruption like pale
bubbles, blooms of strange-shaped gourds, a cornucopia of
unspeakable skinned fruit.

When he saw what it was, El Dopa fell back, shouting
incoherently, shooting wildly, his mind ticking off the limited options still available to him and his men. The way he
saw it, the only feasible one was that they all jump overboard and blow up the submarine. Blow it up whether they
could find a usable boat or not, whether they could get clear
or not. *Blow it up blow it up blow it up.* Just go!—there was
no time for anything else.

But in the time it took him to think it, even that time
ran out—ran out like his ammo, like his last hope—and
the roiling, bulging, breaking mass of undead flesh fell
upon him.

CHAPTER **TWENTY-FOUR**

OCTOPUS'S GARDEN

In the last extremities of panic and exhaustion, with day-light receding above and only green depths below, Sal De-Luca tried to breathe by gulping the cold, cold water. It was nauseatingly salty, heavy as wet cement, and his lungs rebelled at receiving it. He convulsed, his chest heaving to expel the alien fluid, then slacked and opened wide to the sea.

For a few more seconds he was still conscious, strangely calm, feeling the cold radiating outward from his flooded core, and the soothing dark stealing over him—there was nothing to be afraid of, and never had been. A rush of joy filled his skipping heart . . . and then, just like that, he was gone.

There was a momentary lull, when Sal's dead body gent-ly touched bottom and began to sway slowly in the current. Then, suddenly, he started to dance, to flail and twist, to jerk limply in all directions as if tugged by invisible strings. Pieces of his outer suit ripped loose, leaving puffs of inky liquid as they flapped against their metal fastenings, unzip-ping themselves and tearing away, only to spin haplessly in the gloom, trailing bits of metal and fabric. In a few minutes Sal was stripped naked, having kicked off the last few shreds of rebelling Xombie tissue along with his clothes.

He was back.

Snapping his sprung joints into place, feeling the teeming armies of his body forging soft new cartilage and tougher ligaments, he looked around at the interesting surroundings. *Awwwwwsommmme,* he thought.

The river, which had seemed so murky and dark to his former sight, now glowed with a hundred thousand sources of pale light. Luminous bodies filled the green depths like so many oil lamps, a vast migration sweeping slowly out to sea.

They were all Xombies. And Sal was one of them.

There was an explosion—then another. The shock waves slammed Sal into the muddy riverbed, ringing his skull like a gong. Within that deafening sound, he could hear the crane barge shearing apart, its steel containers ripping like tinfoil as huge bubbles of force ballooned outward and upward, casting tons of scrap far out onto dry land. In a second, all that was left were black ribs of settling wreckage and oily whirlpools spinning apart downstream.

He could see bodies and parts of bodies floating down all around him, all the myriad bits and pieces moving independently, a glowing exodus from the barge's ravaged hull. His attention was drawn to the surface, up to the brightest lights of all, a great raft of votive candles bobbing on the waves. A human chandelier of living beings, survivors— fast-burning tapers of mortality, soon to be snuffed.

It was a fleet of boats to which the men had escaped and where they were now consolidating their survival, gathering their forces, and planning their next move. The futility of this effort wrung Sal's dead heart like a tragic chord of music: *If they only knew.*

Sal wasn't the only one; all the Xombies yearned to

intervene, but they were too heavy to swim, and in any case, the ebb tide was against them, pushing them downstream like a powerful wind. It was more than the tide: There was something else drawing them that way, a distant choir calling for them to come. So they walked with the current as though the river itself was the glorious force of their longing, as marchers in a vast candlelight vigil, parading down a valley to a rendezvous at sea. A final revival.

Across the intervening depths, Sal could sense many familiar auras: Lulu, Kyle, Russell, Derrick, Freddie, and most of the other boys from the shore party; Ed Albemarle, Julian, Jake, Lemuel, and Cole; Voodooman and a whole host of former Reapers, as well as Chiquita and many fallen Kalis, now shed of their masks and the mortal fear that imposed them. Even Uncle Spam was there, his riven body made strangely graceful in this octopus's garden of algal mats and junk cars. All were innocents again, baptized by the purifying waters of Agent X. Children of Uri Miska.

Born again, Sal was called back to the steel womb from which he had come, to the place they were all being shepherded: back to the boat.

CHAPTER **TWENTY-FIVE**

I AM THE WALRUS

The next day they went for a walk. It was easier getting out of the cylinder than it had been getting in; turned out there was a small padlocked door at the base, hidden behind the bushes. Bobby felt funny, but for once he wasn't the least bit afraid.

Downtown Providence was dead, totally deserted, and as they strolled down Fountain Street, Bobby and Joe had to tread carefully over broken glass and other wreckage that had issued from burnt-out shells of buildings. Most structures were still intact, however, particularly two enormous masks of comedy and tragedy, which had been fashioned out of steel mesh and hung above the sidewalk. The masks contained black nests of bones—the charred remains of many women.

Circling back, they came to a massive brick edifice, the Providence Place Mall, which had been designed to resemble the mills that once dominated the city skyline, and it did, overshadowing even the great marble State House. The mall overlooked an artificial pond, and actually straddled its polluted tributary canal, which meandered sludgily under an archway beneath the soaring windows of the food court.

The old man was whistling a familiar tune, "This Land Is Your Land," when they saw the horsemen.

There were four of them, tattooed berserkers on blinkered police horses, and they burst galloping from a hidden tunnel by the skating rink. There were vehicles there, too, and other, more monstrous beings on foot: steel-stitched grotesqueries charging from every direction.

Man and boy didn't move, standing their ground as the horde swept down upon them.

"STOP WHERE YOU ARE," croaked an amplified voice. "SURRENDER AND YOU WON'T BE HARMED."

The boy was still not afraid; he found all this very interesting. There was an unearthly beauty to the scene: those brilliant horses and riders, bodies glowing like molten metal, and the flesh-armored infantry glimmering through their seams like banked coals. They *burned* with life—it was consuming them from within as though they were walking, talking jack-o'-lanterns. Which in a sense they were. If nothing was done about it, they would soon burn out and turn to mush. So sad.

One of them had a megaphone. "I AM MAJOR KASIM BENDIS OF THE NEW UNITED STATES. KEEP YOUR HANDS WHERE I CAN SEE THEM."

Surrounded, covered by dozens of automatic weapons, Joe and Bobby stood in the center of a shrinking circle of long, bladed pikes. The sight of all those sharp points triggered a knotty feeling in Bobby's stomach—a thing he realized was fear. It was like remembering something from long ago, a regression to infancy: the forgotten dread of potty training or something equally ridiculous. He could only grin in embarrassment.

The leader handed off his megaphone and approached them. "Uri Miska, I presume?" the man said, keeping his distance. He was a tall, handsome man, with wavy black hair and a neatly trimmed mustache. "You can't imagine how much this means to me, finally meeting the great man in the flesh. Father of the Mogul Cooperative, chief engineer of the Maenad nanocyte, architect of the Xombie apocalypse—the list goes on and on. But you don't like to take credit for that, do you?

"You probably don't recognize me, but then I'm not surprised—Colonel Sanders probably didn't know who plucked his chickens, either. I've served your organization for a number of years now. A private contractor, one might say, strictly freelance. But it's not really your organization anymore, is it? Not since Sandoval took over the project. Is that why you unleashed the plague? Personal revenge? Did you think you could just vanish into the blue? That's an interesting condition you have, by the way—blends right in. Very clever. As a soldier, I appreciate the value of camouflage.

"But maybe you don't need camouflage. No one walks in the open anymore unless they have confidence in their own immunity. Look at us, burdened with the crude instruments of our resistance. Now look at you: no guns, no protective gear, acting like nothing could be more natural than taking a pleasant stroll on a sunny Sunday morning. It's obvious that you've found a cure—and kept it for yourself.

"Well, the time has come, the walrus said, to talk of many things: of lack of sex since Agent X, and lonely buggerings. That's the New World as we know it, Uraeus, and I am the walrus."

Averting his eyes, the old man said, "Yes, yes, I know you. You're the handyman—the one who will fix anything for the right price. I know they bought you, just like they tried to buy me. Now they want to steal what they couldn't buy. But I tell you what I told them: Everything comes to he who waits."

"I've waited long enough," said Bendis. "This is a barter economy, so I'm offering you a trade: your Tonic for the boy's life."

Bendis gave a signal, and suddenly a noose was around Bobby's throat, dragging him backward.

Hemmed in by a ring of spears, the old man just shook his grizzled head in disappointment. He looked broken and pale. Very pale—in fact, white. And as the blue pigment evaporated, Joe Blue's face seemed to fill out, it's withered features smoothing and hardening until he resembled another person entirely . . . until he was Uri Miska. In the flesh.

"Can't you people take a hint?"

All at once, everything stopped. The Reapers froze, quivering in place as though their Xombie suits had suddenly turned to stone. They couldn't move. Muffled cries of alarm could be heard from their helmets.

Then, haltingly, they began to dance.

Jerking around like clumsy marionettes, they formed pairs and tottered from foot to foot, making stiff curtsies and pas de deux. Grabbing Bendis and his mercenaries, they launched into a violent tango, twisting the protesting men's arms from their sockets and snapping their spines. Dragged from his horse, Bendis realized his mistake and managed to pull the pin of a hand grenade. It went off at his belt, blowing bits of man and horse in all directions, kicking the party into high gear. The street was a monster's ball, with men's harrowing screams as the orchestra.

Stooping over the major's mangled body, Uri Miska said, "Silly to steal what is freely given." He leaned close, whispering into the other's ear.

Barely alive, Bendis nodded frantically, desperate to listen, to cooperate, until his face suddenly contorted in a violent spasm. Something peculiar was going on inside his ear canal: a long snakelike thing had emerged from Miska's mouth and was burrowing its way down his eustachian tube, cutting off Bendis's airway and patching his circulatory system to Miska's. A joint umbilical cord, mixing blue blood with red.

In a moment, it was done.

Standing up, Miska wiped his mouth and went to find the boy. Bobby Rubio was unharmed, sitting at the curb with a dreamy expression—the rope still around his neck. Miska took it off and led him down to the waterfront promenade under the mall. The stilted dance continued behind them, the screams occasionally punctuated with an explosion or random crackle of gunfire.

There were fires on the river; some fleeing sentry had lit the braziers. Others would come now that the message was out: Miska Was Here.

"What's that?" the boy asked.

"WaterFire," the Blue Man said.

There was an unusual boat there—a long black gondola. Taking the boy down to the dock, Miska helped him aboard and told him to lie low. Then he untied the line and pushed the boat in the direction of the current.

"Aren't you coming?" Bobby cried, sitting up.

"I can't," Miska said. "I'm sorry."

"What am I supposed to do?"

As the boat slipped out of sight beneath a low bridge, the old man held up his arm and called back, "Go forth and multiply."

CHAPTER **TWENTY-SIX**

YES, VIRGINIA, THERE IS A SANTA CLAUS

"**A**ttention Virginia-class submarine. This is a U.S. naval vessel under the command of Admiral Harvey Coombs. Please acknowledge."

There was a long pause. Then a sharp, hostile voice: *"What is your vessel's call sign?"*

"We have no call sign. This is a decommissioned ship salvaged for an emergency mission, code name SPAM. We have no official existence, our orders are classified, and we are operating under conditions of strict radio silence. This communication is a breach of operational security, so let's keep it short: If you represent the interests of the United States of America, then we are here to offer whatever assistance and support you may require."

There was no answer for long minutes, just a quiet wash of static.

Then the voice said, *"You guys got any food over there?"*

"We've got whatever you need," said Coombs. "Come and get it."

"Are you serious?"

"Yes, Virginia, there is a Santa Claus."

ABOUT THE AUTHOR

Walter Greatshell has lived in five countries and worked many odd jobs across America, including painting houses, writing for a local newspaper, managing a quaint old movie house, and building nuclear submarines. For now, he has settled in Providence, Rhode Island, with his wife, Cindy; son, Max; and cat, Reuben. Visit Walter's website at www .waltergreatshell.com.

It's the end of the world—unless you're a zombie.

XOMBIES:
APOCALYPSE BLUES

by Walter Greatshell

When the Agent X plague struck, it infected women first, turning them into mindless killers intent on creating an army of "Xombies" by spreading their disease.

Running for her life, seventeen-year-old Lulu is rescued by the only father she has never known and taken aboard a refitted nuclear submarine that's crew has one mission: to save a little bit of humanity.

Now available from Ace Books!

M588T1009